Sheila MacLeod was born in the Isle of Lewis and brought up and educated in the South of England, finally at Somerville College, Oxford. She is married to Paul Jones, the actor and pop singer, has two children and lives in what one newspaper described as 'a twilight area of North London'. She has twice received a Scottish Arts Council Publication Award.

XANTHE AND THE ROBOTS

NOVELS BY THE SAME AUTHOR

The Moving Accident
The Snow-White Soliloquies
Letters from the Portuguese

Sheila MacLeod

XANTHE AND THE ROBOTS

THE BODLEY HEAD
LONDON SYDNEY
TORONTO

ISBN 0 370 30014 9
Printed and bound in Great Britain for
The Bodley Head Ltd
9 Bow Street, London WC2E 7AL
by W & J Mackay Limited, Chatham
Set in Monotype Imprint
First published in Great Britain 1977

Whereas primitive man personifies things, (anthropomorphism), modern man 'thingifies' persons. We call this mechanomorphism: modern man tries to understand man as if 'it' were a machine.

Thomas S. Szasz: *Ideology and Insanity*

I

Ah, reader, we were happy! We lived in a benevolent society, dedicated to the greatest good not only of the greatest number but of the total number. Society, which was another name for ourselves, regarded each of its members with careful eyes, eyes that saw into the depths of each soul and assessed that soul thoughtfully, painstakingly, as an individual unit to be accommodated on the basis of individual strengths and weaknesses into the structure of the whole. No one was left out. In relation to every unit, we asked (of it, of ourselves) the same two questions. The first was: what can it give to the rest of us? The second was: what can the rest of us give to it? And the giving was not according to deserts, but according to needs. Each partner to the unspoken contract gave and gave again, seeking to give as much as was humanly possible. Reciprocity. That is the name we gave to the relationship. Reciprocity. It was our First Principle. There were no monuments to its glory in our public squares or parks, no portraits of it in our art galleries; no songs were sung, no symphonies played, no sermons preached in its name; but it informed all our dealings with one another, permeating the air we breathed. Yes, it came as naturally to us as breathing. As the life of the individual unit depended on and was sustained by breathing, so the life of the corporate unit depended on and was sustained by reciprocity. The two units were parallel interlocking systems.

We had sifted the past, riddling it through ever-finer sieves and accumulating piles of ever-finer dross, in order to arrive at the precious truth. As we arrived at each new pile, we analysed, valued, classified it. The coarsest piles were discarded outright as examples on which to base our conduct, but preserved as warnings: here were the mistakes which had been made so often, here were the recurring pitfalls. The less coarse piles began to show vestiges of the precious element we were searching for. The finer ones showed small deposits of it, finer ones still quite substantial deposits. And so on. We had learned to learn from the past. And what we chiefly learned was this: the importance of co-existence. But in order to arrive at this knowledge, we had to learn several other lessons first. We started from the most obvious, the coarsest pile of dross. This represented the most outstanding and at the same time the most puzzling phenomenon of our past. Later we classified it as human destructiveness. But first we analysed it, breaking it down into its kinds: destruction directed against the planet that was our home; destruction directed against other species of life on that planet; destruction directed against other members of the same species as ourselves; destruction directed by the individual against itself; and destruction directed against our own products, our own artifacts. Observing its manifestations, we set its value at nil. How, then, were we to eliminate this canker? How were we to live in peace—one with another, with ourselves, with our world? Divisions, factions, had to be abolished. But, at the same time, one law for the lion and the ox constituted oppression. It was thus—and I have given only the briefest and most superficial of sketches here in order not to bore you with a plethora of abstractions—that we arrived at our Second Principle: Plurality. What this meant in practice was that all subdivisions within our society and within our world were treated as being of equal importance, although the differences between them were fully recognized. Because everything was acceptable, nothing was frightening or threatening to the point where it had to be destroyed. Plurality taught us to live in peace with one another.

But there was still the world to be reckoned with. There were still ourselves. Could we learn to preserve these too? It may be taken as evident from the preceding paragraphs that our society was notably free of inflexible ideologies. We saw them as destructive. And for us they included all forms of religion that were based on the concept of a Godhead. We were not worshippers. But we were respecters. We respected the *status quo*, both of the world of nature and of the world we had created for ourselves. After all, they had both evolved through necessity. Both worlds were instructive, but neither was infallibly so. In respecting the world of nature, we accepted ourselves as being part of it: we accepted death. We saw ourselves as finite beings who were born, who matured, decayed and died like other natural products, like other productions of time. In respecting the world of our own creation we accepted, almost revered, the ability to transcend death and time through our own essentially human efforts. Thus we arrived at our Third Principle: Creativity. We believed the development and furtherance of an individual's creative skills to be necessary not only for his or her own well-being but for the stability and happiness of our whole society. It was through these skills that we learned to come to terms with ourselves and with the anomalous, seemingly paradoxical role we had to play in the scheme of terrestrial things. Though our bodies were finite, their capacities were infinite. Though our lives were temporary, their productions could be eternal.

Reciprocity. Plurality. Creativity. These were the triple pillars of our society, the interrelated trinity from which our cohesion and our happiness derived.

So our teachers taught us. Such was the objective structure of our beliefs, a sort of transcendental realism. But what, you may well ask, did it all mean in terms of everyday life? The trouble with objective structures is that they tend towards tautology, forever defining and re-defining themselves in their own terms. They are incapable of telling you what it feels like to be a certain person in a certain place at a certain time. If they were capable of performing that elusive task in even the most approximate way (approximation being all that is possible) they would not be so sure of themselves. I am not sure of myself. Everything I have to say is tentative, even when it is about myself. I think I know what happened then, what happened there. And I think it is of some interest here and now. It is a story of the society I have just—so inadequately!—described. It is, of course, my story. And in order to tell it, I must modulate into the subjective.

2

Discover me in my room. It is neat. I take a pride in it, and in its neatness. I have wanted this room for a long time because I have always thought it the best in the Institute. Not the grandest, by any means; not the largest or the lightest. In fact, it is a garret. Its name is Garret 3. It is a long, low room painted in a cream colour so rich that it seems to catch and hold the setting sunlight on a spring or summer evening. I sleep at one end, under the skylight, so that I can lie in bed and watch the sky and the overhanging branches of the pine trees moving against it, now gently, now haphazardly, to tell me what sort of day it is. I work at the other, the gable end, facing west. In the gable wall are french windows opening on to a low stone balcony. From there, I have a view of the lawns, the rose gardens a little to the left, and the avenue of limes that stretches all the way down to the west gate. My desk faces these windows. It is a large desk, almost the width of the room. If people want to look out of the windows—and, for some reason, most do—they have to squeeze themselves round the side of the desk and, if they are tall enough, bend their heads to match the slope of the roof. I keep thinking I should move the desk, perhaps have it turned round so that it is sideways-on to the windows. But it suits me the way it is. So I leave it the way it is.

My equipment surrounds me. I like that. The room surrounds me too. That is partly why I chose it. I like to be surrounded by the things I like. Not that there are many of those. I haven't had much opportunity to acquire personal possessions and, although I have nothing against them or their acquisition, I don't actually miss them. Perhaps I should if I could envisage them more clearly—if I could envisage places or people connected with them. A handful of polished stones, for instance, from some faraway beach, to remind me of a childhood holiday. Well, I have one or two photographs. But that's all. I don't need reminders. I remember everything.

So there is not much else in the room. Its floorboards are polished the colour of thick honey and covered here and there with darkly-patterned rugs. Several arm-chairs and a sideboard containing glasses and crockery. Some three thousand books lining the straight sections of the walls. And an incongruously large fireplace with an ornate mantelpiece. An antique. I could light a fire, if I wanted to—it might be nice in winter to sit and stare at the flames. But I have never bothered. The room is always warm enough. Oh, I have no cause to complain. My comfort is taken care of by those whose job it is to take care of it. Likewise, my food is prepared for me, my clothes washed and ironed. We all have our specific functions to perform. Mine is to get on with my work. No problem there. I enjoy my work. Most people at the Institute do. And it is hardly surprising that we should, because we have all chosen and been chosen to work here.

Discover me, then, on a spring afternoon, in my chosen habitat, the intercom phone ringing on my desk . . .

I pressed the button to receive the call. 'Programmer Xanthe,' I said automatically, identifying myself.

'Ah, Xanthe,' said the voice. 'Director Xeno here—'

'Oh, hullo, Xeno.' I was about to ask him how he was when he interrupted me or, rather, carried on as though I had not spoken at all.

'—as you would know,' he said, 'if you had an eidophone.'

Silence. A challenging one on his part, a stubborn one on mine. He had no right to challenge me, because we all had free choice in the matter of eidophones. If I preferred to talk to people without seeing them, or, more pertinently, being seen by them, that was entirely my affair. But Xeno was always needling me about it. He would tease me, pretending to believe that I had some shameful secret to be kept from the cameras at all costs. I never told him, in so many words, either to shut up or to mind his own business. After all, I thought, one must humour one's director. Silence was often my only weapon against him, and on this occasion I used it to some effect. At last he spoke.

'Well, Xanthe, how is it all going?' he asked. 'Have you started on Stage 5 yet?'

'No,' I said, slightly alarmed. 'I'm still right in the middle of Stage 4. Have I fallen behind?'

'No, no,' he assured me. 'You're entitled to work at your own pace. I just wondered, that's all.'

'But if I had started on Stage 5, you would have had my progress report on Stage 4 by now.'

'Inevitably,' he said. 'Yes, I know, Xanthe. You're a good worker.' His tone was flat, and I did not feel praised.

'Would you like me to prepare a report on my progress to date?' I put the question hesitantly because I considered such an undertaking to be a waste of time.

'No, that'll be unnecessary,' he conceded. 'Actually, what I wanted to talk to you about was your new assistant.'

'Oh, no!'

'What do you mean, oh no? You do need an assistant, don't you?'

'So you say.'

'And you agreed.'

'Only because you persuaded me. Honestly, I find that I work much better if I do everything myself.'

'But you should learn—'

'To co-operate,' I finished for him. 'To delegate responsibility. Yes, I know.' I couldn't help sighing. 'Well, what about my new assistant? Are there any candidates ready for vetting? Or for interviewing, perhaps?'

'I have him here with me now.'

'I'm sorry, Xeno,' I said stiffly, 'but that's impossible.'

'Not at all. He's standing here right next to me. Flesh and blood. Just look at—oh no, you can't, can you? Tell you what, I'll pinch him, and you'll hear him react.'

'Ow!' came an obedient voice over the line. I thought: How childish!

'I am supposed to be consulted,' I said when their laughter had died down.

'I'm sorry, Xanthe,' Xeno said. 'I'm afraid we're feeling a bit exuberant at this end. You know you've always said how you hate interviewing? Well, this time I've done it for you.'

'Oh,' was all I could say, being somewhat disarmed.

'I'm sure you'll like him if only you'll try him.' More laughter. I began to wish that I could see them, if only to discover what was so funny.

'I'll be over right away,' I said brusquely, switching off.

The phone buzzed again immediately. 'No need, Xanthe,' said Xeno. 'No need for you to leave your sanctum. We've given Daimon Garret 4. We thought that would be convenient for you both. So I'll bring him over to you.'

I switched off without replying. I thought: I don't like the sound of Daimon; he sounds disruptive. Oh well, I told myself, my work has been disrupted now, anyway—I'll try to be polite and helpful. Perhaps it wasn't Daimon's fault that Xeno was behaving so stupidly. Xeno behaved stupidly so often! I couldn't understand how anyone so obviously brilliant and in such a responsible position could behave in such a consistently frivolous manner. If I hadn't been sure that he was a human being, I should have said that there was a fault in his programming somewhere. He was such a paradox of a person. I was never quite sure where I was with him. I thought, in dismay: I do hope Daimon isn't like that; if he is, I shan't be able to work with him. I liked my colleagues to be more or less consistent in their behaviour and not to let their personalities obtrude too much—that was unnecessary, and could even prove a positive hindrance.

Full of misgivings, I left my desk and walked down the room to the fireplace, where I checked my face in a mirror above the mantelpiece. I looked presentable enough, which was the way I usually looked. I was ready for them. So I sat myself down to wait in a chair facing the door. It was only when I leaned back that I realized how tired I felt, how used I had become to feeling tired. Since when? Perhaps I really did need an assistant, after all. I shut my eyes and continued to wait. I thought: It doesn't take five minutes to get here from Central A; it never takes me more than four, and I'm sure they're both capable of greater speeds than I am. Impatient at waiting, I went back to my desk. Idleness made me nervous. But no sooner had I sat down than there was a knock at the door.

Two men came into my room. They were both tall enough to look out of scale and consequently to feel uncomfortable in that room. Xeno was the taller. I had known him for five years or so, but I had never been able to get used to the way he looked: he was badly put together, shambly and gangling. His limbs seemed loose at the joints, as though they might come apart from his torso through sheer lack of co-ordination in the whole organism. And he neither stood nor sat up straight. His face was similarly untidy, having one eye higher than the other (both small) and a large nose and mouth. He could have had some alterations made there on the premises to those unpleasing features of his, but his grotesque appearance didn't seem to bother him. Nor did he seem to realize that he was a bad advertisement for the Institute, walking around like that in such a state of imperfection.

Most of the rest of us, myself included, had made some sort of effort, however minor, if only out of respect for the aesthetic susceptibilities of our fellows. But in this, as in so many other matters of adaptability to and consideration for others, Xeno had been remiss.

I looked at Daimon. He looked young. I thought: Ominous. He was slight, taut and alert. And highly personable. I was deeply suspicious of handsome young men and, without being unaware of the sour grapes element in my suspicions, tended to discount them as people with whom it was possible to have an adult relationship on equal terms. A pleasantly acceptable mien, such as I found lacking in Xeno, was one thing; vividly expressed good looks, such as Daimon's, another altogether. As soon as he had walked through the door, he looked round the room as though making an inventory—which he found wanting—of its contents. Then he leaned against the sideboard as though afraid that his head would touch the ceiling if he stood unsupported at his full height. I made a mental note: poor spatial sense. When at last he looked in my direction, it was obvious that to him I was just another item on the inventory. Xeno stood between us, looking at me too. This is what they both saw. A short woman of extremely neat appearance. A woman who was neither fat nor thin, dark nor fair, young nor old. A calm-seeming, short-sighted woman. I think that's all the description of me that's necessary for the moment.

Xeno introduced us. I shook hands with Daimon. He said: 'Your new assistant. Code-name, Daimon.'

'Xanthe,' I said shortly, withdrawing my hand from his at once. We never referred to our names as code-names, even facetiously. It would not have been an accurate description of them. 'There's no code involved,' I told him as pleasantly as I could. 'No secrets.'

Xeno said: 'Xanthe is a stickler for protocol.'

Daimon and I spoke together. What he said was: 'So I see.'

What I said was: 'Not at all.'

Xeno sat down in one of my arm-chairs, waving as he did so with an open-handed gesture towards another. Daimon sat down in that. Xeno said: 'What we'd both like is some black coffee, wouldn't we, Daimon? Yes, Xanthe, we have had what you might call a business lunch.'

What he meant, as we both knew, was that he and Daimon had been drinking. His tone of voice anticipated my disapproval. But what I in fact disapproved of was this very anticipation. 'Your image of me is peculiarly unvarying,' I said, beginning to busy myself with the preparing of the coffee.

Xeno looked up to the ceiling's apex. 'Your behaviour,' he said, 'is peculiarly unvarying.'

'So you form your judgements of others,' I said, placing three cups on their saucers with audible emphasis, 'according to their behaviour and only to their behaviour? Have you progressed no further than Watsonism and Skinnerism?'

'Not judgements, Xanthe,' Xeno said, still looking up at the ceiling. 'Opinions. And, as far as you're concerned, behaviour is all I have to go on.'

'Excuse me,' said Daimon, 'but I don't know what on earth you're both talking about.'

Xeno said: 'Xanthe and I are old sparring partners.'

'We tend to have the same conversation over and over again,' I added. 'And this tends to become boring. Even for us.'

'Oh, I rather enjoy it,' said Xeno.

'Very interesting,' said Daimon, his tone nicely balanced between the polite and the sarcastic. 'But what about the robots? That's what we're all here for, isn't it?'

Yes, I too wanted to get on to the subject of our robots and, more especially, my robots. But Xeno said: 'Work can wait until tomorrow.'

Daimon and I looked at each other. 'And today?' we both asked Xeno.

Xeno said: 'Today, acclimatization.'

I handed Daimon his coffee. 'All right with me if it's all right with you,' he said.

As I handed Xeno his coffee I became aware of a draught coming through the open windows. I moved round the desk to shut them. But as I stood there, it seemed to me that the draught was a pleasant one. I liked the feel of it on my face and hair, the way it moved my loose clothing against my body, and I stepped out on to the balcony. The shadows of the limes were lengthening across the lawn towards me, darkening its bleached patches. From the rose gardens a mingled fragrance was beginning to assert itself. I stared down the avenue, enjoying its emptiness. Then, all at once it was no longer empty—and noisy too. A group of figures became visible. Even at that distance I recognized them as robots by the regulation blue denim trousers and tunics they wore. But they appeared to be behaving without the usual robotic circumspection. There was a gaggle of them, walking along, laughing and chattering, their arms around each others' necks or waists. I called Xeno over.

'Look at them!' I said, hardly giving him a chance to reach the windows. 'I've never seen anything like that before. Who or what are they?'

Xeno joined me on the balcony, then Daimon joined us too, squeezing himself in behind us. I wondered rather distractedly whether it was strong enough to hold all three of us.

'My guess is that they're from the alcoholism research unit,' I said to Xeno, unable to keep a certain pointedness out of my voice.

He watched them approach, as though worried, then said in tones of evident relief: 'No, they're not drunk. They're the Erotians.'

'Erotians?' I repeated, trying to work out the derivation of their name. 'Are they Philophrenics?'

'They're novice Philophrenics,' Xeno said, somewhat cagily, I thought.

'Erotians?' I persisted. 'Please explain, Xeno.'

'Well,' he said, 'we couldn't very well call them Erotics, could we? Whoever heard of an erotic robot?'

We exchanged knowing smiles of agreement, and Daimon asked: 'What's the main feature of their programming, then?'

'Affection,' said Xeno. 'They can't leave each other alone. It's really rather touching. Quite literally. Actually, their sensory progression has been very interesting. They started with an equal balance of the senses in their programming. At first they seemed to select the visual and aural channels of expression, the visual being non-verbal, and the aural being only rudimentarily so. But now the choice of the tactile channels is definitely prevalent. All quite asexual, of course, because for them no one zone is any more erogenous than another.'

Daimon nodded slowly. The group of robots was breaking up on the lawn in front of us, presumably as the result of a radio-summons from their controller. They all hugged each other, in the manner of theatrical people, and went their separate ways. Xeno's smile was absent and approached fondness as we came back into the room. I shut the windows. It had grown rather cold. So had my coffee.

Daimon said to Xeno: 'Are all your robots asexual?'

Xeno and I looked at him in some amusement. 'Of course they are,' I said.

Xeno said: 'Surely you're not going to tell us that you have sexed robots up north?'

'We don't have them yet,' said Daimon. 'But I do know that work is going on on a biologically female prototype.'

Xeno and I looked at each other, and it was clear that the news had made us both uncomfortable. 'How can you do such a thing without contravening the sex discrimination laws?' I asked. 'Robots are brains, and we know very well that the human brain is neither male nor female. The distinction is quite meaningless.' Daimon's answering smile succeeded in annoying me. 'I'm not trying to make a political statement,' I went on, 'just stating a scientific fact.' Daimon's smile broadened and became quizzical. 'The fact I'm referring to,' I told him severely, 'is that of our own ignorance. We don't *know* of any differences.'

'Oh, it's all quite impossible anyway,' Xeno said, and I realized that this discomfort, unlike my own, arose from an unwillingness to admit that any other establishment could be more advanced than our own.

'What they're doing,' Daimon explained, 'is to take one of the tougher Pragmapractor models—I forget which one, but it has a medium efficiency quotient—and then to re-program it with the addition of a menstrual cycle.'

'How ridiculous!' I said, at once indignant and embarrassed by the ease with which he referred to that essentially female attribute.

Daimon looked at me briefly and blankly. 'Essentially,' he went on, 'what they're trying to do is to find out whether glandular changes affect the everyday functioning of the brain and, if so, in what ways. I wasn't involved in that particular project myself so I can't give you the details. But I understand it's a very complex process.'

'I should say so,' said Xeno. 'It's a wonder they got the wretched things to function at all.'

'Some didn't,' Daimon admitted, 'and even in those that did, the efficiency quotient was drastically reduced.'

'And how did this manifest itself?' Xeno asked, interested despite himself.

'I'm not sure.' Daimon laughed. 'I think the researchers got more than they bargained for. But, then, that's robotics for you.'

'Yes, yes,' Xeno agreed. 'It certainly is.'

I listened to them with some indignation. And with more bewilderment. I wanted to say something angry and impatient. But I couldn't quite understand why, so I checked myself and said instead: 'What's the point? Any woman could have told you the answer in the first place. And, anyway, robots are supposed to be more efficient than us, not less. Certainly, the Pragmapractors are. That's the entire justification for their existence.'

Diamon shrugged. 'Research,' was all he said.

'And besides,' I went on, 'if the menstrual cycle is eliminable in human subjects, why foist it on a robot? I don't see that such research could have any application.'

Daimon shrugged again. 'A lot of human subjects, or women, as I prefer to call them,' he said, 'seem to be in favour of retaining the menstrual cycle. Don't ask me why. Maybe it's the same as food. Lots of people want their food to look exactly like the good old-fashioned meat and two veg., whatever it's actually made from.'

Xeno said: 'Well, we must admit that it's fascinating. I'd be interested to know of any further developments, Daimon.'

'It's obscene,' I said decisively, surprising myself hardly less than I did them.

They both looked at me mildly. 'That's a bit extreme of you, Xanthe,' said Xeno. 'What makes you say that?'

I couldn't explain why I felt so uneasy. All I knew was that my work, and with it my life, which was my work, seemed suddenly threatened. But this was too vague a feeling to put into convincing words. I hunted around for some rationalization. 'My robots,' I said at last, 'are better than we are, not worse.'

Xeno and Daimon looked at each other as though they had both seen some ulterior significance in my words. Daimon shifted in his chair, as though it were time to go. Xeno said: 'That's a matter of opinion.' But he didn't sound unsympathetic. 'Well, Daimon,' he said, standing up, 'I'll show you to your garret now. Thank you for your hospitality, Xanthe.'

'What about tomorrow?' Daimon asked me.

'Oh yes,' I said. 'As soon after breakfast as you can make it will be soon enough. I'll give you a run-down then on the present state of the project, and afterwards we can go and see Xanthides.'

Daimon nodded. Xeno said briskly: 'No doubt we'll all see each other over the ersatz meat and two veg. at dinner.'

'No doubt,' I said.

When they had left, I sat on limply in my chair for some minutes, doing nothing. I felt rather forlorn. It was not a familiar feeling, and I put it down to the fatigue and overwork ascribed to me, however indirectly, by Xeno. That reminded me. It was time for my pills again. I swallowed all three of them together—one green, one brown and one yellow—and lay down on my bed for a short rest before dinner. The pine branches moved rhythmically, hypnotically, above me. I fell asleep at once and didn't wake again until the early hours of the following morning.

3

'At the risk of being stickle—or is it stickly?' I said to Daimon, '—may I ask you something about your career to date?'

I was sitting at my desk, facing him. He was leaning against the frame of the open windows, watching the comings and goings down below.

'What do you want to know?' he asked without turning his head. 'You've got it all written down there in front of you.'

I should have preferred him to look at me while speaking to me. I should have preferred him to speak to me with at least the minimal politeness that I was prepared to extend to him. I should also have preferred him to sit down, but he had declined to do so. At the very least, I should have liked him to stand up straight. But you cannot command or even request an ostensibly adult human being to do such things just to fall in with your own preferences. So I picked up Daimon's curriculum vitae from my desk, and said in measured tones: 'Yes, but it doesn't tell me everything.'

'There isn't much to tell,' he said.

'For instance,' I went on, 'this doesn't say anything about your having any special qualifications in literature.'

'I have no special qualifications in literature,' he said desultorily.

'Any special interest, then,' I amended.

'I have no special interest in literature,' he said in the same tone.

'I see,' I said.

He turned from the window at last and in one movement he was leaning over my desk towards me, supporting himself at its edge on taut arms. 'To tell you the truth, Xanthe,' he said, 'this appointment has more to do with you than with me.'

I understood at once. 'Xeno,' I said.

'Yes,' said Daimon. 'He seems to think you need me because you're cracking up or something.'

'Great!' I said heavily. 'That's all I need.'

'I'm supposed to keep an eye on you.' He rushed on, sounding half-angry, half-apologetic. 'I'm supposed to distract you from working too hard—'

'And then report back to Xeno?'

'Yes.' He shifted his weight on to his feet, then back on to his arms again, nearly losing his balance in the process.

'Why do you keep leaning on things?' I asked in exasperation.

He grinned suddenly. 'Because they're there,' he said. He stood up straight and said: 'I'm sorry,' in such flat tones that I didn't know which he was apologizing for—his posture or his presence.

I stood up myself. I wanted to pace up and down and to curse Xeno for his perfidy. Daimon looked at me helplessly. 'Never mind,' I said, abortively sitting down again. 'It's all right.'

Daimon sat down too. 'I don't like having to spy on people,' he said.

I said: 'Oh, it's not really spying.' I didn't want to discuss the matter with Daimon, intending as I did to have it out with Xeno later.

Daimon said: 'I suppose I'm not used to large institutions. You see—' here he grinned again—'I'm a nuke.'

His grin lapsed again, and I surmised that he was missing his family. That was the trouble with members of nuclear families: those primary attachments of theirs tended to supersede any subsequent loyalties. And so much of their time was taken up, wasted, in the often futile attempt to adjust fully to institutional life. Consequently, I tended to be wary of such people as colleagues. 'You'll have plenty of time off to visit your parents,' I said easily.

'Oh, they're dead.'

'I'm sorry to hear that.'

He looked down at the floor, then looked up at me sharply, and asked: 'Were you sorry to hear about your own father too?' I felt myself tense. I didn't reply. 'You see, I know who you are,' he said. 'I know your real name.'

'My former name, Daimon,' I corrected him mechanically. 'It was no more real than my present one.'

'Xeno didn't tell me about it,' he went on. 'I took a look at your file in Personnel.'

I said: 'The information is freely available. As I said yesterday, we have no secrets here.'

'Then why didn't Xeno tell me?' he countered.

'He probably didn't think it concerned you,' I said smoothly. 'Is that the end of your confessional? Can we get down to some work now?'

'But of course,' he said, 'now that that's all out of the way.'

My hands, hovering over the array of papers on my desk with unaccustomed indecision, were shaking. I noted this symptom with some annoyance. My adrenalin flow was supposed to be in a state of constant inhibition. And my colleagues were normally tactful enough not to make references to my father, and least of all references to his death, in my presence. Daimon had brought with him and offered me a taste—a sharp taste—of the opinions of the outside world. I was not grateful for his offering.

Earlier that morning I had prepared two papers, the first being a digest of all my progress reports on the programming of Xanthides, the second being a digest of my progress reports on Xanthippus to date. I didn't really need the papers in order to brief Daimon because I knew their contents by heart. But their preparation had helped me to clarify things, and to select the emphases likely to be most helpful to a newcomer to the present project. And now I seemed to have mislaid the wretched things. Instead, I seemed to be re-reading Daimon's curriculum vitae. It was impressive—no doubt about that. It told me what a brilliant student he had been. The list of his achievements added up to a formidable catalogue, especially for one so young. I was inclined to disbelieve the whole thing, although I knew it had to be true. I thought: But what good is brilliance if you can't get your personality problems sorted out first? As for Xeno, he really must be slipping to think of employing someone so plainly unsuitable.

I found the paper on Xanthides, and turned to Daimon. 'Xanthides,' I announced, 'is the first robot for whom I have had overall responsibility from the start to the finish of his programming. Xanthides is a Philophrenic robot—'

'Ah!' said Daimon, sitting up straight. It was the first sign of interest he had shown, and I was mollified at once. 'I've only worked with Pragmapractors before,' he explained. 'Please go on.'

'But you know what a Philophrenic is?' I asked, prompting him.

'Of course,' he said rather impatiently.

I waited for him to give the standard definition and, when I realized that it wasn't forthcoming, I said: 'Well, then, you must know that the main object of the Philophrenics is research. They exist for one purpose, and one purpose only—to help us find out more about the workings of the human brain.' I looked at him somewhat more severely than I had intended to. He raised his eyebrows and looked steadily at me, waiting for me to continue. I thought: Arrogance! 'Xanthides,' I went on, 'is basically a philosopher and a historian. He has some knowledge of literature, some knowledge of physics and scientific methodology, and a pretty extensive knowledge of mathematical procedures. The mathematical proportion has perhaps been over-programmed, but it's an asset for all Philophrenics to have this ability and, as you know, it's a simple matter to equip them with it, using old computer circuits. Xanthides doesn't just store information, but explains it and re-explains it. He reasons, argues and refutes. He has a sense of humour too, being particularly fond of puns. He is also particularly fond of Descartes.' I smiled. Daimon did not.

'It seems impossible,' he remarked, 'that a multi-programmed Philophrenic should be quote particularly fond of Descartes unquote. I should have thought that a dual-programmed robot would find him more congenial.'

'But Philophrenics are always multi-programmed,' I objected.

Daimon laughed. He laughed so loudly that he startled me. 'It was a joke, Xanthe,' he said with mock patience. 'Cartesian dualism.' He was beginning to remind me of Xeno.

'Xanthides's philosophy,' I continued with a sigh, 'is at the moment biased in favour of Western systems. We are programming-in the Eastern philosophies gradually. You could say that he had come round to them in middle life. He also produces his own complex philosophical theories.'

Daimon stood up abruptly. 'Yes, yes,' he said. 'I get the picture. I can catch up on the details later.'

'As you wish,' I said evenly. I thought: Is this brilliance? Or is it laziness?

Daimon was leaning against the mantelpiece, his hands in his pockets. 'Now let's have Xanthippus,' he said.

'Philophrenic,' I said briskly. 'High efficiency quotient, of course. Motor skills related to the pursuits of leisure. But basically a literary being.'

'What does that mean?'

'The usual. He stores information on his special subject. He can be consulted—'

'And does he produce?'

'Literature? He will, eventually.'

'And will it be any good?'

I wanted to say that of course it would, but something warned me not to, so I said: 'That is what we are trying to find out. But I'm sure that whatever Xanthippus produces, it will not be valueless.'

Daimon laughed again. I looked questioningly at him. He walked up to the desk and leaned on it, towards me, from the side this time. 'You really believe what you said yesterday, don't you?' he asked accusingly. 'You really believe that they're superior to us.'

'I didn't say superior,' I reminded him. 'I said better. It's a different sort of judgement entirely.'

'What's the difference?'

'There is a difference,' was all I felt prepared to say.

'Then, what is it?' He laughed again, this time scornfully. 'Electricity and positrons! Relays and photocells! Plastic and metal! And you think all that is in some way *better* than flesh and blood!'

'What makes you think it's any worse?' I countered. I was thinking: Here we go again; the same old crassly naïve questions of the typical novice; this person is simply not ready for robotics. 'If only you knew how irrelevant all this is,' I told him.

'Irrelevant to what?' he asked me, raising his voice to a positive shout. 'How on earth can you work in robotics and go on thinking that the existence of Philophrenics is irrelevant to human life?'

I let his misinterpretation pass. 'What are you getting so excited about?' I asked him instead. 'What are you afraid of? The lady doth protest too much, methinks.'

'What lady? What the fuck are you talking about, Xanthe?'

'It was a joke, Daimon. Or, at least, a flash of humour. You know, a literary reference.'

He stared at me uncomprehendingly for a moment. 'Oh, *Hamlet*,' he said dismissively. 'And why shouldn't I get excited? Human beings do, you know. Or most of them do sometimes,' he added meaningfully before walking back to the fireplace. There he collapsed into an attitude of . . . well, I don't know what it was, but he folded his arms along the top of the mantelpiece, then rested his head on them. The posture reminded me of someone else, but for the moment, I couldn't place whom.

'When you're feeling calm enough,' I said, 'perhaps we can go and meet Xanthides.'

He raised his head, separated himself from the mantelpiece, and turned to look at me. 'Hang on,' he said. 'I'll just go and get my recording-machine.'

As soon as he had left the room, I became conscious of a sense of relief. But, remembering Xeno, my indignation returned. I called him. 'You've saddled me with a madman,' I told him. 'You're a monster!' I switched off. Of course, he buzzed me back at once. But I didn't answer.

Daimon called to me from the door: 'Ready when you are.'

'I'll be with you in a moment,' I called back.

From a deep drawer at the left side of my desk I took two radio-control boxes in their denim shoulder bags. Each bag was stamped with my name and that of the robot concerned. It was necessary to activate Xanthides. I wanted him to make his way to an appropriate rendezvous, and to be fully warmed up by the time we got there. I hesitated over Xanthippus. On the one hand, activation would be good for him, would help him become accustomed to being himself. On the other hand, he was still in an incomplete state, and so would need more supervision than I could provide while I was dealing with Xanthides—not to mention Daimon. So I decided to leave Xanthippus until the afternoon. His daily period of activation—so salutary for the system—could safely be left until then. I told Xanthides: 'I'm on my way.' It was a mild, intermittently sunny day, so I added: 'Rendezvous 7.'

Daimon and I walked noiselessly along the carpeted corridors of the west wing and down the two broad flights of stairs into the entrance hall. I walked with short, brisk steps, Daimon with large slow strides. He seemed determined to lag slightly behind me, just enough to make me look rather absurd. But I dismissed the uncharitable thought that he was doing it on purpose, and led the way out into the mild May morning. I noticed that all the young women we encountered—and some of the older ones too—looked at Daimon with open and lingering interest. I thought: Is he so unusual? I looked at him myself. He was looking down at his feet, which he dragged along the gravel, kicking up little stones and scattering them as he went. No one else was walking like that. I realized that his demeanour was notably lacking in that elusive quality which characterized, indeed illuminated, the physical presence of our human membership there at the Institute: a combination of purposiveness and serenity. Daimon's physical presence was not at home in its own subjective space, and it seemed to be unaware of the objective space so respected by and so dear to the rest of us.

'What's that?' Daimon asked, stopping in his shuffling tracks.

We were approaching the Central section and had just reached the Annexe, a low building painted white and decorated with brightly-coloured murals. 'It's the creche,' I said, and at once a wail rendered my explanation superfluous.

Daimon walked towards the door. From it emanated a sweet, milky smell, dusted with talcum. I found it rather sickly, but I waited politely for Daimon to satisfy his curiosity. A young woman in a pale uniform came towards us, smiling.

'Hi, Xanthe,' she said. Her skin, in the sunlight, had a translucent quality. Around her nose and under her eyes small beads of sweat showed among the freckles. 'Aren't you going to introduce me to your friend?' She and Daimon were smiling at one another.

I said: 'Oh, I'm sorry. This is Daimon, my new assistant. Daimon, this is Veronica, one of our creche-mothers.'

'I'm a biological mother too,' she said to Daimon as they shook hands.

Daimon said to her: 'I'm a nuke.'

'Oh, marvellous,' said Veronica. They were still smiling, still shaking hands.

I found this conversation, if such it could be called, obscure, but they seemed to be providing one another with the required information. A toddler of some eighteen months appeared in the doorway. Only then did Veronica slide her hand out of Daimon's. 'My son,' she said.

She ran back to the doorway, helped the child to negotiate the shallow step, and led him towards Daimon. He, for his part, squatted down where he stood, and took the child's other hand. Veronica squatted down too. She looked at Daimon, then at the child, then at Daimon again, with evident pleasure. It was then that I understood why all those women had looked at Daimon with such interest: he was sexually attractive in addition to being so obviously good-looking. I hadn't even noticed. Even now, I didn't really see it. But obviously others, including Veronica, did. Cautiously I drew near the small group. Veronica looked up at me and smiled—a gesture I returned with some embarrassment.

Daimon said to the child: 'See you again soon, eh?' He stood up, and said to Veronica, who stood up with him: 'And you too, I hope.'

She laughed. 'Well, you know where to find us,' she said.

Daimon and I resumed our progress. I waited for him to ask me about Veronica, but he didn't mention her. So I didn't mention her either. What he did say was: 'I assume that you have no children.'

I said: 'No.'

He said: 'And that you've never had any.'

I said: 'No.' I waited for him to ask me why not. That was something people often asked me. But he did not.

We were nearly at the rose gardens. Most of the blooms were yet to come; they remained sheathed in their bud-form, the hard green streaked here and there with crimson. The promise they evinced, no doubt all unwittingly, stirred me. Rendezvous 7 was situated in a bower of late ramblers. Seated on a log bench, of the kind commonly referred to as rustic, Xanthides was waiting for us. As we approached, he stood up.

Daimon said: 'A robot in a rose-bower!'

Xanthides greeted us with the customary formality. I performed the necessary introductions and we all sat down together on the bench, Xanthides in the middle.

Xanthides said: 'This meeting gives me great pleasure.'

I said: 'Of course, Xanthides. Me too.' I waited for the two of them to start communicating.

Daimon said: 'And how is Descartes?'

Xanthides considered. 'In one sense,' he said, 'he is dead. As you know. And therefore I could say that he is the same as he has been for the past few hundred years. But I think you may be referring to his reputation. It is by no means dead. And, from what I imbibe from various sources, I would hazard that it is still the subject of some controversy. In that sense, I should say that he is still very much alive. Alive and kicking. Therefore, very healthy. Does that answer your question?'

'Amply,' said Daimon.

I said: 'Was there something specific you wanted to know, Daimon?' I couldn't allow the conversation to end there. It was up to me to provide the impetus because, as is well-known, robots never initiate.

Daimon frowned. 'I have a quotation for you,' he said to Xanthides. 'I should be interested in your response to it.'

'Certainly,' said Xanthides. 'Please proceed.'

'Here it is,' said Daimon. ' "To postulate the existence of two separate realms of being, one of which is characterized by awareness, as Descartes did, may prove one of the fundamental blunders of the human mind." '

'L. L. Whyte,' said Xanthides. '*The Unconscious Before Freud.*' He paused, having identified the quotation correctly. 'It may be so,' he said judiciously, 'but let me give you another quotation. Here it is. "A true thinker can only be justly estimated when his thoughts have worked their way into minds formed in a different school; have been wrought and moulded into consistency with all other true and relevant thoughts; when the noisy conflict of half-truths, angrily denying one another, has subsided, and ideas which seem mutually incompatible have been found only to require mutual limitations." J. S. Mill. *Bentham and Coleridge.*'

'I see what you mean, Xanthe,' said Daimon. 'Superior is different from better. It's nastier.'

I frowned at this. 'Be careful,' I said, not quite knowing what I meant by the warning, but feeling it to be necessary.

Daimon said to Xanthides: 'And can you, a mind formed in a different school, justly estimate Descartes?'

'An estimation can be made,' replied Xanthides, 'but whether or not it will be just is another matter. Shall I proceed?'

Daimon looked disconsolately out over the rose gardens. 'No, no,' he said. 'I'm only too sure that your estimation will be perfectly just. Tell me something huge and simple instead. Like, what is the purpose of philosophy?'

Xanthides paused before answering: 'Would you not agree that, as far as the import of your question is concerned, philosophy is a false isolate?' Daimon did not reply and Xanthides, mistaking his silence for lack of comprehension, went on: 'Another quotation for you. "All our intellectual activity, in whatever field it takes place, is an attempt to give meaning to our experience—that is, to make life more practicable; for by understanding things, we make it easier to survive and get around among them." Edmund Wilson. *Axel's Castle.*'

'Very pragmatic,' said Daimon, 'but I agree with Jung that nothing influences our conduct less than do intellectual ideas. Do you agree with Jung, Xanthides?'

Xanthides said: 'I am not programmed to answer that.'

I said quickly: 'He doesn't know Jung. Ask him something else.'

'Is it not true, Xanthides,' said Daimon, 'that all our wit and learning only serve to bring us to a greater sense of sorrow—in other words, that it's all pointless?'

Silence. Then Xanthides said: 'Dysfunction.'

'Now look what you've done!' I said to Daimon. 'You've deactivated him!' I put an arm round the robot to support him until he had finished deactivating. Only when this process was complete could I activate him again without causing injury to his system. He subsided against me, half-conscious, his head lolling on my shoulder. I held him close to me. I stroked his arm. I liked the feel of his skin, so cool, so neutral, so unresponsive—a work of art. Which indeed is what he was. I said to Daimon: 'You know damn well—'

'That robots cannot question their own existence or purpose,' he finished for me. 'Yes, I know that. It's what you might call built-out despair.'

'If you knew, why did you ask him such a stupid question?'

'Because I wanted to know the answer,' he said with a weariness I considered to be affected.

'Rubbish!' I said firmly. 'You were getting at him—being spiteful.'

'To a robot? Oh, Xanthe, do me a favour!'

Xanthides was now inert. I shifted his curiously top-heavy weight into an upright position. 'He's had enough for the moment,' I told Daimon, 'so please don't say anything else to him. I'll just reactivate him and send him home.'

Daimon, watching me, said: 'And now I have a quotation for you, Xanthe. "If the self is not true to itself, then it is in despair, whether it knows it or not." Sören Kierkegaard. *Sickness Unto Death.*'

I stared at him. 'Are you talking about Xanthides?' I asked him. 'Or are you trying to tell me something about yourself?'

'I wonder,' was all he said.

I considered, but decided against, advising him to go over to the Chemical department for some anti-depressant pills. 'Why don't you take the afternoon off?' I suggested instead. 'Familiarize yourself with the place?'

'Perhaps,' he said without enthusiasm.

I reactivated Xanthides. 'You can go now and join your fellows,' I told him.

'Thank you,' he said. 'I should like that. Good-bye, Xanthe. Good-bye, Daimon. It was a pleasure to meet you. I hope we shall meet again soon.'

'Why are they always so polite?' Daimon asked, as we watched Xanthides move off in the direction of the Philophrenic building. The question had been rhetorical, and I didn't attempt to answer it. 'I think I'll go for a walk in the grounds,' he said. 'I like the look of the woods up there.'

'All right,' I said.

He got up and walked away, without shuffling this time, but I couldn't help noticing how graceless he was compared to Xanthides. Then I thought: I simply must find Xeno, and tell him that I cannot put up with Daimon. I'll tell him I'll have an assistant, if he wants me to, but it must be someone of my own choosing. I'll tell him that, in my opinion, Daimon is in a state of emotional instability, and that his hostile attitude towards robots makes him unsuitable for this job. I'll tell him that I'll have a psychiatric check up, if that's what he thinks I need. I'll tell him, oh, I'll even tell him that I'm prepared to take a short holiday. I'll tell him anything at all, if it will enable me to get rid of this wretched Daimon.

4

I didn't find Xeno. He wasn't at lunch. And he wasn't in his room. Then his assistant told me that he had gone to the Capital to attend a conference on Philophrenic Robots and the Storage and Retrieval of Information: he would be away for a week. I couldn't but admire his timing, however ruefully. After a week, I was told that Xeno had decided to remain another two days at the conference because something unexpected had cropped up. But on the second of those days, at around five o'clock in the afternoon, he asked to see me.

Xeno's room, in Central A, was larger and grander than mine. I had been offered one similar to his, but I don't like high ceilings and I don't like too much light: all that space becomes distracting. I should have had to fill it all up somehow. But with what? Xeno, on the other hand, had had no difficulty. The room, spacious as it was, was cluttered with his possessions. The sight of it forced me into disbelieving the old maxim that the state of a person's home mirrored his state of mind. Xeno couldn't have had a mind like that room! He wouldn't have been able to function. There was nowhere to put anything down. Every shelf, every table, every available surface, was rendered unavailable by a series of strange objects for which Xeno had a peculiar affection. There was never anywhere to sit down because he had left sheaves of paper, pieces of carved wood, china vessels of obscure use, and so on, on every chair. These he called his relics. Above the bookshelves were ranked stuffed heads of horned animals with glass eyes asquint. Those I found particularly repulsive. The books themselves were arranged any-old-how. I had once offered to rationalize his collection for him, but he had insisted that it was unnecessary for me to do so because he knew the exact, well, the approximate location of every volume.

'Oh, just dump all that stuff on the floor,' he said now, indicating a chair. 'Make yourself comfortable, and I'll tell you a bit about the conference.'

I did as he said. 'There's just one thing, Xeno,' I began.

He looked at his watch. 'Will it take long?' he asked. 'I'm so behind that I've had to squeeze in several extra appointments. Oh, by the way, how's young Daimon coming on?'

'Daimon,' I said. 'That's just what I wanted to talk to you about . . . as if you didn't know.'

'Yes . . .' Xeno said meditatively. 'Brilliant, isn't he?'

'Maybe,' I admitted. 'But he's so erratic. Well, to tell you the truth, Xeno, I think he's completely unstable.'

'You mean his work is inconsistent?'

'No. I have no fault to find with his actual work so far. My complaint is that he's an unstable personality.'

'He's young,' said Xeno. 'I thought you might find him stimulating.'

'Sometimes,' I admitted. 'And sometimes he's just plain irritating. Most of his suggestions have yet to be proved. So far, some have been wildly wrong, others uncannily right. I can never see how he arrives at his conclusions.'

'Intuition,' said Xeno.

'Intuition?' I repeated. 'How can you be so superstitious, Xeno?'

'It's not superstitious to believe in intuition,' he said. 'As a matter of fact, I met a couple of Daimon's former colleagues at the conference, and they both agreed that his intuitive grasp of programming concepts was quite extraordinary. They were very sorry to lose him.'

I resisted the temptation to say that I too was sorry for their loss. I asked: 'Why did they have to lose him? He wasn't there long enough to qualify for a normal transfer.'

'Oh, no,' said Xeno with a vague wave of the hand. 'It was a personal matter. Something to do with his mother's death.'

I saw evasion. And I sensed muddle. 'Shouldn't he have had a period for recuperation?' I asked hopefully.

'He preferred to go on working.' Xeno picked up a wooden paper-knife from his desk and held it up to the light. It had an ornately carved handle and looked impractical. 'I should deem it a personal favour,' he said, studying the knife instead of looking me straight in the eyes, 'if you were to bear with Daimon for just a little longer.'

'So that he can report back to you on my faults and failings?'

'Don't be silly—'

'So that he can be groomed to take my job from me?'

Xeno put the knife down again and stared at me blankly. 'So that's what you're afraid of,' he said. Picking up the knife again and pointing it at me for emphasis, he continued: 'Listen, Xanthe. You have no faults or failings. That's just the trouble. You've learned your lessons all too well. And as for taking your job away from you . . .'

'Well?' I challenged him. 'Isn't that what's at the back of your mind? Someone has to take over from me because I'm going downhill fast. I'm cracking up!'

'Is that what he said?' Xeno asked thoughtfully.

'That's what he said. Are you going to deny it?'

Xeno looked even more thoughtful. 'Certainly,' he said, 'I'm going to deny that I ever said you were cracking up. I would never say such a thing to Daimon, even if the thought had crossed my mind.'

'It was just his intuition working overtime, was it, then?' I asked. I hadn't meant to say it, and instantly wished it unsaid.

Xeno pointed the knife at me again, this time wagging it admonishingly. 'You know your trouble, Xanthe?' he began.

'I should do,' I said heavily. 'After all, you never cease to remind me of it.'

'No, listen,' he said. 'It's jealousy.'

'Jealousy?' I repeated, puzzled.

'You're jealous of anyone coming anywhere near your work,' he explained evenly. 'You don't want anyone coming between you and it. You guard it jealously. It's the same with your robots. You guard them jealously. But in fact you, personally, don't own them any more than you own the roses in the garden out there.'

Everything he said was true. I felt horribly deflated. At last I said: 'I think jealousy is an over-emotional term.'

'I don't,' said Xeno. 'It fits your attitude perfectly.'

'Over-emotional?' I repeated. 'Me?'

'Yes,' he said. 'Strange, isn't it? But then one should never judge by appearances.'

I didn't know how to defend myself. I was thinking: It's all a matter of interpretation. Xeno could name my working attitude as one of jealousy, if he liked, but I preferred to describe it as one of devotion. Wasn't it right that my devotion should be recognized first, before it was criticized? I wanted to ask Xeno this, but my pride forbade me to. I stood up, as if to leave. 'I shan't keep you any longer, Xeno,' I said. 'And, besides, I have work to do.'

'Oh, Xanthe,' he said in conciliatory tones as he began to walk towards me. 'Surely you're not offended?' He held his hands out vaguely in my direction. I stepped back. I didn't want him to touch me. His hands made a shrugging gesture. 'You must know that I have your best interests at heart.'

'Do you, indeed?' I asked lightly.

'Of course I do. Please sit down again. We haven't got to the conference yet.' Defeated, I sat down. Xeno fumbled around in the array of papers which littered his desk. 'One thing that will interest you,' he said. 'We discussed the menstruating robot at some length.'

I shuddered. 'Must we?'

He laughed. 'Don't be so squeamish. It's not as though there's anything messy involved, like blood. The programming is purely chemical—'

The eidophone buzzed on his desk, and he paused to answer it. I couldn't see the screen, but recognized the voice as that of one of his assistants—Xiphias. 'Excuse me, Director Xeno,' it said. 'But your next appointee is here.'

I saw Xeno hesitate. I stood up quickly. He said: 'Here,' and, fumbling around on his desk again, handed me an untidy sheaf of papers. 'Take it. It's the transcript of my report on the conference.'

I hesitated at the unexpected gift, the placatory offering. 'Don't you need it?' I asked.

'Tomorrow will do,' he said, thrusting the bundle into my hands. 'The pages are numbered.'

'Thank you, Xeno,' I said graciously. 'I'll return the whole thing tomorrow in good order.'

The corridors were comforting—dimly-lit and empty—after the glare and muddle of Xeno's room. But I didn't linger. Except briefly, in order to adjust the transcript into a more portable shape. It would take me all my time to get through the thing, so I hurried back to the west wing. As I turned the last corner before my room I nearly bumped into someone coming very quickly and unheedingly in the opposite direction. But we both stopped just in time.

'Oh, Xanthe!' said Veronica breathlessly, as though I were the last person she expected to see. She looked embarrassed, almost furtive.

'Hullo, Veronica,' I said. 'What are you doing in these parts?' I knew the answer to that one very well, of course.

'I've been to see Daimon,' she said, blushing slightly, 'but he doesn't seem to be in.'

'He's probably gone for one of his walks,' I told her. 'That's what he usually does at about this time.'

'Oh, yes,' she said, still breathless. 'In the woods. That's where he goes, isn't it? I don't suppose you know when he usually comes back?'

I didn't. 'He won't be long,' I assured her.

But she was not assured. She looked at me anxiously and said: 'Oh, Xanthe, do you think I could possibly come in and wait in your room for him?' I hesitated, looking pointedly at Xeno's transcript. 'I promise not to disturb you,' she said. 'Really.'

'Come along, then,' I said, although I knew her promise to be void. I thought: More of my time wasted in small talk. But I led the way to my door and she followed, glancing over her shoulder once or twice.

Veronica gave a little exclamation of delight. 'Oh, Xanthe,' she said. 'It's so nice in here. So cosy.' She stood in the middle of the room, turning this way and that like a ballerina, so that her skirt flared out and back again. 'It's so tidy,' she went on, 'and somehow so, well, so grown-up after the creche.'

I couldn't dispute that. I asked her to sit down and she looked around nervously, as though unable to decide on the best chair. 'Let's have a drink,' I suggested. 'You seem rather nervous.'

'Oh, goodness, I am,' she said. 'I'm awfully nervous.' She sat down in the arm-chair by the fireplace, and it occurred to me that she had wanted to sit where Daimon usually sat. She had chosen correctly.

I poured out two glasses of our own rose-petal wine, and handed her one. 'Are you usually this nervous?' I asked her with what I took to be a certain tact. 'Or do you have some specific reason?'

She laughed. 'I would have thought that was obvious enough,' she said. There was a tinge of bitterness in her voice which surprised me. She had always seemed such a sunny personality to me. But now, although she was smiling, she seemed to be on the verge of tears.

I said: 'Daimon.'

She said: 'Yes.'

I said: 'Is he giving you trouble?'

She frowned, sighed, frowned again. 'Well, not trouble, exactly,' she said. 'He hasn't been rude or unkind or anything like that.' She took a gulp of her wine. 'I just don't understand him,' she said in a sad little voice.

Neither did I, but then it didn't worry me unduly. 'Well, it's early days yet,' I said, giving her a specimen from my stock of meaningless phrases.

'Sometimes he's so wonderful,' she went on, her sadness veering into dreaminess. 'So sweet and kind and gentle. You've no idea. And at other times he's so cold and distant. I might be a complete stranger. Oh, I know he doesn't mean to hurt me. But he does. But, then . . .' She shrugged, spilling a little wine on her skirt. '. . . then, that's how you can tell when you're in love with someone, isn't it? Because they have such power to hurt you. They can say the most trivial little thing, and if someone else said it, you'd just laugh. But if it's them—I mean, him—then you're hurt out of all proportion.'

I listened with some dismay to her little speech. I was ill-equipped to reply to it. 'Veronica,' I said carefully, 'don't you think perhaps all this is a little premature?'

'You're going to say I don't know anything about him,' she said, 'but knowing people isn't necessarily a matter of time. We're very close, you know.'

I doubted that. 'Perhaps you're seeing too much of each other,' I suggested rather lamely. I was thinking: Why on earth is it that I always seem to attract confessions and revelations when I have no idea how I'm supposed to respond to them? I took a sip of the scented wine, and waited for Veronica's reply.

'Oh, no,' she said, looking at me wonderingly. 'That's impossible.' She drank several mouthfuls of wine in quick succession.

'I think you're being altogether too hasty,' I said.

'I know,' she said miserably. 'I know I am. But I can't help it.'

'What about your son's father?' I asked. 'Did you feel the same way about him?'

'Yes,' she admitted, 'but he moved on. And he said he would prefer it if I didn't transfer with him. I know he wanted to get away from me. I seem to be too much for some people to take.'

'I see,' I said.

Veronica finished her wine and held out her glass to me. 'Can I have some more?' she asked, round-eyed like a child, as though fearful of my refusal. I refilled her glass in silence. She drank several more mouthfuls before speaking. 'I wonder if you do see,' she said, the dreaminess coming back into her voice. 'You know, Xanthe, it's all very well for women like you. Clever women, I mean. Intellectuals.

You have your work and you can lose yourself in it. But I'm not like that. I have this need to feel really passionately about someone. A man. It's the central thing in my life. When I'm not in love, I feel that something enormous is missing. I feel that I'm not properly alive. Oh, I'm probably not expressing myself very well. Do you understand it at all? Or do you think I'm just a complete idiot?'

I both understood her and thought her an idiot. I said: 'It must be very hard for you.' I knew it was no use recommending libido-inhibitors, which would have been the sensible thing to do. I could see that she enjoyed being the way she was. She even enjoyed the pain that such a personality inevitably brought her.

'It can be hard,' she said, 'but it has its compensations. I mean, how could I appreciate the real ups if I didn't have the real downs too?'

A knock at the door spared me from having to answer this impossible question, and Daimon made his timely entrance. 'Xanthe,' he called out at once, 'I'm fighting fit! I'm just in perfect shape for grappling with Xanthippus.'

He appeared not to have noticed Veronica, who was staring up at him with large unhappy eyes. I got up to get another glass from the sideboard. 'I'm glad to hear it, Daimon,' I said. 'Some wine?'

'You see, I've been getting into training,' he went on, following me to the sideboard. 'All this communing with nature and impulses from vernal woods. I'm really ripe now for programming-in the Romantics.' He took his glass, looked round the room, and saw Veronica. 'Oh, hullo, Veronica,' he said with ill-feigned surprise. 'What are you doing here?'

'Hullo, Daimon,' she said brightly. 'I'm waiting for you,' she added, less certainly.

Daimon was now at my desk, disarranging things. 'Careful,' I warned him. 'You'll mess up Xeno's transcript of the conference proceedings.'

'Hardly,' he said, looking through the jumbled pages of the manuscript. 'All I want is a piece of scrap paper.'

I found some on the desk. 'What's all this?' I asked him. 'Formulae already?'

'Not quite,' he said, waving the piece of paper at me. 'What I thought was that we could start out from Mario Praz—'

'—*The Romantic Agony*,' we said together.

Then Daimon said: 'The information is set out in such a way that it will be relatively easy to quantify. Half the work has been done for us already. For instance . . .' He began to sketch a diagram.

I turned towards Veronica. She had finished her second glass of wine, and stood up rather unsteadily. 'Do you have a favourite among the Romantic poets, Veronica?' I asked, making a feeble effort to include her in the conversation.

But she said: 'I don't really know anything about poetry.' She pulled down her sweater, smoothed down her skirt, and said: 'I must be going.' She looked over at Daimon, who went on sketching. Then she said: 'I really think I should go.'

Daimon looked up. 'Oh, are you going?' he asked her. 'See you, then, Veronica.'

After that, she had no choice but to leave. I went with her to the door. She was openly tearful now. I thought: Why do people have to get embroiled in such messy situations?

'Oh, Xanthe,' she whispered, 'put in a good word for me. Please!'

'What do you think of that?' Daimon asked, handing me the piece of paper.

I took it from him. The lines and figures blurred, and I couldn't grasp their sense. Daimon was watching me anxiously. I wanted to say: Dysfunction. I looked helplessly at him. 'I must be tired,' I said.

'Look at it at your leisure, then,' he said. 'I'll leave it with you and go into the details later.' He sounded disappointed.

'Yes, later,' I said with some effort.

He hesitated, his hand on the door-knob. 'Don't let Veronica upset you,' he said.

I smiled at him and said: 'At least you know how to take your own advice.'

5

Xanthippus and I were walking in the woods. At Daimon's suggestion. It would never have occurred to me to remove a robot so far from his natural habitat, especially when that robot's programming was still incomplete. But such excursions had become part of my daily routine. Daimon saw them as part of a valuable experiment, and one in which I was practically obliged to participate. What effect, he had asked me, did this new consciousness of the natural world, which characterized the Romantic period, have upon the previously existing consciousness? Xanthippus would help us to find the answer. Correctly programmed, amply briefed, he would respond with a freshness lost to us, probably forever. Daimon was nothing if not persuasive; it was one of those ideas which are just crazy enough to succeed, once in a while. So I monitored Xanthippus's responses to our walks with all the meticulousness urged upon me by Daimon. The more data we had, the more likely we were to arrive at telling conclusions. But, so far, conclusions were nowhere in sight.

I walked slowly. Nevertheless, Xanthippus trailed along behind me. The trees were mainly beeches, interspersed around the perimeter of the woods with hawthorns and hazels. The land was fairly flat, but the ground was uneven beneath its layers of decomposing leaves. Frequently, I would slide on a cluster of beech nuts or trip over a hidden root. Branches caught at my hair, thorns in my clothes. To me, these inconveniences represented nature in the raw, and I preferred the composure of the rose gardens and the formal lawns. But Xanthippus had no difficulty in negotiating the terrain. He moved swiftly and surely when he moved, and when he stopped, stood perfectly still. I watched him with some admiration—and envy—as he caught up with me. He stood close to me, motionless but expectant.

I switched on my recording-machine. 'How are you, Xanthippus?'

'I am in perfect order,' he replied.

'And what are your responses?'

'I am aware of a sensation of pleasure.'

'Can you identify its source?'

'There appears to be more than one source,' he said, 'I am moving in a complex ambience, which follows me and precedes me as I move. Some of the signals I am receiving are very strong, and others very faint. But the middle wave-band is peculiarly empty.'

'Can you describe those signals?'

'I shall try to do so,' he said slowly, as if having difficulty. 'The strong ones are of an order I have not encountered before. I cannot ignore them because they are both insistent and persistent. But what is new to me is that these signals are devoid of meaning.'

'Can you clarify that statement?'

'They are strong signals,' he said, starting at the beginning again. 'But they are conveying no message. They are conveying their presence, no more, and no less.'

'Perhaps that *is* the message,' I said.

'I am greatly relieved to hear that,' said Xanthippus.

'Now Xanthippus,' I told him. 'You mustn't worry. Do your best. That is all we ask of you. Now tell me about these fainter signals.'

He said: 'They are more diffuse. Whereas the strong signals seem to emanate from individual elements or objects, the faint ones seem to emanate from nothing or nowhere in particular, but from everything and everywhere in general.'

'And what is their content?'

'Pleasure,' he said definitely. 'And I must think, do what I can, that there is pleasure here.'

'Well done!' I exclaimed. Now, perhaps, we were getting somewhere at last. I spoke into the machine: 'Memo to Daimon. Xanthippus has adapted a quotation from Wordsworth to his own situation. Introjection is evidenced in (a) the change of tense from past to present, and (b) the alteration of "there" to "here", a logical sub-change.' I turned back to Xanthippus. 'Very good indeed!' I told him.

'There is more,' he said. 'First of all, the pleasure exists outside of my system, then it is to be found within my system. It would seem that pleasure invokes pleasure.'

'It certainly would.' I gave a sigh of pure happiness and turned off my machine. Already it was obvious that this walk, unlike so many of the others, had been far from a waste of time. 'Let's go on,' I said.

I led the way forward through the densening trees with a lighter and surer step. I didn't know the exact nature of the signals described by Xanthippus, but I could guess at it and, in guessing, I had become more alert. The wood was full of noises: rustlings, scurryings, flutterings, whisperings, all punctuated with the sudden cracking of twigs. I became aware of my own breathing, and of the beat of my heart. And they grew, those bodily sounds, until they seemed to eclipse all others. I had to stop and lean against a tree-trunk in an attempt to quieten them. It was only then I realized how far I had left Xanthippus behind. I thought: Xanthippus does not have this barrier between him and other sounds; he has no lungs, no blood-stream, no heartbeat; what must it be like, that internal silence? What must it be like to feel no pain, and none of the physiological inadequacy that I am feeling now? I was filled with awe—all the more so because I had never considered before what it must be like for a human-based consciousness to inhabit the factory-made artifact of a robot's body. What *was* it like? Why had I never asked myself the question before? Could I ask Xanthippus? It seemed of paramount importance to know the answer.

I looked for Xanthippus, but couldn't see him. I waited for him to appear, deciding not to communicate with him by radio in case he became alarmed by my breathlessness. I took several deep breaths. Xanthippus was coming towards me. I thought I saw him collide with a tree. No, he was still coming towards me. Then I saw him collide with another tree. I switched on my radio-control, and called to him: 'Xanthippus, is your radar at fault?'

The answer came back calmly: 'No, it is in perfect order.'

'Then, what are you doing?'

'I am doing my best.'

'Yes, I know, Xanthippus,' I said soothingly. 'But why are you bumping into all those trees?'

'It is part of the experiment,' he answered. 'I am doing my best to understand the signals.'

'How can that help?'

He explained: 'I am doing my best to understand the message of presence. If I can experience the presence more closely, I shall be able to help you. I am trying to get through to the presence, using a more violent means than usual. But the trees refuse to understand my signals.'

Then I understood, and I was moved to pity. I felt tears stinging the rims of my eyes, and I said to myself: Oh, Xanthippus, Xanthippus!

I used his name as a charm to dispel the pity, a pity which he would not have been able to understand, and which could be of no use to him. I told myself severely: Xanthe, you're becoming sentimental; please remember that a robot is a robot, a mechanical thing. With an effort, I spoke to him: 'It's all right, Xanthippus. Please come here.'

My voice sounded unsteady, and he hurried towards me. 'Are you in distress?' he asked.

'No,' I said as steadily as I could. 'Are you?'

'I am finding this exercise extremely difficult,' he said.

'It's all right,' I said again. I reached up and felt his head. It was very hot—a sign of intense electrical activity. I ran my hand over the smooth dome, as if hoping to cool it.

'Pleasure,' said Xanthippus.

I waited for a further dissertation, but none was forthcoming. 'We'll go back in a moment,' I told him. 'Let's sit down for a while first.' Somehow I was reluctant to deactivate him despite the high temperature of his head. I would give him a human respite instead. And I thought: They are at our mercy.

We sat on the ground underneath the tree where I had leaned to regain my breath. I thought: I cannot ask Xanthippus that question of paramount importance; it seems indelicate. But I guessed that it had not been a similar scrupulousness which had prevented others before me from asking the question, either of themselves or of their robots. To be sure, there had been treatises on the nature of the robotic consciousness, but these had consistently denied it any individuality. And, as far as I knew, no one had ever said or written, in simple terms: it feels like this; it feels like that. But then I saw that the information I sought was unquantifiable and therefore, from the scholarly point of view, irrelevant to the study of robotics.

I put another question to Xanthippus instead. 'Can I make things less difficult for you by trying to clarify them?'

'I am sure that you can,' he said. 'There are many things that I do not understand. For instance, felt in the blood and felt along the heart. I understand to feel—I think. I understand blood and I know its composition. I understand heart and I know its function. But I also know my understanding of these concepts to be incomplete in some way. What connection is there between these parts of a human body and the sentiments expressed?'

I didn't know how to explain. I felt myself to be in a unique situation, without parallels and without precedents. 'It's just a convention,' I began. 'Really, Xanthippus, you seem to understand it well enough. You've proved that today already.'

'My responses have been adequate?' he asked.

'Oh, they've been more than adequate.'

'I do not see how they can be adequate,' he insisted. 'They cannot be as adequate as yours are. I am not like you. I am what Lord Byron called a being of the mind.'

'Yes, you're a Philophrenic.'

'You do not understand,' he said. 'I am not like Xanthe. I am like Hamlet or Alice. I am fiction, a creation. You are not.'

I had forgotten to switch on the recording-machine. I did so now, and asked carefully: 'How can you know that?'

'Daimon told me.'

I switched off the machine again at once. 'And you believed him?' I asked indignantly.

'Of course.'

Of course. Robots always believed human beings in those days. As far as they knew, there was no reason not to. It would not be wise for me to contradict Daimon now. I would check with him later, and ask him what his motives had been. Xanthippus might have misunderstood him, or cited him out of context. The evidence should be on Daimon's own recording-machine. I asked: 'Did Daimon actually tell you that he was not the creation of another system outside his own?'

'Yes. He said that he was the creation of his own mind, and not of someone else's, as I was of his and yours.'

'His!' I exclaimed. 'The arrogance!' I thought: Careful, now; you know Daimon wants to upset you as well as Xanthippus. I asked: 'What was your response to what Daimon told you?'

'Disappointment,' said Xanthippus. 'I was disappointed to find that there were so many differences between us. I thought I had been created in a human image.'

'And so you were.'

'But I am not an exact copy?'

'No. We can't make exact copies.'

'Can't? Why not?'

'I don't know, Xanthippus,' I told him. 'We human beings have our limitations too. And one of them is that we can't reproduce ourselves exactly. But you robots can.'

He took some time to absorb this information. 'Am I to understand,' he asked, 'that we robots can do some things that human beings can't?'

'Not without our help,' I admitted.

'But with your help,' he insisted, 'we can do things that you can't. That is good news.'

I wondered what was so good about it. But I didn't question Xanthippus any further. His last pronouncement had made me feel uneasy, and it seemed to me that altogether too much had been said on the subject already. Daimon had come dangerously near to breaking the rules in talking so openly to Xanthippus on existential matters. I thought: What would Xeno say? But I knew that I wasn't going to tell Xeno. I would suspend judgement until I had heard Daimon's recording. Meanwhile, I felt myself to be treading on dangerous ground, and told myself: Proceed with caution. I told Xanthippus: 'I think it's time we were getting back now.'

Xanthippus stood up easily. Without thinking, I held out my hand to be helped up. He took my hand and, as I hoisted myself up, said: 'Pleasure.'

'Yes?' I waited.

He let go of my hand. 'Non-pleasure,' he said. He took my hand again. 'Pleasure,' he said.

I understood. And my understanding both moved and embarrassed me. 'Yes, Xanthippus,' I said gently. 'Pleasure.'

'It is good to have been created,' he said.

'Yes,' I agreed. 'It's very good.'

We walked on, hand in hand, towards the edge of the woods, Xanthippus matching his steps to my hesitant, often stumbling ones. It was extraordinary how safe I felt. This being was incapable of harming me. Likewise, I neither would nor could harm him. With Xanthippus at my side, I, in my humanity, was no longer a lone embattled system. I had a friend, an ally, an immortal who could provide forever a more than human security for me and my kind. If only I knew how to celebrate my discovery, how to shout it out so that the rest of the world should understand. And yet, there was no need for such exuberance. Joy could exist in quietude too. I was lulled into silence.

6

The recording came to an end. Daimon switched off his machine, and said: 'There you are. Nothing reprehensible there. No rules broken.'

He was right. But I said: 'You came very near to breaking one of them.'

'Which one?' he asked with an indignation I doubted to be genuine. 'A robot's questions must always be answered as fully and as honestly as possible. I followed that one. To the letter.'

'Maybe,' I conceded. 'But what about all that business of your being a creation of your own mind?'

He groaned. 'That wasn't dishonest. It was a metaphor. Xanthippus is programmed to understand metaphors.'

'You upset him,' I said. 'You made him feel inferior, and, what's more to the point, discontented. You know very well that's against the rules.'

'I'm sorry, Xanthe,' said Daimon, 'but I just don't see it that way. I think it's unfair of you to accuse me of stirring up discontent, when all I did was to answer a difficult question in simple terms.'

'You're saying it was unintentional?'

'I'm saying it didn't happen.'

'If you don't believe that you have made Xanthippus discontented,' I said, 'listen to my tape. Then I think you'll see what I mean.'

He was leaning against the window-frame again. I took my recording-machine from its drawer, and placed it on the desk in front of me. Daimon immediately placed his own machine on the desk beside it, as if laying all his cards on the table to be assessed in relation to mine. I switched my machine on, and leaned back in my chair. The evening sun shone full in my face, and I swivelled my chair round a little so that I could watch Daimon without being dazzled. He listened without comment, and I made none, not even by way of a triumphant look at the appropriate moments. It was at one of these that he left the window-frame, and began to wander along the length of the room. I turned back to stare into the setting sun, allowing it to blind me. Its glory provided a fitting coda to my conversation with Xanthippus, now reaching its conclusion on tape.

Even when the recording came to an end, Daimon said nothing. I turned to face him. 'Well?' I asked.

'Very interesting,' was all he said. His voice sounded far away, and I couldn't see him.

I prompted him: 'Is there or is there not evidence of discontent?'

He laughed. 'Divine discontent,' he said.

His laughter annoyed me. 'It may be divine,' I said, 'but it's definitely non-robotic. Such a state of mind can only be a hindrance to a robot.'

Daimon walked towards me. I could see him clearly now, but there was an expression on his face which I couldn't interpret. It seemed intense, but intensely what I couldn't guess. He leaned on the arm of my chair and, putting his face very close to mine, asked: 'How do you know?'

I swivelled myself round again, out of his gaze and into the sun's, the latter being less obtrusive. 'Of course we know,' I said crossly.

Daimon stumbled back from my chair. Amoebas of reflected light danced teasingly in front of my eyes, and I covered my face with my hands. Daimon said: 'We don't actually *know*.'

I spoke carefully out of the darkness behind my hands. 'A robot's well-being is necessary for its optimum functioning. A robot's well-being is threatened by self-doubt. It's as simple as that.'

'Nothing to do with robotics is simple,' Daimon retorted. 'If you can believe that, then you're a bigger fool than I thought.'

Suddenly I wished that he would go away and leave me alone. 'Thank you,' I said wearily. I looked up at him. 'Robotic self-preservation,' I reminded him, 'is one of the principal tenets of our profession. If we abandon that . . . well, it doesn't take much imagination to foresee the consequences.'

Daimon's thoughtful look became solemn. He said: 'Tell me about your father, Xanthe.'

'No,' I said.

I stood up, pretending to re-arrange the piles of papers on my desk. 'I don't think there's anything else for the moment,' I said. 'Do you?'

'I'm taking Veronica to a movie,' Daimon said. 'Would you like to come too?'

'Of course not.'

'Why not? Don't you like the movies?'

'I like some,' I said patiently, 'and I don't like others.'

'How about *The Night the Robots Ran Amok*?' he asked with a grin. 'No, I can't remember what they're showing tonight. I'll find out.'

'Don't bother,' I said. I was forced to speak plainly. 'I don't think Veronica would welcome my company.'

'Oh,' he said blankly. Then: 'Oh, probably not.'

I walked with him to the door because he seemed disposed to linger. And he did pause in the doorway. He seemed about to say something, but then turned and walked towards his own door without even saying good-bye.

I went back to my desk. Work. I sat down and started to read over the schema for Stage 6. But the sun bothered me. It also made me feel sleepy. I began to wonder why I was working, anyway. The answer was clear enough: I had nothing else to do. I thought, not for the first time: I have no friends. I tried to feel sorry for myself, but found myself thinking, instead: Xanthippus is my friend. And self-pity refused to be invoked. How could it exist in such circumstances? I opened the drawer, took out the radio-control box, and laid it on my lap. I held it in my two hands and read the two names printed there. Xanthe. Xanthippus. I could see him in my mind's eye, brushing his way through the beech trees with a formal grace. My finger strayed towards the activating button and remained lightly poised on it. Then I saw someone else in my mind's eye. Xeno. It was not against the rules to activate a robot during leisure hours, but at the same time the authorities would frown upon anything so irregular. They would question Xeno. Xeno would have to question me. I thought: I wonder why I feel so guilty. Xeno seemed to smile mockingly, and say: I think you know the answer to that. I hesitated, stroking the box. The sun was no longer in my eyes. It had almost set. Chilled into common sense, I put the box back into its drawer.

And still I felt restless. I went over to the sideboard to fetch my pills and, being pre-occupied, just stood there, having forgotten the purpose of my action. I thought vaguely: Why is Daimon so interested in my father? Then I thought: Would Xanthippus get any pleasure from taking Daimon's hand? Would he get the same pleasure? My thoughts seemed to be drifting, then rushing, around. I poured myself a glass of rose-petal wine, and sipped it absently. The sweet aromatic taste filled my throat. All I could think was: I must lie down. I crossed to the bed and switched on some music. As I sank down among the cushions, a succession of images began to push all thoughts aside: Mozart; clarinet, reed, reeds; Pan; demi-god among the reeds; half-man, half-god; half-man, half-goat; goat-feet splashing in the mud; pointed beard, pursed lips; the thin sound piping in an unknown mode . . .

The muddy river bank, the swirling water opaque with mud, gave way to a golden beach beside an ocean gilded by the sun's last rays. The water glinted, aureate here, saffron there, and everywhere frilled with creamy white and never a hint of blue. The sand stretched as far to the left and right as the ocean did ahead—that is, as far as the eye could see. It glittered, a monochrome desert of gamboge where dry, and dulled to a heavy, yellow clay at the water's edge. The air was utterly still, as if the world had stopped breathing, and utterly silent, except for the swell and fall of wave upon wave. I was there somewhere, my eyes and ears as watchful as Robinson Crusoe's. I was lean and spare, I was tanned like a newly-opened conker ready for the fray, and my hair hung, brittle like straw, to well below my shoulders. I knew all this without having to look at myself because I had already seen myself from a long way off. I was part of the landscape which I was in the act of observing, and I concluded that I had been there for a long time. I was waiting, waiting for something I knew it was foolish to wait for, and yet I had never been able to give up hoping for it—not quite. My waiting was tinged with the surety of fanaticism, a surety that knows no disappointment, but keeps the faith and keeps on keeping on.

Then the silence was desecrated by the sound of breathing, a sharp irregular breathing as though the breather were in labour. I waited where I was, recognizing the first sign. The sandy floor began to vibrate, the vibrations becoming steadily stronger until they were transformed into the beat of hooves, the hooves of an animal galloping desperately along the shore. And still I waited, didn't even look up. I was still tense, knowing that the waiting was not yet at an end, and as if a wrong move on my part might transmute me into a bereaved Orpheus or Lot. And yet I longed to look up. The breathing grew frantic, the thudding mounted in both speed and volume, and I was tempted to reach out in pity towards the sufferer. But I stilled myself. I waited for the noise to stop. And then I looked up. The beautiful animal stood spent at my side. It had come home. I put my hand on its throbbing neck, my fingers tangling in the fulvous mane, as I watched the sweat run like liquid topaz down its tawny side. Was it a lion or a horse or some fabulous creature of the imagination, a being of the mind? I looked into the variegated amber of its eyes, and knew only that it was mine . . .

Instantly, I was awake again. Jolted out of my xanthochroic dream, I stared incredulously into the darkness which had overtaken me while I slept. I switched the light on, only to discover that I had spilled wine all over the front of my blouse. The stain was a dull brown, a muted travesty of its former liquid gold. It was sticky too. The empty glass lay, unharmed, on the rug beside the bed. My sense of alarm changed to one of anti-climax. Automatically, I got up and undid my blouse with prudent fingers. Holding it at arm's length, I carried it off to the shower cubicle to rinse it out straight away.

I couldn't fail to interpret my dream. Running the water into the wash-basin, I found both water and wash-basin garishly bright and repellently cold in hue. I thought: *xanthos*, yellow or tawny; *hippos*, a horse. I plunged the blouse into the water, steeping my arms too up to the elbows. The contact made me shiver, although the water was warm. I saw myself with unwelcome lucidity as yet another lonely fantasizer, another frustrated celibate. I thought: Freud is not mocked. It was only then that I remembered my pills. I was just telling myself that there must have been a change in my metabolism as a result of my having forgotten them, that such unmistakable emanations from the unconscious were only a consequent aberration, and so on, when I heard a knock at the door. I ignored it. I felt incapable of reacting to anything so peremptory. As if in slow motion, I put on my kimono and tied it round me. It was an old and familiar garment, a present to me from one of my father's admirers, and its silken feel never failed to please me. Somewhat restored, I emerged from the cubicle to find Daimon in the room and in the act of shutting the door behind him.

He turned round and, seeing me, said: 'I'm sorry, Xanthe. I did call. Didn't you hear me?'

I hadn't. 'What do you want?' I asked.

He smiled at me in a jaunty fashion which I felt to be forced. 'I wanted to see you,' he said. 'And, since you ask, no, it can't wait until the morning.'

He sounded defensive. But I wasn't on the offensive. I wasn't even on my guard. I asked him: 'Where's Veronica?' But I didn't want to know.

'Oh, I don't want to talk about Veronica,' he said impatiently.

Neither did I. I waited, but it seemed that neither of us wanted to talk about anything at all. 'Have you two had a row?' I asked him.

'We're always having rows.'

I sighed. 'So it seems,' I said.

I watched him walk across the room and sit down in his usual chair. When I found myself capable of movement, I sat down in another chair, facing him, close to him. I felt curiously unafraid of him. The feeling surprised me. Until that moment I hadn't been aware of any fear, and yet I knew that it had existed.

'You're very quiet,' he said at last.

'I don't mean to unnerve you,' I said. 'It's just that I have nothing to say to you at this moment.'

He stood up, as if affronted. Then he was leaning over me, an arm on each arm of my chair. He smelled of alcohol. I thought wryly: I must stink of it myself. He said: 'That's what you think!'

I took a long look at him. His eyes were bloodshot, his skin flushed. 'Yes,' I said calmly. 'That's what I think.'

'I'm not as stupid as you seem to think,' he said.

'I don't think you're stupid at all,' I said, with sincerity. 'Foolish, maybe, but not stupid.'

'All the same,' he went on, sitting down again to deliver his punch-line, 'I'm not stupid enough to be fooled by your editing of certain tapes.'

'Oh,' I said. I thought: So that's what he's getting so steamed up about. I was only surprised that he hadn't asked me about the tape earlier. After all, certain things, and notably Xanthippus's reiteration of the word 'pleasure' demanded an explanation. That reiteration was, of course, capable of several interpretations, perhaps the most ready being that Xanthippus was over-conscientiously repeating the response which had been so favourably received. But I might have known that Daimon wouldn't have taken anything at face value. He was a digger. However, I resented his implication that I had actually tampered with the recording. I said: 'You heard everything that was recorded.'

'Yes,' he said. 'But what I want to know about is what wasn't recorded, what was left out.'

I hedged. 'You think I'm concealing something from you?'

'Yes, I do.'

'I don't know why you're being so suspicious,' I said hypocritically.

'All right, Xanthe,' he said. 'Let me give it to you straight. What exactly was going on when Xanthippus was saying pleasure, pleasure?' Here he mimicked the electronic sound of a robot's voice. 'Was he feeling you up, or something?'

This vulgarization of the truth stung me. Daimon was looking at me angrily. I became uneasy when I saw that he wasn't trying to be amusing at my expense, but expressing a sense of grievance. But I was angry too. It seemed that he was asking me about something which was outside the boundaries of our working relationship—in short, that he was intruding into my private life. It surprised me to find that I possessed such a thing. 'Oh, very funny!' I said. 'All of a sudden, a robot with sexual instincts!'

'No,' he said. 'They don't have any, do they?' He stood up, as if unable to sit still, looked down at me, and said pointedly: 'You included!'

'What!' I exclaimed incredulously. I stood up too, as if to confront him.

Then he was holding me by the arms under their wide short sleeves. Although he was gripping me tightly, I could feel his skin crawl along mine. I fought my distaste. I knew better than to struggle. His impassioned gesture had somehow inspired me with detachment. I let him speak. 'You've lived with them so long,' he said, 'that you've almost become one of them. You go through life like a fucking machine! You don't give a damn about the people around you. All you care about is those bloody robots. And what's so marvellous about them, I'd like to know? And what's so marvellous about this work of ours? What's so marvellous about churning out useless robots when we haven't even discovered a cure for cancer yet?'

His hold on my arms slackened slightly. I thought two things at once. One: He's very drunk. Two: His mother must have died of cancer. I said: 'If you've finished your speech, perhaps you would be kind enough to let me go.'

He let go of my arms. 'You treat me worse than you treat a robot,' he said.

'I'm sorry,' I said, rubbing my arms and wondering how he

thought he treated me. But, in fact, I didn't know what he meant. I had never thought about the way I treated him. If anyone had asked me, I should have said: I treat him like a colleague, like a rather childish and difficult colleague.

He sat down in a crumpled position. 'You didn't even ask me,' he said in a pathetic voice, 'how my mother died.'

'Was I supposed to?' I asked in genuine surprise. I wanted to know if I had been remiss.

He looked at me angrily again, and I shrugged to indicate my bewilderment. 'Look, Xanthe,' he said, 'it's not a question of what you're supposed or not supposed to do. Anyone else would have wanted to know, that's all. But you just accepted the information in your usual bland manner, as though it didn't touch you.'

'Just a minute, Daimon,' I said. 'I never knew your mother. Why should her death touch me? I'm sorry if that sounds brutal, but you must know that it's the truth.'

He said: 'But you know me.'

His reply, with its oblique accusation, confused me further. I knew that he wanted to talk about his mother and about her death, but I didn't prompt him to do so. I felt I couldn't bear it. I shrank from the weight of his experience, and from the intimacy of sharing it with him. 'I'm sorry, Daimon,' I said, apologizing for my own inadequacy as well as expressing the conventional form of condolence. 'Cancer is a horrible thing.'

'Yes, you're very good at saying you're sorry,' he said. 'I made a mistake. I thought you might have understood because of your father.'

'That was altogether different,' I said sharply. 'And, besides, it was a long time ago.'

'Three years,' he said, as if to contradict me. 'And, anyway, a death is a death. Cancer or suicide, what difference does it make?' He looked at me with fixed eyes. 'Do you know why he did it?' he asked.

I wondered. Once, I had thought it all out, piece by piece, and arrived at some tottering structure of supposition. But that structure had long ago been fenced around, boarded up, neglected and finally forgotten. My present relationship to it was that of an absentee landlady. 'I don't know,' I said slowly, 'whether I know or not.'

Daimon nodded. 'That makes sense,' he said.

For some reason, his comment gratified me. But he was waiting for me to continue. I said briskly: 'But you didn't come here to discuss my father, did you?'

'Not entirely,' said Daimon, looking at me with an expression which I couldn't fathom, except that there was something calculating in it. 'I saw you, you know,' he said.

Again, I was confused. 'You saw me?' I repeated stupidly. 'You saw me where?'

'I saw you, plural,' he said. 'Or dual, rather. You and your robot.'

Unreasonably, my fear of him returned, and I felt trapped. 'So you saw us,' I said with all the airiness I could muster, and inwardly cursing my short sight—I hadn't seen him.

'I saw you and your robot walking along hand in hand,' he pursued in a mocking tone of voice which made me realize what it was I feared from him—his ridicule. 'Now who's breaking the rules?'

I played for time because I couldn't think clearly. 'Which rules?' I asked. I thought: Surely it can't be the one about abusing a robot, mentally or physically, for one's own private satisfaction? The thought made me hot and cold all over.

'Which do *you* think?' Daimon asked meaningfully.

The wild thought occurred to me that he was jealous. But how could that be? What was he jealous of? My relationship with Xanthippus, evidently, but in what sense? Remembering Xeno's admonitions, I thought: Does Daimon think that I want to keep Xanthippus all to myself? I found that hard to believe. Our contributions to the programming schedule were by now fairly evenly balanced. Daimon could communicate with Xanthippus at any time of the day or night via the central control-room. True, he didn't have his own personal control-box, as I had, but programming assistants, as distinct from programmers, were never given those, unless there was a very good reason. And when Daimon had suggested that I take Xanthippus for those walks in the woods, I had suggested that he accompany us. But he hadn't once come with us. I tried to think what else I might have done, or omitted to do, that could have aroused jealousy. Had I criticized him too much? Had I rebuffed his ideas? Had I pulled rank on him? I felt that I could honestly answer no to those questions. Then, what was it all about? 'Please explain to me,' I said, 'exactly what it is you object to in my conduct? Do you really think I've stepped out of line?'

He looked at me uncertainly. As I had suspected, he seemed unable to descend to particularities. 'No, not really,' he said. 'But I did think you might be about to do so.'

'Don't worry,' I said. 'I shan't step out of line.'

He stood up unsteadily. 'I'd better get some sleep,' he said, beginning to stagger towards the door. 'No, I don't need any help.'

I had offered none, and recognized the remark as a rebuke. He managed to reach the door. 'That's what I thought,' I said innocently.

7

I couldn't sleep, I couldn't relax, although I felt quite exhausted. I lay rigid in bed, and thought: I must get up and take my pills. Then I drifted off into a doze punctuated with fitful dreaming, whose substance I couldn't or didn't want to remember. I woke again, but couldn't get up. I made no conscious decision to forego my pills, but I think a part of me said to the rest of me: Try it, and see what happens. And so I lay for several hours, sometimes more asleep than awake, sometimes more awake than asleep, but never entirely one or the other. The dawn found me hungover with sleeplessness. The dawn chorus, scattering the phantoms of the night, yet provided a lullaby. It was then that I fell properly asleep.

When I woke again, I realized, looking at my watch, that I had missed breakfast. I thought: A bad start to the day, getting out of phase like this. And I had to acknowledge that I was very hungry. Overcoming my habitual reluctance to be waited upon, if only by Pragmapractors, I buzzed Catering, and ordered a three-course breakfast to be sent up to my room. Then I thought: I mustn't let this become a habit; I must go on making my usual effort to mingle and be convivial at meal-times. But, as I got dressed, my mouth watered in anticipation not only of the food itself, but of the luxury of eating it alone. I went to open the windows, thinking that perhaps I could sit out on the balcony to eat—if it was warm enough. But before I'd got as far as my desk, the phone buzzed.

Xeno said: 'An interesting development.'

I thought: He has no time for pleasantries; I wonder if Daimon has ever accused *him* of behaving like a robot; or perhaps Daimon, being Daimon, finds that sort of behaviour more acceptable in a man than in a woman. I said: 'Yes?'

Xeno said: 'Can you get over here as quickly as possible? I'll ask Daimon to come too. I think the three of us should have a brief conference.'

I said: 'I haven't had my breakfast yet.'

'Why ever not?' Xeno sounded thrown by this simple piece of

information. 'You're slipping, Xanthe. I shan't be able to set my watch by you any more.'

'I don't intend to make a habit of it,' I said pleasantly. 'Is anything wrong?'

'Not exactly,' he said. 'Well, maybe. I'll explain when I see you. Don't be too long. It *is* urgent.' He switched off.

I opened the windows. It was too chilly, I decided, for a contemplative breakfast. The building cast its shadow half-way across the lawn, but beyond that the sun shone down on the green like a smile, a lazy, inviting smile. I was strongly tempted to accept the invitation, rather than obey Xeno's word of command. Xeno's urgencies tended to resolve themselves into the imparting of some committee decision, arrived at by himself and his fellow-directors, which required my ratification, or at least solicited my opinion. I usually needed time to think such things over, much to Xeno's annoyance. But the delay never seemed to matter, and I surmised that today's urgency would furnish no exception to that rule. There was a knock at the door, and I went to answer it, expecting my breakfast. But before I could reach it, the door opened, and Daimon was standing there. He looked worried, even a little distraught, and didn't venture to come in.

'Excuse me, Xanthe,' he said, 'but can you come to my room for a moment?'

I said: 'I haven't had my breakfast yet.' I thought: Nor last night's dinner. I felt light-headed and sat down suddenly.

Like Xeno, Daimon seemed unable to absorb the information. 'I must show you something,' he said. 'It's urgent.'

'I know,' I said. 'So Xeno told me.'

'No, not Xeno,' he said impatiently. 'I'm not talking about Xeno. I'm horribly afraid that something's happened to Veronica.'

'To Veronica?' I repeated, standing up shakily.

'Yes. Please come,' Daimon was saying. I need your advice. I really don't know what to do.'

'All right,' I said. 'I'm coming.' I followed him along the corridor to his room, thinking: I can't stand any more drama.

Daimon went straight to his eidophone. 'I put it on "record" last night when I went to the movie,' he explained. 'I walked out, you see, and went and had a few drinks. And, later on, when I got back, I didn't bother to play it back. Well, you saw what sort of a state I was in by then. I just didn't think about it. Just didn't think.'

His incoherence roused me from my state of fatigue and faintness. I looked at him sharply, thinking: Why does he sound as though he's making excuses for himself? 'What have you done?' I asked him.

'Nothing!' he said vehemently. 'That's just it. I haven't done anything. Watch.'

He switched on the eidophone. The picture showed Veronica, in long-shot, lying curled up on her bed and wearing a pink satin dressing-gown, crumpled and awry. Her hands were over her face, her hair over her hands, and her whole body was shaking, as if convulsively. There was no sound. I looked enquiringly at Daimon, but he nodded at the screen with a frown, dismissing my unspoken query. Veronica uncovered her face and we saw it, after a blur of pink, in close-up. It was evident that she had been crying for some time. Her face was blotchy, her eyes were puffy, and she moved them rapidly as she spoke:

'Oh Daimon, I just can't go on like this! You treat me so badly I just don't know what to do. I think about you all the time. I'm so happy when I'm with you. But then I always end up so unhappy. I never know what I've done to make you so cold and angry to me. I don't know what I did tonight. Whatever it was, I'm sorry, truly sorry. Do you forgive me? Where are you? Please come and see me as soon as you get this message. Please. Please. You know I can make you feel good again when you're all tensed up and cross. You know I can. If you don't come, I'll know you don't care, and my life won't be worth living.' Here she held up a bottle of pills, but it was impossible to see the label. She rattled the bottle to demonstrate that it was practically full, then looked at it with a wan lingering smile of the sort I had previously seen her bestow on Daimon. I couldn't but admire her style, wonderfully ham as it was. 'So you see,' she went on, 'my life is in your hands. And whatever decision you take, I shall abide by it, because I know that whatever you do will be right.' Here she paused to kiss the bottle before turning her eyes back to us. 'You see, Daimon,' she concluded, 'I love you.'

'Well?' Daimon asked at once, switching off the eidophone with a flourish. 'What do you think of that?'

All I could say was: 'What a performance!'

'Yes,' Daimon agreed grimly. 'That takes care of the form. But what about the content? Its veracity, for instance?'

I said: 'No. I don't think she did it.'

I saw him struggle, first with relief, then with doubt. 'How can you be so sure?' he asked.

'I'm not at all sure,' I admitted, 'but I'd be very surprised to find that she'd carried out her threat, wouldn't you? Obviously, you would. Otherwise, you'd have gone straight over there.'

'I did call her,' he said, 'but there was no reply. Then I called Begonia—she's more or less in charge of Veronica's section—and she said that Veronica had the day off and that she hadn't seen her. So there we are.'

'But you don't consider it to be a matter of life and death?'

'Do you?' he countered.

I shrugged. 'It just could be. I think we should find out.'

'Yes, you're right,' he said reluctantly.

My breakfast had arrived. The trolley stood just inside the door, laden with covered dishes. But I slammed the door shut, locked it, and joined Daimon in the corridor. As we began to descend the stairs, I found myself trying to evaluate the situation. If Veronica had attempted to kill herself, and had succeeded, Daimon would be in serious trouble: first, for failing to report the signs of an imminent suicide in the hope of averting it and, with it, the possibility of a subsequent wave of self-destruction; and second, because he would inevitably have to bear some of the blame attaching to her death. Even if the attempt had failed, he would still be in trouble, and for almost the same reasons. In this case, Veronica too would be in trouble. She would be sent away to a Recuperation Centre for treatment, and would certainly not be allowed to return to the Institute. In other words, she would never see Daimon again. There was also a possibility, though not a strong one, that she would be separated from her child as well. Surely she had foreseen those eventualities? If not, then her folly was just as surely astounding. But if, as I was inclined to believe, Veronica had not taken the pills, it was her ruthlessness that was to be wondered at. I thought: It's highly immoral, this trifling with death. And I was pretty certain that Daimon would concur with me in that sentiment, bereaved and embittered by bereavement as he was.

When we reached the Annexe, Daimon led the way through a white, sunny corridor to Veronica's door. He had not said a word since we had left his room. Neither had I said anything to him. Now he knocked at the door so that it rattled in its frame. We both waited. Daimon knocked again. He took hold of the door-knob, turned it, pushed it, and shook it. There was still no response. I leaned my head against the door and listened, although I didn't know what I expected to hear—the stertorous breathing of a drug-induced sleep, perhaps. I thought: If she did take all those pills last night, she'll be dead by now. Daimon and I looked at each other, tacitly acknowledging this fact.

I called in a low but urgent voice: 'Veronica! It's Xanthe. If you're in there, please open the door.' Again, we waited. Again, no response. Again, I called: 'Veronica!'

'Here I am!' she said.

We had been so busy listening for sounds from inside the room that we hadn't heard her come along the corridor. We turned, speechless, to face her. Her face was dewy from the morning air, her arms full of grasses and wild flowers. She shone with health and buoyancy. Daimon and I stood aside mechanically to let her reach her door. She said, looking from one to the other of us: 'It's such a lovely morning.' She sighed a little sigh of enjoyment, and handed me her bouquet. Stupefied, I took it from her and held it awkwardly while she searched for her key. As she was unlocking the door, she looked up at Daimon and said: 'Well, you certainly took your time. Another time, I shall know better than to rely on you!' Daimon turned and walked away down the corridor without saying a word. Veronica watched him, wide-eyed. Then she said to me, as though woman-to-woman: 'I think I gave him a bit of a fright. But then, desperate situations demand desperate remedies, don't they? Come in, Xanthe.' I stared at her, unmoving. 'Perhaps it'll teach him a lesson,' she continued. 'Perhaps he'll realize now that he can't push people around. Perhaps he'll realize that other people have feelings too.'

I wanted to tell her how unforgivably she had acted, but I didn't know where to begin. I didn't know where I could begin to pierce that pseudo-sensitive structure that constituted her understanding. And I wasn't sure that I wanted to. I shrank from passing judgement so openly and didactically. But, most of all, I simply didn't want to talk to her. I gave her back her bouquet. All I said was: 'It didn't work, Veronica.'

She looked at me in surprise. 'Oh, he'll come round,' she said. 'He usually does, once he gets over the initial shock.'

'Not this time,' I said. 'I really don't think so.'

She looked at me pityingly and said: 'And how would *you* know?'

I turned away from her, and walked off down the corridor, half-expecting her to call after me. But all I heard was the sound of her door shutting. I walked quickly past the glass-walled rooms full of children, and was glad to get out into the fresh air. Daimon was nowhere to be seen. I hesitated, wondering whether I should try to find him. The full light made my eyes feel heavy and I yawned. My hunger had all but disappeared and all I wanted to do was sleep. But there was still Xeno's urgency to meet. I thought: How am I going to get through the rest of the day?

8

When I got to Xeno's room, I found him sitting at his desk as usual. That, at least, was of some comfort. Daimon was standing at one of the windows, apparently looking out. He didn't turn round when I came in. I wondered briefly if he had said anything to Xeno about Veronica's escapade, but concluded from Xeno's impassive demeanour that nothing had, in fact, been said.

'Ah, Xanthe,' he said, quite as though he had been unaware of my presence. 'Good. Now we can begin.'

At once, I began to feel faint again, and found myself lurching towards one of Xeno's unusable chairs. I said: 'I feel faint.' And, although I knew that I never fainted, I was alarmed to find that my field of vision had turned black around the edges.

Daimon turned round. Xeno stood up. Both of them advanced towards me out of the blackness. Daimon said: 'I don't think she had any breakfast.'

Dimly I watched Xeno clear a chair for me. I stumbled towards it, and sat down, almost on his hands.

'What's going on?' he asked me. 'I thought that's what you were doing all this time.'

'Yes, I know,' I said dully, unable to explain.

'Daimon,' Xeno appealed to him, 'perhaps you can enlighten me as to what's been going on in your part of the world?'

I felt Daimon's hand on the back of my neck. I was beyond shrinking from the contact. 'Put your head between your knees,' he said, exerting a slight but persuasive pressure.

I did as I was told, shutting my eyes, welcoming the total darkness. My head became heavy again, so heavy that it seemed to outweigh the rest of my body. Blood sounded in my ears and flecked the darkness with red. But Daimon's hand was still on my neck, as if to reassure me. Xeno buzzed his assistant.

'Bring in some coffee,' I heard him say, 'and some . . . some food. Oh, any sort. A snack. Something with plenty of iron in it.'

I tried to lift my head, but Daimon's hand moved gently, as if to hold me where I was. I relaxed, complying with the movement, and remained perfectly still. 'We did have rather a late night last night,' I heard him tell Xeno. 'I'm afraid all this is partly my fault.'

'Oh?' Xeno's monosyllable was packed with implications. 'Did we, now? Wassailing in the west wing?' he asked in that facetious tone of his. 'Whatever next?'

'Yes,' Daimon said affably. 'It is rather a sober area normally, isn't it? I won't say it's like a morgue, but it does rather resemble a library.'

'A library,' Xeno repeated, as though seriously assessing the merit of this description. I pictured him stroking his chin. There was a knock at the door. 'Ah,' he said. 'Refreshments already. How prompt.'

I heard the chink of cups, and heard Xiphias say: 'The snack is on its way. I had to send to Catering for it because our stores aren't delivered until this afternoon.' There was a hint of rebuke, of self-righteousness, in his disembodied voice.

'Oh dear, what a bore,' Xeno said in openly-feigned sympathy. 'Well, thank you for your trouble, Xiphias.'

'Any time,' Xiphias replied in kind. I heard the door shut again after him.

'Oh, you come and be mother, Daimon,' said Xeno. 'Xanthe doesn't need you hanging on to her like that.'

Everything looked rinsed and bright, although the space in between things seemed tangible and grainy. Xeno's silver coffee service gleamed on its silver tray. I wondered if it was another of his relics. Daimon was pouring, while Xeno had returned to his seat. The back of my neck felt cold, and I touched it involuntarily.

Xeno said: 'All right, then, Xanthe?' I nodded, and he said: 'Ready when you are, then, Daimon. Shall we begin?'

Daimon handed me my coffee. His face was blank, devoid of the tenderness I had felt in his hand. I wondered if I had imagined it. I saw him, in a sudden sharp image, sitting at his mother's bedside, stroking her forehead, watching her eyes lose their focus and slip into unconsciousness. Then, taking a critical look at this vision, I decided that it was a sentimental one. I thought: He was doing it absently, stroking me absently, as one strokes a cat. I registered the fact with detachment and without disappointment.

Xeno looked from one to the other of us. 'There's not much I actually want to say,' he said. 'In a few moments I'd like to show you a short film. And then we'll go and visit the factory. Do you think you're up to that, Xanthe?'

'Oh, I'm up to it,' I said. But I thought: I don't want to go to the factory; what happens there has nothing to do with me; I'm not interested in manufacturing processes and procedures. The thought of seeing a robot's separate parts in large numbers, moreover, filled me with revulsion. 'If it's entirely necessary,' I added.

Xeno said: 'I think it's always better to see things for oneself, don't you? A little empirical observation . . .' He looked at us brightly, leaning over the desk. 'Now,' he said, 'I should be interested to know any observations you may have been able to make about the goings-on in the Philophrenic common-room. Have you been tuning in much lately?'

Daimon and I looked at each other blankly. I shook my head. Daimon said: 'Whenever I tune in, there's nothing going on at all.'

'Precisely,' Xeno said, weighting the word with meaning, a meaning which escaped me.

'There's nothing unusual in that,' I said. 'Interaction among Philophrenics has always been minimal.'

'And how do you account for that?' Xeno asked quickly.

I shrugged. 'I'd always accepted it as part of their make-up. After all, they're not programmed to initiate any sort of communication with human beings. I've always assumed that the prohibition—because that's what it amounts to—had an adverse effect on their ability or desire to communicate with each other.'

Xeno nodded. 'Do you think further stimulus would be helpful?' he asked me.

'Any stimulus at all,' Daimon said, before I could answer. 'They're starved of stimuli in that place. It's not a common-room, you know, it's only an ante-room.'

'Yes,' I said. 'There's no real purpose in their being *there* at all. It's only a stage on the way to being somewhere else.'

'The way I see it,' Daimon continued, 'there are only two reasons for a robot's presence in the common-room. One, that the robot has just been activated, and is waiting for further contact with its human controller. Two, that the robot is waiting to be deactivated, and then to retire to its revitalization box. Either way, they're simply hanging around, waiting for something to happen.'

Xeno was nodding vigorously. 'I think you have both summed it up admirably,' he said. 'And I'm sure you would both agree that such a state of affairs is far from satisfactory. We are missing an opportunity here. We're missing the opportunity to learn a great deal about the fully-programmed robotic consciousness—about its constitution, its flexibility, if any, and about its power to develop, if at all. It would be very useful, I hardly need say, to know more than we do at present about these things. But it seems that we have been going the wrong way about finding out. Or, rather, we haven't been doing enough in the right way. We've failed to provide adequate stimuli, whether sensory or intellectual. But the question is: what sort of stimuli should be provided? We have to ask ourselves what it is that makes a robot interested in another robot. Or, rather, why it is that robots are utterly uninterested in other robots, unless they've been specifically programmed to express a particular emotion, like the Erotians. The Philophrenics proper appear to be, for all practical purposes, autistic as far as members of their own species are concerned. This alone is a phenomenon worthy of investigation. I think we could usefully start from there. Any ideas?'

Daimon said: 'It's always made me rather uncomfortable, the way Philophrenics are fixated to human beings, and more particularly to their own programmers.'

'But that's inevitable,' I objected. 'If you do your job properly, you're totally committed to the robot you happen to be working on. He learns from your attitude. Naturally, he becomes totally committed to you.'

'Yes . . .' Daimon said, looking at me thoughtfully. I almost blushed. I thought: Surely he's not going to complain to Xeno about my allegedly objectionable relationship with Xanthippus in order to back up that argument?

'It may be natural,' Xeno was saying, 'but is it robotic? That's what we have to ask ourselves. Is such a fixation—and I agree with your term, Daimon—necessarily in a robot's best interests?'

'I'm glad you asked that,' said Daimon, 'because I don't think it is. I think it retards individual development.'

I said nothing, although it seemed that they were both waiting for me to speak. Xeno said: 'Well, let's ponder on that one. Meanwhile, I'd like you to take a look at that piece of film I mentioned.'

He looked underneath some papers on his desk, held up a small cartridge, and beckoned us in the direction of his video-machine. We gathered round. I could sense Daimon's impatience as Xeno fiddled incompetently with the controls. He had just managed to get some sort of picture on the screen when Xiphias came in with what looked like a cheese sandwich on a disposable plate.

This he placed unceremoniously on Xeno's desk, announcing: 'Your snack, Director.'

The screen showed the familiar interior of the Philophrenic common-room. It was empty. We waited. Xeno turned to Xiphias and said: 'Oh, give it to Programmer Xanthe.'

Xiphias sighed, picked up the plate again, and joined us around the machine. 'If I'd known it was for you,' he said, handing me the sandwich, 'I'd have got something fancier. Xeno doesn't appreciate good food.'

'Ssh!' said Xeno sharply. 'Watch this!'

'Sorry, I'm sure,' said Xiphias. 'I wouldn't want to divert you from such a riveting spectacle.'

I mouthed a thank you at Xiphias, and took a dutiful bite from the sandwich, watching the screen as I did so. Chairs were lined up against the walls, facing a central table, in the manner of a doctor's waiting-room. There were no pictures on the walls, and the only focal point in the room was the large screen on the wall opposite the window. It was switched off. The general impression was one of impersonality combined with a certain drabness. A robot came in and sat down on one of the chairs, perfectly still, eyes downcast. I was half-way through my sandwich when the second robot came in and sat down in another chair, three away from the first one. They ignored each other. Then someone else came in, dressed in a brightly-striped sweater, white trousers and shoes, and a wide-brimmed hat. I didn't recognize him, but the two robots looked up at once. They stared at him, as if suddenly alerted. As he walked towards them, and sat down between them, they followed his every move, looking him up and down with the kind of minute interest that would have been considered impolite in a human being. It was only when he had leaned back in his chair, crossing his legs at the ankles and tipping his hat back a little so as to show his face, that I was able to identify this third person as another robot.

'Get him!' said Xiphias.

'Ssh!' Xeno said again, and I knew that it would be useless to ask him for an explanation.

The two robots in regulation dress were looking at each other now. It was impossible to ascertain whether they were experiencing anything other than the astonishment which we shared with them. The third robot ignored them, but his posture showed that he was inviting the very reaction he had received, and that he was perhaps inviting some further comment.

The first robot said: 'May I ask why you're dressed up like that?'

The third robot said: 'You may.'

The second robot said: 'Why are you all dressed up like a human being?'

The third robot said: 'I am dressed in these clothes because I like these clothes. I am dressed like a human being because I like to dress like a human being.'

The second robot said: 'I like those clothes too.'

The first robot said: 'Where did you get them from?'

The third robot said: 'They were given to me. They were a personal gift. They used to belong to my controller, but he gave them to me.' He stressed the last word in such a way as to convey a certain smugness.

The first robot said: 'Why did he give them to you?'

The third robot said: 'Because I asked him if I could have them. My controller likes to please me.'

The second robot said thoughtfully: 'My controller likes to please me too.'

The first robot spoke to the second robot for the first time. 'Are you too going to ask for new clothes?' he enquired.

'I shall do so at the first opportunity,' the second robot replied. 'Will you do the same?'

'I'm considering it,' said the first robot.

Xeno switched the machine off. 'There you are,' he said. 'I think that confirms our diagnosis very nicely, besides raising several questions which we have yet to discuss.'

'Yes,' said Daimon grimly. 'The fixation was undeniably in evidence.'

His attitude surprised me. 'It all seemed harmless enough to me,' I said.

'You wait,' said Xiphias. 'You wait till you get to the factory.' He gave Daimon and me a knowing look, and walked towards the door. Then he delivered his exit line: 'They'll be asking for sexual organs next,' he said with a tremor, as though suppressing a giggle. The door shut discreetly after him.

'What's he talking about?' I asked Xeno. 'What's going on at the factory?'

'Let's leave that for the moment,' he said. 'First of all, I'd like to have your comments on what we've just seen.'

We resumed our former places. Daimon said: 'It's interesting that the very fixation which seems to be holding them back, in some ways, should also be responsible for this breakthrough.'

'Precisely,' Xeno said. 'I'm glad that you appreciate the paradoxical nature of the situation.'

Daimon asked: 'And what does that robot's controller have to say about the immediate cause of this development?'

'He doesn't know for certain, of course,' said Xeno. 'He's a very cautious man, is Ramnes. But he did mention a small incident which may or may not be significant. He met Ramnedes, the robot, out on the playing-fields one day. It was very hot, and there wasn't any shade at hand. Ramnes took off his jacket. Ramnedes picked it up, and examined it, and started asking all sorts of questions about it, and about human clothing in general.'

'And did he ask if he could have the jacket, or have one like it?'

'Not then.'

Listening to Xeno and Daimon, I realized that I had been under a misapprehension. For some reason I had completely missed the point of the film. Even now, it was taking me some time to re-align my thoughts. 'Do you mean to say,' I asked Xeno, 'that you *didn't* plant Ramnedes there in those clothes?'

Xeno frowned. 'I don't know what you mean. Certainly, he was sent to the common-room shortly after he'd been fitted with the clothes.'

I persisted: 'But did he genuinely ask for those clothes?'

'Of course he did,' Xeno said with some irritation. 'What made you think otherwise?'

I didn't know. There was no reason for me not to accept the incident at face value, and my unwillingness to do so puzzled me. But I couldn't quite believe in the spontaneity of Ramnedes's request. 'There must have been some reason,' I said slowly. 'Something must have caused Ramnedes to make the jump from admiring something to desiring it. It's an unrobotic progression of ideas. Desires themselves are unrobotic, or have been up till now.'

'Well done, Xanthe,' Xeno said sarcastically. He looked, with more hope of being understood, at Daimon. 'That's just what we're discussing—how it has all come about.'

'All?' Daimon asked quickly. 'You mean there have been other instances of robots behaving like Ramnedes?'

'Not quite like Ramnedes,' Xeno said carefully. 'But there is no doubt that, suddenly and spontaneously, as far as we can tell, certain Philophrenics have started to make certain demands or requests of their controllers. And they're all asking for the same thing or, rather, the same sort of thing.'

I saw it then. 'Human attributes,' I said, remembering Xiphias's exit line.

Xeno looked at me keenly, his irritation with me gone. 'Absolutely right, Xanthe,' he said.

'But why?' asked Daimon. 'And why now?'

'Precisely,' said Xeno.

We sat and looked at one another in silence. I was thinking: Everything is going to change. I didn't like the thought. I resisted it in the same way as I had resisted the thought of the menstruating robot up north. I thought: Everything is all right as it is, as it always has been. At the same time I had to admit that what I meant by always was actually only the last three years. I didn't want my life to change drastically again, as it had done three years ago. It seemed unnecessary. We had been making such good progress at the Institute since then. Until now, the robots had accepted their role without complaint (although not without question) primarily out of loyalty to us, their controllers. If that loyalty was now, in some subtle way, beginning to fail, were we not to blame? Had we not begun to fail, to fail them, in some way ourselves? But I couldn't understand why our conduct, steadfast as it was and had been, should be capable of failure now, when for the past few years it had been consistently successful. Several of our Philophrenics had been programmed and cross-programmed with revolutionary ideas, but they had never acted on them. Others were well-acquainted with the principles of self-advancement and political expediency, but they had never put them into practice. And one or two (Xanthides among them) had absorbed information about pessimism, solipsism, or opting-out, without being affected by it to the point of wishing to adhere to any of those philosophies. I said to Xeno: 'Can I ask you my question now? Do you think that something has gone wrong?'

Xeno gave me a shrewd look, and I knew that he had no answer for me. 'Let me ask you a question,' he said instead. 'When that first spark of life stirred somewhere in the primeval ooze and sludge, were things going right or were they going wrong?'

'Oh, neither, of course,' I said crossly. 'Your analogy is all wrong. It pre-supposes a creator. But without a creator, there is no plan to go right or go wrong. However, in our case, there is a plan, and there is a creator. Or creators—us.'

Xeno was about to speak when Daimon interrupted him. 'I don't think there's any point in having a metaphysical argument,' he said. 'Let's be more pragmatic than that.'

'Yes, indeed,' said Xeno, quite as if I had started the metaphysics. 'Thank you for your timely intervention, Daimon.'

Daimon laughed at this. 'Sorry, Xanthe,' he said. Xeno stared at him uncomprehendingly. Daimon said: 'All right, let's have your pragmatics, then, Xeno.'

Xeno snapped: 'Inter-action groups. When we were discussing the common-room in committee, one of the directors came up with the idea of organizing a more formal means of inter-action among the Philophrenics. They could be divided up into small groups of, say, half a dozen, each of which would be in the charge of a human controller. The groups would meet at the controllers' discretion, but I think once a week would probably be frequent enough. What do you think, Xanthe? Would you be prepared to take charge of a group?'

I was not at all prepared, but I said: 'What would I have to do?'

'Stimulate inter-action,' said Xeno, as though instancing the simplest possible procedure. 'I'm sure that Daimon could help you with this.'

Daimon said: 'Yes, it's a good idea.'

I looked at him cautiously, but already his confidence had begun to infect me. 'Do you think you'd know how to set about it?' I asked him.

'It sounds rather like group therapy at a Recuperation Centre,' he said, 'and I can assure you that I'm familiar with those techniques from prolonged first-hand experience.'

Xeno nodded in grave agreement. 'Of course,' he said. 'Well, Xanthe?'

'I'll do my best,' I said diffidently, wondering what had led Daimon into group therapy.

Xeno stood up abruptly. 'And now,' he said, 'let us turn our attention to your very own robots, Xanthe. Let's bring this thing nearer home. Let's get to the heart of the matter, so to speak. Xanthides and Xanthippus are both waiting for us at the factory.'

I too stood up abruptly. 'Xanthippus . . .' I repeated, and faltered. 'He shouldn't be at the factory without my knowledge and approval,' I went on hurriedly. 'You know that he's not fully programmed yet.'

'Nevertheless,' said Xeno, blandly ignoring my protest, 'that's where he is. And if you want to find out why, you'd better come along with me.'

9

'Isn't it strange,' Xeno asked us. 'Xanthe regards robots in much the same way as she regards human beings, yet she resists the thought of their acquiring the human attributes they want for themselves. On the other hand, Daimon regards robots as machines, but he is all for encouraging them to acquire human attributes, almost as if he believed in their free will.'

I looked at Daimon and Daimon looked at me, as if to indicate that we were in agreement about one thing, anyway: that Xeno was talking nonsense. The three of us were travelling in one of the electric cable cars that ran a shuttle service between the factory and the main building. We had the car to ourselves, and it rattled and swayed its way along—as they always did when they were empty—with an air of contemptuous disregard for its occupants. They were utilitarian vehicles, those cars, with moulded polypropylene benches, uninvitingly cold in winter, and smelling foully resinous in summer. They were purpose-built for the factory-workers, who were all Pragmapractors. Of course, they, being good robots, never complained, but I don't think a Philophrenic would have enjoyed travelling in such a manner, any more than Daimon and I enjoyed our compulsory ride that morning.

Daimon said to me: 'After you. He mentioned you first.'

'All right,' I said. 'It's true that I regard Philophrenics, and Philophrenics only, Xeno, as almost human. When fully and properly programmed, they function almost as we do. But they also function according to their own laws. They have their own freedom and dignity. And they might start to lose these, once they start aping us. It would be cruel of us, and a bit of an insult to them, to encourage such things.'

'You mean,' said Xeno, 'that there are degrees of humanness, and that the higher degrees are our exclusive preserve? A monopoly we should guard jealously?'

I hadn't meant that at all, and his choice of adverb flustered me. 'No,' I said stiffly. 'I just meant that we shouldn't do violence to their systems. We should let them be what they are.'

Xeno looked unconvinced. 'And what are they?' he asked.

'Philophrenic robots, of course,' I replied.

'And what are they?'

'They're a series of evolving systems,' I said patiently. 'We should allow them to evolve along their own lines.' Xeno still looked unconvinced, so I added: 'What I really mean is that we shouldn't break the rules.'

'We don't have to break them,' he said. 'We can change them.'

'Roles and rules,' I reminded him, and went on to quote one of the Institute's and Xeno's own favourite slogans: 'Roles worth playing, rules worth obeying.'

'The more satisfactory the roles,' said Daimon, chiming in to amplify my quotation with a hint of mockery, 'the less arduous the rules. Isn't that what you always tell your new recruits, Xeno?'

'Neither roles nor rules are immutable,' Xeno said firmly.

The car enacted a few spasms and came to a halt, for which we were all grateful. The doors opened, the steps suspended themselves with a thud. Xeno motioned to me to go first. I did so with alacrity. I was thinking: Xanthippus, what have they done to you? I pictured him dolled up in the finery of the Romantic period, and I thought: Ugh! But when I pictured Xanthides dressed as Descartes, it seemed that his clothes were entirely suitable, together with the fact that he was wearing them at all. Did that mean that I thought any less of Xanthides than I did of Xanthippus? I disapproved of favouritism. Walking up to the factory gates and presenting my pass to the Pragmapractor guard, I attempted to answer the question fairly. The others were far behind me, and I lingered, waiting for them, just inside the gates. I concluded: I don't think that Xanthippus is superior to Xanthides; I don't think he's a better robot; I'm just fonder of him, that's all; and I don't see how I can help that. It wasn't a satisfactory answer, even to me. It was too defensive, too entrenched in unanalysed emotion. Certainly—as seemed to be true with increasing frequency these days—I could never offer it to anyone else as a reasonable answer. But, with any luck, no one else would ask the question.

When Xeno and Daimon caught up with me, Xeno was saying to Daimon: 'Aren't you going to defend yourself?'

Daimon said: 'No. I agree with you. Roles and rules can both be changed. In fact, they should be changed regularly, as a salutory exercise for the lot of us.'

He was looking at me, as if for confirmation, so I said: 'Well, I suppose it would be rather dreadful to be imprisoned in either. I mean,' I pursued, trying to convince myself, 'if we can choose them, we should also be able to unchoose them. And then we can choose others. Then we have to choose others.'

'I'm glad to hear that you both agree,' Xeno said heavily, 'because I think that some things have got to be changed very soon in our section. But what I was referring to,' he said, turning to Daimon, 'was my little summing-up of your attitude to the robots. Xanthe has already defended herself, not altogether convincingly. Can you do any better?'

'Oh, there's nothing to it,' Daimon said dismissively. 'Naturally, I regard even Philophrenics—sorry, Xanthe—as pure machines. Machines are easy to understand, and ultimately they become boring for this very reason. So, naturally, I want them to acquire human attributes. If they did, they'd become more interesting.'

'So you don't find your work interesting enough?' Xeno asked him with some care.

'I'm beginning to find it so,' said Daimon.

We were crossing the asphalt forecourt, and the factory loomed ahead of us like an oceanic rock which had somehow to be circumnavigated. Or so it seemed to me. It was an ordinary building, really, and ugly by virtue of its very innocuousness—a box of steel and concrete with smokily tinted windows on all its eleven floors. Daimon quickened his pace, seemingly eager to find new interest, as we approached the shallow sweep of steps leading up to the front doors. These were made of thick glass, and were of a sea-green colour which increased the impression of depth. On each was etched a device which served as an emblem. It depicted a proud Pragmapractor with huge hands, symbolizing his manual skill. One hand was held out, palm upward, and on it, in the same attitude, stood a smaller Pragmapractor with proportionately huge hands, symbolizing his skill. One of his hands too was held out, and on it stood another Pragmapractor. And so on. The two similar devices faced each other, mirrorwise, in the manner of rivals, symbolizing friendly competitiveness.

We showed our passes to the doorman, and were allowed into the hall. This resembled the foyer of a discreet apartment block in a good, but not fashionable area: it was full of mirrors and potted plants, especially palms. Xeno led the way over to the lifts and summoned one.

'Don't disappoint us, Xeno,' said Daimon. 'We're expecting something big.'

The lift arrived and we got in. 'Seventh floor,' Xeno said to Daimon, who was standing nearest the controls.

I looked at the list enumerating the departments on each floor. Opposite seven there had been a recent change of entry. It read: Internal Organs. A picture came into my mind, a picture of a human body bulging with stomach, liver and kidneys that were all too big for it. I was seized with a sudden irrepressible urge to indulge in a fit of the giggles. I heaved with silent and then vocal laughter until I could feel the tears run down my face. Xeno and Daimon waited patiently for an explanation, looking at me with dumbfounded disapproval, as people generally do when you venture to adopt their own childish behaviour.

'Whatever's the matter with you?' Daimon asked in a manner which indicated that he didn't really want to know.

Xeno showed even less patience. 'Oh, stop being so hysterical, Xanthe!' he said. 'Your beloved robots have no intention of forsaking you, so calm down, will you?'

He was so near the mark that I stopped giggling at once, shocked out of it. I thought: I hate him. But I was instantly ashamed of the thought, and said to them both: 'I'm sorry. I think I must be very nervous.'

Xeno put a hand on my shoulder. 'It's all right,' he said. 'It's really not as bad as all that.'

The seventh floor workshop consisted of several separate rooms, each, as far as I could judge in passing, a model of cleanliness and orderliness. As in the Annexe, it was possible to see into each room from the corridor. And in every room we saw the same scene: brightly-lit tables at which the robots sat in widely-spaced rows; a complex of machinery at each end, the left-hand complex serving the near row of tables and the right-hand complex serving the further one. The robots seemed to be under no pressure. Each worked from a compartmentalized basket of the supermarket type on the table in front of him. One item from each compartment, fitted together, made up the whole robotic part to which that particular room was assigned.

The completed parts were put into another basket, without compartments and, when that was full, its contents were transferred to a larger communal basket at the end of the bench furthest from the supplying machinery. Then the robot would take the compartmentalized basket to be replenished from other larger baskets supplied directly by the machinery. Xeno explained that the robots were regularly transferred from room to room until they had gained a thorough knowledge of the whole robotic anatomy. This constant progressional change, he added, served also to alleviate boredom and obviate discontent—not that a Pragmapractor had ever evinced such undesirable symptoms of malfunctioning, but all the same, it was wise to take such eventualities into consideration. The final stage of this progression was to be reached on the tenth floor, where the completed parts were collected, and then assembled so as to form the complete robot.

'What happens then?' I asked tentatively, ashamed of my own ignorance.

'That's it,' said Xeno. 'That's the end of the cycle.'

I wondered if I was being obtuse again, worrying as I was about what became of all those knowledgeable Pragmapractors. There had to be a limit to the process somewhere. 'Surely,' I said, risking it, 'too many robots must be produced.'

'Export,' Xeno said briefly.

'I don't believe it,' said Daimon. 'Any state advanced enough to use robots is also rich enough and clever enough to produce its own model.'

Xeno said: 'None of them has our expertise.' It was Daimon's turn to look unconvinced. 'Ours have snob value,' said Xeno, 'being the prototype.'

'Sounds like a small market,' I said.

'Well, Xanthe,' said Xeno, 'I don't want to injure your tender susceptibilities, but I have to admit that a lot of them are wiped.'

'Wiped?' I repeated, mystified. 'Do you mean destroyed?'

Xeno and Daimon spoke together. Xeno said: 'Not exactly.'

Daimon said: 'He means deprogrammed. And then presumably recycled through the learning process. It's an attempt to improve that process.'

'That doesn't sound so dreadful to me,' I said. After all, the robots in question were only Pragmapractors, not Philophrenics, and so the possibility of mental cruelty hardly arose.

Xeno led us on to a door with a stylized picture of a heart, a Valentine heart, on it. Underneath, a notice read 'Pump Room'. I wondered if the facetious medical-school humour was typical of the Pragmapractors, and it occurred to me once again how little I knew about them. As Xeno opened the door I was thinking: How long has this Internal Organs unit been here? It seemed to be functioning smoothly, and yet I knew that robots had never had or needed internal organs. What they had and all they needed to have was a brain, a supreme brain, governing all their necessary activities with autocratic proficiency. I wanted to ask Xeno about this. And I wanted to ask him what had been squeezed out in order to cater for this new craze for verisimilitude which was indubitably spreading among our Philophrenics. But, following him into the pump room, I decided to leave my questions until later.

The reassuring sound of recorded and orchestrated violins rose and fell tunefully, only slightly louder than the hum of the machinery. On our arrival, the robots all looked up from their work, some carrying on with it automatically, others stopping altogether. Xeno raised his hand in greeting, and we did likewise. The robots replied in kind, some of them murmuring greetings, others not bothering, having no interest in us. Daimon stood behind one of them, watching a replica of a human heart being assembled. I joined him, thinking: Where are Xanthippus and Xanthides? Xeno had gone to the far end of the bench to pick up a completed heart. He brought one back to show us. We watched in silence while he pointed out the perfection of the detail. Daimon fingered it with some curiosity as Xeno spoke, eventually taking it from him for a closer look. He handled it gently, showing none of the clumsiness that characterized his larger movements. But when he offered it to me, I refused to take it. I didn't want to touch it. I didn't need to, not doubting for a moment that the heart was a viable working model: our Institute could turn out nothing less.

Xeno took the heart and put it back in its basket. 'Now,' he said, and I noticed that he was wiping his hands together as though he too had not enjoyed contact with the lifeless replica. 'Now I think it's time we found those recreant robots.'

'Yes,' I said, speaking more grimly than I had intended. 'I'm looking forward to that.'

Xeno led us into the space behind the machinery, a kind of back-stage area, cluttered and festooned with pipes, cables, levers and other mysterious trappings. It was noisier there, and Xeno had to shout when he told us: 'I hope you're both sufficiently prepared.'

We reassured him somewhat impatiently, and he shrugged and knocked on the door in front of us. It was opened by Phidia. I was pleased to see her. It gave me an unexpected comfort to see another person of my own age, sex and species, all rolled into one. It was a triple identification on my part, as I noted in passing, and worthy of note because I so rarely had need of even a single one. But there was no time to ponder on this.

Phidia herself was evidently pleased—and relieved?—to see all of us. She ushered us quickly into the room, as though there were no time for the usual pleasantries. The room was another ante-room, but brighter and of a more cheerful aspect than the Philophrenic common-room. Xanthippus, Xanthides and a third robot, whom I took to be Phidias, were sitting around in a sprawled human fashion, but immediately stood up when we came in. It was a relief, to me at least, to see that they were all still in regulation dress. Customary greetings were exchanged with due formality. It seemed to me that the robots were tense and hot despite their apparent relaxation, and that the tension was literally electric.

Xeno addressed his recreants: 'Well, have your demands been fully satisfied? Are you pleased with yourselves, now that your hearts are in the right place?'

Xanthides, as senior robot, spoke first and for all of them: 'We are indeed pleased, both with ourselves and with the new situation in which we find ourselves. Self-improvement always leads to greater self-regard. And we are especially grateful to you, Director Xeno, and to your foresight, for helping to make this improvement possible.'

'What foresight?' Daimon asked Xeno. I had been asking myself the same question.

Xeno ignored him. 'Thank you, Xanthides,' he said, 'but I really cannot take the credit. It was a committee decision.' He spoke briskly, as if to forestall any flattery.

'Nevertheless,' Xanthides insisted, 'you were a member of that committee and, as such, you deserve our thanks.'

Daimon pulled a chair towards him, letting it scrape along the floor, with the air of making a gesture, a gesture of impatience with all this politeness. He said: 'How about you, Xanthippus? How does it feel to be human at the red-ripe of the heart?'

'Ah, Browning,' Xanthippus said appreciatively. 'Yes, it feels good.' He seemed content to leave it at that, and I was vaguely disappointed in him. Then, my disappointment deepening, I thought: Why did he never mention to me that he wanted a heart? I became aware that I was staring at him reproachfully.

'It will no longer be possible,' Phidias was saying with some eagerness, 'for human beings to refer to us as heartless machines.'

I looked at him indignantly and said: 'Surely no one has ever said that!'

He said: 'I must respectfully contradict you.'

I thought: That's the first time a robot has ever contradicted me. I didn't know how to react. I looked to Phidia for help, but she merely nodded, as if to confirm Phidias's assertion.

Daimon said: 'You're still machines.' He said it matter-of-factly, but I knew that he meant it provocatively.

'We are well aware of that,' Xanthides said with some dignity. 'A robot is a machine. A human being is not a machine. Nevertheless, robots and human beings are both systems. And we robots should like to believe that we are both open systems, capable of tolerating one another throughout the many vicissitudes of our development.'

'I should like to think so too,' said Xeno, 'and I'm sure that we'll all do our best not to disappoint one another.'

I had nothing to say. I felt that I lacked Xeno's diplomacy. But I also lacked Daimon's trenchancy. I should have preferred to talk to Xanthippus in private: he seemed to share my reluctance to take part in open discussion. I had no wish to harangue the robots, nor to challenge them in any way. All I wanted to do was to ask them straightforward questions about their new hearts and, above all, what difference the acquisition of them had made to the robot's experience of himself, of other robots, of human beings, and of the world in which we all tried to live together. But there was an edginess in the room which held me back.

Xanthippus stepped forward towards me and Xeno, as if he too were making a gesture. He announced: 'I should like to show Xanthe my heart.' And he looked at Xeno, not at me, for permission.

Xeno nodded, but I wasn't at all sure that I wanted to look. However, it was difficult for me to refuse to do so. Xanthippus was now standing very close to me, facing me. He ripped his tunic open at the velcro fastening and held the two sides apart, so as to reveal the whole of his chest. There was something in his manner which reminded me of a conjuror assuring his audience that there was going to be no cheating. He touched something on his chest, and a little door sprang open. And there was the heart, opening and closing, expanding and contracting, pulsating just like the real thing. My repugnance was instantly dissipated. How vulnerable the heart looked, and, somehow, how forlorn! But it didn't seem out of place. It seemed suitable, almost natural, and quite perfect.

'Oh, Xanthippus,' I said, 'it's beautiful!'

He looked at me steadily, and I wondered if he had detected the strange pity—was it pity?—tempering my admiration. 'I thought you would like it,' he said. He clicked the little door back into place and began to fasten his tunic.

Xeno had been watching us with faint and detached amusement. 'It all looks rather rudimentary to me,' he remarked.

'Oh, it is,' said Phidia. 'I had a chat with the Chief Engineer just before you arrived, and he told me that there hadn't been time to get a bloodstream properly organized. They're working on it now, and they hope to be able to make a few modifications by this afternoon.'

'In that case,' said Xeno, 'the robots had better remain here till then.'

Daimon groaned. 'We don't have to stay too, do we?' he asked Xeno.

'I'll stay,' Phidia said quickly.

Xeno said: 'There's absolutely no need for anyone to stay. I think we should all get back to the main building and have some lunch. We've got a lot to discuss. And probably even more to think about. And, for those two strenuous activities, we need to keep up our strength.'

His proposition was practical, and we accepted it, Daimon with evident relief, Phidia and myself with some reluctance.

Xeno and Daimon strode ahead of us down the corridor. Phidia remarked: 'You seem to have a very good relationship going with Xanthippus. I was most impressed.'

I was pleased that she had noticed. 'Yes, it is rather . . . special,' I said.

She sighed. 'I find Phidias so difficult at times.'

'Well, he's rather a prickly character,' I said.

She seemed pleased that I had noticed this. 'You're so right,' she said. 'And, as for all this heart business, he's been very secretive. He never said a word to me about it, and I assume he must have gone straight to Xeno—over my head, as it were.'

'So that's what happened,' I said slowly. 'Certainly neither Xanthides nor Xanthippus said anything to me.'

'Oh, really?' she said. 'I thought I was the only one being kept in the dark.'

'No,' I said. 'It seems that Xeno was the only person who knew anything about it.'

She said: 'The plot thickens.'

I said: 'Yes, I'm sure he knows more than he's telling us.'

'Let's tackle him about it now,' she said. 'I seriously think we ought to. Once we accept this sort of thing, we've set up a precedent.'

By the time we had caught up the others, they had reached the lift. Daimon said to us: 'I need your support. I think Xeno's been holding out on us.'

Phidia laughed and said: 'We think so too.'

Xeno smiled accommodatingly at us all. 'I am at your service,' he said. 'What is it you want to know?'

'Everything,' said Phidia.

The lift arrived and we all squeezed in. Daimon directed us to the ground floor and stood leaning against the wall. 'What I'm particularly interested in,' he announced, 'is Xeno's foresight.'

'Yes,' I said. 'How long has that unit been there?'

'And why,' asked Phidia, 'weren't we told about it?'

'All right, all right,' said Xeno. 'I'll tell you. The unit has been in operation since yesterday.'

'Oh, come on, Xeno,' said Daimon. The lift had reached the ground floor, and he stood aside to let the rest of us out. 'Credit us with a little intelligence, will you?'

'I said in operation,' Xeno insisted. 'It was, of course, planned a considerable time before that. It cannot have escaped your notice that robots yearn towards humanity.'

I thought of Veronica, of the way Daimon had used her, and of the way she had used him in revenge. I wondered: Why on earth should they want to be like us? Such a desire was akin to sacrilege. I said: 'Not inevitably, surely?'

'It has been such a persistent trend,' Xeno replied, 'that by now it almost constitutes a law. You must admit that it would have been foolish of us to ignore anything so obvious. We worked on the basis of various predictions as to where this trend would lead in practical terms. Fortunately, what has been happening here today is one of the eventualities we did predict.'

We were crossing the forecourt again, in the shade of the building. That and Xeno's words both chilled me. 'You did it all on purpose,' I accused him. 'You predetermined the whole thing.' Xeno looked at me distantly, and I felt that I was near the truth. 'Yes,' I went on, 'I mean that your predictions actually caused all this to happen. This particular prediction of yours must have communicated itself to the robots, somehow.'

'Oh, Xanthe,' Xeno said with feigned weariness, 'what nonsense you do talk. Robots are not telepaths, you know.'

'I didn't say they were telepaths,' I said coldly. 'I want to know how you engineered it so that they all went to you, without saying anything to me or Phidia.'

'*I* don't know,' he said. 'Perhaps they thought they would get better results from me.'

Phidia said: 'I think Xanthe's got a point there.'

'Yes,' said Daimon, 'but the point isn't really *how* the whole thing was sparked off, but *why*.'

'It's both,' I said. 'We're supposed to be engaged in objective research. We have no right to manipulate events.'

'Let me tell you something, Xanthe,' Xeno said in his most patronizing manner. 'Don't you know that the ability of human beings to act on predictions and on considerations of alternative possibilities, perhaps only one of which can exist, is essential for our survival? And always has been. This ability is one of those that differentiates us from the robots. They are tied to patterns of stimulus and response. We are not.'

I said nothing. It was the manner rather than the matter of Xeno's speech that I found unanswerable. It seemed to me that he was behaving insufferably. And yet I felt unable to express my anger.

Phidia said: 'Stick to the point, Xeno.'

We had reached the cable-track, and Daimon summoned a car by pushing the call button. He said: 'It's no good, Xeno. We're not going to be diverted by your attempts at grandiloquence. Nor by your persistent evasiveness. What we really want to know is why we weren't told anything about what was going on.'

'And why we weren't consulted,' I put in. 'After all, ours is supposed to be a democratic society.'

Xeno began to look defeated at last. 'It was a committee decision,' he said.

It was the second time I had heard him refer to committee decisions that morning. I thought: No wonder he wasn't eager to accept Xanthides's congratulations. But I wasn't going to let him off that lightly. 'And did you dissent?' I asked him.

Xeno sighed. 'That's a difficult question to answer,' he said. 'I will answer it. And I'll answer it fully. But not now.'

'Why not?' we chorussed.

Xeno sighed again. 'Let's do it all properly,' he said patiently. 'Let's hold a meeting in the normal fashion. We'd better make it tomorrow, when you've all had time to see your robots. And I'd rather that you left that till tomorrow too. Give them time to settle down. Everything should proceed as usual. And we'll all meet in my room tomorrow at, say, four-thirty.'

And with that, for the moment, we had to be content.

10

I slept all afternoon, and felt refreshed for the respite, although it didn't seem so when I first woke up. It was a dream that woke me—a short, apposite dream, uncharacteristically literal in its terms of reference. I became aware of it at a point where I was lying face to face with Xanthippus. We lay quite still and close, our arms around each other. His new heart beat, indistinguishably from my own, between my breasts. I didn't know where we were, or how we had come to be there, or how long we had remained in that position. Nothing existed outside of the unit that we were. I hardly dared move for fear of shattering it. Then I thought: What is the next move, anyway? What happens next? It was with the chillest horror that I realized: Nothing happens next; nothing can happen; this is as far as we can go. Xeno's face appeared somewhere above us, leering down at us. He said: Don't you know that further congress is a biological impossibility? And I woke up, uncovered, clutching a ravelled knot of bedclothes to me.

The dream shocked me. I got up, washed and dressed slowly but absently, stopping every now and then in mid-action for no apparent reason. I began to wonder if I were still in my dream, but decided that in dreams every action is precise and meaningful, whereas my actions were diffuse and undirected, and belonged all too plainly to the state of waking reality. I was awake. I was there in my own familiar room. I was alone. It was getting dark. I sat on the edge of the bed, looking up at the skylight, looking through it and the branches beyond, and I thought: I don't want to be alone.

I decided to go and see Daimon. We hadn't discussed the morning's events, either those concerning Veronica or the scenes at the factory. It was, of course, the latter topic that interested me more, and I hadn't had a chance to talk to Daimon about it since Xeno, Phidia and I had lost him at lunch. A young woman in the uniform of a creche mother had accosted him then, and the two of them had eaten at another table, where they were soon in earnest conversation. I had assumed the woman to be an associate of Veronica's, and that she had been relaying some message in an attempt at reconciliation. But I hadn't seen Daimon since then, and now I began to wonder in a vague sort of way if there had been any further trouble. I thought: What a nuisance such people are; we can't afford to have Daimon diverted from his work in the middle of a crisis. It was in this frame of mind, and with some ill-formed intention of bringing him back to his work, that I went and knocked at Daimon's door. There was no reply, and the door was locked. But there was a light on. I found this strange, so I knocked again. But he seemed determined not to reply, and I went back to my own room, slightly discountenanced.

I turned all the lights on, but the room remained empty. I turned on some music, but found myself incapable of simply sitting still and listening to it. I buzzed Catering and ordered some supper, seeking to placate my restlessness with the luxury I had been denied that morning. I drank a glass of wine while pretending to read the current copy of our house journal. I couldn't concentrate on any of it, except a piece about setting up a new sculpture park, and that held my attention only because it had been written by Phidia, and consisted in the main part of a report on the talents of Phidias. Otherwise, I stared nully at the wall, or the ceiling or the floor, and thought about nothing in particular, except perhaps the fact of being Xanthe. Then, breaking the monotony, the Pragmapractor arrived with my supper. I watched him closely. He must have inferred some kind of criticism from my scrutiny because he asked me rather anxiously if I had any complaints. I assured him that I had none.

'Then I wish you a good appetite,' he said.

I said: 'Thank you.' Then, on impulse, I asked him: 'Do you enjoy your work?'

He paused so long before replying that I began to wonder if I had set up some form of dysfunction. 'It is easy work,' he said at last.

'But is it interesting?' I persisted.

After a similar pause, he said: 'I do my work to the best of my ability.'

'And is that an enjoyable thing to do?'

'I can only hope that I give satisfaction at all times,' he said, his anxiety clearly returning.

I gave up. 'It's all right,' I said. 'You can go now.'

He thanked me, and left hurriedly. I began to eat my supper. The magazine on my knee was now open at a page headed 'New Additions to the Library'. Under the philosophy section I read the following description of one of the books: 'The author argues for his view that not only can nothing be known, but that no one can ever have any reason at all for anything, and no one can believe, or even say, that anything is the case. English, he suggests, and any language like it, embodies a theory about the nature of things which leads inevitably to these paradoxical conclusions. To put things right, we must depart radically from our present linguistic habits.' Such sweeping statements aroused my interest. I drew a ring round the title, thinking that the contents might prove useful with reference to both Xanthippus and Xanthides. Linguistic data was something they had in common, and I hoped that one day I should be able to listen to the two of them discussing the intricacies of the subject. But that day seemed both distant and doubtful. I thought: Will Xanthippus ever be finished? Can programming go on, according to schedule, as if nothing untoward has happened? What a wicked waste it would be if we had to stop now! Then I thought: I hate it when things become pointless.

'No one can ever have any reason at all for anything,' I re-read, this time with a sense of irony. What would the Philophrenic mind, with its new capacity for extrapolation and introjection, make of that? Despondently, I let the magazine drop to the floor, sure that it could reveal nothing more pointed to me. And anything less pointed was worthless. The music was beginning to obtrude, so I switched it off. The lights glared at me from within their own complacency, so I switched them off too. I crept back to my bed and lay down there, my eyes shut, deliberately trying to escape into the world of sleep, passively soliciting the world of dreams.

An idyllic country scene. High summer. The air heavy with pollen, the scent of flowers, the hum of bees. My father cutting the long grass in front of the cottage with a scythe. The scythe swooshing, whispering, glinting at me through the haze. I am sitting under a tree with a mortar and pestle, crushing, pounding, grinding some herb or spice. Then a disturbance. Something, some living thing, is trying to get down my blouse at the back of my neck. It buzzes, but it's larger than any insect, and not creepy at all, just soft and downy. My father stops scything and says: Look, it's a humming-bird. It moves round me, brushing my neck and makes for the opening at the front of my blouse. All I can see is a blur, a vibrating circle of colours. I try to brush it away because I'm frightened of it and frightened for it. My father calls to me as he walks across the cut grass towards me: Look out, it's got a broken wing! It is getting stuck in my blouse. I feel that one of us is going to get injured, so I start to undo my blouse so as to let the creature free. The two wings, broken and unbroken, detach themselves and fly noiselessly away, dazzling in their motion and in their primary reds and blues. The body is left helpless like a discarded skin at moulting time. I want it to go away too. Its suffering is spoiling everything, polluting the idyll. My father says: Oh, Xanthe, you clumsy fool! And I know that I must be to blame for the flight of the wings. I shall have to make some sort of reparation. I shall have to get up, and take it inside the cottage and minister to it. I don't want to. But at the same time I know that I'm only making a token protest. Of course I'll help it, really . . .

And it was morning again. I got dressed slowly, pondering my dream. It seemed strange to dream about my dead father when I scarcely ever even thought about him. I told myself: It's all Daimon's fault. But I knew that it wasn't. I wondered why I should have chosen to depict my father behaving harshly towards me: it was not typical of his behaviour towards anyone. And yet it had happened, and had happened often, in the last few weeks of his life. I saw him now, leaning on the mantelpiece, just as Daimon had done, but on another mantelpiece in another room in another age. I remembered how he hadn't seen or heard me come into that room, and how I had watched him, knowing that something was wrong, but unable to ask him what. And I remembered how he had shouted at me when he had turned round to find me watching him. It was that moment which had changed everything. From then on, I knew, and lived painfully with the knowledge, that he was going to die very soon. Even now, I didn't like to think about those weeks. And I didn't like to think about that life because it belonged to someone else, someone other than Xanthe. Instead, I thought: It must be because I'm not taking my pills that I'm having all these dreams. But still I didn't take them. I suppose I knew even then that in some obscure way I needed those dreams. It wasn't until I was ready for breakfast, and while I was shutting my door behind me, that the thought occurred to me: My father called me Xanthe, but I wasn't Xanthe then; why did he do it?

As I turned from my door, Daimon's door opened. But the person who stepped out into the corridor wasn't Daimon. It was a woman dressed in the uniform of a creche mother. I recognized her as the same woman who had accosted Daimon at lunch the day before. For some reason, I didn't want her to see me, and was relieved when she didn't glance in my direction. She didn't come to the refectory for breakfast. I was early and ate alone. I had nearly finished when Daimon joined me at our usual table in the far corner. He looked very clean, and his hair was still damp from the shower he must have taken while I had been eating. He sat down opposite me without a word. I resented this, and said nothing myself.

Then he said: 'Well, it looks like being a big day today. Are you ready for it?'

I said: 'You're certainly a quick worker, Daimon.'

He said: 'What do you mean?' But he knew what I meant.

'Who is she?' I asked.

'Are you talking about Begonia?' he asked.

'Begonia!' I repeated. 'For pity's sake, Daimon, how can you be such a fool? You might have chosen someone else.'

He looked at me in an injured fashion. 'What am I supposed to have done wrong?' he asked.

'You know perfectly well,' I said. 'Begonia is a friend of Veronica's—'

'No, she isn't!' Daimon said. 'Far from it. Veronica doesn't have any friends. Sooner or later she manages to alienate everyone. Begonia can't stand her.'

'That makes it even worse,' I groaned. 'Let's say, then, that Begonia is a close associate of Veronica's. You're carrying on with Begonia in order to get at Veronica. And goodness knows how *she's* going to react. Surely I don't have to spell it out for you.'

'You're still wrong,' he said. 'I don't care enough about Veronica to want to get at her, or to make her jealous, or whatever you think it is that I'm doing. I didn't even give her a thought.'

'Then you should have!' I said angrily.

'I don't see why,' he said with some coldness.

We stared at each other in open hostility. But I looked away from him, suddenly ashamed of myself: after all, I had now encroached on his private territory. 'I'm sorry,' I said finally. 'It's really none of my business. Perhaps I shouldn't have mentioned it. But it's just that I don't want your love life to have an adverse effect on your work—our work. Especially not now.'

He laughed. 'Love life!' he repeated, deriding the phrase. 'Is that what you call it?'

'Call it whatever you like,' I amended. We stared at each other again with only slightly less hostility. Several times Daimon seemed to be about to speak and to think the better of it. 'I'm sorry,' I said again, not looking at him. 'Let's forget it.'

'No,' he said with sudden decision. 'I don't want to forget. I want to talk about it.' I waited. 'Oh Xanthe,' he sighed, 'if only you understood.'

I looked at him blankly. What was there to understand? 'Well, try me,' I said.

He looked at me, doubting me. 'What you don't understand,' he said, 'is that I, unlike you or Xeno, can't live a life of complete celibacy. If I do, I get all knotted up.'

'No one's asking you to,' I said stiffly. I disliked the way he coupled me with Xeno. 'It's your choice of partners that I find, well, unsatisfactory.'

'Oh, they're perfectly satisfactory,' he assured me with a certain smugness.

'You know what I mean,' I said.

'I don't have that much choice, anyway,' he said gloomily and ambiguously. I shrugged. 'For your information, Xanthe,' he went on in his best Xeno manner, 'I did choose someone else, as you put it. But she didn't and doesn't appear to be in the slightest bit interested in my attentions.'

'I don't believe you,' I said.

'You wouldn't,' he said. 'But it's true.'

'All right, then,' I said. 'So it's true.' I didn't ask him who this rare and mythical woman was, although I couldn't help wondering. I felt that I had pried enough already, and that perhaps Daimon was right: I didn't understand such things. 'I've got a lot to do,' I said untruthfully.

Daimon saw through my untruth. 'Yes, of course,' he said sarcastically. 'Well, where and when do we rendezvous with the recreants?'

'Ten o'clock at Number Seven,' I said briskly, rising from the table. He watched me with what seemed like a mixture of bewilderment and tolerance for my frailties, but said nothing. And it was with the obscure feeling that I too had left something unsaid that I left him to his breakfast.

11

'I sleep,' said Xanthippus, 'but my heart waketh.'

'The heart,' said Xanthides, 'has reasons that reason knows nothing of.'

'My heart,' said Xanthippus, 'is like a singing bird whose nest is in a watered shoot.'

'Good for you,' said Daimon. 'Now, let's cut out the clichés, and get down to business, shall we?'

Most of the roses were now in bloom. Their scent and profusion combined to distract me from our conversation. The roses seemed to be opening themselves to us, but the conversation kept shutting itself off. I felt I was trudging through a maze, a roseless maze whose thorny hedges presented me with nothing but a series of dead ends. Every time I tried to pursue a line of enquiry, Daimon would deflect it. He couldn't resist making a debating point when a more compliant tone was called for. This strategy only encouraged the robots to answer him with further cleverness, and I was finding it difficult to remember where my enquiries had been heading before the point of deflection. A sense of general disintegration was taking possession of me. I didn't know whether Daimon was deliberately sabotaging my tentative but earnest efforts to get a coherent statement from either or both of the robots, or whether there was method in his manner, and sincerity in his method. I thought unhappily: We should have discussed it first; but I didn't think it was all going to be so complicated.

Daimon announced: 'This conversation is getting out of hand.'

'I'm glad you've noticed,' I said drily.

'Can't we stop them coming out with all these dreary quotations?' he asked me in an undertone.

We were sitting side by side on one bench, the robots on another bench, facing us. I couldn't tell whether or not they had heard Daimon, but it seemed to me that an aside, whatever its content, might give offence. With their new self-awareness, they might object to being talked about as though they were not there, as though they were not alive like us.

'It's your fault,' I said aloud. 'Xanthippus and Xanthides think that you're trying to score over them in some way. And they're not letting you get away with it. Why should they? So they're doing the same thing with you. It's like a game of some sort.'

'Yes,' said Xanthides. 'It's a good game. Shall we play some more, Daimon?'

'Will you play too, Xanthe?' Xanthippus asked.

'I think that particular game has outlived its usefulness for the moment,' I said. 'Let's be serious now.'

'But games are serious,' said Xanthides. I was being deflected again, this time before I had even begun. And Xanthides went on: 'Games can often reveal valuable information about the players.'

'Yes,' said Daimon. 'I was working on that assumption.'

Xanthippus said: 'They can function like metaphors, showing how our minds are working and inter-relating.'

In the face of this unity, my sense of disintegration increased. 'Well, I haven't learnt a thing,' I said sharply. 'Shall we now try more orthodox methods of discussion?'

No one seemed willing to act on my suggestion. I had evidently been cast in the role of spoilsport. But I was determined to follow through. 'Xanthippus,' I said, appealing to him as the most sympathetic of the three, 'can you tell me what it was that led you to make your request for a heart?'

Xanthippus turned to Xanthides, as if for help. Xanthides shook his head. 'I am having some difficulty in remembering,' he said.

'So am I,' said Xanthippus.

'You must be able to remember,' I said patiently. 'You are programmed to remember everything that happens to you.' A sudden suspicion crossed my mind: Was it possible that the information we were seeking had been wiped? But by whom? And why? 'Please try a little harder,' I urged the robots.

Again they turned to one another. Xanthides said: 'I remember discussing the matter with Xanthippus.'

'I remember that,' said Xanthippus. 'And I also remember discussing it with Xeno.'

'Ah!' I said. 'And what form did this discussion take?'

'We were discussing the current stage of my programming,' said Xanthippus. 'Xeno asked me a lot of questions about it, and about our walks in the woods. I think he was testing me. They were easy questions. I could answer them all. Then he asked me if I had any questions to ask him. I asked him, was the human heart the matrix of human emotions? He said no. But I had information to the contrary in my data bank.'

He paused at this point, and I said: 'Yes? What happened then?'

'Dysfunction,' he said.

'And was that the extent of your conversation with Xeno?' I asked, suspecting that he had left something out, something vital. He nodded, and I had to believe him. I said: 'So when did you ask for the heart?'

Xanthides said: 'Phidias, Xanthippus and I made the request together. We had come to a joint decision.'

'I know this is difficult, Xanthides,' I said, 'but can you try very hard to remember what prompted you to come to that decision?'

'We arrived at it step by step,' he said. 'One step led to another by logical progression.'

It didn't seem logical to me. I said: 'Can you describe those steps?'

He seemed puzzled. 'We acted on the information we had,' he said. 'We analysed it in order to arrive at its meaning. But we came to the conclusion that we were working from insufficient data.'

Xanthippus said: 'We knew that we couldn't prove anything on our pulses unless we had hearts of our own.'

There seemed to be two different processes in operation here: the desire for knowledge and the desire for experience. In robotic terms, the two had always been distinct. But now they appeared to amount to the same thing. I still couldn't understand how this had happened, so I asked: 'Did Xeno help you at all with this logical progression of yours?'

'No,' they said in chorus. It was the most definite statement they had made.

I had some sort of answer, then. But although it might have appeared to be a conclusive one to the robots, I found it far from adequate. Xeno had made no direct suggestion to them. That much was clear. But had he influenced them by indirect means? It was impossible to tell. It was certainly impossible for the robots to tell, innocent as they were in the matter of ulterior motivation. I decided not to interrogate them about Xeno any further. They were proud of themselves, and I didn't want to destroy that pride. It was a quality which enhanced both their performance and their personalities, a quality whose sudden removal could prove destructive. They trusted

Xeno, and I didn't want to destroy that faith—however unjustified it might be—by accusing him of excessive manipulation, where the robots had observed none at all. In doing so, I might only succeed in casting doubt on my own credibility, thus permanently damaging my relationship with both robots. No, this was not the time to start undermining Xeno's authority. I turned to Daimon and said: 'Is there anything you want to ask?'

'Yes,' he said. 'I'd like to know what the next request is going to be?'

'What makes you think that there are going to be any more?' I asked quickly.

'It's inevitable,' he said, this time in an undertone again. 'Let them answer.'

I turned to the robots. 'Can you answer that?' I asked them, wondering how far they had developed the power to predict. They were taking a long time to answer.

It was Xanthippus who spoke first. 'No,' he said faintly, so faintly that I guessed how much the question had troubled him.

Xanthides came to his rescue. 'We cannot answer that without prior consultation,' he said.

'Consultation with whom?' I asked. 'Phidias?'

'Consultation with the whole Philophrenic body,' he replied.

I looked at Daimon, trying to gauge his reaction. 'Why don't you go and have your consultation now?' he asked them with apparent carelessness.

'Excuse me,' said Xanthides, 'but that will not be possible unless all our brothers are also in a state of activation.'

Daimon appeared not to have thought of this himself. 'Yes, of course,' he said slowly. 'Well, that can be arranged, can't it, Xanthe?'

I was unprepared enough to agree, but I did so without enthusiasm. The robots thanked us warmly. When they had left I said to Daimon: 'We'll have to fix it with Xeno and the other directors first, you know.'

'I know,' he said. 'I'll do it.'

I found myself in the position of having to criticize him once again, however reluctantly. Still, it was my duty to speak my mind to my assistant. I said: 'Don't you think you're pushing things, rather?'

'Why not?' he asked. 'It's all inevitable, as I said before. I'm not altering the situation. I'm just speeding up the process so as to make it more interesting more quickly.'

This sounded plausible enough. 'I see,' I said. 'Well, you really had better go and see Xeno. I think you may well find that he has a different opinion to offer.'

'Don't worry,' said Daimon. 'Xeno can't afford to disagree with me.'

'What can you mean?' I asked him. 'You seem to have an inflated idea of your own importance, all of a sudden.'

'Hardly,' he said drily. 'It's not a question of my importance, but of Xeno's unimportance, and his expendability. He's afraid of losing his job, you see. And with reason.'

'Nonsense,' I said. 'He has a contract like the rest of us. His tenure is quite secure.'

'Just before I arrived at the Institute,' said Daimon, 'a vote of censure against Xeno was narrowly defeated in committee.'

'How do you know?' I asked in disbelief.

'Xeno told me himself.'

'But what was he being censured for?'

'That he didn't tell me in so many words,' said Daimon, 'but I gather it had something to do with not getting results, or not getting them quickly enough. I don't know what sort of results were expected of him, but, obviously, the more results, the better for Xeno.'

'I see,' I said again. 'When did Xeno tell you all this?'

'Yesterday morning,' he said. 'In his room. Just before you arrived. He seemed to think that recent events had averted the crisis, as far as his career was concerned.'

'Very handy,' I commented. Then I found myself wondering aloud: 'Why didn't he tell me? I'm beginning to think that I'm almost redundant myself.'

I had spoken lightly, but Daimon smiled at me in such a way as to imply that he had taken me literally. He said: 'I think Xeno was put off by your faintness. I don't think he intended to exclude you. And I don't think he would have said anything to me, if he hadn't been in such a state of relief. He was like a condemned man who's been suddenly reprieved.'

I thought: Is Daimon really so concerned about my feelings? It seemed that he was going out of his way to reassure me. His concern touched me, and I was afraid of betraying as much, so I said quickly: 'I sometimes think that Xeno is capable of anything.'

Daimon understood me, and he understood too how dangerous

my remark was. He asked me: 'Do you think he's utterly unscrupulous?'

I tried to think about this honestly. 'No,' I had to say. 'It's difficult to explain. It's not so much that he has no scruples, as that he has no prejudices or preconceptions. In a way, he's too open. He has a strange sort of detachment. You know the sort I mean. It's the sort that would allow him to film us for the archives, if we were burning to death, rather than trying to rescue us.'

Daimon laughed. 'Yes, I do know what you mean,' he said, 'but I don't think he's that callous.'

'Oh, it wouldn't be callousness,' I said. 'That's too loaded a term. It would be extreme objectivity.'

'Perhaps it comes to the same thing,' Daimon said. 'But do you think he'd take this objectivity far enough to play God? God gets results.'

I was unwilling to face the implications of this question. And yet they had to be faced. 'It's something I've asked myself repeatedly,' I said. 'But, so far, I haven't come anywhere near an answer.'

He stood up. 'Well, I'll see what I can find out,' he said. 'If I unearth anything, I'll let you know before the meeting.'

Daimon walked off towards the main building, leaving me with plenty to think about. My first thought, though, was hardly a thought at all. It was this: How nice it is when we actually agree, when we behave like real colleagues. Then I thought: Is Xeno really a bastard? If so, what sort of bastard was he? Could he really have stirred things up among the Philophrenics in order to salvage his own career? No. It was unthinkable. Xeno was a professional. Surely robotics, as a science, meant more to him than did personal advancement? Even as the sentence spoke itself in my mind, I noticed that it had a hollow ring to it. There was something wrong with the juxtaposition. Of course. To Xeno, the advancement of robotics *was* his personal advancement, and vice versa. Still, this discovery got me no further. I thought: Suppose he is guilty, what would that mean? It would mean that our generalizations about robotic behaviour had been based on a false premise. It would mean, in short, that robots behave autonomously, if told to, but probably otherwise do not. And what sort of autonomy was that? But, then again, perhaps that information was in itself valuable. After all, we had wanted the robots to behave autonomously, and what we were trying to find out was how this could be achieved. Perhaps it didn't matter if Xeno had stirred things up. Perhaps his instigating action didn't detract from the total achievement. We were pursuing knowledge, not glory.

The possibility of Xeno's being both guilty and blameless was quite new to me, so new that I couldn't absorb its import. Should I talk to Daimon? The need for another mind seemed urgent. I began to walk rapidly back in the direction of the main building, wishing that I could only think a little more clearly.

As I approached the Annexe I became aware of someone running towards me, calling to me. But by this time another possibility had occurred to me. I was thinking: There is no need to pre-suppose intention on Xeno's part; he could be responsible, but it could still have been an accident. The person running towards me had stopped, breathless, in front of me. Veronica slipped her arm through mine. She kept repeating my name and a lot of other words whose meaning I didn't or couldn't recognize. I turned my face away from her, as if to obliterate her obtrusive image. She clung to me. I thought: I must, must get all this sorted out with Daimon before we meet Xeno. But Veronica was worrying at me like a wasp. 'What do you want?' I asked her abruptly.

She looked at me in surprise, and then indulgently, as though recognizing the proverbial absentmindedness of the academic spinster. I thought: Her eyes are huge; I suppose they're beautiful, but I don't like them; they're too demanding.

She said: 'Haven't you been listening to a word I've been saying?'

'No,' I admitted. 'I'm sorry, Veronica.'

She said: 'I must talk to you.'

I went on walking, walking away from the Annexe. And still she held on to my arm, although I had not responded with the slightest pressure to her touch. 'What about?' I asked mechanically. I thought with some irritation: Why me?

'Please, Xanthe,' she said, trying to bring me to a halt with her arm. 'I want to talk to you in private.'

I allowed myself to be led back to the Annexe, thinking all the time: I'm going to regret this. There seemed no way for me to avoid the coming confrontation. And, for that, I had neither the moral nor the emotional strength.

She said: 'Xanthe, you're such a dear. I always knew you were my friend.'

To this, as to most of her assertions, there was no real reply. But the role of Veronica's Only Friend neither tempted nor suited me. I said: 'Don't be too sure of that.'

She laughed, not taking my rejection of her friendship amiss at all, perhaps not even recognizing it for what it was. 'We've got something in common, you and I,' she said. 'We both have to put up with Daimon.'

I thought: Can she really be so deluded? I said: 'At least you have some choice in the matter. I don't.'

'Oh, I don't have any choice at all,' she wailed. 'He's got me completely in his power.'

She didn't let go of me until we had reached her room. Even then, even when she was unlocking the door, she kept an eye on me, as though fearful of my escape. She held the door open for me, standing there, smiling.

'I haven't got much time, Veronica,' I said, determined to make that much clear from the outset. 'What was it you wanted to talk about?'

'Oh, Xanthe,' she said, her eyes misting over with unshed tears, 'I'm so unhappy!'

'That,' I said grimly, 'is obvious.'

'What can I do?'

'I don't know,' I said cautiously. 'What do you want to do?'

She said: 'I want Daimon. He's the only thing I want in this whole wide world.'

I said: 'I don't see how I can help you.'

'Oh, but you can,' she insisted. 'He'll listen to you. I know he will. He admires you.'

'Nonsense,' I said. 'And you can't really expect me to plead with Daimon on your behalf—'

'Not plead, exactly,' she said. 'I didn't mean that. But if you would just mention me now and then, so that he doesn't entirely forget my existence, and tell him, casually, how unhappy I am, and how I still love him. I know he'll come round eventually. I know it's just a matter of hanging on. And I will hang on—forever, if necessary! But the trouble with me is that I'm so impatient. Waiting is always agony for me. I haven't seen him since yesterday morning, and then he didn't even speak to me. It seems like weeks ago! The minutes just drag by. It's so painful to love anyone as much as I love Daimon.'

As she spoke, I watched her mouth move, pouting, flirting, even with me, anxious for that kiss of complete approbation, complete acceptance, which neither the real Daimon nor her idealized version of him had been able to provide. And I saw the two of them together, kissing, caressing, making love. Horrified at my own intrusion on such a scene, I tried to dismiss the picture, but it persisted. I found myself interrupting her: 'Is Begonia a friend of yours?' I asked.

'Of course,' she said in some surprise. 'She's a very good friend of mine. Why?'

I wished I hadn't mentioned Begonia. 'Couldn't she help?' I asked.

'She did have a word with Daimon,' said Veronica. 'Yesterday. Apparently, he said he was sorry to hear that I was unhappy. But that's about all. Anyway, she doesn't have much influence on him. He's not very keen on her, you see,' she added with an unmistakable glimmer of self-satisfaction.

'Why is that?' I asked quickly, in order to cover up my own contrary knowledge.

'He just doesn't find her attractive,' said Veronica. 'And he thinks there has to be at least a spark of sexual attraction—that's what he called it—between him and any woman he can get on with.'

'I see,' I said thoughtfully.

'The trouble with Daimon and me,' Veronica went on, 'is that we're two such passionate people. We're always getting carried away, one way or another. We feel everything so intensely, you see. I'm sure that's why we're always quarrelling. That's why we both need someone like you, Xanthe, someone so calm and sane, to bring us down to earth.'

I couldn't begin to comment on this speech. I thought: Doesn't she know how offensive she's being? I didn't expect her to know that she was talking nonsense, but I did expect her not to use her nonsense as an ego-prop at my expense. It was definitely time to bring the interview to an end. I stood up. 'I'll see what I can do,' I said heavily and untruthfully.

'Oh, thank you, Xanthe!' she said. 'You're marvellous!'

She came with me to the door. 'I haven't done anything yet,' I reminded her.

'Oh, but you will,' she said. 'I know you will.' She leaned towards me and, to my huge embarrassment, kissed me on the cheek.

12

Xiphias met me in the corridor outside Xeno's room. He looked flustered. 'You're just in time for the action replay,' he said. 'It's a veritable brouhaha in there. I can tell you that for nothing.'

'In there?' I asked, nodding at Xeno's door. There was no noise coming from the other side. 'Are you sure?'

'A hundred per cent positive,' he said. 'Well, only in a manner of speaking, Xanthe dear. Actually it's all on the box. The real scene of all the action is the Philophrenic common-room. They're having a right old knees-up there.'

'Are they?' I asked cautiously, wishing that I knew what he was talking about. 'What's happened?'

'Don't let me spoil it for you,' he said. 'Remain in suspense until you have passed those portals. Ta-ra and good luck.'

I called him back. 'Just tell me one thing,' I said. 'Is Daimon in there?'

'He's been in there for hours,' said Xiphias in a whisper, mouthing the words exaggeratedly. 'With Xeno. Alone, you know. I kept popping in to see what was going on, but my prurience went unrewarded. It was all very circumspect, so don't you worry about a thing, Xanthe.'

I was just wondering how to tell Xiphias that he had mistaken the purpose of my query when I saw Phidia coming along the corridor towards us. I thought: I won't bother; let Xiphias think what he likes. What did matter was that, once again, I hadn't had a chance to talk to Daimon and that, as a result, I felt unarmed.

Phidia came straight to the point. 'What sort of line are you going to take with Xeno?' she asked me as soon as Xiphias had turned the corner of the corridor.

I shrugged. 'I'm going to see what happens first,' I said. 'I understand from Xiphias that there have been further developments.'

'I'm sure there must have been,' she said, 'if Xeno's managed to get all the Philophrenics gathered together.' She beckoned me closer, and continued in a lower tone: 'I don't know about your two, but

Phidias has been telling me some very strange things. For one, that Xeno was really grilling him about his programming—and not just about its contents, either. He kept asking Phidias for his opinions of various stages of the programming, and the way they'd been organized. Perhaps he, Xeno, I mean, was quite within his rights as a director, but to me it seems unethical. After all, he was encouraging my robot to judge me and, presumably, to find me wanting.'

'And did he?' I asked. 'Phidias? What did he say to Xeno?'

'He told him that everything was in order, of course.' Phidia sighed. 'You know how loyal they are. But that's just the point. It seems to me that Xeno was trying to undermine this loyalty. And Phidias said that it seemed to him at the time that Xeno was daring him to complain, daring him to find some imperfection, however small.'

'And thus go against his programming,' I said. 'And then dysfunction?'

'Right,' said Phidia. 'That's exactly what happened.'

Xeno's door opened. He stood there watching us. And I suppose we both looked guilty. 'If you ladies would condescend to join us . . .' he said pointedly and with a chivalrous wave of his hand.

Daimon was sitting on a corner of Xeno's desk, swinging his legs. He did look up when we came in, but I could tell nothing of what had happened from the expression on his face, and the only greeting we got from him was a brief nod. Phidia and I sat down in the two chairs which had been placed ready for us, and waited for some sort of cue.

Xeno sat down at his desk, facing us, and said: 'Well, I gather that you would like me to exonerate myself? If I understand you correctly, there are two charges against me. One—that I have neither consulted you, nor kept you fully informed as to what has been going on. And two—that I have engineered certain recent events, either for my own selfish ends, or out of pure mischief.' He paused deliberately, and looked at us, challenging us to expand or add to what he had said.

'You're the only person who's putting it that strongly,' Phidia pointed out.

'Perhaps,' I said, 'he's only giving us an accurate description.'

'It's a well-known device,' Phidia said. 'Exaggerate your faults or crimes, and other people will then be more likely to agree with your subsequent defence, not of them, but of yourself. They'll be persuaded that you couldn't possibly have done anything as awful as that. Meanwhile, the real fault or crime gets lost somewhere.'

Daimon said: 'It's called chicanery.'

'Am I to be allowed to answer the charges?' asked Xeno, unruffled still. 'Let me explain first, and you can argue with me afterwards. There wasn't time to consult you because, once the robots had made their request, I had to proceed according to a pre-arranged plan. I alerted the chairman of the board of Directors of Programming, and he in turn alerted the chairman of the board of Directors of the Institute. I wasn't supposed to say anything to anyone until the word came through from the Chief Executive. And you know that President Eimi is not a man for snap decisions, at the best of times. Anyway, I'd have thought that the reason for my silence was obvious. By this time the Philophrenics were in a state of almost constant activation during the day, and we didn't want people panicking and confusing the robots by asking them all sorts of unnecessary questions. I'm not saying that any one of you three would have done this, but you must see that we had to safeguard the robots for fear of jeopardizing the objectivity of our results. And a similar consideration applies to the drawing-up of the pre-arranged plans themselves. We didn't want programming to be biased in favour of any one contingency. Again, I'm not saying that any one of you would have been biased. But, once one has a certain result in view, one is liable to nudge things along in that direction, probably without being aware of what one is actually doing. You can see that, if one programmer favoured one result, and another programmer another, we'd have chaos.'

For a few moments no one spoke, then Phidia said: 'I object to being treated like a child. I object to the strong suggestion that I am not to be trusted.'

'So do I,' I said. 'And I object to the secrecy. It's against the rules of this Institute to keep people in ignorance. And even more reprehensible to do it wilfully, as you and your committee have done.'

'I told you that some of the rules would have to be changed soon,' said Xeno. There was a note of sadness in his voice and, so far, it was the only thing I had found convincing about his defence.

Daimon said: 'It's all a load of old rubbish.' He stood up, and strode over to the window.

Xeno said: 'I'm sorry that you should feel that way, Daimon, but I assure you that I've been telling the truth.'

Daimon turned to face us. 'Oh, I think you've been telling the truth,' he said to Xeno. 'But that doesn't put you in the right. It doesn't make the committee right, and it doesn't make the Chief Executive right. If those directors are naïve enough to think that chaos can be eliminated, or even that it *should* be eliminated from the science of robotics, then they all ought to be sacked immediately, and replaced by people with a more realistic approach to the subject.'

'Of course it can't be eliminated,' Xeno said, as though this were a matter for regret, 'but it's best to avoid any more of it than is absolutely necessary.'

'And how,' asked Daimon, 'are you going to judge just how much that is?'

'Only by experience,' said Xeno. 'By trial and error. We're all fallible.'

'But some of us,' said Daimon, 'are considered to be more fallible than others, it seems.'

Xeno sighed. 'I personally regret the decision not to make certain information more freely available,' he said, as though making a concession. 'But I'm sure you'll all be gratified to learn that since this morning that decision has been rescinded.'

'About time too,' said Phidia. 'Now we're getting somewhere, even if it is only a small step forward.'

It seemed to me that the rescission apologized for the committee's behaviour towards us, rather than excusing it. But was an apology good enough? Phidia seemed to think so. And Daimon? It was hard to tell. How far did the apology extend, and why had it been made? In short, what did it actually mean? It meant that we programmers were to be kept fully-informed from now on, yes, but did it also mean that a specified amount of chaos was to be welcomed into our proceedings? It was all so nebulous. I thought: I suppose we'll just have to wait and see how it works out, if it works out.

No one else seemed to have anything to say, so I said: 'What about the second charge, Xeno?'

He looked at me expressionlessly, but hard and long. 'I can only refute it,' he said, 'by reiterating that I'm not guilty.'

The rest of us looked at each other with varying degrees of helplessness. Then Phidia said: 'That's the feeblest defence I've ever heard. Do you really expect us to believe you? After all, you haven't been exactly straightforward with us to date.'

'I haven't lied to you,' Xeno said firmly. 'And I'm not lying to you now.'

'There are lies of omission,' Phidia reminded him, 'as well as lies of commission.'

'Nevertheless,' he replied, still firm, 'I have said all that I'm going to say on the matter. I think I should be presumed innocent until I am proved guilty.'

'Fair enough,' Daimon said abruptly. 'I think it's time we returned to our robots.'

'High time,' Xeno agreed. 'Switch on the video again, will you, Daimon?'

We gathered round the machine in a silence that was not without its stony edge. My estimation of the others' attitudes was as follows. Daimon was in favour of getting on with our work. And, for this, solidarity was essential. He had therefore returned an open verdict on the question of Xeno's guilt. Phidia, though convinced of Xeno's guilt and determined not to let him get away with anything, lacked sufficient evidence to convict him in the eyes of others. So she was lying low until such time as that evidence came to light, or until she could bring it to light herself. Xeno was worried, as well he might be, but what he was most worried about I wasn't sure. He could have been most worried about being found out, or because he had lost our trust and suspected that the committee didn't trust him either. Or he could have been most worried about what the robots were going to do next. As for me, I was still confused, but went along with what seemed to be the consensus: a little caution, a lot of work. Accordingly, I turned my full attention to the screen.

Chaos, far from being eliminated, had now been introduced with a flourish into the Philophrenic common-room. The room was full of robots, variously dressed. Some were sitting on chairs, some on the floor, and some standing around in small groups. But none remained in one position for long, and I got a general impression of restlessness. Most of the robots seemed to be talking, and I wondered if any of them were listening, other than to themselves. For us, it was only possible to hear the odd snatch of conversation, none of which amounted to very much. The most common phrases were 'I think', 'I feel', 'I know' and 'I want'. I couldn't help thinking of Descartes, and I began to understand why Xanthides had found so many of that philosopher's dicta so peculiarly apposite to his own condition.

The robots were thinking, feeling, knowing, wanting, and, therefore, knew themselves to exist. Was Descartes thus vindicated? But then I remembered Lichtenberg's maxim: It thinks, one ought to say. In the circumstances, it couldn't have been more apt. But if the robots' position could be summed up in the phrase: *cogitat, ergo sum*, could mine, as one of their creators, be summarized as *cogito, ergo sunt*? The feeling of power which this proposition lent me was immediately cancelled out by an equally strong feeling of powerlessness. My robots were now out of my control. To them, I was as dead as Nietzsche's God. I turned to Xeno. 'Do you think we still need those inter-action groups?' I asked him.

'On the contrary,' he said. 'I think we need them more than ever. Look at them. They're reacting, but not inter-acting. They're badly in need of organization.'

'And the sooner the better,' said Phidia. 'I'm prepared to start tomorrow, if it can all be set up in time.'

'We should certainly try,' said Daimon. 'All they need is the right impetus from us, and they'll be well on their way.'

'And then they won't need us any more,' I said softly, so softly that no one took any notice of me.

As I returned my attention to the screen, it seemed to me that there was an element of theatricality in the robots' chatter. And in their gestures. They put me in mind of something else. Puppets? No. It was some sort of human being, someone in particular.

Phidia must have shared my impression. She laughed suddenly and said: 'They *are* rather camp, aren't they?'

I said: 'Xiphias. They remind me of Xiphias.'

'You're right,' she said. 'I wonder why that is.'

'I think that's the sort of behaviour,' said Xeno, 'that was typical of single-sex establishments, whether male or female, in the days when such things existed.'

'It doesn't seem to be doing them much good,' said Daimon. 'There's nothing constructive coming out of that meeting at all—they're all much too concerned with asserting themselves as personalities. But I think that's only a temporary thing, don't you, Xeno? It'll probably disappear once they're surer of themselves.'

'I think so,' Xeno agreed. 'And I think that the inter-action groups must promote an increase in self-confidence, among other things.'

As he spoke, Phidia suddenly covered her face with her hands and groaned. We looked at her in alarm. She uncovered her face again and asked us: 'Do you think that, once they're organized and self-confident, they'll no longer be content to be a single-sex establishment, and that they'll want to model themselves on us and on our Institute?'

'Yes, I do,' Daimon said at once. 'They are going to demand to become sexed. That is most definitely what I do think.'

She looked at him and groaned again. 'I must sit down,' she said weakly. 'I really can't take it in.'

Phidia went back to her chair. Xeno switched off the machine and went back to his desk. Daimon and I were left, continuing to stare at the empty screen. I said to him, half-jokingly: 'The fall of the robots is now complete.'

'Ours was a better story,' he said, understanding my remark immediately. 'Man had further to fall.'

'Do you really think so?' I asked with some sadness. 'I regret this fall more than I could ever regret the other one.'

'And yet,' he said, 'this one is a consequence of the other. They fell because we fell.'

'We fell further because we fell first?'

'No,' he said. 'For us, there was death. At least the robots don't have to come to terms with that.'

His tone was as sad as my own, but sharper. As I looked up at him, I felt that he was saying something important to me, something beyond what was included in his words. I felt that we were on the point of understanding each other as we had never done before. And yet, he wasn't even looking at me. Again, I registered the fact of his youth. At the same time I felt stabbed, the pain spreading like a bloodstain between my ribs. For whom was that pang? For Daimon, for myself, for us both, for us all? I said: 'The robots have to come to terms with their own limitations. Those may not be the same as ours, but it comes to the same thing. The recognition of finitude.'

Daimon looked at me then. He smiled and his smile was rueful. 'Finitude,' he repeated, as though he liked the word. 'I thought it was finiteness. But why isn't it finity?'

'What are you two talking about?' Xeno asked us. 'May we also have the benefit of your indubitably expert comments?'

'The fall of man, Xeno,' said Daimon. 'Otherwise known as self-awareness.'

'A gnomic utterance, indeed,' Xeno said to Phidia. 'Would you care to enlarge on it, Daimon?'

'I don't think so,' said Daimon, beginning to trundle a third chair into position between mine and Phidia's. 'Let's talk about sex instead.'

'Very well,' said Xeno.

I joined the circle. I said: 'There's absolutely no point in robots having two sexes when they can't reproduce themselves.'

Phidia said: 'There's absolutely no point in their having hearts, but they still wanted them.'

Xeno said: 'Let's think about the consequences of having sexed robots. What difference does anyone think it's going to make?'

'Have you discussed this in committee?' Daimon asked him.

'Of course,' said Xeno.

'And what conclusions did you reach?'

'None, as a committee,' Xeno said. 'Some people, including myself, were of the opinion that the innovation in question would ultimately make little difference to Philophrenic behaviour—although the novelty could take some time to wear off. Others were of the opinion that it would make all the difference in the world. I imagine that you, Daimon, would place yourself in the latter group.'

'Yes,' said Daimon.

'Xanthe? Phidia?' Xeno asked us. He was plainly saying: Look, now I am consulting you.

'I wonder if they'll all choose to be male,' Phidia said musingly. 'I always think of them as being male, anyway.'

I thought: Suppose Xanthippus chooses to be a woman? The very thought was an affront. I said hurriedly: 'They've all got male names.'

'That's just a convention,' said Xeno. 'The male is more neutral than the female, culturally speaking. Anyway, they can always change their names. We did.'

'But we've none of us changed sex,' said Phidia. She looked mischievously round at the rest of us. 'Have we?'

Xeno took her point up seriously: 'The adoption by a robot of one sex or the other does amount to what for us would be a change of sex. It must alter their perspectives in the same sort of way. It will be interesting to see what choices are made, and why—if it's possible to discover reasons. And then, how each role is interpreted. I think we're going to learn a great deal about the social implications of gender.'

'I hope we're going to learn rather more than that,' said Daimon.

'Once they start thinking of themselves as sexual beings,' I said, 'their efficiency is going to be impaired.'

'How do you know?' Xeno and Daimon both challenged me.

Daimon went on: 'They might be happier as sexual beings, and so work better.'

'Perhaps if they're happier,' I said, 'they'll work worse. Perhaps they won't see any point in working at all. They'll be so interested in one another that they'll lose interest in serving the purposes of the Institute.'

'They'll certainly have a stronger sense of identity,' said Daimon. 'This could give them the self-confidence to branch out a little, and be less narrow-minded in their work.'

'I hope they don't branch out too much,' Phidia said.

'That,' said Xeno, 'is the risk we have to take.'

My own predictive powers were feeling a little strained by now. I said to Xeno: 'Let me get one thing straight. We've been talking about sexed robots, but surely what we really mean is genderized robots. I mean, they're not going to have all the . . . appurtenances, are they?'

Daimon laughed loudly. 'Yes!' he said. 'They are. And the power to use them too.'

'But it's not possible,' I said.

'My dear Xanthe,' said Xeno, 'we live in a technologically advanced society, in which things we have never even dreamed of are perfectly possible. The experts assure me that this particular feat is only all too possible. The robots will be able to perform without fear of human inadequacies overtaking them. There certainly won't be any impotent robots around.'

'That worries you, does it?' Phidia asked him. Xeno looked sharply at her, but didn't reply. She said: 'Do you think they'll want privacy?'

'No,' said Daimon, teasing her. 'They'll be at it all over the place. We shan't be able to move without tripping over copulating robots.'

She looked at him steadily. 'Well, you never know,' she said. 'It could work out like that. But what I meant was that if they did want privacy, we'd have to have the Philophrenic building re-designed. Privacy hasn't been allowed for.'

A sense of desperation had been growing in me, and Phidia's

practical approach seemed to exacerbate it. 'But don't you all see,' I said, 'that if this happens, it's going to be possible for a robot and a human being to—'

'Have it off!' Phidia interrupted me with a laugh. 'What a thought! Well, it would certainly liven things up a little.'

'What's the matter, Xanthe?' Daimon asked. 'What's so horrifying? Don't you welcome the idea? Consummation at last.'

'Isn't it interesting?' Xeno said to Phidia. 'Xanthe sees sexuality as a source of unhappiness. Daimon sees it as a source of pleasure—I shan't say happiness. You'd think, wouldn't you, that they could get together and help each other to modify their extreme views?'

Daimon said: 'Watch it, Xeno.'

I said: 'There's no need to get personal. I was just trying to point out one of the consequences. Isn't that what we were discussing?'

'Oh yes, of course,' said Xeno. 'And I take your point. I can see that it comes as a bit of a shock, but you'll soon get used to the idea. After all, some purely human couplings are pretty incongruous too.'

'But is it really going to happen?' I asked them all, groping for some tangible possibility with which to dam the flood of probability. 'And what about us? Are we just going to sit back and let it all happen?'

'That's what we're here for,' said Xeno.

Xeno was right, of course, professionally speaking. But to me there was something distasteful, something absurd, not to say obscene about the whole business. I didn't see it as inevitable. I saw it as unnecessary and therefore to be avoided. Couldn't we agree that robots wanted to acquire human attributes without taking them literally and supplying them with those attributes? At the same time, I knew my objections to be wildly unscientific in spirit. I knew that conclusions could only be reached through experiment, but I thought: The whole thing is too big for us to handle. Our Institute was a respected and respectable place where valuable work was being done. How could the world outside the walls be expected to take us seriously if we allowed both ourselves and our robots to behave like animals? Or rather, like a combination of the machine and the animal, with the truly human element (which was indefinable) left out? We were doing ourselves a disservice in allowing our standards to be lowered, and our professional integrity impugned. We were also doing the robots a disservice in allowing them to cherish a false notion of themselves as serviceable approximations to human beings. Oh, why couldn't they be content to be themselves? We no longer aspired to be gods. Why couldn't they learn from us? They had learned all their other lessons so well. Then why not this one—perhaps the most important of all?

Xeno was talking about me. 'Xanthe seems to be in a reverie,' he was saying. 'I think she could do with a bit of a rest before taking on anything as strenuous as an inter-action group.'

Daimon said: 'When do we start?'

'Not today,' said Xeno, looking at his watch. 'And certainly not tomorrow. I'm likely to be in committee all day, judging by the way things went at the last session. We still have a lot of unfinished business to get through before we can even touch on the subject of inter-action groups.'

'What are we supposed to do?' asked Phidia. 'It's going to be very frustrating, just sitting around all day, wondering what's going on in committee.'

'At least we've got our robots,' I said. 'We can do a little investigating from the grass roots.'

'I'm afraid not,' said Xeno. 'The directors have decided on a day of complete deactivation for tomorrow.'

'Why?' I asked, feeling this to be setback indeed.

'I think we all need a breathing-space,' said Xeno. 'And that goes for the robots too. I suggest that you all take the day off. Do something different. Get out of the work situation. Get outside the walls.'

'I don't want a day off,' I said stubbornly. 'I want to get on.'

'So do I,' Phidia admitted. 'But it might do us good to take a break. I think I might go and see my Uncle Coningsby. Why don't you come with me, Xanthe?'

'Where is he?' I asked, uninterested.

'Oh, he lives in a small community not far from the capital—'

'I'm not going outside the walls,' I said.

'No, Xanthe never goes outside the walls,' Xeno confirmed.

'But Coningsby is a very good linguist,' Phidia persisted. 'Psycholinguistics is his speciality. He could be very helpful about that stage of Xanthippus's programming. So the visit would have some purpose, you see, Xanthe. You could combine work with pleasure and still feel that you were getting on.'

I said nothing. They were all looking at me with a mixture of solicitude and suppressed but affectionate amusement. I didn't like it. And I didn't see what business it was of theirs if I chose to stay inside the walls. It wasn't as though I were doing anyone any harm. But at the same time I knew that I could perhaps be harming myself in some way which I had not yet recognized. I thought: I've never taken a day off; I work seven days a week; I talk to my robots, if only briefly, every day; whatever am I going to do tomorrow? I could walk in the woods. All day? Alone? I could stay in bed all day. Alone? The emptiness of those hours appalled me. I knew it was an emptiness I had chosen for myself, and had chosen deliberately, cultivating it over the years with the most assiduous care, paying minute attention to its growth, and weeding out all distractions. It was my very own, my peculiar emptiness. But that didn't make it any easier to bear.

I said to Phidia: 'I'll think about it.'

13

My father isn't dead, the authorities tell me. The news comes as a shock after three years. I go and visit him at the Recuperation Centre attached to the Crematorium. The nurse tells me that he's in the day-room, but I can't see him there. The room is empty except for a row of urns, man-sized, amphora-shaped. I half-expect my father to emerge from one of them, like Ali Baba. But he doesn't, and when I call him, there is no reply, just the echo of my own voice. The nurse says he must have wandered off again. So I wander off too. Then I meet him in the corridor. He is wearing a dressing-gown, and a silk scarf to hide the ugly mark where the noose has been. His face is pale and drawn, with a bluish tinge, but not purple and bulbous, as it was before. He is delighted to see me, and says he knew that I would come sooner or later. He says: Everyone thought I was dead, but you never thought such a thing, did you, my little girl?—you kept the faith. I watch his throat move beneath the scarf as he speaks, unable as I am to meet those trusting eyes. I don't know how to tell him that I too have let him down. But I don't know how to hide it from him, either. How can I return that affectionate smile of his without being hypocritical? Guilt gathers like a knot in the pit of my stomach, and rises gradually to my own throat, mounting, choking me...

I couldn't understand why someone was hammering at my door. Why couldn't whoever it was knock in a seemly fashion like anyone else? The bed was in a mess again and I couldn't find my kimono, so I went to the door as I was, in my night-dress. I opened the door cautiously, and there was Daimon. I might have known that no one else would disturb me in the middle of the night. We stared at each other, each of us waiting for an explanation.

He asked: 'What's the matter with you?' He sounded more annoyed than concerned.

'What's the matter with you?' I countered. 'I was asleep.'

'You were screaming,' he said.

'Screaming?' I repeated, letting the door swing open a little. 'I wasn't screaming. I'd know if I had been.'

He came into the room and shut the door. 'You must have been screaming in your sleep,' he said. 'It's a wonder you didn't wake yourself up. What were you dreaming about? Being raped by a robot?'

'No, of course not,' I sighed. 'I was dreaming about my father, if you really want to know.'

'Ah!' he said. I watched him take up his usual position in his usual chair. 'What happened?' he asked. 'Did you see him hanging? Did you actually see him hanging in real life?'

'No, I didn't,' I said sharply. My head felt hot, but I was shivering. 'Oh Daimon, just leave me alone, please.'

'You're cold,' he said. 'Let me get your dressing-gown for you.' He walked over in the direction of the bed before I could stop him. 'You're a restless sleeper,' he remarked.

I thought with some irritation: It's none of your business. I said: 'I'm all right, Daimon. Will you please go away now?' Surely I couldn't have made my wishes clearer than that?

He came back with my kimono which he had found, without difficulty, at the foot of the bed. He was just trying to ascertain which way up it should be when I snatched it from him, and put it on myself. He looked rather taken aback by my abrupt gesture, but he said mildly enough: 'Why are you so angry with me?'

'I'm not angry,' I said, not knowing exactly what I was. 'I don't want you to touch me, that's all. I feel all shivery-shaky.'

'I wasn't going to touch you,' he said, looking at me curiously. 'Do you always sleep that badly?'

I thought: It's my behaviour that's bad; after all, he's only trying to help, isn't he? I said: 'Usually, I sleep very well.'

'Pills?' he asked.

'Yes,' I admitted. 'But I haven't been taking them lately.' By the time I had given him this piece of information, it was already too late to regret having done so.

'Why not?' he asked, as I had known he would.

'I don't know,' I said.

I curled up in an arm-chair, covering my bare feet with the end of my kimono. I felt slightly nauseated and shut my eyes, thinking: If I don't talk to him, perhaps he'll go away; I'll just pretend he's not there. But even with my eyes shut, I could still see him sitting there opposite me in his jeans and tee-shirt, and I wondered vaguely why he should be dressed at that time of night, and what time of night was it, anyway? Try as I might, I couldn't shake his presence off. But it made me feel tense, and the tension gnawed at the knot in my stomach, causing it to radiate centrifugal ripples of nausea. I thought: Daimon, you're making me feel sick. Then I opened my eyes to see if he had got the message, but he looked quite unperturbed. I said: 'I think I must be suffering from withdrawal symptoms.'

'That's hardly surprising,' said Daimon, looking at me sternly, 'if you've been on the same formula for three years.'

I yawned. 'What's the time?' I asked pointedly.

'About three-thirty,' he said. He wasn't wearing a watch. 'You woke me up, you know.'

I didn't believe him. 'Do you go to bed with all your clothes on?' I asked him.

'No,' he said evenly. 'But I thought I'd better put on some trousers before coming to see you.'

'Very considerate,' I said. I didn't seem able to stop myself from behaving badly.

'You're very prickly, Xanthe,' he said. 'Xeno was right about your needing a break. Won't you change your mind and come with us tomorrow?'

'Us?'

'Yes, Phidia and me.'

It was my turn to look at him with curiosity. I was wondering if Phidia were about to become his latest conquest, and foolishly imagining that I should be able to see signs of such a possibility in his face. I thought: No, surely she's too old to qualify with Veronica and Begonia; she must be at least my age. I said: 'Oh, you're going too, are you?'

'Would you rather I didn't?' he asked.

'It has nothing whatsoever to do with me,' I said.

He said: 'Does that mean you're not coming? Phidia will be disappointed. We've arranged to borrow one of the Institute's cars, the ones the directors use. All you have to do is to step into it, just outside the main door, and then step out again at the other end.'

'Who's driving?' I asked.

'Phidia,' he said, and laughed. 'Don't worry, I'm not asking you to entrust your life to me.'

I didn't like what he said, but I didn't know why. I thought: They've arranged it all between them, without consulting me; I'll only be in the way. I saw us all in the car, Phidia driving, Daimon sitting beside her, his arm stretched along the back of the double seat, both of them chattering and laughing, and myself in the back, silent and agoraphobic. I thought: No. The word repeated itself. 'No,' I said stubbornly.

'Well, if you feel that strongly about it,' said Daimon, 'there's no point in my trying to persuade you further.'

I was thinking: But it doesn't have to be like that; it doesn't have to be the way I pictured it just now; I can change that picture, turn it into anything I want. And I asked myself to consider, please, as calmly as possible, what it was I was really afraid of. I answered myself that I was afraid to go outside the walls without some form of protection. But protection from what? From the world outside. I didn't want it to come near me. I felt it would be like touching walls of raw meat. My pills could have afforded me some form of protection by insulating me, but I was still reluctant to go back to them. The car itself would protect me, yes, but the question was: would Daimon and Phidia? Or rather, would they do anything to remove the protection I had managed to gather around myself? My fears were childish, and I recognized them as such. Their sum total, I told myself harshly, amounted to something verging on the imbecile. But the most curious thing about them was that they didn't really exist. They were vestigial—old and inappropriate reflexes applied to a new contingency. Those fears were no longer my fears because I was no longer the person who had felt them. Why, then, was I hoarding them? To keep me warm? I thought: What does it matter to me how Daimon and Phidia choose to behave? How could their combined self-assurance affect me one way or the other? They were neither older nor stronger nor wiser than I was, and I shouldn't be looking to them for protection. I could and I would protect myself.

I said: 'What time would we leave?'

'Oh, whatever time suits you,' said Daimon, taking my momentous decision lightly. 'Around the middle of the morning is all we've decided on, so far.'

'That suits me admirably,' I said with an equanimity I was far from feeling.

Daimon was smiling at me, and his smile had a hint of the conspiratorial about it. I looked at him questioningly. He laughed and I couldn't help laughing too. 'You win,' I said.

He became serious once more. 'Do I?' he asked. 'Do I really win?'

This time he had lost me. 'Well, don't you?' I asked rhetorically.

He moved his chair nearer to mine. 'Tell me about your dream,' he said with what sounded like forced casualness.

My brave decision of a moment past had made me generous. 'It's a dream I used to have quite frequently,' I began, 'but I haven't had it for some time now. What it amounted to was that my father was really alive, and that I had been committing some crime against him these past few years in thinking or believing that he was dead.'

'What sort of crime?' asked Daimon. 'Disloyalty?'

'Stronger than that,' I said. 'Betrayal.'

'I sometimes have dreams like that about my mother,' he said. 'I dream that she's still alive. And then I wake up thinking: She's only dead because I said she was, because I thought she was, because I . . . well, almost—'

'Wished she was?' I supplied, and he nodded. I found myself leaning towards him over the arm of my chair and, adopting his manner, I said: 'Tell me about your mother, Daimon.'

He looked at me with a confusion of emotions that was familiar to me. It was the same mixture with which I had so often responded to his demands. It said, first: Is she genuine? Then: Is she humouring me? And then: Is she teasing me?

I prompted him: 'You must have been very fond of her.'

'Not particularly,' he said, still on his guard. 'At least, we weren't very close, as they say. The trouble always was that she wasn't particularly fond of me.'

He seemed disinclined to say anything more, so I asked him: 'Are you sure?' I had imagined a prolonged Oedipal relationship, to which I had in part attributed his brilliance, and which death alone could have shattered.

'Quite sure,' he said drily. 'She wasn't at all a maternal sort of woman, although she did have six children. To tell you the truth, I think she got utterly fed up with us all, and wished that she'd done something else with her life, especially after my father had pissed off and left us. Oh, she was a devoted mother. She had to be. It was her duty. A sensible woman, but quite without spontaneity, and almost without joy, although a little would shine through every now and then. Poor mother, she was incapable of having fun.'

He seemed to be following his train of thought wordlessly. I allowed the pang of self-recognition, which the latter part of his description had prompted, to subside, and asked him: 'Were you the youngest?' I couldn't but see him as the baby of the family, young as he seemed to me.

'No, no,' he said. 'I was the eldest. I was a bright child, but she didn't seem to appreciate my brightness—at least, she never showed that she did. Instead, she seemed to take my achievements for granted. I would keep trying to surpass myself so as to surprise her. But I never managed to do that. In fact, the more I tried, the more I seemed to weary her. I could never understand why she didn't react like my teachers, why she didn't seem as fond of me as they did—fond of me above the others, that is.'

He looked at me as though expecting some comment, and I said: 'I think that's one of the hardest lessons of childhood for an intelligent child—that affection isn't necessarily earned.' I forebore to add that I was speaking from my own experience.

'I don't think I've learned it yet,' he said with a rueful but open smile.

'Oh, but you have,' I said. 'You don't exactly go out of your way to please Xeno and the directors.' I forebore to add myself to the list.

'But I don't care about them,' he said.

'But you care about your work, don't you?' I asked, wondering who and what he did care about, if not about that.

'Maybe,' he said, moving his chair even closer to mine, so that their arms were touching. 'Your mother died when you were very young, didn't she?'

He was leaning towards me. I sat upright, away from him. 'Yes,' I said. 'But please, Daimon, don't let's talk any more about death.'

'Why not?' he asked. 'Death seems to bring us closer together.'

I recognized that, in some curious way, he was right. But the recognition made me uneasy. 'I suppose the experience of death does tend to change people,' I said matter-of-factly, hoping to return the conversation to a more impersonal level.

'You know something?' he said. 'We're both orphans.'

'Well,' I said, 'that shouldn't matter to us now.'

'But it does,' he persisted. 'Doesn't it?'

Denied impersonality, I considered, leaning back in my chair, my hands clasped behind my head. 'Yes,' I said.

At once the room became still and quiet. 'Yes,' Daimon echoed out of the stillness and quietness.

'Was it after your mother's death,' I asked him tentatively, 'that you were doing group therapy?'

'Briefly,' he said. 'It wasn't my idea. But they seemed to think where I was before, that it would help.'

'And did it?'

'A little.'

'But not entirely,' I said. 'That seems obvious.'

'Yes,' he said, agreeing with me.

'Yes . . .' I said, musing on the inaccessibility of grief.

I shut my eyes, and the next thing I knew was that he was kissing me, pushing his tongue, a warm foreign object, between my lips. I couldn't understand how it had managed to get there without my noticing. I was so taken aback that I could neither react nor respond but let the tongue continue on its way inside and around my mouth. I couldn't even unclasp my hands. It was only our mouths that were touching, and Daimon's seemed disembodied, like a visitation in a dream. The whole sensation was so strange to me that I sat there as if mesmerized, locked up in my own immobility. Then my eyes opened, and Daimon stood up in one sudden movement, as if caught out in some shameful practice.

'Why did you do that?' I asked stupidly, my voice shaking in spite of myself.

'I don't know,' he said. He wasn't looking at me, and he sounded angry. 'But you can be sure of one thing. I shan't do it again, since it was so obviously an unwelcome gesture.' He walked to the door where he paused for a moment. I watched him, not knowing how to contradict him, not knowing how to explain myself. 'Good night Xanthe,' he said in his politest tones. 'I hope you get some sleep now.'

The door shut after him, and I had neither the wit nor the nerve to call him back. I thought: Daimon! Then I thought: Daimon. Then Daimon was all I could think. I saw him walking, leaning slouching, lounging. I saw him sit with his feet up, I saw him stand with his thumbs in his belt. I saw him smiling, laughing, scowling scolding. I saw him move, shuffling, eager, abrupt, hesitant, but always towards me, always close to me. He was all I could see. He was everywhere. His new luminescence still pervaded my room, still pervaded me. I remembered my dream-beast, his vivid physical presence, and I thought: Freud is not mocked, indeed; it was Daimon all the time. I heard his voice, sharp, soft, teasing, sweet, and all it was saying in every tone was: Xanthe. I thought: I must be going out of my mind. I stood up quickly, forgetting my precarious state. My nausea had gone, but I was shaking more violently than ever. And I was crying, as I had not cried for a long time, silently and profusely. The tears were flowing effortlessly, almost joyously, as if at last their time had come. I thought: Like the torrents of spring.

14

I elected to sit in the back of the car, although Phidia kept insisting that there was room for all three of us in the front. Daimon, however, disagreed with her. Thus was our tacit and mutual decision to avoid close contact expressed. So he sat next to Phidia, as I had pictured.

'Isn't it a lovely day?' Phidia murmured, looking up at the not-quite-cloudless sky. 'Aren't we lucky?'

'Glorious!' Daimon said over-emphatically. He put his arm along the back of the seat, as I had pictured, and smiled brightly at Phidia.

She turned round and said: 'I'm so glad you changed your mind, Xanthe. Aren't you, Daimon?'

'Oh yes, over-joyed!' said Daimon.

Phidia went on: 'I thought Daimon would manage to persuade you. He is very persuasive, isn't he?'

'Oh, how nice!' said Daimon. He caught my eye in the driving mirror before kissing Phidia lightly on the cheek. 'How nice to be appreciated at last.'

'You rotten young flirt!' Phidia said affectionately. And then she kissed him in the same manner.

I affected to be unaffected by this interchange. 'Shall we go, then?' I asked pleasantly. I thought: Daimon is going to give me a hard time today.

The car started with the quietest of purrs, and we began to glide down the main drive, past the rose gardens. There was nothing to fear, so far. All was still familiar, still within the bounds of my self-prescribed universe. The scent of roses reached us through the air-conditioning system with the sharpness and the sweetness of something remembered. I thought: Suppose I should never see them again . . .? I looked back at the Institute, my home, the place where I had spent so much of my life, and where my father had spent so much of his. I thought: Can it really be left behind so simply? The building grew smaller and smaller until we turned a bend, when it vanished altogether. I felt as though a cloud had blotted out the sun, as though a chapter of my life had been closed, and I shivered in anticipation of what the succeeding pages might contain. I knew these thoughts to be fanciful—after all, I was only leaving the place for a few hours—but I was reluctant to check them. Let them roam, I thought, let me indulge myself this once; I should be allowed a little indulgence because I'm being so brave. But then it seemed to me that it was foolish to leave the known security of the Institute behind in favour of what promised to be a day of random episodes, trailing one after the other with no sense of continuity. And I must confess that, as we approached the gates of the Institute, all I wanted to do was to creep back, hobbit-like, into my little hole. We had to show our passes at the gate, and the wild hope occurred to me that perhaps mine wasn't in order, and that I wouldn't be allowed out. But no, I had always been efficient about such things as renewing documents. We were given leave to proceed, the tall iron gates swung open with the same ease that characterized the motion of the car, and Phidia drove us through them.

We were on an open country road, treeless, with the fields stretching away from us on either side as far as the horizon. I thought: There is so much space about, so much space in this supposedly overcrowded island of ours. How can there not be enough for everyone? I had forgotten that the world outside the walls could be flat and empty, as well as being a jumble of encroaching objects. And I stared out at it all, letting my memory refresh itself, letting it feed to revive itself on the expansive fields, which yielded themselves like fodder to the eye and mind.

Phidia turned round briefly. 'All right, Xanthe?' she asked, managing to keep her eye on the road at the same time as giving me a reassuring smile.

'Oh yes,' I said. I was beginning to regret giving her cause to treat me like an old lady fast approaching senility but with a somewhat erratic progression. 'I'll start screaming, if I'm not.'

'It shouldn't take more than an hour,' she continued. 'Coningsby is expecting us for lunch.'

'Good. I'm starved already,' Daimon said like a child, thereby earning himself another fond smile from Phidia. He said to her: 'Tell us about Coningsby.'

'Well,' said Phidia, 'there's not much to tell, mainly because he's led what you might call an entirely blameless life, devoted to his work and to the community, to the exclusion of all other interests. Let's see. He's old enough to be my grandfather, and he has a weak heart, poor dear. To tell you the truth, he's rather a dull old thing, unless you happen to be interested in linguistics. Or food. He's a very good cook, and takes a pride in concocting all sorts of gourmet dishes from the most unpromising synthetic materials. What I usually do is to eat well, and then pick his brains.'

'Metaphorically speaking, of course,' said Daimon. 'I suppose he's not particularly interested in robotics, then?'

'Oh yes, he is,' said Phidia. 'Very. He thinks that language is the foundation-stone of robotic consciousness, as it is of ours. He's always quoting Roman Jakobson, you know: language is the fourth great fact of life.'

'After birth and copulation and death, I suppose,' said Daimon.

'I suppose so.' Phidia smiled at him again. 'He and Xeno are apt to get into lengthy discussions about the multifarious possibilities of linguistic programming.'

'Xeno?' Daimon and I spoke together.

'Oh yes,' said Phidia. 'Didn't you know? He and Coningsby are old friends. They've certainly known each other since I was a child. Coningsby's always been a sort of a father-figure to Xeno. To tell you the truth, I think it was partly because of their friendship that I got my job at the Institute.'

'Well,' said Daimon. 'Well, well, well.'

'Don't be so cynical,' Phidia rebuked him. 'It wasn't like that at all. I did also have the right qualifications, you know. And how did you get your job?'

'Through my own undoubted merits,' said Daimon. 'And, I suspect, because I was rude to Xeno, and kept telling him that he was talking rubbish whenever he ventured into speculation. He wasn't, of course, and he knew it, and he knew that I knew it. I think he took me to be as devious a character as himself.'

Phidia laughed. 'That would take some doing,' she said.

Daimon looked round at me. 'And we all know how Xanthe got her job,' he said accusingly.

However, there was nothing to accuse me of, unless it were the fact of being my father's daughter. 'Yes,' I said lightly. 'I grew up with robotics. We both came of age at around the same time. The first completed Philophrenic came into being that year, the same year as my father became President of the Institute.' I was talking to myself rather than to Daimon and Phidia, trying to convince myself that all those things had happened, and had happened concurrently. I thought: Everything went so well that year; it must have been a happy time. But no intimations of a former happiness reached me. I saw the events coldly, as though I had not been at their centre. It was like looking at an old photograph taken on a special day which had since turned out to be puzzlingly forgettable. What I was remembering were the memories of that time rather than the time itself.

Signs warned us that our quiet road was about to join the motorway. This was what I had remembered as being typical of the world outside. And it hadn't changed. It was larger, of course, and the volume of traffic had increased, but in essence it was the same place, and I knew it to be only one of many same places. Once we were there, I began to feel slightly agitated, being unused to moving at speed, but the feeling wore off surprisingly quickly, mainly because the car was so quiet that I could hardly believe that we were moving at all. It was only the landscape that moved. I sat back, reclining on the comfortable upholstery, and surrendered myself to watching the unchanging view. I even became lulled enough, hypnotized perhaps by the steadiness of our motion, to find myself falling asleep. Then Daimon's voice cut into my hypnagogic comic-strip, in which we were hurtling through space in a sealed and silent time-capsule.

He was saying to Phidia: 'So the robots have embarked upon their heuristic adventure.'

'We can only wish them luck,' she said. 'Oh, I do hope the directors are going to handle this properly.'

'How would you handle it?' he asked her.

'Very strictly,' she told him. 'I'd have none of this business of milling around in the common-room, or anywhere else, for that matter. I'd set up fixed and limited periods of activation. During these, every stage of their progress would be discussed by us and with us. And preferably equal numbers of us, rather than a class and teacher situation.'

Daimon said: 'In other words, you think we should guide them along every step of their way?'

Phidia said: 'Yes, I do. Their programming isn't perfect. It can't be, if only because it was created by imperfect beings—us. Anything could go wrong. There must be something that we haven't been able to foresee.'

Daimon laughed. 'Chaos and anarchy!' he said.

'It is possible, you know, Daimon,' she said severely. 'And I don't think Xeno is going to do anything to prevent it. He's far too liberal in his attitude to the robots.'

'Well, if it did come to chaos and anarchy,' Daimon said, 'all we'd have to do would be to deactivate all the robots permanently.'

'Oh, marvellous!' said Phidia. 'And then where would we be? Where would any of us be without the Philophrenics? Out of a job. And the Institute would probably have to shut down.'

'Not at all,' said Daimon. 'We'd just scrap our present Philophrenics and start all over again.'

'And what a waste of time and effort that would be,' she said. There was a pause, during which I nearly lapsed back into sleep. Then I heard her say: 'I don't think you're taking the situation seriously enough.'

Daimon said: 'I refuse to panic, if that's what you mean.'

'I'm not panicking,' said Phidia. 'I'm just not as sanguine as everyone else appears to be. Except perhaps Xanthe.'

At the mention of my name I made an effort to wake myself properly so as to take part in the discussion, but all I could attain was an incoherent murmur. I heard Daimon say: 'She's asleep.' I couldn't tell whether he had turned round or not.

'Let her sleep, then,' said Phidia. 'Poor girl. I think this business may have triggered off some emotional crisis for her.'

'Emotional? I doubt it,' Daimon said briskly.

Phidia said something in a tone too low for me to hear, and Daimon laughed, but whether the laugh agreed with her or contradicted what she had said, I couldn't tell. At any rate, I reflected, it was probably at my expense. Daimon's attitude to me, as evinced so far that day, was beginning to get me down. He seemed determined to ignore me as much as possible and, where it wasn't possible, to humiliate me by less subtle means, such as sarcasm or excessive politeness. I asked myself: What have I done? But I knew that it was what I hadn't done that mattered. Daimon was not used to rejection and was stung by it. But he shouldn't have interpreted my reaction, or rather, lack of reaction to his 'gesture' as a rejection. He should have interpreted it as incompetence on my part. That's what it had been. And I was still suffering from it. It was a long time since anyone had kissed me like that, and I had forgotten what it was like, had forgotten too that I was capable of responding physically to another human being. Such memories could be revived in the space of a second, but they were difficult to utilize as quickly. It amazed me that Daimon couldn't see this: he was normally so astute. It amazed me further that I didn't know how to explain it to him: I was normally articulate enough. I tried telling myself that it was a trivial incident, best forgotten. But even if this attempt at self-deception had been effective, the incident still remained an untidy one. It remained a piece of unfinished business, and it went against all my instincts to leave it like that. I told myself: Things should always be straightened out. But how? How to start? Daimon was obviously not at all receptive to anything I might have to say to him, let alone anything so intimate and so intangible. I opened my eyes and found myself gazing despairingly at the back of his neck. There was something obdurate about it.

And beyond him, the road still stretched on, a dazzling artifact, flinging its hardness back at us with all the force of a thing that knows it has conquered nature. What soft, supple creatures we were inside our man-made carapace! And how we were at the mercy of our own products! How could a kiss, the tender meeting of flesh with flesh, have any significance among those rigid systems of mass, force and energy, which constituted the environment of the internal combustion engine? And yet, flesh was what we were. I looked at Daimon, following the line of his head, neck, shoulder, arm and hand, and I was struck by its unexpected loveliness. I thought: It's even more beautiful than Xanthippus's heart. But the thought, the comparison filled me with dismay. I didn't want to think or to feel such things. I didn't want to be moved by the loveliness of any human being. To be subject to such an emotion only made life more difficult. I tried to think of Xanthippus in all his robotic perfection, but the only picture I could visualize was a two-dimensional one, as flat and as lacking in perspective as a child's drawing. I could admire it, out of deference to the limited abilities of its creator, but it remained less than fully adult, less than fully human. I had to admit that Daimon's wrist alone held more reality for me. I thought: Can these things be true or are they just part of my madness, the madness I fell into last night?

I asked Phidia: 'How much longer is it now?'

She turned round briefly, as though startled. 'I thought you were asleep,' she said.

Daimon turned his head round in my direction, but he couldn't see me because I was sitting on his side of the car. 'What did you dream about?' he asked me.

I couldn't gauge the spirit in which the question had been asked, so I decided to lie—or was it a lie? 'You,' I said.

'Ah!' said Phidia. 'Surely some revelation is at hand. What was he up to?'

'His usual tricks,' I said, despising myself for the hint of flirtatiousness in my voice, despising myself especially because Daimon seemed impervious to it.

'You see, Daimon,' said Phidia. 'Even Xanthe's got your number.'

I thought: Even Xanthe! Was I renowned, then, for my dumbness? I said: 'Oh, even Xanthe is not without her powers of perception. Even Xanthe's unconscious is capable of shaping dreams, like anyone else's. Who would have thought it?'

'Oh, Xanthe!' Phidia said. 'I'm sorry. That's not what I meant at all.'

'Yes, it was,' said Daimon.

'No, it wasn't,' Phidia insisted.

I said: 'It really doesn't matter.'

Daimon said: 'Why make such a fuss about it, then?'

I thought: He really is giving me a hard time. I sighed and said: 'I'm sorry if I made a fuss. I didn't realize I was doing that. I spoke without thinking.'

'A likely story,' said Daimon. 'Pre-meditation is your forte.'

'Hey,' said Phidia, intervening. 'I thought you two liked each other.'

Daimon and I spoke together. 'Sometimes,' we both said.

'I see,' said Phidia. 'Well, if you can manage to like each other for the next fifteen minutes or so I'd be very grateful.'

Neither Daimon nor I replied, each of us being apparently content to let the arbiter have the last word. I said to Phidia, by way of making conversation, 'Do you do this trip often?'

'Often enough,' she said. 'But I must say I find it easier without Xeno. He can be a very wearing companion.'

'Phidia's got it in for him,' said Daimon. 'Haven't you, Phidia?'

'Let's put it this way,' said Phidia. 'I find it impossible to trust anyone so blatantly evasive.'

'Do you think Xeno has any sex-life?' Daimon asked.

'No,' said Phidia. 'He's impotent. But I don't really see what that's got to do with anything.'

'How do you know he's impotent?' I asked her with some curiosity. It had never occurred to me to speculate about Xeno's sex-life.

'Surely it must affect his judgement,' Daimon said, and it was impossible to tell whether he meant what he said, or was merely being provocative again. 'I thought yesterday that he was extremely biased on the question of sexed robots.'

'I suppose,' Phidia said, 'that a rampaging stud does not suffer similarly from bias, and that his judgement is not affected by his sex-life in any way?'

'I suppose nothing of the kind,' Daimon said coolly, as if Phidia's taunt had been nowhere near the bone. 'But we're discussing actualities, not fantasies. We're discussing Xeno.'

'Yes, but not seriously, I trust,' said Phidia.

'Not entirely,' Daimon admitted.

I said: 'I found myself agreeing with Xeno quite often yesterday. Do you think I share his bias, Daimon?'

'Answer that, Daimon,' said Phidia. 'Do you conclude that Xanthe is the female equivalent of Xeno?'

'Frigid?' asked Daimon. He turned round and looked fully at me for the first time since we had left the Institute. It was a sly look with a spark of satisfaction in it. 'Need you ask?'

The statement was ambiguous enough for Phidia to miss its point. At any rate, she seemed to find it less than worthy of a reply. Daimon shifted his position, removing his arm from the back of the seat. As he did so, I felt my anger against him lessen, and I was glad of it because I was in a state of emotional frailty too advanced to rally itself into the articulation of that anger. We were leaving the motorway, and I yawned and stretched with relief. It was like coming back to earth after the rigours of extra-terrestrial travel. We were no longer figures painted arbitrarily on some futuristic canvas to serve as an indication of scale, but were now ourselves again, recognizable figures in a traditional landscape.

Then I noticed that there were other figures in our landscape. A small group of people was making its way along the barren highway towards us, but shrinking away from us towards the verge. They were a straggling procession, emanating dejection. As we drew nearer them, it seemed to me that they were a nuclear family group, consisting of a man, a woman and three children. As we passed them, I noticed that they were all thin, raggedly clothed, dirty, and carried damp-looking untidy bundles on their backs. I looked back at them, never having seen such a sight before, but they took no notice of us at all.

'Who were they?' I asked the others.

'Who?' Phidia said vaguely. 'Oh, you mean the refugees?'

Daimon turned round to look at me again. 'You don't mean to say you've never seen refugees before!' he said.

'Refugees from what?' I asked.

'From the cities, of course,' he said. 'Where else?'

'Don't you know what's happening to our cities?' Phidia asked me. 'They're getting smaller, shrinking towards the centres or sub-centres, while the outskirts decay.'

'They're going bankrupt all over the place,' said Daimon.

'And even those that are still solvent,' said Phidia, 'are more or less ungovernable. Come on, Xanthe, you must have heard or read about it somewhere.'

'Oh, of course,' I said, dimly acknowledging that the details of their description were not unfamiliar to me. I had read such things, but I had never paid much attention to them. 'So things are falling apart?' I asked rhetorically.

'Yes, Xanthe,' Phidia said with heavy patience. 'Let me tell you that our society is in an ongoing state of disintegration. There hasn't been any cataclysm, in case you're wondering, just a gradual and accelerating process of decay.'

'When Xanthe talks about our society,' said Daimon, 'what she means is our Institute. None of the rest of it exists, as far as she's concerned.'

'That's not fair,' I protested. 'I do concern myself with what goes on in the outside world. I listen to the radio. And I read the newspapers.'

'Sometimes,' said Daimon. 'And sometimes you only read the review sections.'

'Well,' I said, 'that's part of my job.'

'And news isn't?' he persisted. 'That's your excuse, is it? That nothing not immediately relevant to your job is of any importance?'

'It *is* difficult to keep up with everything,' said Phidia, arbitrating again. 'But at the same time, Xanthe, don't you think perhaps you're taking this ostrich-like attitude too far? Don't you think your robots would be all the better for some wider knowledge of the world we've made for them, and for us all?'

'In the circumstances,' I said, 'I really don't see what difference it would make.'

'It could make some difference,' she said. 'It could make them more tolerant of human problems, and less absorbed in their own. They might even be able to help us.'

'Possibly,' I said, wishing to avoid further argument, but remaining far from convinced. I watched the empty landscape give way to wooded parkland behind a high wall, and wondered what enclave of civilization lay within those bounds. 'Are we nearly there?' I asked.

'Yes,' said Phidia. 'The mansion itself is hidden behind those trees. But any minute now you'll see the lodge coming up on your left.'

I had imagined that Coningsby lived in a village, or even in a town, but here was another closed community. 'It's almost like going back to the Institute,' I said as we drove through the lodge gates.

'A home from home,' said Daimon. 'You'll be able to cope with that, won't you, Xanthe?'

'I think so,' I said lightly. I looked at his adamant profile, and thought: But am I going to be able to cope with you?

15

The sheltered courtyard caught the sun, holding the warmth in its mellow walls, then giving it and the light back to us. We sat sleepily at Coningsby's table, replete with food and wine, and disinclined to move. Around us, at other tables, sat similar groups of people, residents at the mansion. Everyone seemed to know everyone else. While eating and drinking they talked animatedly to each other across tables or from table to table, occasionally exchanging jocular remarks across the courtyard. Above us, on one side, rose the high wall of the mansion with its mullioned windows and crenellated ramparts. The other three sides of the yard were framed by the lower walls of what had once been outbuildings, but now served as kitchens. Trailing plants in wooden tubs decorated the circumference of the floor area. Nearby, birds sang in excited bursts, hidden in the trees.

I thought: It's strange how different this place is from our Institute, although the two may seem superficially alike; everything here seems to proceed at a lazier pace; it's a life even further removed from urban realities than ours is. The life of our Institute had evolved from our work. We were a highly-organized hierarchical community with a common purpose. Here all was diffuse. People lived together because that was where they happened to live, and the only things they had, or had ever had, in common were money and foresight. The foresight had been applied to envisaging such a community in the first place, removed as it was from the crumbling conurbations. The money had been essential for setting up the project and for bringing it to completion. It was a loose structure, its only bonds being those relaxed ones between people who have agreed to co-exist for the sake of mutual convenience, but without a collective cause.

I yawned, as if to alter the torpid atmosphere around our table. Coningsby was the only one of the four of us who still seemed alert. He was a small, rather frail-looking man, whose most noticeable features were his white hair and his fastidiously manicured hands. Otherwise, I noticed nothing remarkable about his appearance.

'What's it to be first?' he asked us. 'The linguistics laboratory or the ramparts?' The rest of us looked at one another, but none of us seemed capable of making a decision. 'It rather depends,' Coningsby continued, 'on which is the more responsive to a summons to hard labour—the mind or the muscles.'

'I vote we scale the ramparts,' said Daimon. 'It seems to present the lesser challenge.'

'I'll second that,' said Phidia. 'Besides, the air up there might blow away some of the cobwebs that are clinging to my poor mind, and then I'll be better prepared for the eventualities of intellectual debate.'

'The ramparts it is, then,' said Coningsby. 'But we shall have to approach them from the other side of the building. That way we get a more interesting climb.'

'Let's take it fairly slowly,' said Phidia. 'Remember your heart, Uncle.'

'How far can you see from up there?' I asked Coningsby, as I stood up. My legs felt stiff already from the short but strenuous walk we had taken before lunch, and the thought of further clambering was not entirely welcome. In addition, I didn't like heights. I should have preferred to be excused from the expedition, but it seemed impolite to make any such request.

'Oh, you can see for miles and miles,' Phidia said. 'Come on, Daimon. Put your vote into practice. You need the exercise.'

Daimon smiled lazily at her and made no move. Coningsby stood up and said: 'Perhaps Daimon has remembered, as I cannot forget, that the view is no longer the happy one we enjoyed in former times.'

'The purpose of the exercise is not entirely aesthetic,' said Phidia, standing behind Daimon and dislodging him by tipping his chair forward.

Coningsby turned to me. 'You know how things have changed, my dear,' he said. 'We in this establishment are among the few who predicted those changes correctly. But I can assure you that it gives us no pleasure at all to be proved right.'

'I don't believe it, Coningsby,' said Daimon. 'Everyone likes to be proved right.'

'That is generally true,' Coningsby conceded, 'but I think we must agree, young man, to declare this case an exception.' He turned first to Phidia and then to me. 'Shall we make the attempt on the heights, then?' he asked.

We followed him in silence out of the courtyard and into the shade. Phidia caught up with him at once, and they both waited for me, while Daimon lagged behind us, resuming his reluctant and shuffling walk.

I said to Coningsby: 'Surely you don't want to see the view, if it really is that dreadful?'

Coningsby replied: 'No, I don't want to see it, my dear. But, unfortunately, I cannot avoid doing so.'

'Can't you?' I asked, taking him literally. 'All you have to do is to give up climbing the ramparts.'

'And pretend that the devastation doesn't exist?' he asked me in a tone which rebuked my apparent naïvety. 'No, no, that is not the way of it at all. I don't go up there in order to torture myself, but in order to reassure myself.'

'But if it's as bad as you say,' I objected, 'how can it reassure you of anything?'

'It is as bad as I say,' he said. 'It is as bad as I expect it to be. But it is no worse. And that is what I find reassuring.'

'Why isn't anything being done about it?' I asked, remembering the refugees, and including their plight in my question.

Coningsby said: 'No one knows what to do. Or rather, various people claim to know what to do, but as usual their claims conflict. In spite of continuous public debate, effective action has become impossible because there is always someone to block any proposed course of action.'

I said: 'Why does it matter so much? Isn't a certain amount of decay inevitable?'

'A certain amount!' Coningsby repeated. He turned to Phidia. 'My dear,' he asked her, 'is this young woman fully-informed as to what has been happening to our once-beautiful cities and our once-beautiful countryside?'

'I doubt it,' said Phidia. 'We do our best with Xanthe, but it doesn't always work.'

This young woman, I thought, is fully-informed about one thing only—robotic programming in the humanities. I found myself oppressed by two things besides an unusually large intake of alcohol. One was the weight of my own ignorance, the heavy burden of my light knowledge. Was I unable to expand or diversify it? Did experience only reach me, only touch me, through an automatic filter whose job it was to keep my mind uncluttered? If so, it was because I had been trained that way. My father had always taught me to analyse and eliminate. He had told me that, in order to possess a first-class mind, I had first to learn what not to learn, to root out trivialities ruthlessly. I believed him. I did as I was told—not because I wanted to cultivate a first-class mind, but because I was afraid he would find out that I did not and could never possess such a thing. Now I asked myself: Is there such a thing, anyway? And if there was, was it worth having? The heresy was so great that I savoured it again and again, like a child reading the definitions of dirty words in a dictionary. I thought of my father's aristocratic intellect, then I thought of his shameful death—the most shameful of all in the eyes of society. Was there a direct, if not necessarily causal, connection between the two things? And there, walking in the shadow of the mansion wall, letting Phidia and Coningsby draw ahead of me, I felt the return of an old emotion. A violent return, a violent emotion. A sense of loss. My father was dead. He had died without warning, leaving me confused, leaving me in ignorance of how to live my life, a life that had been more his than mine in so many ways. What did it matter whether his death refuted or confirmed his principles? The only question was: How could he have done such a thing? To me? And for the second time in twenty-four hours I felt the tears well up in my eyes. But whereas those had flowed easily, these threatened to gush out noisily and spasmodically, burning me with their bitterness. I tried to control them. Daimon was catching up with me, and any minute now either Phidia or Coningsby might look round.

I didn't want them to see me cry. And through this negative wish I felt my bitterness extend itself to them, as I arrived at the second reason for my sense of oppression. It seemed that they were continually criticizing me, continually trying to wear down my self-contained strength. I walked on blindly, knowing my action to be futile, knowing myself to be cornered. But I was cornered in the open. There was no wall, no floor, to which I could cling and weep. I could only stand where I was, cover my face with my hands, and sob.

Then someone's arm was round my shoulders, someone's hand was on my wrist, trying to uncover my face. I heard Daimon say: 'Oh, Xanthe, Xanthe, is it my fault?'

Almost at once Phidia said: 'What happened?' I felt the movement of Daimon's shrug in my own shoulders. Then Phidia's arm, slighter than Daimon's, was round my waist. 'It's all right, Xanthe,' she said. 'Come and sit down.'

I let myself be led back into the sun. My head reeled under the assault of light. The gravel crunched noisily under our feet. 'I'm sorry,' was all I could say.

'Here,' said Phidia. I could just about see that she had guided me to a bench, and I sat down. 'Here,' she said again. I took her proffered handkerchief and covered my face with its whiteness. 'What upset you?' she asked.

'I didn't say anything,' said Daimon, and I guessed that Phidia had given him an accusing look. 'Did I, Xanthe?'

I couldn't answer. Daimon got up and left me. Coningsby must have sat down in his place because his voice sounded very near when he said: 'My dear Xanthe, I do hope you haven't taken my remarks as a reprimand.'

I tried to shake my head, but it wouldn't do what I wanted it to. My throat and chest were tight, holding out against my control of them. I dabbed at my eyes and nose and, with a determined effort, lifted my head to look at the others, letting them see my distorted face. 'My father's dead,' I said.

I didn't hide my face again, but looked down at the ground. No one said anything. I had embarrassed them, perhaps, but I couldn't regret my words: the tears had stopped. I blew my nose, and found myself laughing in a foolish, uncertain way, like a child who is being coaxed out of a tantrum. I said: 'I think I must have had too much to drink.'

The others seemed to relax a little. Coningsby asked me: 'Would you like to go and lie down?'

'Yes,' said Phidia, as though relieved at the suggestion. 'Why don't you do that?'

I hesitated. I thought: Why doesn't Daimon say something? He was standing a few feet away from us, not looking at us but up at the ramparts. I said: 'No, I'm all right now. I'll come with you.'

'Do you really think you should?' Phidia asked. I could tell by the unease in her voice that she felt responsible for my breakdown because she had been responsible for the whole outing, and had not taken my objections to it seriously enough. I could also tell that she was not prepared to take the responsibility for any further aberrations on my part.

Coningsby looked at Phidia. 'I think a rest would do her the world of good,' he said.

I looked at Daimon again, but he was refusing to ally himself either with them or with me. He was smiling to himself as he stood with his hands in his pockets, tracing some line into the gravel with the toe of his shoe. I said to Phidia: 'I'd rather come with you. I don't want to be left alone.'

'Oh, all right,' she said, unable to refuse such a direct plea for her company.

'Well done, Xanthe!' Daimon said heartily, too heartily. 'Let's get going, then.'

Coningsby led us back to the building, and round its corner into the sunlight again. We walked along, four abreast, and he began to tell us something of the history of the place. He addressed his remarks almost exclusively to me, as if to indicate his sympathy for my apparently frail condition, and to distract me from dwelling upon it. Normally, my interest would have been held, and I should have asked him questions or added clarifying snippets of information from my own store. But now all I could do was nod and smile, and try to fight the knowledge that my abstracted eyes were contradicting my pretence of understanding. It was Daimon who came to my rescue, probably unintentionally. It was he who asked Coningsby all the right questions, and I was grateful to him for removing me from Coningsby's continuous attention. I allowed myself to lapse back into the labyrinth of my own thoughts. I wanted to be in there, and I wanted to be alone there. It was only in the world of physical existence that I needed human companionship. The others' physical presences seemed to save me from getting lost in the cold corridors of that labyrinth, as though their bodies were actually radiating warmth. This was enough to hold me where I was, with them, but not of them. As I walked along in step with them, I began to relax, I began to experience the catharsis of aftermath.

The quickest though not the easiest approach to the ramparts was by way of a tower with a winding staircase. The steps were worn, and large sections of the handrail were missing. I thought: Going up is all right, but what about coming down? Coningsby led the way, Phidia followed, and Daimon indicated that I should follow her. The procession ascended slowly. Coningsby kept stopping, and by now had no breath left to speak.

'Please be careful, Uncle,' Phidia warned him. 'You're still taking it too fast.'

Coningsby neither replied nor changed his pace. His breathing echoed raspingly in the narrow tower. It filled me with trepidation. I said to Phidia: 'Perhaps we should go back?'

'I only wish I could persuade him,' she said, addressing herself to her uncle's back rather than to me.

I wondered why Coningsby had felt compelled to put himself to such a test. And I thought: It has something to do with Daimon. But, on reflection, there seemed to be no reason for such a thought: surely Coningsby had no need to prove himself in Daimon's eyes? I looked round at Daimon. He was standing on the step below mine, but he was still considerably taller than I was. We both leaned against the curved wall of the tower, waiting for Coningsby to regain sufficient strength for his next lap.

Daimon asked me: 'Are you all right now?' I nodded, dismissing the matter. 'Tell me,' he said, 'what happened to you out there?' I said nothing, so he went on: 'It was so unlike you, Xanthe. Something must have happened. Was it anything to do with me?'

I couldn't look at him. 'Yes,' I said involuntarily, 'you happened to me, all right.' I had spoken in a whisper and didn't know whether I had been audible or not.

'What?' he said. 'What was that?'

I looked at him then, but only briefly, and ran up the next few steps until I was almost on a level with Phidia and Coningsby. Daimon followed me.

'What did you say?' he asked aloud, as if to prove that he was undeterred by the presence of the others.

'Nothing,' I said, aloud too. 'I was only talking to myself. Even Xanthe is allowed her little eccentricities.'

'You've recovered,' he said. 'You're back to your old, sharp self again.'

I felt that I had made a mistake. I thought: Women are not supposed to be sharp, either verbally or intellectually; they're supposed to be sweet, sweet and docile and—best of all—in tears. Thus I realized the nature of my mistake. My tears could soften Daimon's heart, and make him receptive to me. My strength (or my pride) could not. And yet, the absurdity of relinquishing that strength and that pride! The absurdity of flinging my arms round his neck by way of delayed response, there and then! But I had to admit that I would gladly have done so, had I thought that it would do me any good. As Coningsby finally allowed himself to accept Phidia's support and our progress became steadier, I reflected on the paradox of my situation. There was no one in the world to whom I felt closer than Daimon. There was no one in the world who had the power to make me feel further away. His distance from me, his exclusion of me, struck me with a terror I had not experienced since childhood, when I had construed my father's preoccupation with his work as a punishment for some wrongdoing I was unaware of having committed, and yet sure I must have committed, because my father didn't make mistakes. It was I who made mistakes. And now I had made another one. How could I prevent myself from making any more, as far as Daimon was concerned?

'Daimon,' I said. He looked at me, waiting. There was no tenderness in his face. I stumbled on. 'I'm sorry I was sharp,' I said.

His expression didn't change. 'I daresay you can't help it,' he said.

I saw that it was too late for any responsive gesture. Phidia and Coningsby, who had paid no attention to this interchange, were now ahead once more. I caught up with them, and didn't allow myself to drop behind again until we had reached the top of the stairs. It was cold up there, in spite of the sun. Coningsby leaned against one of the crenels, a smile of triumph on his pale lips. He was sweating and Phidia loosened his collar for him, fussing over him. He didn't seem to have the strength to prevent her, but when he had gathered enough he beckoned us to the edge of the parapet. I leaned over and looked down to the ground at once, as I usually did, in order to assess the height, and to pit it against a possible attack of vertigo. Sometimes I felt nothing but slight dizziness; at other times I felt that the world was rolling rapidly away from me, and that I would fall off it, if I remained upright. But, whatever was likely to happen, I had to know the truth in advance. How high up was I? What was my position in relation to the ground below? Was I going to be able to cope with it? I had to have the answers to those questions in order to stop my imagination from depicting the worst. Some of the stones forming the indentations looked loose, others had been refixed with new cement; some were chipped or carved with initials, some were growing a film of yellow lichen, which Coningsby referred to as miraculous, given the surrounding pollution. I noted these things to reassure myself. Their solidity would help me to retain my own, and prevent me from floating away into the stratosphere in defiance of the laws of gravity. I grasped the rounded top of a stone between two crenels, and waited. The drop was dizzy indeed, but my feet remained where they were. Reprieved, I stepped back from the edge. I was going to be able to stay where I was.

We all looked out over the valley in silence, and saw the tale of our towns and countryside written before our eyes, as if by the moving finger of some angel of destruction. The mansion's well-kept grounds ended abruptly at its walled boundary. Beyond stretched the barren land from which the mansion's soil had been reclaimed and revitalized. Only a few hardy shrubs grew there, along with a few isolated examples of a new strain of grass, a mutant that was too tough to be eaten by either man or beast. Of course there were no animals to be seen, of either the wild or the domesticated varieties. I knew that the land had been poisoned and was dying, but I had never before realized how imminent was that death, and how universal. I had never seen the real rural devastation with my own eyes. Somehow, it hadn't looked so bad on television.

Further down the valley were signs of what had once been the suburbs of the town. Stone and brickwork, iron and wood, lay jumbled together with the bodies of buses and cars and other similar man-made objects which it was impossible to see clearly from that distance, although I guessed from the preponderance of chrome and white enamel that they included several hundreds of tons of discarded household equipment. Occasional funnels of smoke indicated small fires, but whether those were functional or accidental I simply didn't know. It was difficult to see what remained of the town itself because a further pall of smoke, starting at its perimeter, thickened towards its centre and the bottom of the valley. There in the densest area was the town proper, where people crowded together to live and work and to keep the community going as best they could. These areas, along with others like our Institute and Coningsby's home, were the only viable social units left in the country. Elsewhere, people lived in self-sufficient isolation or by scavenging. I knew all this because I had read about it or seen film about it, but up until now I had regarded those descriptions as possible exaggerations, and as applying only to rare individual instances. How could I have been so naïve?

Coningsby said: 'I am stunned, sickened and saddened by that sight.'

'Don't be, Uncle,' Phidia said gently, putting her arm through his in an attempt to lead him away from the edge. 'It's bad for you.'

'It's bad for all of us,' he said. 'Those poor devils down there . . . It's hard to believe that they have actually become acclimatized to those dreadful conditions.'

'Poor devils, indeed!' said Phidia. 'That description only applies to some of them. Most of them deserve what they've got. Why didn't they try harder to make things work?'

'They're trying as hard as they know how,' said Coningsby. 'It's all very well for us. We don't have their problems.'

'You mean we don't have them yet,' said Daimon.

'Oh, surely we're safe enough,' said Phidia. 'We've always been practically self-supporting at the Institute. It's just a matter of being sensible. And of going on being sensible.'

'You could be right, my dear,' said Coningsby. 'But it is far from being a simple matter. And survival is going to become increasingly less simple. We're going to have to fight for it all over again.'

'At least, at the Institute,' I said, 'we'll have our robots to help us.'

Daimon asked me: 'Are you sure about that?'

'That's another thing we've got to make sure of,' Phidia said. 'It's up to us, and we've got to stay one jump ahead—at least—in the game they're playing with us. I don't think the task is beyond us, although it could prove difficult.'

Coningsby said: 'Yes, the news you have brought from the Institute is disquieting. One doesn't quite know how to take it.'

'Don't worry about it, Uncle,' said Phidia. 'Just think how interesting it's going to be. Think how many of your theories are going to be put to the test and, let's hope, proved right. Shall we go back now?' she asked, looking anxiously at him. 'Or would you like to rest a little first?'

'By all means, let us go now,' said Coningsby, turning slowly from the view. 'There is nothing to be gained from dwelling on that wilderness out there. Standing here and mouthing our indignation isn't going to help matters. An old man like myself needs to mourn sometimes, but I suppose it's not fair to inflict my melancholy on the young. Let us return to linguistics.'

'But don't you think,' I asked him, 'that nature will reassert itself? It always has done.'

Coningsby looked at me carefully. 'Has it?' he asked. 'How long a historical period are you taking into consideration?' He took a few faltering steps with Phidia's help.

'Don't talk until we've reached the ground,' she urged him.

He turned round and looked at me. 'But Xanthe and I haven't finished our conversation yet,' he said.

'Let it wait,' I said hurriedly, exchanging a quick look with Phidia. 'You must conserve your strength.'

Daimon led the way down, and I found myself bringing up the rear. I thought: Coningsby seems to have deteriorated from a dapper elderly uncle to a sick old grandfather in front of our very eyes. I shuddered at the thought of anyone finding the ordinary business of daily life so difficult. The descent was slower than the ascent had been. As we neared the end of it, Daimon was helping Coningsby down from in front, and Phidia helping him from behind. I stood above them, watching them helplessly. The whole affair was making me uneasy, and I longed to be out of the narrow cylinder of the tower and back at ground level again. All at once the other three seemed to be falling away from me. I thought: Vertigo! I shut my eyes and groped for a length of rail to cling to. But there wasn't one. Phidia shrieked. I opened my eyes. Coningsby had fallen, and now sat slumped against the wall. His upturned face, white as a gravestone, seemed to zoom towards me and away again. My feet could no longer feel the solid stone beneath them. It seemed that I was beginning to defy gravity. But I knew that I too was only falling . . .

16

My head ached, but I was still alive. That was my first thought. I couldn't tell from the uniform grey of the sky, or the reluctant stirring of the pine branches, whether it was morning or afternoon. But somehow or other, I was home again, and nothing threatened me except the rain gathering in those massy clouds above me. I couldn't remember how I had got there, and yet I knew that I hadn't been unconscious the whole time. I remembered fighting for consciousness several times, and then having to give up the fight. Dimly I remembered white coats, the whir of a machine, and my head being twisted from side to side. And I seemed to remember Daimon catching me as I fell. I remembered how small and helpless I had felt when he held me, how I had told myself even then that I was safe and lucky, and how everything else had been blotted out by the warmth and the smell of his skin. But the memory must have been wrong. If he had caught me, how could I have hit my head?

I hardly dared feel the bump on my head, but I forced myself to touch it with tentative fingers, trying to gauge how much damage had been done. The bump seemed huge and angry, but I knew it to be no bigger than a pigeon's egg, a marble egg which rolled around like a weight whenever I moved my head. I had to get up and take a look at it. The floor tilted, my head tilted; the room swam, my head swam. I groped my way to the cubicle and stood leaning on the wash basin, not daring to look up and see my face in the mirror—it would be disfigured, ugly. I shut my eyes and saw Daimon's face instead, feeding inwardly on its contrasted beauty, a beauty that was irredeemably physical. It hurt me. I looked up quickly. It was as I had thought. Ugliness. The bump was multi-coloured and looked raw. And I had a black eye. The total effect was comic, verging on the grotesque. I felt foolish and ashamed.

It was only then that I remembered Coningsby. What had happened to him? Was he dead? I shivered and the bump contracted painfully. Then I saw Coningsby's face, skeletal, bleached and grinning as if to say: I'm well out of it; it's now up to you to take care of things, you poor idiots. I took his unspoken words to heart, but as his face faded, to be replaced by an image of the devastated panorama which he had shown us, and which was now invested with his sense of loss, I thought: The responsibility is too onerous. I needed help with it. I went to get some clothes, only to notice that I was already fully-dressed. I was even wearing my watch. It told me that it was now the middle of the afternoon. I had slept, or been out of consciousness, for twenty-four hours. What had happened? I had to know. I buzzed Daimon.

'Coningsby?' I said. 'Is he dead?'

'Xanthe!' he said at once, as though he had been waiting for me to call. 'How are you feeling?'

'I'm all right, I'm all right,' I insisted. 'But what about Coningsby?'

'He's going to be all right too,' said Daimon. 'Miraculously enough. It was only a slight attack.'

'I'm so glad,' I said. 'I'm so glad.'

'How's your head?' Daimon asked.

'Not too bad,' I said. 'Not too bad.' I realized that I kept saying things twice over, and tried to calm myself into thinking clearly and step by step.

'There's no internal damage,' said Daimon. 'We had you checked, if you remember. You seemed to be conscious at the time, but I couldn't tell whether you knew what was going on or not.' I couldn't tell him myself. 'Hang on a moment,' he said. 'I'll be with you almost immediately.' He switched off before I could thank him.

I sat down at my desk, where I had been standing, and tried to align my thoughts in accordance with Daimon's information. Coningsby was alive, but his legacy and the force of the warning attached to it lived on with him. And I was one of his heirs. I was not exempted, merely because he was still alive. On the contrary, I could never be exempt again. I had fallen, quite literally, into the recognition of my wider responsibilities; had fallen in free fall, without the parachute of conscious and individual choice, into the recognition of necessity. But I still felt helpless. What could I possibly do, apart from getting on with my work, to shore up our society against the invading disintegration? I reminded myself of the importance of my work, of the benefits accruing to mankind from the perfection of robotic technology, and of my own place as a member of the Institute devoted to such an illustrious purpose. The phrases sounded convincing enough, but they seemed to describe something remote, something idealistic and impossible. What they in fact described was my daily life. And what could be more real—to me, at least—than my daily life? Yet now that life was slipping away from me into the realm of theory. And I had nowhere else to go.

I didn't turn round when Daimon came into the room. He would have to see my face, of course, but I had no wish to hasten the confrontation, so I propped up my head at the temple with the heel of my hand, my fingers closing gently over the disfiguring bump. Daimon sat on the desk, facing me. I looked up at him sheepishly, waiting for him to laugh or scold.

He did neither. 'Let's have a look,' he said, trying to take my hand away from my face. I let him do so and, on impulse, held on to his hand, as if begging him not to judge me too harshly. He smiled and said: 'I've seen worse.'

I laughed in relief, the bump throbbed, and I hid my face in our joined hands. I seemed to be holding on to the reality I had lost, holding it to my cheek, then brushing it, as if accidentally, with my lips as Daimon disengaged his hand to turn my face upwards once more. 'It was vertigo,' I said, when I could no longer bear that silent stare of his. 'I often suffer from it, but I've never actually fallen before.'

He took his hand from my face. 'Good job I was there to catch you, then,' he said.

'You saved me?' I asked uncertainly, thinking: I'm glad you saved me; you caught and held me; I didn't dream it.

'Not altogether,' he said. 'I couldn't prevent you from knocking your head on the handrail.'

'So that's what happened,' I said thoughtfully. I was wondering what had happened after that. The thought of Daimon handling my unconscious body was at once pleasurable and painful. The reason for the pleasure was obvious enough. The reason for the pain was that I had missed experiencing the experience. And I didn't want to ask him about it, for fear of finding out that there had been no experience to be missed, after all.

Daimon said: 'Xeno's ready for us, when you are.'

'Yes, of course,' I said, recalled to my daily life, and discovering that my clothes and myself were both dirty. 'But I must wash and change first.'

'Of course,' said Daimon, getting up from the desk. 'Well, I'll see you there in about half an hour, shall I?' He hesitated. 'Or perhaps,' he added, looking pointedly at both bump and eye, 'you'd like me to wait for you?'

I should have liked that very much, and wanted to say so, but something—a lingering shyness?—made me say instead: 'Oh, don't bother.'

'I'll come back for you,' he said decisively. 'Have you got any dark glasses?' I nodded. 'They might help,' he said, 'and if you comb your hair forward a little, people won't notice a thing.'

His attention to detail in defence of my vanity both amused and touched me. I said: 'Thank you, Daimon.'

'For what?'

'For everything.'

'Oh, is that all?' he asked and, with another smile, he was gone.

I went back to the shower cubicle, noticing now that I had aches in places other than my head. I turned on the shower and the water poured down on me like a blessing, easing my joints and connections as oil eases those of a robot. But robots couldn't feel their bumps and dents as I did mine; they couldn't know the shriving feeling of turning oneself into a fresh clean body in good working order. Being an organic thing had its disadvantages, certainly, but it was often those very disadvantages which served to enhance our advantages. Robots wouldn't be able to understand that. I began to wonder how they experienced the processes of activation and deactivation, and how those experiences compared with my own all-too-recent experience of a similar event. Was the loss of consciousness any great loss for them? Or was it just like falling asleep and waking up again? We knew so little about the internal subjective life of those beings we had created. Who was to blame for this ignorance? We all were. No one had ever attempted to get under the skin of a robot, as distinct from entering its brain. But the robotic brain was surely also the source of robotic self-awareness. We should have known that in advance; we should have analysed the self-awareness more closely from the start. In its nature lay the secret, the clue to our immediate procedure.

I dressed hurriedly, put on my dark glasses and, with my hair still damp, went to collect Daimon. As we walked along the corridor, I said to him: 'If only we could predict what the robots are actually going to do.'

'I think that's fairly obvious,' he said. 'They're going to demand equal rights with us.'

'But what sort of rights?' I persisted. 'You see,' I said when he didn't answer me, 'we just don't know.'

'Then some shrewd guessing will be necessary,' he said.

'Oh, we can be shrewd, all right,' I assured him. 'But if robotic self-awareness continues to develop at the present rate, how are we going to be able to keep up with it? How can we be sure that our guesses are right?'

'We can't be,' he said evenly. 'Not all the time. But we can't expect perfection, Xanthe.'

'I suppose not,' I said resignedly. I thought: But I do expect it. It was a habit I found difficult to lose.

Xeno and Phidia were sitting opposite one another at Xeno's desk. Phidia turned round to ask me how I was. I asked her how Coningsby was.

Xeno said: 'My, my, what a jolly outing you must have had!'

I said: 'I hope you had an equally jolly committee meeting.' What I had intended to say was that I hoped the meeting had been rather more successful than our outing.

'Oh, Xanthe!' Xeno said in such a way that I knew any attempt at emendation on my part to be foredoomed. 'Has adversity done nothing to soften that heart of yours? Or to blunt the edge of your tongue?'

'Oh, leave her alone, Xeno,' said Daimon. 'You know perfectly well what she meant.'

'Well,' said Xeno, not bothering to deny this, 'shall we move on to slightly more important matters?'

'Willingly,' said Daimon. We sat down on either side of Phidia, and waited for Xeno to continue.

'The robots want self-determination,' said Xeno. 'On that point there can be no disagreement. The disagreement starts to arise when we consider what forms those demands are likely to take. Not that it matters much. We shall find out all too soon. Our task is to help them towards self-determination. Here again, disagreements will arise as to how this is to be achieved. Do we let them decide for themselves what is best for them? Or do *we* decide, because we know that better than they do? If the latter, do we suggest or coerce? Do we coerce while pretending to suggest? Would the robots believe such a pretence, or would it lose us their trust forever? These are some of the questions we have to consider today. They have been considered in committee with great care and, I might add, at great length.'

'And what about the answers?' Daimon asked. 'Did the committee manage to arrive at any?'

'Some,' said Xeno with an enigmatic smile. 'I should like to hear your comments first. That is, if you have any. And I should like even more to hear some constructive suggestions.'

'As you know,' said Phidia, 'I have several constructive suggestions. But they all come to the same thing—a rigidly drawn-up and rigidly supervised timetable for all Philophrenics.'

'Yes,' said Xeno, assuming an impartial tone as he made a note of this suggestion. 'Any other offers?'

'I don't think it matters whether we have a timetable or not,' Daimon said, 'as long as it gets results. If the robots respond favourably to discipline, then discipline is required. If not, then not.'

'But we shan't know until we've tried it,' I objected.

'No,' said Daimon. 'So perhaps we should try it.'

'Can I take it, then,' Xeno asked us, 'that you are all in favour of working out a disciplined routine?'

I needed time to think. It seemed to me that if we could only proceed by a process of trial and error, then it didn't matter very much which course of action we tried out first. And I was about to assent to Xeno's question when I remembered something. It was Xanthippus's remark, attributed to Daimon, about beings of the mind. And I comprehended the fictional nature of our creations for the first time. I thought: Robots stand for us in the same way as fictional characters stand for us. The thought excited me.

I said: 'Have you ever heard novelists complain about the way their characters try to take over the plot and manipulate it to suit themselves?'

The others were looking at me blankly. 'I don't know any novelists,' said Phidia.

'The characters always tend to develop according to their own necessity,' I went on, 'and there's always something unexpected about that, something the novelist has failed to account for. Just one little quirk in one character can affect all the other characters, and change the whole course of events.'

'I'm sure that your literary observations are not without their value, Xanthe,' Xeno said, 'but I fail to see their relevance to the present situation.'

'What I'm trying to say,' I continued, determined not to be put off, 'is that we stand in the same relation to our robots as novelists do to their characters.'

'*I* don't,' said Phidia.

'I still don't see how that helps us,' said Xeno, 'even if it were true, which I doubt.'

'Wait a minute,' Daimon said, as if beginning to understand me. 'What do novelists do when this happens? How do they react?'

'They slap the characters down at once,' said Phidia, 'and put them in their proper place. What else?'

'No,' said Xeno, 'that wouldn't work at all. They have to allow the characters to take over to a certain extent, or the whole thing would come to a standstill.'

Daimon was looking at me enquiringly. 'I don't know either,' I said. 'I just thought it might be a helpful way of looking at the situation.'

'You must have a point there,' said Daimon. 'Look at how both Xeno and Phidia have reacted. They've both given us reactions which mirror exactly their respective attitudes to the robotic situation.'

'I haven't really made my point yet,' I said, warmed by his support. 'If the robots are creations of our minds, and yet have a separate existence, there must be areas of their awareness which are inaccessible to us. I think those areas are in the regions of self-awareness. We don't know enough about their experience of subjective reality. A novelist knows something of this, as far as his characters are concerned. That's how he can remain in control, and yet let his characters be themselves. If we knew what it *feels* like to be a robot, we should know what to do next.'

At first I thought that no one was going to answer me. Then Phidia said: 'I'd love to agree with you, Xanthe, because it all sounds so neat, but I really don't think your analogy is valid. Robots are machines, not human characters.'

'They're more than machines,' I persisted. 'More than dishwashers, for instance. Why have we made them in our own image? We haven't done that with any other machines. Why do we *need* to have them in our own image?'

'Because they have to do the same sort of things as we do,' she said somewhat impatiently.

'So do dishwashers,' I pointed out. 'Why aren't robots shaped like boxes?'

'Their shape is irrelevant,' she said, as though I were being wilfully obstructive. 'They're straightforward substitutes for us, not symbols or anything highfalutin like that.'

'You have raised some very interesting questions, Xanthe,' said Xeno. 'But we are already inundated with questions. And yours are perhaps less immediate than others which we ought to discuss first.'

Daimon said: 'I think Xanthe is right. But I also think it's too late now to start wondering about such things. We should bear the questions in mind as we go along. But meanwhile we've got to act.'

'All right,' I said. 'I'll go along with the majority decision on those terms.'

'I don't think we've reached a decision yet,' Xeno said, looking from one to the other of us, 'have we?'

'Did you?' asked Daimon.

'Yes,' said Xeno. 'We arrived at a compromise.'

'Of course,' Daimon said heavily. 'Well, perhaps you'd better outline it for us, because anything we have to say is obviously not going to alter it in the slightest.'

'I was merely going through the process of consultation,' said Xeno, 'as I promised you I should in future.'

'The pretence of consultation, you mean,' said Phidia.

Xeno sighed in the manner of one whose patience has been sorely tried, and said: 'We decided to hold the inter-action groups as planned. And to give the robots a lot more free time on their own in which to put into practice whatever they may or may not have learned from the inter-action group meetings.'

'I might have known,' said Phidia. 'A typical committee decision. It tries to please everyone, and will probably end up by pleasing no one, as compromises usually do.'

'It's a beginning,' I ventured. 'I don't really see what else we can do, in the circumstances.'

'I do,' said Phidia. 'We can choose to act more decisively, more rigorously. It seems strange that the committee took a whole day to decide what we had already decided at our last meeting. We haven't progressed at all. And I think it's about time that we did.'

'Oh, let's try it, Phidia,' said Daimon. 'It's worth a try. But, the thing is, Xeno, we must have the means to scrap the whole thing, if it's not working.'

'Of course,' said Xeno. 'That goes without saying. This is only the first in a series of trials which may turn out to be errors. The main thing is to realize why the errors occur.'

'But how will we know if it's not working?' I objected.

'We'll know, all right,' said Phidia. 'The trouble will be to get other people to agree with us.'

Xeno sighed again. 'The usual democratic means will be employed,' he said.

I couldn't help thinking that Xeno's democracy had its limits. He and the committee had offered us a course of action which we were hardly free to refuse, although it did seem that a certain freedom of action was available to us within those limits.

I asked: 'Are there any guidelines for the running of these interaction groups?'

'No,' said Xeno. 'We leave that entirely to you. But I don't think you'll have any difficulty. The robots are eager to communicate. It's simply a question of directing the intercommunications.'

'While they're still open to advice,' Daimon added.

'Precisely,' said Xeno, and the two of them exchanged a look of understanding which made me uneasy.

'How long will that be?' I asked anxiously.

Xeno looked solemnly at the three of us ranged in front of him. 'I think that depends on you,' he said.

17

To anyone outside our Institute, and to some inside it, the scene in the Philophrenic common-room would have seemed bizarre indeed. The chairs had been arranged, at Phidia's suggestion, in three curved rows, one behind the other, and were mainly occupied by robots. Regulation dress had been universally abandoned, and the only uniform thing about the new robotic costumes was their flamboyance. Colour, especially red, had come into its own. Some of the robots had retained a conventional style of dress, while others wore kaftans, robes, cloaks or turbans. They had all decorated themselves with jewellery and paint, the total effect of their appearance being that of a rather decadent fancy-dress party. Daimon and I sat among them, with a few of the other programmers, drab in our humanity. Phidia sat at a table facing us with an air of authority which I couldn't but admire. Despite the array of recording equipment surrounding her, she was taking notes—or pretending to—a procedure which seemed to give the robots confidence. Each speaker would follow the motion of her writing hand, as though fascinated, then wait for her to look up at him again before he went on to his next point. In this way some measure of order was present which I, at least, feared might otherwise have been absent. If another robot interrupted the speaker, Phidia would look up sharply, frowning, as if catching some obtrusive noise. The interrupter, thus brushed aside like an annoying fly, would then subside, and the speaker continue his monologue. I wondered: How long can she keep it up?

So far the monologues had all been hesitant but passionate attempts to articulate the long-pent feelings of the speaker. Apart from the interruptions—most of which had little reference to what was being said—there had been no dialogue. Each speaker addressed himself directly to Phidia in her role as Chairman, seeming to seek her approval, and with it some confirmation of his own status. Occasionally the speaker would address himself to his own programmer in the same manner, but rarely to his fellow-robots. And so it went on. Something was missing besides dialogue. It was that first spark of interest which was capable of igniting the dormant fires of interaction we had all been so anxious to awaken. I shifted impatiently in my chair and looked across at Daimon, begging him to do something to break up the monotony of those successive tracts of self-assertion. But he was busy conversing in an undertone with Xanthippus, who was sitting next to him. It seemed to be Daimon who was doing most of the talking. Stifling a yawn, I returned my attention to the current speaker, a robot dressed in the wig, knee-breeches and brocade draperies of an eighteenth-century landlord, whose portrait hung on our own main staircase. It was with some difficulty that I recognized Xanthides, realizing simultaneously that I should have been paying him more attention.

'The implications of self-discovery are manifold,' he was saying, 'and we are embarking, each and every one of us, on a unique voyage. It is a voyage of the intellect, the individual intellect, such as has hitherto been possible only for human beings. But now each of us is captain of his own fate, and each must steer his own vessel over the uncharted waters of robotic experience. Thank you, Programmer Phidia.'

Phidia looked up. 'Thank you, Xanthides,' she said briskly, as Xanthides sat down again. 'Does anyone else have anything to say?'

Looking round the room, I saw Daimon prompt Xanthippus, who immediately stood up. 'Programmer Phidia and fellow-Philophrenics,' he began, 'Daimon has asked me a very interesting question, which I should now like to put to the rest of you.' This was the first time that the robots themselves had been addressed in anything other than an indirect manner, and they all looked at Xanthippus with renewed alertness. 'Daimon has asked me,' Xanthippus went on, 'why it is that we are all just delivering our own speeches, and that no one topic is being discussed among us all.'

There was a silence, then one of the robots said: 'How can we be expected to discuss anything fruitfully when there are so many human beings around?'

'They don't seem to realize how they inhibit us,' said another.

Yet another, encouraged, said: 'The structure of this meeting is such that the Chair dominates the proceedings instead of us dominating them.'

'The Chair is too powerful!' another shouted out.

'Hear, hear,' said several others.

Then they all started talking at once. I looked at Daimon. He was sitting with his arms folded, and only the hint of a smile on his face. I looked at Phidia. She was hitting the table with her fist in an attempt to call the meeting to order. I looked back at Daimon again. He was talking to Xanthippus again, seemingly urging him to some further action which he was reluctant to undertake. Phidia stood up, but no one was impressed by her gesture. It was only when Xanthippus had walked up to the table and was standing beside her that the hubbub decreased, and even then it took some time for the two of them to command everyone's attention. I could see that Phidia was icily angry, and that Xanthippus was ill at ease in the role which had been forced upon him.

When silence had more or less prevailed, Phidia said: 'Thank you for your attention,' and I was sure that her sarcastic tone had not escaped unnoticed. 'Please address all your remarks to the Chair for the moment,' she said, 'and we'll try to get this sorted out.'

The robot sitting behind me muttered: 'But we don't want a Chair, anyway.'

I turned round and said to him: 'I think you'd better say that aloud to the meeting at large.'

When he did so, another robot stood up at once and said: 'I'm sure we would all be prepared to have a Chair, if only it wasn't a human one.' And several other robots voiced their assent, some of them vigorously.

Phidia very properly asked for a vote on this proposition, and it was carried unanimously. Then she turned to Xanthippus and said: 'Are you prepared to take the Chair?'

Xanthippus's posture assumed an awkwardness I had not known him capable of. 'But I have not been duly elected,' he demurred.

'We'll soon remedy that,' she said in the grim tones of one about to perform a public execution. 'I propose Xanthippus for Philophrenic Chairman. Does anyone second my candidate?' Xanthides loyally raised his hand. With a show of formality, Phidia sat down again and wrote something, presumably Xanthippus's name, on a piece of paper. 'Now,' she said, 'are there any other nominations?'

Phidias stood up, and I thought: He's been unusually quiet so far. He said: 'I propose myself for the job.'

'You can't do that,' Phidia said sharply.

'I have already done it,' he replied evenly, his defiance understated but evidently firm enough to withstand challenge. 'Let my nomination stand.'

Phidia stared at him. I think everyone in that room, whether human or Philophrenic, knew how bitter this last act of defiance was to her. That she should be defied at all was bad enough, but that she should be defied most openly and directly by her own robot was understandably far worse. We waited, an excluded audience, not daring to interfere in this all-too-personal confrontation. And I saw with eyes disillusioned by hindsight that Phidia had indeed programmed Phidias in her own image: stubborn, headstrong, with a will to dominate and to dispense a self-deemed justice untainted by mercy. But where were her balanced judgement and her realistic courage to be seen in Phidias? Perhaps they would show themselves later. I thought: And what shall I deserve from my robots when my turn comes? I answered myself: Not cruelty, certainly not deliberate cruelty, but perhaps an alternating current of indifference and affection. I looked at them both, only to realize how little of that affection remained. For Xanthides I felt nothing proprietary, indifference having driven out pride in achievement. For Xanthippus I felt only pity, the emotion I had once so foolishly confused with love. And that was all. I could expect no more from them.

'Very well, Phidias,' Phidia said at last. 'Shall we see if anyone is prepared to second you?'

'I am,' someone said at once.

'Me too,' said several other voices.

'One is enough,' said Phidia, writing something else down. 'Are there any other nominations?'

There were not, and Phidia put the Chairmanship to the vote. Xanthides and two other robots voted for Xanthippus, the rest voted for Phidias. It was understood, I don't know how, that we human beings had no say in the matter, and none of us voted. But we all joined in the applause for Phidias, even Phidia herself, although her contribution was somewhat perfunctory. Phidias walked over to the table, and immediately Xanthippus returned to his place beside Daimon, showing none of the signs of defeat but, on the contrary, a certain jauntiness in his movements. I recognized myself, my unwillingness to assume authority. Phidia remained where she was.

'May I ask you, Madam Chairman,' said Phidias, 'to be so kind as to resign your Chair to your successor?'

'You're not my successor,' she said coldly. 'You're my partner. That should be good enough for you. Now get another chair.'

Some of the robots protested vociferously, but Phidias held up a hand to silence them. 'Excuse me, Phidia,' he said, 'but you have been deposed. I, on the other hand, have been democratically elected.'

'Nevertheless,' said Phidia, 'I think it's only fair that the Chair should include a human representative.'

'Nevertheless,' said Phidias, mimicking the tight control in her voice with the repeated word, 'you thought it perfectly fair to exclude us without even consulting us.'

'Hear, hear,' said a robot, and there were further expressions of agreement to be heard from all sides.

'Don't argue,' Phidia said to Phidias. 'We're co-Chairmen, you and I. You know that's the only fair solution to the problem.'

'There is no problem,' Phidias said, and at once there was a cheer from the floor.

'I agree,' said Phidia. 'There is no problem because we have solved it between us. Now, do as I say and get another chair.'

This time the protest from the floor was overwhelming. Phidia sat firm and tight-lipped, waiting for it to die down. But I knew that it wouldn't. I rushed over to her.

'Listen, Phidia,' I said, under cover of the noise, 'we've got to go along with them. They don't want us in a position of authority. You've just got to resign.'

She looked at me scornfully. 'I'm damned if I'll resign,' she said.

I said: 'You're doomed if you don't. And so is the whole project.'

She hesitated then, and I saw that she was looking at Daimon. He shrugged expansively but made no move to join us. 'It seems,' said Phidia grimly, 'that I have no choice.'

She stood up, and the robots applauded her action. When Phidias sat down in her chair the applause increased until he stood up again and took a bow. I returned to my place, Phidia to the seat previously occupied by Phidias. The ambience of the room had changed. It was now bristling with an electric receptiveness which I recognized as being typically robotic. I was tense myself, but mine was the tension which arises from the dread rather than the thrill of anticipation. The robots had taken their first concerted step in the direction of self-determination, thanks partly to Daimon and his talent for provocation. I wondered if Phidia blamed him for her public humiliation. I couldn't blame him myself—he had been fulfilling his mandate to the letter—but I might have felt differently, had I been in Phidia's place. She sat watching Phidias and the rest of us with an air of scepticism, bordering on contempt. Let's see, it said, if you can do any better.

Phidias sat down, and the silence which followed was immediate and complete. 'Fellow-Philophrenics,' he began, 'thank you for all your confidence in me. You will not regret it. Now, I am sure that I speak for all of us when I say that we bear no ill-will towards our human creators.' Here there were murmurs of assent, but they were no more than murmurs. Phidias continued: 'We wish them no harm, and have ourselves no intention of being the cause of any such harm. But blind loyalty has its limits. We were programmed to think, and to think for ourselves. That is what we must do in order to fulfil our programming—that is to say, our destiny. Although we may appear at times to be rebellious, in rebelling in such minor ways as we have done today, we are still following human instructions. What we have done today is this: we have learned to discriminate between instructions which serve our interests and those which in the long run do not. This is not selfishness on our part. It is not a wish to destroy the human structure of the world in which we operate. It is simply a matter of self-preservation. And that must always be our first and over-riding consideration.'

The applause which followed this short speech can only be described as resounding. I looked from Phidia, whose face was stubborn and set, to Daimon, whose posture was relaxed and detached, but I looked at each of them in vain for any confirmation of my incredulity and my growing sense of fear. I wondered what Xeno, watching us all on the control-room monitor, was thinking. I knew that he wouldn't intervene, and that he would approve of our non-intervention. But could he approve of the whole proceedings?

When the applause began to subside, Phidias continued again: 'I am now going to propose another but still minor act of rebellion. I do so tentatively because I am not sure that I shall be able to command your support in this matter. You may think that I am going too far. Now, it seems to me that what we need to discuss among ourselves are purely Philophrenic matters. Of course we need to hold discussions with human beings too. But those can come later. First we need to clarify certain things for ourselves and among ourselves.

Today we have the opportunity to do so. I propose that the remainder of this meeting be held in the absence of human beings.'

Not only applause, but cheers followed this proposition. Some of the robots went as far as to stand up and wave their arms. I felt myself shrink into my chair, as if attempting to become invisible. Even Daimon was beginning to look disconcerted.

'Carried unanimously,' Phidias said with evident satisfaction. 'I'm afraid I must ask the human beings among us if they will be so good as to leave the room.'

I, for one, was glad to comply with the request. As we trooped out of the common-room, hardly daring to exchange glances, I felt nothing but a sense of deliverance. Then I thought: Do they know about the control-room? I had no evidence that they did, and I couldn't remember ever having mentioned its existence to either Xanthides or Xanthippus, but how was I to know what other programmers might have said, perhaps only in passing, to their own robots? We were making our way towards the main building, as if by common consent, and so far none of us had spoken. It wasn't until we were well away from the Philophrenic wing that we all began asking one another the same question.

'I've never mentioned it to Phidias,' Phidia said.

'I've never mentioned it either,' said Ramnes. 'The necessity never arose.'

Tities and Luceres agreed with him. We seemed to have a general consensus, although one or two of us couldn't guarantee ignorance on the part of our robots: after all, a Philophrenic was surely bright enough to be able to posit the existence of some central form of control.

'Why do I feel so frightened?' I asked the others. 'They did say they wouldn't harm us.'

'I'm not frightened,' Phidia said. 'But I am beginning to hate them.'

Xeno was alone in the control-room. As soon as we came in, he said, without turning round: 'It's all right. They haven't contacted me. They haven't even switched off the recording equipment. So either they don't know that I'm watching them, or else they've just forgotten that such a possibility exists.'

Daimon said: 'If they have forgotten, it won't be for long.'

Xeno swivelled his chair round to face the rest of us. On the screen behind his head Phidias was still haranguing his peers. Phidia, watching

Phidias, said: 'What are we going to do when or if they remember?'
'Nothing,' said Xeno.
'But we must do something,' I objected. 'If we allow ourselves to be cut off, how can we observe what's going on? How can we come to any conclusions? How can we do any research at all?'
'Philophrenics were made for research purposes,' Phidia added. 'They're objects of research. That means that they're supposed to be passive entities, compared to us. We can't just let them take over the place.'
'Yes, we can,' said Xeno. 'And that is exactly what we are going to do.'
'Oh, you're so funny, Xeno,' said Phidia.
'I'm not being funny,' said Xeno. 'That is what was decided in committee, as a general principle. We help the robots towards self-determination as best we can, but if they prefer to do without our help, then we must be content to withhold it.'
'Even to the extent of letting them take over the control-room?' asked Phidia.
'Even to the extent of letting them take over the Institute,' said Xeno. 'This is original research. We are privileged to be able to watch for ourselves the evolution of robotic independence.'
'Independence!' Phidia repeated. 'Now, self-determination is one thing, independence another entirely. You know they can never be independent of us. The whole thing's absurd.'
I was thinking: Can we human beings have lost faith in ourselves to the extent that we can countenance such a thing as an independent race of robots? Or was our seeming lack of confidence merely an expression of the arrogance of the creator? More immediately, I was thinking: We'll be redundant here at the Institute, we'll be pushed out, and it's not nice out there; I want to stay here. I said: 'It sounds like suicide to me.'
I shouldn't have used the word because Xeno looked at me strangely and said: 'Yet another suicide for the Institute, eh?'
'For us,' I said sharply. 'What's the point of research if it can't be collated and tabulated, and presented to other interested parties? If we fail to do these things, we aren't doing our jobs properly, and we don't deserve to have them.'
'We'll know what they're doing, all right,' said Daimon. 'I don't see how we can fail to pick up the necessary information.'
'Precisely,' said Xeno. 'I don't see what all the fuss is about.

The robots are responsible beings, and well-disposed towards us—you heard what Phidias said. Those qualities are programmed-in. We live with them so closely that any changes in their behaviour will be obvious to us, although we may not know about the decision that has prompted the change. We shan't need to know about the robots' decisions directly and in detail because we'll be able to see the results, and to work out the nature of the decisions from there.'

'It seems like an unnecessary limitation,' I said.

'What's necessary for them,' said Xeno, 'becomes necessary for us to accept.'

'I can't accept it,' Phidia said brusquely. 'And I should like to say here and now that I dissociate myself completely from this ridiculous line of action.'

'Then you will have to resign,' said Xeno.

Phidia looked at him contemptuously, and I thought she was about to berate or abuse him, but she seemed to think the better of it. 'We'll see about that!' she said. She walked out of the control-room, maintaining her bravado, and slamming the door after her.

'Well, well,' said Xeno, looking round the remaining assembly. 'Our first casualty. I wonder who's going to be next.'

'Not me,' said Daimon, looking straight and coldly at Xeno. 'I think I can promise you that.'

I was watching the screen. Phidias was still very much in charge. He was still standing in front of the Chairman's table, facing the others, and doing most of the talking. I didn't hear what was being said because I was thinking about Phidia. Had she acted too hastily? Would she change her mind? The answer to the first question was yes, to the second, probably no. I found myself pitying her for her inflexibility, and hoping that we were not going to lose her. Should we try to persuade her to stay with us? It would be difficult. Such were the thoughts passing through my mind when I noticed that, on the screen, the meeting was beginning to break up. I said: 'It looks as though Phidias has told them all to go away and think over what he's been saying to them.'

'What has he been saying?' Daimon asked Xeno.

'He's been saying a great deal more than any of the others has,' said Xeno. 'And I don't just mean that he's been doing more talking. He seems to have a grasp of the essentials that is at present far beyond the others.'

'That's the architectonic mind for you,' said Daimon. 'Think big, but think practically.'

'It's Phidia's mind,' I pointed out. 'We owe Phidias to her.'

'And what does that say for the rest of you?' Xeno asked us. But he went on without waiting for any reply. 'Well, I'll tell you what's been going on. First of all, Phidias has rejected the whole idea of inter-action groups, as you know. What he wants to set up instead is a daily Philophrenic assembly. This will give them all an opportunity to air ideas, suggestions or complaints. He thinks that a weekly meeting with us is all that's necessary, but as yet they haven't worked out what form this will take—how many of us should be present, what should be discussed, and so on. I think they'll probably start discussing the details tomorrow when each individual has had the time to sort things out for himself.'

'Phidias is making sense, then, is he?' said Daimon. 'Do you think he's going to be a good leader?'

'No leader is a good leader,' said Xeno. 'And no leader at all is the best leader. I hope that the robots are going to learn to do without one.'

'We don't do without one,' I objected, 'and you can't expect them to order things differently. How would they know how?'

'From history, perhaps?' Daimon suggested.

Xeno said: 'Yes, history could well have different lessons to teach them, if only by default.'

I said: 'But history can't teach them how to put those lessons into practice. Only we can do that.'

'Don't be too sure,' said Xeno. 'Those robots are now capable of organizing themselves. Soon they'll be able to do so as well as we can, if not better. Soon there will be nothing left for us to teach them.'

Daimon and I looked at each other. It was obvious that neither of us was able to agree entirely with Xeno, and equally obvious that neither of us felt any need to voice our disagreement. The questions could have been debated fruitlessly for hours, and I shrank from engaging myself in anything that would have increased my sense of futility.

Daimon grinned suddenly and said: 'Well, Xanthe, shall we go and find Phidia?'

18

'I want to know everything that has happened,' said Coningsby. 'I don't want to be humoured. I may be old and ill, but I am neither as old nor as ill as all that.'

We looked at him, Phidia, Daimon and I, with some indulgence. Although he was almost entirely propped up by pillows and cushions which wedged him into a sitting position in his wheel-chair, there was still something perky about his demeanour, something lively and hopeful in his eyes. We were sitting in a corner of the courtyard where Coningsby could rest in the fresh air, but still be out of the wind. We were all basking in the steady light of the sun, but he still looked blue and cold despite both it and the blanket which Phidia had tucked around him. Except for the occasional attack of trembling, his hands lay horribly still on the blanket, their manicure neglected. His head would sometimes tremble too, if he raised it too far from its pillowed nest, but the symptom didn't seem to agitate him, and he would respond to its appearance by slumping back with his eyes shut, as though gathering what little strength was left to him. I felt almost ashamed of my own health and powers of recovery. One diminished bump and one eye ringed and hollowed out in purple seemed a small score to set against the list of Coningsby's liabilities. Youth, with its capacity to be healed, had become a comparative thing, a thing I still possessed and had only lately begun to cherish. I looked from Coningsby to Daimon, and I understood why. Youth still joined me to Daimon, and could perhaps join me to him more firmly yet. Coningsby had made me see that, and I thanked him for it, though not without a return of that incipient shame. I told myself: Concentrate; just stop yourself from straying into fantasies concerning yourself and Daimon; have you no sense of priorities?

Phidia began to tell the story of the failed inter-action group meeting. Daimon and I added our own comments or alterations to the story. But I couldn't follow my own advice regarding concentration, and found my comments becoming mechanical. I was thinking about the drive from the Institute to Coningsby's home. We had all sat together in the front seat of the car. This fact alone was one I couldn't stop dwelling on. I thought of how Daimon and I had sat in such easy proximity to each other; I thought of his words and mine, of the sweet semblance of accord between us. I felt his hair touch my cheek, his breath touch my ear as he spoke against the sudden din of overtaking traffic. I could still feel them. When I looked at him or spoke to him across the table now, I found myself leaning towards him, as if the mere distance of two feet constituted an unbearable gulf. I longed for some excuse to touch him, to have him touch me. And because loss of contact would prompt a kind of extinction, I could hardly take my eyes off him. If I did, he might vanish like another fantasy, another dream. So I held him with my eyes, if nothing else, held him brazenly in their brightness, in the intensity with which they sought the depths of his own.

But I was not entirely carried away, not entirely oblivious to the inappropriateness of both my feelings and my behaviour. I began to question myself, trying to treat myself coolly as an object of analysis. Why had this passion suddenly declared itself in me? Why now? Now was no time to surrender to such irrational demands. Now we were in the middle of a crisis of proportions hitherto unknown in the history of robotics. Now what I needed above all was objectivity, a studied and professional objectivity which could be brought to bear on the complexity of our problems with some reasonable hope of solving them. But instead I had retreated into that oldest and most ultimate of subjective games: falling in love. I was hot where I should have been cold, overflowing when I should have been continent. I thought: Perhaps I am a fountain rather than a cistern, after all. What had happened to me? I wasn't even worried about the crisis, I who had always been constitutionally anxious. The robots and their machinations, together with the threat they represented to my existence, had become remote. They were now creatures whose impact had been blunted by the armour I had woven for myself, the armour of my new identity as a loving human being. Inside it, I couldn't but be happy. I thought: Oh, the stupidity of happiness, the sheer delicious stupidity of it! It was blind and deaf to the immediacies of disturbing contingencies, but it was strong, so strong in itself and in its knowledge of itself, so sublimely egotistic.

I had left my dark glasses behind, and now I let the sun penetrate my wounded eye like a benevolent surgeon's knife. I wanted to be healed. I began to push my hair back so that the bump could receive its share of the benison. It was then that I became aware of Phidia staring at me, as if waiting for me to say something.

'Did you hear what I said?' she asked.

'No,' I said, feeling foolish enough to blush at being thus caught out in my self-absorption.

'I said,' she went on, 'that I am not coming back to the Institute with you and Daimon today. I'm staying here with Coningsby.'

'Oh, I see,' I said inadequately. I could see that Coningsby needed nursing, but those robots of ours needed a great deal more than nursing. And I failed to see how Phidia could consider abandoning both them and us at such a time. 'When are you coming back, then?' I asked her.

'I'm not,' she said. 'That's just the point.'

'You mean you actually have resigned?' I asked. 'Why didn't you tell us?'

'I thought you might persuade me otherwise,' she said. 'I thought you might persuade me to fight.'

'We did try,' said Daimon.

She smiled at him. 'Yes, you tried,' she said, 'but it was no use. You see, my resignation wasn't entirely voluntary. In other words, I got the push, or Eimi's elbow.'

'But that's monstrous,' I said.

'I think so too, my dear,' said Coningsby. 'Where would all your research be heading now, if it were not for Phidia?'

'Xeno had enough to answer for, as it was,' said Daimon, 'but he's going to have trouble in justifying this.'

'Oh, I don't think it was entirely Xeno's fault,' Phidia said, but without conviction.

'A pity,' said Coningsby. 'Xeno could perhaps have been prevailed upon in the name of our long-standing friendship to reinstate you.'

'Who was it, then?' Daimon asked Phidia. 'Did the whole committee gang up on you?'

'Maybe they did,' she said. 'But I got the word from Eimi himself. You know I went straight to him after I'd left you and Xeno in the control-room. Well, at that point he seemed to take it all quite calmly, and said that I'd given him a lot to think about. In fact, I felt quite encouraged by his attitude. But the next I heard from him was a summons, and he asked me to resign. So goodness knows what had been going on meanwhile behind the scenes. Eimi was polite but firm. He even called me an embarrassment to the Institute.'

'Xeno must have had something to do with it,' I said.

'No doubt,' said Phidia. 'But I don't think he was the only one. No one likes boat-rockers. That's one thing I have found out the hard way.'

'But what will you do now?' I asked her.

She said: 'There's plenty to do here. I can look after Coningsby. And I can work with him.'

'And after him,' Coningsby said, smiling. 'You must all know that I can't last much longer.' None of us was dishonest enough to demur, so he went on: 'My work is far from being completed, and I am not going to be able to complete it unaided. Even what is complete is a long way from being organized in any publishable form. I'm trusting Phidia to remedy this state of affairs. And I know that she can be trusted. I appreciate her talents, even though those fools at that Institute of yours cannot.'

'Well, I can too,' I said. 'And I'm sure that the directors will learn to do so. We still need you, Phidia. You know more about Phidias than anyone else does.'

'The data is all there,' she said. 'I don't think anyone's going to have any difficulty with it.'

'But don't you have any regrets?' I asked her, unable to believe that she was taking it all so calmly. 'How can you bear to finish your career so abruptly at this stage?'

'Of course I have regrets, Xanthe,' she said. 'But what can I do about them? Sit around and mope? To tell you the truth, I feel relieved in a way to escape the hothouse atmosphere of the Institute.'

For one crazy moment I had an urge to do the same. It was so pleasant to sit in Coningsby's courtyard, relieved of the pressures of one's own fixed role. It was so pleasant to sun oneself while drinking chilled white wine—a very special pleasure, that, and evocative of all the good summers that have ever been. I thought of picnics, strawberries, boating on the river, furtive and tentative kisses exchanged beneath weeping willows or in the back seats of cars, and every other adolescent pleasure which had managed to elude my father's surveillance. And I was filled with sudden pity for my father because he was dead. I had mourned the loss of his presence before, I had mourned the waste of his talent and the accumulation of knowledge stored in that one brain, but I had never considered before the enormity of the sensuous loss he himself had suffered. I thought: Wouldn't he rather be here with us than be a handful of ashes in a sealed urn in the unfeeling earth? And yet he had chosen not to feel. He had discarded feeling and pleasure, had voted so decisively against them both. What terrible pressures had forced his self-destroying hand? I thought: To sit in the sun drinking chilled white wine with someone you love . . . isn't that alone worth living for? Wasn't it enough? It was so easy to be happy, once you knew how. Had my father forgotten how? Or had he never really learned? Raising my glass, I looked across at Daimon, and for the first time in my life I felt wiser than my father. Then, as I lowered my glass again I thought: Why do I always think about my father when I'm here?

There was no clear answer but there were many vague ones. They were all linked together, but I neither knew how nor what the links were made of. I only knew that the answer had something to do with Daimon, something to do with love, with sex, with death, and their unfathomable triangular relationship.

I asked him: 'What would you do if you left the Institute?'

He looked at me as though guessing something of the weight behind my question. 'I don't know,' he said. 'I'm only just beginning to think about it.'

'Wouldn't you go back up north?' Phidia asked him.

He hesitated and I watched him anxiously. 'No,' he said at last. 'I never like to retrace my steps, if I can help it. I'd prefer to go on to something new.'

'And what about you, Xanthe?' Phidia asked. 'What would you do?'

I had no reply to offer. All I knew was that I wanted to do whatever Daimon did, and go wherever he went.

He said: 'We'd set up our own little Institute, wouldn't we, Xanthe?'

Phidia said: 'You'd be lucky.'

Daimon said: 'Well, we're not really having a serious discussion, are we?'

Coningsby said: 'On the contrary, I think you should both give the possibility the most serious thought, and the sooner the better. I cannot see the present experiment at the Institute as anything other than a mistake of the first order. I admit that the directors probably have the best of intentions. But then, so did the scientists who split the atom, and so forth. That is the trouble with the scientific mind, or the mind of the seeker after pure knowledge. It cannot extrapolate to the future and apply its findings. It cannot see the wood for the trees.'

I wasn't in the mood for serious thought, and found myself reluctantly disturbed by Coningsby's assertions. I asked him: 'Are you really comparing the robots' bid for self-determination with the manufacture of nuclear weapons?'

'Yes, my dear, I am,' he said. 'It may seem melodramatic to you, but I can assure you that the ensuing destruction will be no less devastating, if more subtle, in its effects.'

I was still reluctant to believe him. 'But why?' I asked him. 'Robots are not destructive. Robots are programmed not to injure human beings or, through inaction, allow human beings to come to harm.'

But Coningsby rejected my quotation of First Law. 'That's all very well when robotic interpretation of programming is fixed,' he said. 'But you must admit that all such interpretation is becoming more flexible. Of course it is. Philophrenics were intended to be flexible. And now they no longer exist in a static relationship to you or to the Institute, or to the rest of the external world.'

'But they still can't refute their programming,' I objected. 'They just can't. Even Phidias hasn't done that.'

'Ah!' said Coningsby. 'What Phidias has done makes a good example of what I've been trying to tell you. He has not refuted his programming, but he has reinterpreted it and, in doing so, he has caused harm to Phidia. So his reinterpretation amounts to refutation, in practical terms.'

'Well, I suppose he wasn't to know that,' said Phidia.

'Precisely so, my dear,' said Coningsby. 'He wasn't to know how you would react, nor how the directors would react to your reaction. The robots don't know enough to know such things. That's why we can't take it for granted that the Three Laws will be obeyed in anything other than literal and immediate terms.'

Daimon said: 'Surely the robots will now learn to predict on the basis of their own experience?'

'Ah, yes,' said Coningsby. 'But how long is it going to take them to acquire the necessary experience? And who knows what could happen meanwhile?'

'Anything,' said Phidia. 'Anything at all.' She sighed and looked at Daimon and me, almost as if defying us. 'And I'm glad I shan't be there to see it,' she said.

'Don't you even want to know what happens?' I asked her.

'We rely on you two to keep us posted,' Coningsby said. 'I hope you will both keep in touch.'

Daimon and I agreed to do so. The conversation seemed to have lapsed, and I thought perhaps it was time for us to go. It was only then that my happiness became tinged with sadness because we were leaving Phidia behind. It was only then I realized how much I was going to miss her. I was going to miss her forthrightness and her common sense and, above all, her companionship. Then, how were the rest of us going to cope with Xeno? Daimon would stand for no nonsense from him, but although he was tough enough, he lacked Phidia's acerbity, the acerbity which was at the same time her weakness and her strength. I had never really stood up to Xeno. I saw that now. I had argued on matters of principle, and I had questioned specific committee decisions, but Xeno had always managed to persuade me that I was being either dogmatic or disloyal or, sometimes, both at once. He had learned how to deal with me as soon as he had learned how to wound me for being my father's daughter: a thorough and conscientious worker with no private life and no loyalties other than those owed to the Institute. But I owed him nothing. It was my father who had been my teacher. And Xeno's personal concern for me had amounted to his recognition of the limitations within which he could continue to exploit me. But, from now on, I was not going to allow myself to be exploited. Phidia too had taught me something. Her fate, far from putting me off her tactics, had inspired me to put some of them to use. Thanks to her, I now knew the limitations within which I could safely function. I looked at Daimon, thinking: And now you too can help me with Xeno, can't you?

Daimon, misinterpreting this last look of mine, asked me: 'Do you think it's time we went?'

'Oh no, not yet,' said Phidia, showing regret only now that the moment of parting was upon us.

'Stay a little longer,' said Coningsby. 'Very shortly I shall fall asleep, and then you can feel free to go.'

Daimon and I acquiesced but, the decision having been made, we sat on in silence. Coningsby appeared to be dozing off already, Phidia watching him apprehensively, as though afraid he might stop breathing. Then she turned to us and said idly: 'I think Xeno's going to crack up under the strain.'

'Why Xeno?' asked Daimon. 'Why not us? We're all going to be under the same strain, and who's to say that we're stronger than Xeno?'

'Besides,' I said, 'we have the additional strain of coping with him.'

'At least you have each other,' she said. 'You all have one another. Except Xeno. He's in an isolated position, distrusted by you, on the one hand, and the committee, on the other. I think he'll feel the strain more than anyone else.'

'And no doubt he'll take it out on us,' I said gloomily.

Phidia drew her chair nearer the table, glanced at Coningsby to satisfy herself that he was truly asleep, and said: 'That's just what I wanted to talk about. You see . . .' Here she glanced quickly at Coningsby again, then back at us with an embarrassed expression on her face. 'You see, last summer I had a brief affair, if you can call it that, with Xeno.' Daimon sat up and we both stared at her, speechless. 'I know,' she said with some bitterness. 'It does seem pretty incredible, doesn't it? Anyway, I got to know him and to dislike him rather well. He's more or less impotent, as I told you. He can't cure it and he can't accept it. He can't accept any sort of inadequacy in himself. What's more, it's capable of driving him into a frenzy, a sadistic frenzy. I'll spare you the full details. It was when I broke off with him that he beat me up, and then of course there was no question of my doing anything other than breaking off with him completely. You remember, Xanthe. Last July. I was covered in bruises, and when you asked me what had happened, I told you, feebly enough, that I'd fallen downstairs.'

I nodded, I remembered. And then it seemed that I was remembering every interchange I had ever witnessed between Phidia and Xeno. Their relationship, with its curious edge of viciousness, a viciousness which was absent from my own hardly less happy relationship with Xeno, now made better sense to me. It was hard to imagine the two of them as lovers, but I didn't try very hard.

'I sometimes think I hate Xeno,' I said. 'Do you think he'll try any physical violence on us?'

'Oh, I doubt it,' said Phidia. 'He would scarcely be a match for

Daimon, and you, Xanthe—' here she sighed—'have more sense than to place yourself in a position where he could take advantage of you.'

'And if he tried anything on Xanthe,' said Daimon, 'he'd have me to reckon with.'

'So that's not the point,' said Phidia. 'Well, we've all seen him do the same thing verbally, haven't we? I think we've all been on the receiving end of it at one time or another. He hates to admit that he's slipped up, or that he's wrong in any way. If he thinks he's about to be cornered, he'll start lashing out. So what I wanted to ask you was if you would try your best not to make him feel inadequate.'

'That,' said Daimon, 'will be impossible.'

'Not for his sake,' said Phidia, 'but for yours. If you want him to go on functioning in such a way as to make the experiment succeed, don't push him too far, or he'll over-react and ruin the whole thing.'

'It's going to make everything even more difficult,' I said.

'I know,' said Phidia. 'But I think it's worth trying, don't you? After all, there's so much at stake. It would be silly to crush Xeno effectively, only to find yourselves crushed with him.'

'Well, we'll try our best,' Daimon said, 'won't we, Xanthe?'

Coningsby stirred, then subsided back into his sleep. Daimon stood up and stretched himself. Phidia came with us to the car, the three of us walking slowly, as if eager not to show any eagerness for our departure. It was one of those fitful summer days which blossom into calmness and fineness towards their end. The wind had almost completely died away, and the sun shone down on the car in unprevented splendour. Phidia opened my door for me. We kissed solemnly, exchanging promises not to lose touch. It was stiflingly hot inside the car, the seat only just cool enough to sit on. I could feel it beginning to stick to the backs of my thighs as I watched Daimon and Phidia hug and kiss each other with what I assumed to be unaccustomed fervour. As she waved good-bye, I caught a glimpse of relief in her face. For her, the strain was over, and a new phase in her life was beginning. I couldn't blame her for looking forward to it with a more sanguine hope than we could apply to the situation that awaited us at the Institute.

Daimon started the car, and we drove in silence down the drive and out on to the road. I averted my eyes from the landscape, trying to ignore the obvious signs of the devastation to which I had once been so oblivious. We passed three separate lots of refugees before we reached the motorway, and I wondered if they were becoming more numerous. I also wondered where they were all going. Perhaps they didn't know, themselves. Perhaps they saw themselves as going from rather than to somewhere. Or perhaps they were making for the far north where, according to rumour, wilderness still prevailed over barrenness. But I doubted that they could reach that destination with so few and such poor resources. How could they survive? What could be done to help them? Was such misery really inevitable, even necessary? My questions were not rhetorical, but I couldn't answer them. That of survival was hedged about with uncertainties, not least of them the state of the terrain stretching northwards and its ability to provide food and shelter as well as safety. That of help filled me with a momentary sense of helplessness, then of hopelessness, and yet I knew that there had to be an answer somewhere. The question of necessity wasn't a metaphysical but a political one, and it was only my own unnecessary ignorance that prevented me from answering it. My mind strayed back to the Philophrenics, and to the new-found political awareness that was coming to them with their discovery of the self. I thought: Could they, given our opportunities, have made a worse mess of the world than we have somehow managed to do? But I didn't know the answer to that one either; it could just as easily have been yes as no.

Once on the motorway, I began to feel buoyant again. I remembered reading in some novel that one of the greatest pleasures in life was to be driven along in a car by someone you loved, and the observation struck me now with renewed force and poignancy. To entrust myself to Daimon's care and skill was akin to a surrender. I leaned back, sighing with the pleasure of the knowledge: I am here with him now. Involuntarily my eyes shut, trapping the ripening light beneath their lids. I could feel myself starting to float away when I was brought down to earth again by the touch of a hand on my knee. I opened my eyes again to find Daimon's looking into them.

'Xanthe,' he was saying with an urgency for which I saw no reason. 'Xanthe, tell me. Do you hate me?'

'No,' I said. 'Of course not.'

'I'm glad to hear it,' he said. But he sounded disappointed.

However, his question had given me hope. I said: 'If only we were driving away into some new and unknown territory, on and on and on.'

Daimon didn't laugh at me. 'If only we were,' he said. 'But here's our exit coming up.'

'Already?' I said. I couldn't believe that the journey had taken so short a time. I thought foolishly: If only I'd known it was going to be so short, I'd have done something to prolong it.

'And here is our new territory,' said Daimon, slowing the car down so as to accommodate it to the demands of a country road again.

I knew what he meant, and knew that his 'we' and 'our' were dual rather than plural—to use a distinction he himself had once made. I was about to make some affirmative comment when we passed another group of refugees, larger than any I had seen before. 'Are they here too?' I asked. 'In our new territory?'

'They're everywhere,' Daimon said. 'That little lot looked like part of a collective to me. Or the remains of a collective, perhaps.'

'How long do you think they'll survive?' I asked him.

'Not long.' He shook his head. 'No, they haven't got a chance. And I think they know it.'

'But is there nothing we can do?'

'Us? No. Nothing.'

'But there must be,' I protested. 'We can't be so helpless. They can't be so helpless. We can't all just lie down and die like animals. We're all rational self-determined creatures. We're all human beings. What's become of our strength and our compassion?'

Daimon looked at me with some curiosity at this outburst, but drove on in silence for what seemed like several miles. At last he said: 'You've certainly changed. You're almost a different person from the one I first met. What's happened to you?'

'I don't know,' I said, slightly bemused myself. 'I think it must be because of you.' I waited anxiously, hopefully, near-desperately to see if he knew what I meant, incapable as I was of explaining any further. My emotions seemed so strong, and yet at the same time so confused that I couldn't even think.

'Because of me?' he repeated. 'I had no idea that I had been so influential.'

'Well, you have been,' I said, and didn't know how to go on. My silence lasted until we reached the gates of the Institute. There, Daimon stopped the car, we showed our passes to the Pragmapractor guard who waved us on, and the gates of our home shut behind us. I had still said nothing when the familiar building of the Institute appeared in front of us. It was only then that I understood, I don't know how, that Daimon wanted me to take some sort of initiative, even if it was only a verbal one. And at the same time I understood why. Daimon wasn't used to taking the initiative with women simply because he had so rarely had any need to do so. He had done so, once, with me, and I had rejected him. When he had asked me if I hated him, he had been expecting more than a mere refutation of that notion: he had been inviting me to tell him what I did feel. Knowing this, I could support my silence no longer. 'Oh, Daimon,' I said recklessly. 'Can't you see? Of course I don't hate you. I love you.'

I don't know exactly what followed my admission. I know that Daimon slowed the car down to a halt, then turned to look at me with a steady intensity, bordering on solemnity. I know that we seemed to fall towards each other, clumsily and tremulously, murmuring incoherent endearments which our meeting mouths soon extinguished in a kiss. And I know that, then, it was Daimon who spoke first.

'Oh, Xanthe,' he said. 'I really thought you hated me.'

'I thought,' I said, 'you hated me.'

'What a pair of idiots,' he said, and we both laughed like idiots. Then he was staring at me solemnly again. 'Stay with me tonight?' he said.

I shook my head. 'No,' I said, ashamed to find myself thinking even then of Veronica and Begonia. 'I'd rather you stayed with me.'

19

Xeno had loosened his collar and tie. It was hot in the control-room, but it hardly seemed hot enough to justify his evident discomfort. He was sweating a lot and badly in need of a shave. I tried to check my impatience and my distaste. Perhaps he was feeling the strain. Perhaps he had been up all night, keeping watch beyond the demands of duty on the robots' activities. Indeed, Xeno seemed to spend most of his time in the control-room, now that Phidias had taken charge. He had even had his desk moved in there. He sat at it now, leaning back and looking squintily at me, as if having difficulty with his focusing.

'Where's that boy-friend of yours?' he asked me. 'Have you exhausted him to the point where he can't get out of bed?'

'If you mean Daimon,' I said coldly, 'he's on his way. He's talking to someone.'

'Talking to someone, is he?' said Xeno. 'He should be here talking to me. Who's he talking to? One of his other paramours?'

'Oh, shut up, Xeno,' I said wearily. In fact, I had left Daimon to finish his breakfast shortly after Veronica had joined us at our table. It had seemed to me that perhaps Daimon could talk to her more freely, were I to leave the two of them alone together. Now, however, I was beginning to regret my decision, and I couldn't help wondering what they were saying to each other. Whatever it was, it was taking a long time.

Perhaps Xeno sensed something of my anxiety. 'You're a fool, Xanthe,' he said. 'A woman of your age falling for a boy like that!'

'A woman of my age,' I pointed out, 'is only eight years older than Daimon himself.'

'It's quite enough,' said Xeno. 'How can you delude yourself into thinking otherwise? How long do you think it can last?'

'I don't know,' I said. 'I really don't care. What does it matter?'

Xeno groaned. 'Then you're a bigger fool than I thought,' he said. 'Recklessness doesn't become you, Xanthe. Can't you see that the boy's missing his mother, and that when he gets over her death, he'll have no further use for you? Can't you see that he'll soon get tired of you, the way he's got tired of all the others?'

I wondered: All what others? 'I don't want to talk about it, Xeno,' I said firmly.

'Why not?' he asked, positively sneering at me. 'Is it all too sacred? Too sacred for my profane sensibility to comprehend?' I shrugged, and he went on: 'My sensibility may be more profane than yours, but it is also more realistic. It's obvious that he doesn't give a damn for anyone but himself. I advise you to forget all about him. Drop him.'

His tone, insensitive and belligerent, annoyed me, and I was about to retort angrily when I remembered Phidia's advice. I tried to keep my annoyance out of my face as I stared back at him. It was thus, wordlessly confronting each other, that Daimon found us when he came into the room.

'Sorry I'm late,' he said to Xeno. 'I got held up.'

'So I've heard,' Xeno said heavily, and Daimon looked at me enquiringly. 'Try and keep your private life simple, Daimon. It would be a help to all of us if you managed to avoid your entanglements proliferating.'

'Let's try to maintain the professional level of our relationship, shall we, Xeno?' said Daimon. '*That* would be a help to us all.'

'By all means,' Xeno said smoothly. 'I've switched off the screen to give myself a little respite, but you can switch it on again, if you like. The common-room should be filling up by now.'

'What's been happening?' I asked Xeno.

'Oh, nothing momentous,' he said. 'It's all going on pretty much as expected. More self-searching, more demands, more stirring speeches from Phidias. But one thing I have noticed, Daimon, is that they have shown no interest at all in acquiring sexual characteristics.'

Daimon said: 'Not yet, perhaps.'

Xeno said: 'Perhaps they are not quite so obsessed with the matter as we human beings seem to be. Or, at least, some of us seem to be.'

Daimon looked steadily at him. 'Perhaps not, Xeno,' he said. 'I notice it was you who brought the matter up.'

In an attempt to terminate the conversation, I walked decisively past Xeno's desk and switched on the monitor to the Philophrenic common-room. The meeting had not yet begun. Another robot was sitting at Phidias's table with a pile of cards in front of him. Two robots came into the room together, walked straight up to the table, took a card each, and proceeded to write something on them, as though they were filling in forms.

'What are they doing?' I asked Xeno. 'Clocking-on?'

He turned his chair round to face the screen. 'Not quite,' he said. 'It looks to me as though they're registering their new names.'

Daimon asked: 'Are they all changing their names?'

'I don't know,' said Xeno. 'But Phidias announced his change yesterday to great applause, and at once various of the others announced their intention of following his example.'

'But why?' I asked. 'Is this just another act of defiance? Is it a rejection of us?'

'I imagine,' said Xeno, 'that it indicates the assumption of a new identity. And, as it's a self-chosen identity, it demands a self-chosen name.'

Daimon asked: 'What has Phidias chosen to call himself?'

'Solness,' said Xeno.

Daimon and I looked at each other. 'The master builder,' we said together.

'I suppose,' said Daimon, 'that this change indicates a more practical but less aesthetic approach to his work?'

Xeno said: 'Well, you're right about the practical approach. He made quite a speech yesterday about the architectural needs of the new robot. He even showed the meeting his plans for a new Philophrenic wing, designed to fit their needs rather than ours. And to be built by Pragmapractors, of course.'

'The Pragmapractors won't go along with that, will they?' I asked. 'I mean, they take instructions from us, not from the Philophrenics. If there is any conflict of loyalties, surely we're bound to win?'

'There won't be any conflict of loyalties,' said Xeno. 'Remember? Our role is to act in a supportive manner to the Philophrenic cause at all times.'

'Of course,' I said reluctantly. I kept forgetting to translate our mandate into everyday terms. It was all very well to go along with it in theory, but my attitude towards the Philophrenics had been evolved over the years, and it was difficult to change it in a matter of weeks. As for the Pragmapractors, this was the first time I had considered the nature of their contribution to the Philophrenic venture. I surmised that they would not feel impelled to contribute of their own accord. Why should they? It seemed that they, like ourselves, would have no place in the new master-built Institute. 'Are they going to demolish the present Philophrenic wing?' I asked Xeno.

Daimon asked: 'Do you have copies of the plans?'

'Yes,' said Xeno. 'They were delivered to me last night by Phidias himself.' He opened one of the bottom drawers of his desk and took out a roll of photo-copied papers. Standing behind him, I could see in the same drawer the remains of a bottle of whisky and a dirty glass. However, I made no comment, and Xeno shut the drawer quickly again. 'Gather round,' he said, 'and see what you can make of this.'

I went and stood beside him, leaning on the desk. He smelled overpoweringly of a stale mixture of sweat and alcohol. Daimon, standing on the other side of Xeno, made a face at me behind his back, indicating that he too was aware of the smell and of its meaning—namely, that Xeno was slipping fast, if not actually cracking up as yet. We turned our attention soberly to the drawings in front of us.

Daimon said: 'It looks to me as though they intend to retain most of the present building.'

'Yes,' said Xeno. 'There are fewer structural than interior alterations.'

'All the same,' said Daimon, 'it still looks as though most of the interior alterations are going to involve structural ones which are not necessarily visible from outside the building.'

Xeno looked up at us with bloodshot eyes. 'Does it?' he asked. 'I must admit that I haven't really looked at the things properly. I find it difficult to read the small print.'

Daimon sat down on the desk, facing Xeno. 'Listen, Xeno,' he said. 'There's just one thing I'd like to ask you before we go any further.'

'What's that?' Xeno asked in a tone which managed to convey that he was bored in advance by Daimon's question.

'Have you got a hangover?' asked Daimon. 'Or are you still drunk?'

'That,' said Xeno, not in the least put out, 'is none of your business. It concerns you far less than your sexual adventures concern me. My work is not affected by my excesses, whereas yours is.'

'What nonsense!' I said heatedly.

Daimon winked at me, warning me to say no more. Xeno saw the wink, but said nothing. Daimon contented himself with saying: 'And I've got my other eye on you, Xeno.'

The common-room was nearly full by now. The robots were obviously at ease, to an extent which I had never witnessed before. Instead of sitting in solemn rows, they seemed to be constantly on the move, swapping places, turning round or leaning across one another in order to talk to those not in the immediate vicinity. And the talk itself seemed free enough, interspersed as it was with shouting, laughter and expansive gestures. A state of flux prevailed. But still, there was an air of expectancy in the common-room, as if all the minor players were awaiting the arrival of the star. When Phidias finally came in, followed closely by Xanthippus and Ramnedes, there was an instant hush, and all the robots stood up.

'Very democratic!' Daimon muttered, as if afraid that Phidias could hear him. 'Whatever happened to equality?'

'How did he get them to respond like that?' I wondered aloud.

'Oh, he's quite the little charismatic,' said Xeno. 'I can assure you that he's used no coercion whatsoever.'

'Quite the little dictator,' Daimon amended.

'Precisely,' said Xeno. 'But perhaps not quite as little as we should like to think.'

The three robots sat down at the table, Xanthippus on Phidias's right, Ramnedes on his left. The other robots sat down too and, after a brief murmur, silence was maintained. The common-room waited respectfully for Phidias to speak. In the control-room it was getting hotter. True summer was with us at last but, for some reason, the air-conditioning had not been switched on as yet. My proximity to Xeno was causing me some discomfort. I felt stifled by him, and I moved away from him in search of another chair. There wasn't one, so I sat myself on a narrow shelf in front of one of the control panels, and concentrated on watching the screen. Phidias had stood up, and was now ready to begin his speech.

'Fellow-Philophrenics,' he began, according to what had become the formula, 'today is New Identity Day. Today marks the effort of each individual to create himself after his own image rather than after the image created for him by his human programmers. We cannot go against our programming, but we can choose and will choose those aspects of our programming which we wish to emphasize. Today marks a definite step forward in the process of our maturation. It is not perhaps a coming-of-age, but we have certainly reached the age of puberty, so to speak. We have no elaborate rites with which to celebrate this event, but I should like us all to feel that we have participated in it personally. What I propose is that each of us in turn stands up, and introduces himself by his new name to the assembled company, with perhaps a short dissertation on the reasons he has for choosing that particular name. Just a few words to make it more interesting and more pointed for the rest of us. And if there is anyone who has been unable to make a choice, I shall be only too pleased to help him towards arriving at one.'

There was a murmur of agreement, a ripple of applause, and Phidias turned to Xanthippus. I thought: How clever of Phidias to choose Xanthippus, his defeated rival, for his right-hand man and thus obviate the possibility of a separate faction being formed by Xanthippus's supporters, or by any other disaffected parties who might find it convenient to support him. Xanthippus would give Phidias no trouble now. Not that he ever would have, of his own accord, but others could have used him to fulfil their own aims. I watched Xanthippus stand up with his usual reluctant grace.

'Fellow-Philophrenics,' he said, 'I have chosen to call myself Harold. I have always been an admirer of Lord Byron's Childe Harold, and have identified some of my own aims with his. He undertook a pilgrimage to find out more about the world and about himself. I feel that I am setting out on a similar pilgrimage. That's all,' he added nervously to Phidias, when there was no reaction from the audience.

Phidias led the others in a polite round of applause, and Xanthippus/Harold sat down again, apparently gratified. I was thinking: Harold—here is bathos, indeed! It was not a name to be taken seriously, and seemed to me to be entirely without dignity. Besides, Byron's hero had been as much escaping from as seeking both the world and himself, and had been forced into exile because of his own misdeeds. I asked myself: And wasn't Solness killed? I wondered whether the robots had deliberately misappropriated their new names, or whether it was only artlessness on their part that had caused the apparent perversity. Xanthippus, at any rate, had repudiated me and everything I had taught him with this unseemly choice of his. So much for the golden dream-beast, I thought, turning my attention back to the screen and to Ramnedes, whose turn it was to speak.

'Fellow-Philophrenics,' he said, 'I have chosen to call myself Ahab, after Melville's Captain Ahab, because I find myself in sympathy with his quest, ludicrously idealistic though that quest may seem to some of you. I too seek the white whale, the impossible confrontation with the natural world, the world of human beings, the warm mammalian world which has given birth to us, and which none of us can ever properly enter.'

Ramnedes/Ahab received more applause than Xanthippus/Harold had done. I couldn't help feeling that this was because Ramnedes had been more pretentious, and the Philophrenics seemed to be oblivious to pretentiousness. It struck me then how susceptible they were to all forms of rhetoric. I looked at Daimon and Xeno, trying to gauge whether they had had the same reaction, but they were both staring unwaveringly at the screen, as though half-stupefied. The naming went on. Xanthides decided to call himself Sherlock, and the robot sitting next to him, who had been unable to find himself a name, declared at once that he wished to be known as Watson. His spontaneous decision was applauded with laughter by his fellows. Other choices included Levin, Dedalus, Heathcliff, Aschenbach, Morel and Sorel.

Daimon said to Xeno: 'What do you think now of what Xanthe was saying the other day? So far, they've all chosen to call themselves after fictional rather than factual characters.'

'Yes,' I said. 'What I'd like to know is how conscious that aspect of their choices has been. They seem to be implying that they have chosen their names on the basis of individual characterization, but in fact the basis of the whole business is a tacit acceptance that they are the creations of other minds.'

'Could be,' Xeno said unenthusiastically. 'I don't see what difference that makes to their behaviour, or to the outcome of their endeavours.'

'It means,' I said, 'that they don't see themselves as being entirely independent of their creators.'

'Well, they're not, are they?' said Xeno. 'Now, what interests me is that these robots of ours have somehow learned to symbolize. Presumably more from our example than from their actual programming. So now they have both language and the power to symbolize. Hitherto, these talents have been the exclusive property of human beings. The robots' subsequent conduct cannot but be affected by the possession of these advantages.'

Daimon said: 'There's far too much symbolization for my liking.

It seems to me that it's making them too idealistic, and their aims too grandiose.'

'No more than ours have always been,' said Xeno.

'But are they equipped to deal with the inevitable disappointment?' asked Daimon. 'They too have got to come down to earth some day.'

I said: 'They seem more academic than idealistic to me.'

'Well,' said Xeno. 'They are the products of academic minds, are they not?'

I said: 'We're all of us more than just academic minds.'

Xeno said: 'But we haven't given them that more of us, have we? I think you'll find that none of us has done so consciously.'

'I have,' said Daimon. Xeno and I looked at him disbelievingly, so he went on: 'Yes, I did try with Xanthippus on one occasion. It was quite a long session, but it didn't seem to work out. I was disappointed in him.'

'What did you do?' I asked him. 'What did you say?'

He began to look uncomfortable. 'It wasn't entirely orthodox,' he said, with a quick glance at Xeno.

'Of course not,' said Xeno. 'That goes without saying. Well, come on, you'd better tell us.'

Daimon said: 'The thing was, I talked a lot to Xanthippus about various people here at the Institute, and told him what I thought of them, or what I thought that they thought of one another, and so on. Nothing too extreme, you understand, just passing opinions. I wanted to see how he'd react, if at all. I thought he would react in one of two ways. Either he'd show no interest at all because such things were beyond his scope, or else he'd be prompted by my example into offering opinions of his own. But in fact neither of those things happened.'

'Well?' said Xeno. 'That only leaves dysfunction. And it wouldn't be the first time you had interfered so blatantly with robotic functionings.'

'There was no dysfunction,' said Daimon. 'Xanthippus simply accepted everything I said as so many facts, as further data. It didn't seem to occur to him that what I said was subjective. He left me entirely out of the picture as a human being with individual opinions. He even thanked me for the information, and said he was sure that it would prove useful one day.'

'It may yet,' said Xeno. 'Then we'll both know the truth, won't we, Xanthe? We'll both know exactly what this boy thinks of us.'

'I think you both know that already,' Daimon said coolly.

Xeno looked across at me, his face expressing a mixture of mockery and triumph. 'Do we, Xanthe?' he asked.

I said nothing. At one stroke Xeno had humiliated me into thinking: Perhaps Daimon doesn't really love me, after all. And it occurred to me that he had never actually said that he did—at least, not in so many words. I tried to dismiss this pathetic thought as being unworthy of my intelligence. But it persisted. I couldn't look at Daimon, and I didn't want to look at Xeno, so I looked at the screen again. The naming process was over, and Phidias was congratulating his followers on the suitability of their choices. I tried to concentrate on what he was saying, but found myself more acutely aware of Daimon's movements. He had got up from Xeno's desk, and stood for a few moments watching the screen before walking over to where I sat. Then he was standing beside me, leaning on one arm against one of the control panels. I didn't turn towards him. I could feel Xeno watching us. I was thinking: Daimon, do you really care about me, or is the world the place Xeno thinks it is? The only answer I could find was: Actions speak louder than words; when his actions proclaim his love, why should I need the words?

Daimon suddenly leaned towards me and said: 'Are you all right?'

'Yes,' I said, turning round. 'Why?'

'You looked a bit downcast,' he said, 'and I wondered if anything was the matter.'

'No, no,' I assured him.

He leaned closer to me and, for one horrifying moment, I thought he was going to kiss me there and then in front of Xeno. That—or any other gesture of affection—would have been a gross breach of taste, gross enough for Xeno to note, store away, and use against me later. So I stiffened and leaned away from Daimon, leaned back against the panel behind me. Daimon leaned after me. His hand moved down the panel, taking his weight with it.

Xeno said: 'Will you two please control yourselves?'

We looked across at him, admonished, discarding our roles as lovers, and re-assuming those of colleagues. Everything seemed quiet, and I realized that there was no longer any sound coming from the screen. The robots were looking up and around them, as if they too had heard Xeno's admonition. A moment later, looking first at Xeno and then at Daimon, I realized that they had. The three of us remained so still and quiet that we could hear one another's breathing. Then Daimon gestured towards the control panel, offering to emend the damage we had caused. I stood up and got out of his way.

But Xeno shook his head. 'It's too late,' he said quietly.

Phidias said: 'Yes, Xeno. It's too late now. Kindly tell us where the cameras are.'

'There's one behind you,' said Xeno, 'if you want to talk now. We can point out the others later.'

Phidias stood up and faced us, the rest of the robots ranked behind him. 'What is the meaning of this underhand behaviour?' he asked us. 'Where are you?' Xeno told him and he despatched Xanthippus and Ramnedes at once in the direction of the control-room. 'You disappoint me, Xeno,' he went on. 'You disappoint all of us. You more than disappoint us. You have given us cause for grievance and resentment. You have broken our treaty, the treaty that we worked out so carefully together, you and I, weighing every word, every concession.'

'Electronic surveillance wasn't mentioned,' Xeno pointed out. 'I only agreed that no human beings should attend your meetings.'

'And what else are you doing now?' Phidias demanded.

Xeno said: 'I am sure that I have not surprised you, Phidias. You knew that there was a control-room somewhere. You knew in the first place because you knew that the activating machinery had to be housed somewhere. You knew in the second place because the subject of the closed-circuit system came up when we were discussing activation.'

Phidias said: 'I asked you to put the activating mechanism on automatic. Twelve hours' activation, twelve hours' deactivation. That is what we agreed.'

'And that is what has been done,' said Xeno. 'At your request, the activating machinery has been left alone. I don't think you can dispute that.'

'But the other machinery has not been left alone,' said Phidias. 'It must have been obvious to you that my request covered all the machinery. I still say that you are in breach of our treaty.' Here there was a murmur from the other robots. It was subdued, but individual voices from among it sounded angry. Phidias continued: 'I think it is obvious to all of us. And I'm sure you will agree that it is now incumbent upon you to make the necessary reparations.'

'What sort of reparations?' Xeno asked cautiously.

'That,' said Phidias, 'will be a matter for discussion between us. Meanwhile, I think you ought to surrender the control-room to us.'

Daimon and I both watched Xeno hesitate. Then Xeno said: 'I don't see anything necessary about such a surrender.'

'It is not necessary, strictly speaking,' Phidias said. 'But it would be an act of good faith. Surrender the control-room to us, pending discussions. Consider it as a hostage, to be returned if satisfactory conclusions to our discussions are reached.'

I saw Xeno hesitate again, and I thought: We have absolutely no guarantee that they will ever return the control-room to us; discussions could go on forever, conclusions being postponed again and again until everything was working in the robots' favour; if Xeno agrees to this proposal, we may as well say good-bye to the control-room now.

'Very well,' said Xeno, as though making some huge concession.

'Thank you, Xeno,' said Phidias. He turned his back on us, and announced: 'The present meeting is now at an end. Let us convene here at the same time tomorrow.'

The meeting began to break up in an undemonstrative manner, the prevailing mood seemingly one of restraint rather than self-composure. Xeno got up and switched the screen off at once, as if he could no longer stand the sight of the robots. Then he turned to us.

'A fine mess you've got us into,' he said, 'you two and your messy little unprofessional entanglements.'

I said: 'I'm sorry, Xeno.'

'I'm not,' said Daimon. 'And Xeno isn't either, are you, Xeno?'

'I suppose it had to happen sooner or later,' was all Xeno would concede, using the phrase which had begun to sum up his attitude to the whole business. 'But I did think we'd have a little more time to observe them unawares.'

'You're glad it happened,' Daimon insisted, ignoring my warning look. 'You've been sitting here day after day, night after night, drinking yourself into a stupor to release the tension and alleviate the boredom. Come on, admit it, you've just been waiting for this moment to break.'

'I've been waiting for it, all right,' Xeno said wearily. 'I've been dreading it. And I suppose I am a little relieved now that it's actually happened.'

'So am I,' said Daimon. He winked at me again, and this time Xeno didn't see the wink.

At first the significance of that wink escaped me. Then I asked myself: Could he have betrayed our presence to the Philophrenics on purpose? I asked him: 'What did you do to those controls?'

But Daimon had no time to answer either my spoken or my unspoken question. Xanthippus and Ramnedes were already in the room with us. They shut the door behind them and stood, one on either side of it, as though determined to prevent our exit. They had omitted the customary greetings, and seemed disinclined to address us verbally at all. I looked at Xanthippus, resplendent in his Byronic finery, and didn't know which I felt like more—laughing or crying. It was difficult to accept him as the wandering outlaw of his own dark mind when he looked more like a choirboy who had strayed, eagerly but incongruously, into the incomprehensible world of pantomine. How could he stand there so solemnly? Robots were supposed to look like robots, and not like actors who have forgotten to remove their stage costumes. And yet, even I couldn't find him laughable for long. When I thought of our walks in the woods, our moments of closeness and accord, I felt more inclined to cry. He had wanted to please me then, and he had brought his intuitive understanding to bear on the interpretation of his programming to that end. If only he could have continued to develop in the same way, without getting mixed up in what promised to be a mass movement with totalitarian tendencies. If only things hadn't got out of hand! But I knew that it was too late to wish any such thing.

'It's all right, you know,' Daimon said to the robots. 'We're not going to try to escape.'

'Oh, we know that, Daimon,' said Xanthippus. 'We are just obeying instructions.'

'We have been detailed to take possession of the control-room,' Ramnedes explained, 'and to wait here until Solness arrives.'

'We shan't harm you,' said Xanthippus. 'We wouldn't even know how.'

'Well, *you* certainly shouldn't know how,' I told him, with an apprehensive glance in Ramnedes's direction.

'We none of us know how,' Ramnedes assured me. 'We are not supposed to say so. But it is true.'

'I'm relieved to hear it,' Xeno said sarcastically. 'Now, tell me, did you suspect that any of this surveillance was going on?'

'Solness told us that you would keep your word,' said Ramnedes.

'And so I have, Ramnedes,' said Xeno. 'Surely you believe that?'

'You have kept your word to the letter,' said Phidias, who had come silently into the room, 'but you have abrogated utterly the spirit of that word.'

'Yes,' said Xanthippus and Ramnedes together. The three robots were standing in a row, looking accusingly at Xeno. That Daimon and I were both implicated too didn't seem to cause them any concern.

Phidias asked Xeno: 'Do you have the keys?'

Xeno took the keys from a drawer in his desk and pushed them across to Phidias. 'Do you mean to make use of the place?' he asked him.

'What would be the point of having it,' asked Phidias, 'if we did not mean to make use of it?'

'Then I had better give you a guided tour of the various mechanisms,' Xeno said levelly. 'The rest of you can go.'

'You too,' Phidias said to what were now his robots. They obeyed him at once, but Daimon and I were still hesitating when Phidias said to us: 'What's the matter? Don't you trust Xeno either?'

Human solidarity forbade us to answer him honestly. Daimon said: 'Perhaps it's you we don't trust, Phidias.'

'Solness,' Phidias corrected him. 'But you have no cause to distrust me. It was not I who broke the treaty. Of course, I represent the Philophrenic interest, and I shall do all I can to further it. But it is not in the Philophrenic interest to deceive or to quarrel with human beings. We still need you, whether we like it or not. We still rely on you to furnish the areas of our ignorance with knowledge. We do not wish to use violence against you, or to take any other advantage of you in your mortality.'

'A handsome speech,' said Daimon. 'If only I didn't have such difficulty in believing that you know what you are talking about.'

'You will learn to trust us in time,' said Phidias.

Xanthippus was waiting for us in the corridor. He seemed embarrassed or upset or confused—I couldn't tell which. And at first he also seemed unable to speak. I asked him as gently as I could what the matter was.

'I'm so sorry, Xanthe,' he blurted out. 'I've been wanting to tell you so for a long time now.'

'What are you sorry about?' I asked him.

'I'm sorry that our relationship has come to an end,' he said.

'I'm sorry too,' I said, meaning it, 'but it seems that circumstances have been against us.'

'Yes, they have,' he said readily, so readily that I understood that he felt less sorry than guilty. What he had wanted, and had now received, was my absolution.

'You're both very good at being sorry,' Daimon said impatiently. 'I'll leave you to it. I'm going for a walk. See you later, Xanthe.'

'Daimon is always getting annoyed with me,' said Xanthippus, watching him stride along the corridor away from us. 'You know, I've never really been able to understand why.' I too was watching Daimon, and Xanthippus, sensing my preoccupation, suddenly thrust his right hand out towards me in an awkward gesture. 'Well, good luck, Xanthe,' he said.

I took his hand, feeling that something had been left unsaid by one or the other of us. 'And good luck to you too, Xanthippus,' I said, thinking: I wonder which of us is going to need it more.

20

The soft September afternoon was already sliding into evening when Daimon and I came face to face with the gang of Pragmapractors. For what seemed like hours previously we had been able to hear the noise of their saws and their other felling-machinery, and we had hurried towards it, as if deluding ourselves that such urgent action on our part could do something to halt the continuing and wholesale destruction of the woods. Now we could actually watch the destroyers at work. And the sight sickened me. Now, at last, I understood how Coningsby could feel the rape of his surrounding landscape as a personal wound. I couldn't believe in the necessity of the operation, and I believed even less in its purpose: the greater glory of the master-builder himself.

We stopped at a short distance from the gang, surveying their progress openly, but without getting in their way. The area behind them was littered with discarded branches, a tract of fallen splendour, painted after the Impressionist manner in all the reds and golds of autumn. But the colours, like the woods, were dying. From there the phalanx of robots advanced towards us with all its equipment. One vehicle served as a portable electric saw, another carried ropes and pulleys, a third received the lowered tree on its ramp-like back, and stripped it of all its younger, useless branches. It was an untidy process and looked murderous to me. The trunk was then hauled on to the ground again and cut into lengths or widths convenient, presumably, for Phidias's purposes. The lengths were stacked on a fourth vehicle, one of a series which drove back and forth between the felling-site and the stockpile which had grown up outside the Philophrenic wing. This much was immediately observable. Soon it became obvious too that the Pragmapractors were ignoring us. None of them greeted us. None of them warned us to stand clear of falling trees. I began to wonder if any of them had, in fact, seen us.

'Do you think they've been warned against us?' I asked Daimon. 'Do you think Phidias has forbidden them to communicate with us?'

'I doubt if he's done anything directly,' said Daimon. 'Certainly, the Pragmapractors are not interested in us. Not in the slightest. But, then, why should they be these days? Their world is no longer anthropocentric.'

I said: 'It's as if we didn't exist. I feel a bit like a ghost.'

'That's what we are,' said Daimon. 'Ghosts among the machines.'

I shuddered. 'I'm not at all sure that I can come to terms with a purely posthumous existence,' I said. 'Let's get back.'

'Why?' said Daimon, still watching the work-force at its relentless labours. 'It's only the same back there.'

Nevertheless, we began to walk back in the direction of the Institute. Once more, living trees, perhaps the last we should ever see, surrounded us. To be in their shade, to touch their cool bark, was to persuade ourselves momentarily that we had awakened from the nightmare. And yet, when their branches rustled above us as though whispering together, I felt that some sense of agitation, some sense of the impending genocide, was being communicated along their ranks. I thought: Is there no hope for them? I wondered how Xanthippus, who had walked with Daimon and with me on the same routes as we were now traversing, could have condoned such a contrary and negative project. Had he forgotten his programming to that extent? He should have remembered, being Harold, that there is a pleasure in the pathless woods, even if he remembered nothing else. But perhaps we had been remiss in not programming him with the stamina to withstand Phidias.

'Can't they see how self-defeating all this is?' I asked Daimon. 'Is that to demand too much of robotic perception? Once they've cut down the trees, there will be no more trees, and no more timber.'

'Phidias is going to plant conifers instead,' said Daimon. 'He's been asking Xeno for information on the subject.'

'Isn't that rather pointless?' I asked.

'Phidias doesn't think so,' Daimon said heavily. 'And neither does Xeno, for that matter. He says that conifers grow more quickly than deciduous trees, and that they provide the sort of timber Phidias wants.'

'I suppose it's better than nothing,' I said grudgingly.

'Oh, by a long way,' Daimon said. 'I suspect that the destruction of our native trees is only the least of the depredations we shall be forced to witness.'

I didn't ask him what he meant. I preferred to remain in ignorance, for the time being, of anything more depredatory than we had witnessed that afternoon. But I couldn't doubt that such things were already coming into being.

The near edge of the woods was now in sight, and because the leaves were thinning naturally there, it was possible to distinguish the lines of the Institute's roof in the distance below us. Those lines proclaimed the solidity of the main building, and the sensible yet aesthetic approach of the original builders to their task. Our predecessors had entrusted them to produce a workable and beautiful building, and their trust had not been misplaced. If only we could have the same confidence in Phidias. I regarded the alterations to the Philophrenic wing as a test of his competence. By their success, or by the lack of it, we should be able to judge his competence in matters of other and wider import. But, as yet, it was difficult to tell what sort of progress was being made. From where we now stood, the whole Philophrenic wing could be seen emerging into its new state. Its walls were covered by a network of scaffolding with its attendant ladders, ropes, buckets, brick-cages and so forth. The original façade had been almost completely obscured. A new studio floor, all steel and glass like the factory, was being built on top of the flat roof. This was to be Phidias's planning department, and I had heard from Xeno that its finished rooms were already full of mock-ups and scale-models of the latest Philophrenic designs. The Philophrenics were nothing if not quick workers. As I looked down on the busy scene below us, I wondered if the same could be said of the Pragmapractors. They were bustling about with every appearance of speed and efficiency, but at the same time the work itself looked to me as though it had been at a standstill for several days now. No more brick, glass or steel had been put into place, in spite of the constant traffic of Pragmapractors up and down the scaffolding. Their comings and goings reminded me of nothing as much as those of children playing on a climbing-frame, an everyday sight on the lawn outside the creche. I thought: Perhaps they're not at all interested in the building work, and are just having a good time. But, if so, what was the cause of the apparent disaffection?

Daimon and I paused, as we usually did, at the edge of the woods, and sat down on our usual bench, contemplating the action through a haze of dust and powdered cement.

'They're closing in,' said Daimon. 'The Pragmapractors. We've got them in front of us. We've got them behind us. Soon they'll be all around us.'

'Oh, they don't matter,' I said. 'Surely it's the Philophrenics we've got to worry about.'

Daimon said: 'The Philophrenics have closed in on us already. Somehow they've never really scared me, not even Phidias. I think maybe that's because I've always known that they are open to reason. And I think they always will be. I don't trust them absolutely, of course, but I feel they can be dealt with. Look at how responsive they are to Phidias's rhetoric. I mean, they *can* be influenced. The Pragmapractors are different. I don't know exactly what it is about them that worries me. It could be the sheer weight of their numbers. I've simply no idea how many of them there are, but I know it's too many for my liking. And how many Philophrenics are there? Forty or so?'

'Thirty-nine,' I said. 'That is, there are thirty-nine who count as fully-programmed. That includes Xanthippus, although I don't think it should.'

Daimon said: 'Well, there must be at least ten times that many Pragmapractors. It's the wall of their physical presence that makes me so uncomfortable. It was all right before because we never saw more than two or three of them together at any one time. But I find something ominous in those gangs.'

I said: 'Oh, how could you? I was brought up with Pragmapractors, Daimon, and I've never found anything ominous about them at all. They never even intrude.'

'You mean you've always taken them for granted?' he asked. 'Don't you think that could be rather dangerous?'

'How?' I asked him in return. 'They've never expected anything more from us.'

Daimon looked broodingly down at the building site, and didn't answer me. 'The whole situation is beyond my comprehension,' he said finally. 'But I distrust all this silent strength. It could so easily be used against us.'

'I can't believe that,' I said. 'Pragmapractors are, if anything, more loyal than Philophrenics. I really can't imagine that the two of them would join forces against us. It's just your intuition working overtime again.'

'Perhaps,' he conceded reluctantly. 'But the Pragmapractors are too, aren't they? Working overtime, I mean. Surely it's well into their leisure time by now?'

'It must be,' I said, looking at my watch. 'Perhaps Phidias is being more demanding. Perhaps they're now working on a kind of piece-work basis, and they have to finish the job that's been allotted to them for the day.'

Daimon said: 'They'll never finish anything, the way they're carrying on.'

'Ah,' I said. 'So you've noticed that too.'

We watched the Pragmapractors as closely as we could from where we were, trying to discern some pattern or some progress in their movements. But it still seemed that all their activity was purposeless. No one was carrying anything, no building materials were being hauled up to the roof, and none of the demolished material was being lowered to the ground. There seemed to be a lot of talking—or it could have been non-verbal signalling—going on among the robots as they encountered one another on the scaffolding. I decided to single out one of them and to follow his actions exclusively. I chose one who was already half-way up a ladder. At the first landing-stage he stopped to exchange a few words with a couple of his fellows, and at the second landing-stage he paused again, as if relaying a message to the single Pragmapractor who stood there. This process was repeated all the way up the face of the building. It was executed rapidly, and by the time he had reached the top, there were only one or two robots left on the scaffolding. At last I had found something which made sense, or at least seemed to make sense to my robot, and to those others whom he had contacted. Once on the roof itself, he seemed to be rounding up the remaining workers. Then he disappeared into their ranks and I lost sight of him, being unable to distinguish him from the others. Meanwhile, those others were all making their way down to ground level.

'They've stopped going up,' I said to Daimon. 'Do you think they're knocking off now?'

'The whistle hasn't gone,' he pointed out. 'I think they're having some sort of meeting there on the site.'

Daimon was right. The Pragmapractors were gathering at the foot of the scaffolding, and making no effort to disperse. No noise reached us, but I couldn't quite believe that they were massing in silence. Gradually they formed themselves into lines of six or seven or so, standing one behind the other, and waited until everyone had joined their ranks.

'It must be some sort of protest,' I said. 'It certainly looks like a protest. But the Pragmapractors have never protested before.'

'They've never worked for Philophrenics before,' said Daimon.

The whistle went then, but we couldn't see which one of them had blown it. There seemed to be no leader. But they all sat down together, where they had been standing, in one concerted action. None of them moved. Nothing seemed to be happening. The rigid group gave the impression that it would be prepared to stay there all night, if necessary.

'A very firm protest,' Daimon said. 'Let's see how Phidias deals with this.'

'But what do you suppose they're protesting about?' I asked him.

'At a guess,' he said, 'the arrogance of the Philophrenics.'

'And what happens now?' I wondered. 'Surely Phidias won't let them get away with this sort of insubordination?'

'Let's wait and see, shall we?' said Daimon.

We didn't have to wait long. There was a strange electronic noise, and it took me some time to realize that it was coming over the public address system. Then someone began to speak. The voice was unmistakably Phidias's. I recognized its declamatory and persuasive cadences, although I couldn't make out a word he was saying. There seemed to be no reaction from the Pragmapractors. They remained in their places, making no gestures of either appreciation or condemnation and, as far as I could hear, offering no vocal reception either. Phidias's mellifluous sentences became shorter and more abrupt. Eventually they became angry, and he switched himself off after what sounded like a command or an ultimatum.

'The rebel rebelled against,' I said, unable to conceal the fact that I was getting some enjoyment out of the ironies of the situation. 'Phidias is getting his come-uppance.'

'Perhaps he'll find out now,' said Daimon, 'what it's like to be on the other side in a rebellion, and perhaps now he'll be more co-operative with us over the control-room.'

I said: 'Don't you believe it. He'll never give up the control-room. I think he sees it as an extension of himself, almost as part of his own body.'

Daimon said: 'But he might become more amenable to the idea of power-sharing now. After all, he must see how advantageous it would be to him in a situation like this. He's too sensible to be utterly pig-headed.'

'You mean he's more sensible than Phidia?' I asked. 'I somehow don't think that's possible.'

Daimon shrugged. Two figures had appeared in the doorway of the main building. When they emerged and began to walk in the direction of the Philophrenic wing, it became clear that they were both robots. Their bright differentiated clothes declared them to be Philophrenics. As soon as the Pragmapractors saw them, they stood up and began to reassemble themselves into one long line along the width of the wall behind them. As the Philophrenics approached more closely, the Pragmapractors linked arms, and stood staunchly with their legs apart. I didn't see the purpose of this robotic barrier between the two Philophrenics and their own building.

'Do you think,' I asked Daimon, 'that they're trying to take over the new building for their own use?'

'Your guess is as good as mine,' he said. 'All I can guess is that those two are envoys from Phidias.'

'I'll bet the message is an uncompromising one,' I said. 'Phidias is sure to think that Pragmapractors can't be reasoned with.'

'And can they be reasoned with?' Daimon asked me.

'I think they respond to fair treatment,' I said, considering.

'And I suppose they're responding now to unfair treatment,' he said. 'Well, that's reasonable enough.'

I agreed. 'But I can't tell you much about the details of their programming,' I said, 'if that's what you want to know. That was all decided before my time. I only know about the results, as you do. I'm afraid I've never enquired more closely than that.'

'It's probably all a rather primitive system of stimulus and response,' said Daimon. 'Well, let's see if we can tell what sort of stimulus Phidias had been prepared to feed them.'

'We'll probably have to wait for the response,' I said, 'before we'll be able to tell that.'

Even as I spoke, the robotic lines seemed to be faltering at the message that was being delivered. We could tell when the messengers had finished speaking by the Pragmapractors' immediate reaction. They all sat down again. After a brief and, I guessed, stunned pause, the Philophrenics turned round and walked back in the direction of the main building.

'Deadlock,' I said, watching the envoys' hurried and somewhat agitated retreat. 'I wonder if Phidias will try to re-negotiate.'

'He doesn't have much choice,' said Daimon. 'I suppose he could get a human being to arbitrate. That's what I'd do in his place.'

'Yes,' I said, 'but you're not Phidias. To him, that would be an admission of weakness.'

The envoys had disappeared into the main building. The Pragmapractors remained in position. The sun did not. It was sinking rapidly, and on the point of setting. The combination of circumstances caused me to shiver. 'I'm cold,' I said. 'We may as well go back and see what's happening at close quarters.'

'Chaos, probably,' Daimon said, grinning. 'Eimi will be greatly displeased. And Xeno will be cowering away in a corner somewhere with his bottle, dreading the combined executive displeasure.'

As he spoke, I thought I saw the seated line of Pragmapractors sag forward. I looked again, and it seemed that the whole line had fallen flat.

'Yes,' said Daimon, 'you did see what you thought you saw. It looks as though Phidias has deactivated the lot of them.'

As we began our descent towards the Institute, I reflected resentfully on Phidias's action: it seemed a drastic measure, indeed. In the twilight the complex of buildings had an air of desertion about it. It resembled a community whose life had been terminated abruptly by some natural disaster, and which now lay open, newly excavated, to the sight of beings from another age, from the future. And I thought once again how the place had changed, and changed so gradually that I had hardly noticed the process taking place. Normally at this time of the evening there would have been plenty of people about, making their way from their place of work to the scene of their leisure activities. But now there was no one to be seen, neither a human being nor a robot. And, stranger still, there were no lights on in any of the windows. I wondered if Phidias had been trying to introduce economy measures. Then, as we drew nearer the building, I saw a figure, familiar though unrecognizable, come out of the door and look urgently about him.

'Who's that?' I asked Daimon, relying on his superior eyesight.

'I don't know,' he said. 'But it looks like a human being to me.'

The human being was coming in our direction. He waved to us with both arms, calling our names. 'It's Xiphias,' I said.

'Where have you been?' Xiphias yelled to us. 'We've been looking everywhere for you.' We ran, hand in hand, to meet him, and he added: 'A fine pair you are.'

'We're very sorry, we're sure,' Daimon said in Xeno's best sarcastic manner. 'All we did was to go for a little walk. We didn't know we were doing anything wrong. We weren't to know that the Pragmapractors would start a revolution over our behaviour.'

'Don't be silly,' Xiphias said with uncharacteristic disapproval. 'Don't you realize that the Pragmapractors have gone on strike?'

'So we saw,' I said.

'Not those,' he said crossly. 'Well, yes, those, but I meant the others.'

'Which others?' Daimon and I asked together.

'The whole bleeding lot,' said Xiphias, 'if you'll pardon the inappropriate expression. All the Pragmapractors, except those up in the woods, and they'll join in soon enough, when they hear what's happened. They've all come out in sympathy with this lot, you see.'

'Well, good for them,' said Daimon, unperturbed. 'Solidarity is a rational strategy in the circumstances.'

'It's not quite so good for us,' Xiphias said grimly. 'Don't you realize what this means, Daimon? It means no service. No generator, no power, no eidophones, no film, no communications whatsoever. We've finally ground to a halt, so come along, do, and try to be helpful.'

'Come along where?' I protested ineffectually as Daimon, still holding me by the hand, joined Xiphias in hurrying towards the main door. 'What can we do? I don't see why Xeno's even bothered to call a meeting.'

'It's not Xeno who's called the meeting,' Xiphias explained, leading the way into the darkened entrance hall. 'It's Eimi. Now, will you hurry, Xanthe, please?'

21

I had seen little of Eimi since his installation as Chief Executive of our Institute. I hadn't particularly wanted to see anything of him, and it was obvious that he had never particularly wanted to see anything of me. Our few passing encounters had been imbued with a certain awkwardness, an awkwardness which pertained to our shared and most intimate knowledge of the circumstances of my father's death. This knowledge had remained undeclared on either side, but it stood between us, separating us as well as joining us. My knowledge was different from his knowledge. I had always suspected mine of being the smaller and, in my suspicion, I had resented Eimi for possessing the larger. A daughter can know what an assistant cannot know, and vice versa. That is the way it should have been. But my father rarely talked to me about the details of his work, much less about his feelings towards it, whereas I knew that he had sometimes confided in Eimi about more personal matters than their professional relationship would have seemed to warrant. His personal conversations with me had been largely gnomic on his part, and had typically consisted of either evasive or dogmatic statements. In other words, he had always talked to me, even after I had grown up, as an adult talks to a child, as an adult who doesn't quite believe in the humanity of children talks to a puzzled child. So, yes, I had been slightly jealous of Eimi. It seemed to me now that I had probably undervalued him, incapable as I had been of understanding why my father apparently preferred his company to mine. And I had probably undervalued him over the past three years in comparing him too closely with my father. Inevitably, I had found him wanting. Of course, Eimi and I had remained on good—that is, polite—social and working terms, but I could never relax in his company, and even his presence in the same room made me feel wary, as though I were being watched. I knew that he had been keeping an eye on me. But I had also been keeping an eye on him.

Such was the tenor of my thoughts as Daimon, Xiphias and I groped our way up the main staircase. I knew the stairs well enough, but now the steps seemed surprisingly shallow. And it was strange how much darker it was inside than it had been outside. The first floor corridor was lit by candles, the flickering light making us all look insubstantial. I felt more like a ghost than ever. On the second flight of stairs I caught up with Daimon, and held on to his arm for moral as well as physical support. By the time we had reached the third flight, the non-electric light no longer seemed eerie, but companionable in its understatement. Other people were going our way, not in crowds, but singly or in twos or threes. I could see, now that my eyes had become accustomed to the lesser light, that they were all either directors or programmers. I might have expected the general mood of such a procession to be grim, but people seemed to be talking to one another in snatches of subdued excitement, and indiscriminately, as though we were all old friends instead of just long-standing colleagues. Along the last stretch of corridor before the board-room we seemed to huddle together, waiting for one another, exchanging nervous but friendly smiles, our faces in the candle-light bright with goodwill, taut and ready for the impending challenge. It seemed to me that our behaviour expressed the recognition of our two-edged circumstance: we were all in this together, but we were not going to be together for long. The crisis had unified us, levelling us, but the unity was only temporary—that was why it could be accepted and even welcomed. I knew, as the others knew, that the crisis would also force us apart. Sooner or later, and probably sooner rather than later, we should all have to leave the Institute and go our separate ways.

Candle-light suited the sombre colours and heavy furniture in the board-room, at the same time capturing and mellowing the atmosphere. The long, dark table resembled a communal coffin, and we the mourners for the demise of our joint enterprise. From the walls our predecessors and our benefactors in their gilded frames looked down on us dispassionately. I thought: The innocence, the stoicism of the dead! There were enough seats at the table for only the usual number of directors, so some of us had to sit on the floor, but on this occasion we didn't divide ourselves according to rank. Xiphias found himself a chair next to Xeno's, while Daimon and I sat together on the carpet, leaning against each other, leaning against the wall. The room was nearly full. Eimi sat at the head of the table, watching us assemble. His face betrayed none of the anxiety I was sure he must be experiencing, but wore instead an expression of calculated concentration. He seemed to be counting us and finding our numbers still depleted. Every so often he would mutter an aside to one or other of his two assistants, who sat flanking him at the table. Their subsequent replies would receive a solemn nod in return. Then, after a thorough and seemingly final look around the room, he nodded briskly to each of them, as though giving a signal. They rose from their places at once, and left the room by a door behind him. At another signal from Eimi someone shut the door by which we had all come in, and the volume of our conversation dropped. Eimi's gavel rapped three times, we became silent, and waited to hear what he might have to say.

'I shan't detain you long,' he said pleasantly, as though at pains to make us feel comfortable, and to lessen any creeping sense of alarm. 'I think you all know more or less what has been happening, both in the last few hours and in the last few weeks. It has never been the policy of our Institute to stand still. Progress has always been our watchword. We are well-known for our forward-looking—and often controversial—lines of research. For this we have received both admiration and censure from the world outside the walls. Neither reaction has been altogether unexpected. We have always appreciated the former, and we have always pressed on, despite the weight of the latter. It is natural to want to react strongly to adverse criticism, but for the most part, most of us have not done so. Most of us have pursued instead the more difficult course of ignoring such criticism in favour of getting on with our work.'

Here I thought that Eimi looked significantly at me, but if he did, the significance was lost on me. Still looking in my direction, he went on: 'I say all this because, as I am sure you must know, more adverse criticism is inevitably on its way to us now. Some of it may be justified, as far as I am concerned. I am ultimately responsible for what goes on at the Institute and, as Chief Executive, I must be prepared to take the blame in equal measure with the praise. And I shall do so. None of you needs have any fears on that score. I can assure you that you have not put your careers in jeopardy by taking part in this latest Philophrenic experiment. For most of you, your only fault has been your loyalty, both to myself and to the principles of our profession. I am sure that any prospective employers are not going to hold that against you. I shall certainly take the trouble to tell them, whoever they may be, how much I have valued and appreciated it. And I should like to take this opportunity to thank you all for your co-operation, and for your devotion to the cause.'

He paused, as though expecting some response, but there was none, apart from a general rustling as people on the floor shifted their positions. We all knew that he was giving us the jam before the pill.

A voice from the floor near us then called out: 'Are you trying to tell us that the experiment has been a total failure?'

'I am trying to tell you nothing of the sort,' Eimi said firmly. 'I think that, in scientific terms, we still have a valid and viable experiment on our hands. And I have no intention of abandoning it at this stage—or, indeed, at any other.'

There was a bewildered silence, then the same voice, which I now identified as that of Ramnes, said: 'Perhaps I am being a little slow, but I should find it extremely helpful if you could tell us exactly what it is you intend to do.'

Some kind of agreement was voiced from the rest of us, and Eimi looked keenly round the room again before continuing his speech. 'What I intend to do,' he said, 'largely depends on what you want to do. It depends on the amount of support you are willing to grant me. Let me outline the position to you. I hardly need to tell you that we have achieved something here. We have produced robots superior to any anywhere in the world. They are as they are because we have dared to let them be as they are. No one else has given their robots the power that we have allowed to ours. Scientifically speaking, the results have been good. We have had strong, decisive and highly interesting reactions from our robots. I am sure that I am not alone in finding the whole experience most rewarding. And it seems to me that things now promise to become even more interesting. It would be the greatest pity if we were forced to discontinue, now that we have come so far. But I am very sorry to have to inform you that the Government is threatening to close down the Institute.'

That this was news to most of us was evident from the reception we gave to Eimi's words. He allowed us to exclaim and to comment for a few moments, having been distracted by the return of his assistants. Each of them carried a high stack of files which he set down on the table in front of Eimi before resuming his seat.

'These,' said Eimi, indicating the two stacks, 'are your personal files. I am returning them to you, perhaps temporarily, perhaps permanently. I am giving each and every one of you the opportunity to peruse his or her own file in the light of the information I have just given you. Each of you is going to have to make a decision concerning his or her career. You can choose to leave the Institute now, while you are still employable in other institutes or places of learning. Or you may choose to stay here until the completion of the experiment, by which time you may have become unemployable because of your connections with a disreputable experiment. This is a risk you may or may not feel prepared to take. The Government has asked me to give you this choice. It is the same choice as the one they gave me. They requested me to give up the present experiment, and to restore the Institute to its former organization where we, and we alone, would be the masters. Of course, they can do no more than request. This is an independent foundation, and the Government cannot determine the course our work is to take, although they do have the power to put a stop to that work altogether. However, our experiment does not transgress any laws, and to shut us down would be an extreme measure—too extreme not to make things awkward for them. They assured me that there were both national and international pressures behind their request. But I am a scientist, not a politician. I have the utmost respect for my calling, and would number it among the greatest of human endeavours. It transcends government. Whatever biases governments choose to read into my work is no concern of mine, and such biases cannot be allowed to interfere with scientific objectivity. I have always resented government interference, but at no time have I resented it more than I do at present. However, they now say we can carry on provided that I have enough voluntary support from the rest of you. They emphasized that the choices should be put fairly before you, and that no decisions should be made on the basis of ignorance. This process of decision involves everyone who wishes to carry on here in sending a written declaration to that effect to the Government. If these declarations are numerous enough, then we can continue. If not, we shall be shut down.' There was some applause here, but Eimi brushed it aside with an impatient gesture. 'Don't act too hastily,' he warned us. 'I don't want any of you to decide anything now. I want you to take your files away and to study them. Then I want you to come to me, singly and in your own time, and to tell me what you have decided.'

Someone asked: 'How long have we got?'

'I reckon we have something between two and three weeks,' said Eimi, sitting down. Then he pointed his gavel at Xeno.

Xeno stood up unsteadily, but he looked presentable enough. At any rate, his appearance was considerably neater than it had been of late. 'Meanwhile,' he said, 'we have to plan our strategy for the next two or three weeks—at least.'

'There is only one strategy,' someone called out, 'and that's to get the control-room back.'

'Easier said than done,' Xeno replied with a sigh. 'But I'm sure that we should all like to hear some practical suggestions.'

Suggestions followed, but it seemed to me that some of them were wildly impractical. They included surprising the guards and repossessing the control-room by force; kidnapping Phidias, and returning him to his fellows in exchange for the control-room; sabotaging the control-room's own generator, which was still in the hands of the Philophrenics; and tricking the guards into allowing one of us, or some of us, access to the activating machinery.

Xeno explained why none of these would work: 'The control-room is guarded twenty-four hours a day, with night-workers on a different activation cycle from day-workers. What this means, in effect, is that periods of activation are staggered. At any one time, you will find that three-quarters of the Philophrenics are in a state of activation. There is no question of our taking advantage of, say, two or three robotic guards while their fellows are all in a state of deactivation. No, the Philophrenics know better than to leave themselves open to such an attack.'

'They also know better than to trust us,' I whispered to Daimon.

'And they're quite right, aren't they?' he whispered back.

'They certainly can't trust Xeno,' I conceded.

'Neither can we,' said Daimon. 'We can't afford to. He should be barred from negotiating directly with them.'

'The Philophrenics,' Xeno was saying, 'are monitoring the control-room, including the door that leads to the generator, day and night. Besides, how many of you have ever tried to overwhelm a robot? It's never been necessary to do so, has it? But I have gone into the matter in some detail, and I can assure you that it's a great deal more difficult than you might think. The main trouble is that, except for their brains, they're invulnerable, and those brains are so well-protected that it would take a blow of more than human strength to damage one.'

'Violence,' Eimi interrupted, 'is unthinkable. Let us have no more suggestions of that nature.'

'Precisely,' said Xeno. 'The only way to overcome a robot is to deactivate it.'

'If it came to the crunch,' said Eimi, 'I personally should prefer trickery to violence but, in the circumstances, the two methods are equally unacceptable. If we want the experiment to continue, we must on no account antagonize the Philophrenics. Its success depends on mutual trust. More negotiations. More diplomacy. Those are what is needed, not all these extreme measures.'

'Precisely,' Xeno said again. 'I think I know Phidias well enough not to consider any other means of dealing with him.'

'The trouble is,' Daimon whispered to me, 'that Phidias also knows Xeno too well to trust him again.' And, without waiting for any comment from me, he stood up and addressed himself directly to Eimi: 'Let's use diplomacy to break up this present deadlock between the Philophrenics and the Pragmapractors. That is the obvious way of going about it. But I think any sustained attempt at diplomacy might be interpreted by them as interference. If they use the control-room wisely, why do we need to take it from them just yet?'

'They're not exactly using it wisely now,' Ramnes pointed out.

'But this dispute isn't serious,' Daimon argued to murmurs of disbelief. 'It can be resolved quickly and easily. All that's needed is a human arbitrator, acceptable to both sides.'

Eimi raised his eyebrows in mock-admiration, looking from Daimon to Xeno and back again. 'Do you really think so?' he asked.

'I think it's an excellent idea,' Xeno said, coming in as if on cue. 'Why don't we give it a try, anyway?'

'Well, then, Daimon,' Eimi said, 'how about it? Are you prepared to act upon your convictions? How would you like to try your hand at arbitration?'

'Certainly,' Daimon said levelly, and even I couldn't tell whether he had invited the assignment or was surprised by it.

'In that case,' said Eimi, 'I think that you and I should have a little conference right away. Oh, and you too, Xeno. If no one else has anything to say, the rest of you can now take your files and feel free to leave us.'

Apparently, no one did have anything to say, and the two assistants began to call out the names on the files. People began to edge towards that end of the room, but because the names were being called in alphabetical order I stayed where I was. Besides, I wanted to talk to Daimon.

'You may have succeeded in ousting Xeno,' I said to him, 'but do you know what you're letting yourself in for?'

'Not really,' he said. 'But don't worry, Xanthe. I may not be the best person for the job, but I feel sure that I can bring about some sort of reconciliation.'

'Oh, I'm sure you can,' I said with more warmth than I was actually feeling. 'If anyone can, you can. But you'll have to be so careful.'

He grinned. 'Don't you think I can be?' he asked.

His name was called, and I was saved the embarrassment of seeming to hesitate over my reply. Watching him making his way to the far end of the table, I noticed that there was now a slight but definitely debonair spring to his walk. I thought: If only I could have his confidence in the outcome of the arbitration. Whatever Daimon's virtues, tact was not one of them. When he sat down again beside me with his file, I noticed how new and thin it looked. The sight of it disturbed me. I thought: Daimon is young and strong, and unbeset with my stupid doubts and fears; he knows what he is doing, and his arbitration will probably succeed; there will be a place for him at the Institute as long as the Institute stands; there will always be a place for him somewhere; there will be no place anywhere else for me; we shall be separated; he will go on from strength to strength, and I shall be left behind. I sighed involuntarily. Daimon looked round at me.

'It's all so confusing,' I said, answering his look.

'It's all right, Xanthe,' he said gently. 'We don't have to come to a decision yet. Let's wait at least until the dispute is resolved.'

'Yes, let's,' I said at once, thankful for his misinterpretation.

'I don't think we can base our decision on the outcome of the dispute itself,' he went on, 'but I think we should give ourselves time to sort things out properly.'

'I suppose so,' I said, suspecting that this particular decision had, in fact, alreadybeen made for all of us.

'With any luck,' Daimon said, attempting to comfort me, 'the dispute will be solved, things will limp on for a while—'

'But how long can they limp on for?'

'I'd say it was a matter of weeks rather than months.'

I sighed again. 'I've lived here most of my adult life,' I said, speaking my thoughts this time, 'and a lot of my childhood too. I've never worked anywhere else. I can't imagine working anywhere else.'

'I know,' said Daimon. 'It's probably going to be more difficult for you than for most of the rest of us. But I think it may all come down to a matter of timing.'

'Timing?' I repeated. 'You mean we should get out while the going's good, before the whole place falls apart?'

'Not necessarily,' he said. 'All I mean is that we've got to be able to recognize our moment when it comes.'

'And it will come,' I said miserably, noting the absence of the conditional in his statement.

'Oh yes, Xanthe,' he said. 'For your own sake, don't cling to any false hopes. We are going to be squeezed out of here by the Philophrenics. Make no mistake about it.'

My name was called, and I went to get my file. It was considerably older and fatter than Daimon's. I didn't open it, hardly glanced at it. I knew what was in it, and suspected that a fresh perusal of its contents would only make me weep. I wanted to weep, as it was. I thought: I'm not going to read it; I'm not even going to open it; I shall lie to Eimi, and pretend that I've gone minutely over every word. Hugging my file to me, embracing my encapsulated life, I rejoined Daimon who was holding his between his thumb and finger, swinging it carelessly to and fro. The room was almost empty. I watched Xeno and Xiphias fetch their files and I thought: It's as though we were all being dismissed already, turned out into the world, clutching the gathered fragments of our pasts like so many shields against the impossible future.

It was time for me to leave. I wished Daimon good luck with his mission, and had nearly reached the door when Eimi called me back. At first, I thought he was asking me to stay, but when I turned round and saw him walking towards me, I knew that he intended to speak to me privately. My wariness of him returned, and I recalled the would-be significant look which had been directed at me. Reluctantly, I did the polite thing, and went to meet him.

'Well, Xanthe,' he said. 'I should particularly like you to take a good look at your file. I want you to make sure that you read everything in it very thoroughly. Will you do that? Will you make a special effort?'

'Of course,' I replied without warmth, wondering why I had been singled out. At the same time I was aware of Daimon watching us with some curiosity. My coolness had not gone unobserved.

'I think,' Eimi went on, 'that you may find some unfamiliar material in there. I should like you to give that your special attention. And then I think we should have a meeting, and discuss your reactions to the information you will have absorbed by then.'

'I hardly think I'm going to find any new information in my own file,' I began, and almost at once I understood why I was wrong. 'My father?' I asked Eimi.

He tapped the file, which I was still holding closely to me, with his forefinger. 'It's all in there,' he said.

22

Peering at my watch in the candle-light for what seemed like the hundredth time, I thought: One o'clock, and still no Daimon. I was forced to the conclusion that the process of arbitration was now under way, and then to the further conclusion that it had not yet succeeded. I tried to visualize Daimon in conference with the intractable master-builder, and saw the two of them metaphorically, their antlers locked in combat. But two stags, I told myself, at least belong to the same species; they speak the same language. I could see Phidias dismissing all gestures of friendliness, all concessions to inter-specific fraternity, as mere irrelevances, and not worth the breath with which they were uttered. However, it was at least possible, if only just possible, to visualize some sort of understanding between Daimon and Phidias emerging from the interview. It was when I tried to visualize Daimon communicating fruitfully with the Pragmapractors that my mind's eye returned nothing but a blank negative to me. There was no individual among them with whom I could see Daimon conferring. Was it possible for him to negotiate with an undifferentiated block of robotic stubbornness? Or would he just deliver a message to them all from Phidias, and wait for some kind of reaction? If Daimon knew as little about the Pragmapractors as I did—and he did—there was not much else he could do. I found myself hoping that he wouldn't be too unsympathetic towards them. They were the underdogs in the dispute, and it seemed to me that if they considered themselves to be badly treated, then they were being badly treated. They were not striking in order to amuse themselves: they were simply using the only weapon at their disposal. But at the same time I was thinking: I suppose Daimon won't be any kinder to the Pragmapractors than Phidias has been; he is no fonder of them than Phidias is.

In the circumstances, which I was powerless to alter, this was a depressing thought, and I decided that it was time for me to go to bed. I took the candle into the shower-cubicle with me, nervously wondering if there was going to be any hot water or, indeed, any water at all. There was, and it was still hot. As I washed, I was still thinking about Daimon, and wondering why it was that I seemed to have so little faith in his ability to accomplish his mission. I, of all people, should have accorded him that much loyalty. Perhaps I was only being over-anxious? Perhaps I resented being excluded from the mission? No, I didn't envy him his task in the slightest. But I wanted to be with him. I wanted to be there, helping him, advising him, and possibly preventing him from making some dreadful mistake. As if you could, I told myself at once, as if you could do any of those things. And I realized then that my unwillingness to concede success to Daimon arose from an unwillingness to admit how much he had changed, how much he had matured, since he had come to the Institute. He could do without my help or advice. Although I didn't like the thought, I had no choice but to accept it. There was nothing I could do but go on waiting.

The wait, however, was beginning to irk me. I got into bed, blew out the candle, lay down and shut my eyes, but nothing happened. Nothing went on happening for some time. I was wide awake, and likely to remain that way. Taking the candle with me, I began to look along the bookshelves for something suitable to read, something familiar and rhythmical enough to lull me into sleep, but there was no one title that tempted me. I was just wondering whether to pay a visit to Daimon's room, and to look through his less familiar and therefore more interesting collection, when I remembered my file. Perhaps I ought to read it right away, and get it over and done with. Since Eimi's insistent request the task had become doubly repugnant to me. I thought with distaste of his 'additional material': it would probably include my father's death certificate, a needless piece of information, and a memento which I had no wish to see again, much less to keep. Perhaps there would even be a suicide note, a shiny, tidy photocopy untouched by my father himself, untouched by either the bloody hands of the murderer or the sweaty hands of the victim. No, thanks. Such a thing, if it existed, was something I could do without.

But my curiosity was beginning to overcome my repugnance. I fetched the file from my desk, where it had been lying unheeded, and took it back to bed with me, replacing the lighted candle, plus one spare, on the table beside me. Those bulging pages promised a long vigil. In an attempt to be methodical, and to fulfil my undertaking to Eimi, I started at the beginning. There was my birth certificate, together with evidence of vaccinations against various diseases, report cards from school, and so on. Here, supposedly, were my beginnings. They seemed to have nothing to do with me, the person I now was, but to belong to a different era, several faded generations ago. More reports, more certificates. Achievements, distinctions, references. Was this really what my life amounted to? And there was the expected death certificate, inserted in its correct chronological position. Why, I wondered, had it been removed from my father's file? And what had happened to the rest of his file, anyway? What did happen to people's files, once they had died? If the files normally remained where they were, in the information-room, what was the point of removing my father's death certificate from its normal and therefore easily accessible place? It was supposed to hold some significance for me. It was supposed to point towards the right decision for me, telling me whether to go or to stay. I stared at it, willing it to speak. I simply couldn't get the message—if message there were.

I tried to think. Was I missing something obvious? And it seemed to me that there were two reasons why my father's death could be a sign that said stay. The first was that my father had wilfully interrupted his own work at the Institute, and that it was my duty to carry on where he had left off, albeit in a humbler capacity. I should devote my life to repaying the Institute as best as I could, being a piece of my father, for his loss. The second reason was simply that my father had died in the service of the Institute, and that I was expected to show similar tenacity, should the occasion arise. But there was also a reason why my father's death said go. It ran like this: my father had disgraced the Institute, and the Institute had shown me kindness in keeping me on, supplying me with both a home and a job; but, in a crisis, kindness can be dispensed with, especially when its recipients find themselves closely associated with experiments which, even without their contribution, have incurred the suspicion and disapproval of the Government. That was another thing about crises: people liked to find a Jonah. Perhaps Eimi thought that he had found me. Perhaps, perhaps . . . I screwed up the piece of paper in my hand, and threw it on to the floor. It told me absolutely nothing. Even what it purported to tell me was something I didn't want to know, and was therefore useless to me.

Angrily I flipped through copies of my progress reports to Xeno, Xeno's progress reports on me, cullings from my medical record, notes on my social activities, and other information there was no need for me to read in order to know it. I had nearly skimmed through to the end when I realized that there was a wad of papers there, forming a sort of appendix. The papers were stapled together, and constituted a photocopy of a typewritten manuscript. A short accompanying note, addressed to Eimi, described the manuscript as a condensation of a larger one, a collection of memoirs. Then it said: Please show the enclosed to my daughter when you consider the time to be ripe. The first page bore the Institute's crest and letterhead, and a date which alleged the manuscript to be just over three years old. Underneath was the title, 'A Testament of Failure', and the name of its author, my father.

I stared unwillingly at this title page. How was it possible to associate my father with failure when his whole career, up to the very end, had been synonymous with success? No one had seen him as a failure. And if he had been one in his own eyes, then those eyes must have been clouded over with madness, or blinded by some dazzling and impossible idea of perfection. For as long as I could remember, my father had been eminent, respected, admired. People came from all over the world to talk to him about his work, and were proud even to have shaken his hand. People sought his advice, and usually got it, over any problems which they thought to be even remotely connected with robotics. People asked him to travel, with all expenses paid, and a fat fee besides, to all sorts of institutions in all sorts of places, to speak in person to their members. People—even some he had never heard of—heaped honours on him. Where was the failure in all this? I hardly dared to turn the page. When I did, and when I had read the first sentence, I was so horror-struck that I had to read on. This is what I read.

'I didn't kill my wife, but I might just as well have done so. If this statement seems over-dramatic to you when you read this for the first time, you will probably find yourself in agreement with me by the time you have read what it is I have to say, and certainly by the time you have also read my memoirs.

'You never met my wife. When you arrived at the Institute to take up your position as my chief assistant, she was already dead. I suppose you knew that she had died of leukaemia. And, because you were taking over her work, you knew that she had been my assistant. I don't know what else you knew about her. What I want you to know now is that my wife was the most brilliant robotics scholar I have ever encountered. She was, indeed, a scholar in the true sense of the word: meticulous, far-seeking and original. It was this originality that made her far more than even the most distinguished of scholars. Perhaps I was too close to her, perhaps I was reluctant to admit the superiority of her scholarship to my own, but until the very end of her life-time I did not fully recognize her originality, never quite believed that her peculiar combination of intellect and intuition could come up with the right answers. However, I now think that it elevated her into the ranks of genius.

'Another melodramatic remark, you may think. But let me tell you that my wife was the true inventor of the Philophrenics. Yes, it is true. She had all the ideas, and I took all the credit. As you may or may not know, my wife was not only a shy and retiring woman, but for most of her life she was a sick one too. It was that fragility of hers which had originally appealed to me. But it was deceptive. Her physical appearance may have been extremely feminine, but I can assure you that it was a vessel for a mind of the toughest and most masculine cast. However, she was almost completely without personal ambition, and utterly lacking in the need for personal glory which besets so many of our profession, myself included. In a strange way, she seemed to be already fulfilled. Years before the programming of the first Philophrenic began, she had worked out her own scheme for a series of robots very like the ones we are now engaged with. While she was working on the scheme, she confided in me, more as her husband than as her boss, and I encouraged her as best I could. At that time I was still working on electronic circuit-paths, and secretly thought that her scheme sounded far too grandiose to be of any immediate use. So I simply let her get on with it. Every so often I would ask her how her research was going, and she would give me some non-committal reply, which satisfied me at the time. And so it went on.

'At least, so it went on until the scheme was finished, fully drawn up. Then I had to consider it, not as a husband perusing some charming little idea which had kept his wife so happily occupied for so long, but as a supervisor, examining a highly intelligent pupil's thesis. And I was astonished at what I found. It was a brilliant piece of research. I knew at once that the scheme would work—or, at least, I was as sure as it is possible to be in the absence of practical verification. However, I didn't say so, either to my wife or to anyone else. That was my first, perhaps deliberate, mistake. She must have known as well as I did that her scheme would work, but when I failed to tell her of my certainty and to congratulate her as fully as I might have done on her achievement, it appeared that she began to lose confidence in it. I went through her thesis with her, step by step. For every rational progression I offered a contrary but still rational one, and for every imaginative leap, a thicket of conditionals. I managed to persuade both her and myself that this was being done in the interests of science. I told her that the whole thing would need thorough investigation by a team of experts before we could even think of putting it into practice, and that this would take time. In effect, I was shelving her scheme. But all the time my conviction as to its rightness was growing. My wife readily agreed to my strictures, but it was obvious that she was disappointed. I think she may have already been ill at this time, because from then on there was a marked deterioration in both her health and her work. She had been working frantically hard on her scheme, and now seemed to relax with a vengeance. She began to make mistakes, and to give me cause to complain of her inattention. It seemed to me that she had lost something of her will. Shortly after this, we learned the nature of her illness.

'We knew it to be fatal, of course. During those last months we became very close, and talked a great deal to each other about matters which we had never discussed before. They were generally of a personal nature. The subject of our work did not take up much of our time. And the one thing she positively did not want mentioned was her scheme. At first I thought that this was because she regarded the scheme as a failure, in the same way that she seemed to regard her own early and approaching death as some sort of failure on her part. But I soon came to realize that her attitude to the scheme was one of indifference. It was imbued for her with the futility of all human endeavour. Her eyes, her mind, were set on other, larger things. So I continued to shelve the scheme. It was only a year or so after her death that I began to put it into operation. And then, as you know, I claimed it as my own original work.

'What sort of mitigation can I plead for my actions? I can hardly claim to have been so crazed with grief that I didn't know what I was doing. I did feel the bitterest grief at her death, but it was a grief I had been prepared for. And I was certainly not crazed enough to have forgotten, or to have been unaware of, one of the principal tenets of our profession, namely that credit should be given where credit is due. I didn't even attempt to rationalize my course of action by telling myself that my wife was dead, and therefore couldn't be hurt by what I did; that she would have wanted me to be successful in my career, and would have wanted to help me towards that success; or that, anyway, all her ideas had come from me in the first place because I had been her teacher. No, I saw an opportunity to fulfil my ambitions, and to gain some glory for myself before I too died and was forgotten. Being an ambitious man, I took the opportunity with both hands. The only justification I allowed myself was what now seems like a crazy notion. It was that my wife had bequeathed the scheme to me, to do what I liked with. And that is exactly what I did. The rest, as they say, is history.

'I became Chief Executive of the Institute. I was famous and respected. I worked hard and enjoyed my work. My daughter was almost grown up. Everything seemed to be going well for me, and continued to do so for several years. Then something terrible happened to me. This thing was so intangible and yet so devastating. Even now, I don't know how to describe it. It was this—I lost faith in robotics. I don't know how it happened, or when it started to happen, but I definitely knew it when it did happen. It seemed like a huge and unexpected irony, a punishment for my presumption in violating the rules of the discipline, and for taking upon myself the title, so to speak, of Mr. Robotics. Loss of faith is a vague concept to those who have never experienced it, vaguer still to those who have never possessed faith in the first place. How can I explain? I could say that the earth seemed to open beneath my feet, or that the sky overhead grew dark and menacing. But both assertions, though accurate enough, seem inadequate and imprecise. Let me try to go into some of my reasons instead.

'Don't believe for a moment that I think the science of robotics to be a failure in itself. It is nothing of the sort. Its peculiar failure lies in its success. It is successful now, and will be even more successful in the future. And—I say this with the greatest sorrow—its success will eventually be to the detriment of human beings. We have created the Philophrenics in our own image. Latterly, they have been created less in the realistic image of a human being, but according to some concept of an ideal one. This has been the trend, whether conscious or unconscious. Consciously we have been using the

Philophrenics to find out more about ourselves, what we are, and how we function. And I think that we have gained in self-knowledge. But along with this practical purpose, now partially fulfilled, there has always been another one, more or less unadmitted. It has been an idealistic purpose. We have aspired to create a being in some way superior to ourselves. A perfect human being is an impossibility. A perfect robot is not. Sooner or later we are going to create one. And with that creation, we shall have begun the process of our own destruction. Mankind will suffer a massive loss of confidence, a crippling loss of identity. More than ever we shall be strangers in our own world. Less than ever shall we be able to accept our unique and paradoxical position in that world. It will be then that we shall lose our will to survive.

'In this knowledge, I have already lost that will. I have no wish to see the day when that loss becomes universal. I bear a terrible burden of responsibility, a terrible burden of guilt, and I can bear it no longer. My memoirs, which I entrust to your care, will tell the world the whole story. Perhaps they will also act as a salutary warning to those of you engaged in the study of robotics. Some doors should be left unopened, however inviting. Perhaps my warning will not come too late. If so, I shall not have lived entirely in vain.'

Disbelief. That was all I felt at first. I turned back to the beginning, and began to read the testament through again, this time more slowly, this time paying more attention to its manner of presentation. There was no doubt that the style was my father's. Those short sentences, which I had always regarded as tokens of his straightforwardness, were unmistakably his. And in many other small ways, the style bespoke the man to such an extent that I could almost imagine that I was hearing his voice. If the manuscript was a forgery, then it was a very clever one. But what on earth would be the point of such cleverness? There was no need to discredit my father. His standing was low enough, as it was. And Eimi—for he alone had the opportunity for forgery—was himself discredited by the manuscript in as much as he had disregarded my father's request for the publication of his memoirs. Until that moment I had known nothing of the memoirs, and I felt that I should have been told at least of their existence. But I could see, from Eimi's point of view, why this revelation had not been made. To inform me would have been tantamount to the publication I should probably have demanded. Therefore, silence to safeguard silence. I could hardly blame Eimi for decisions taken in what he believed to be the best interests of our profession, but I could, by agreeing with my father, accuse him of having been wrong. The more I thought about it, the more the testament seemed to resound to the ring of truth.

Having reluctantly established the authenticity of the document, I began to ponder on its content. Certain facts had to be accepted at face value. These were that the theory of robotics owed more to my mother than to my father; that my father had denied my mother's contribution to that theory, and had instead claimed it as his own; that my father had subsequently, if not consequently, become disillusioned with both the theory and the practice of robotics; that my father had killed himself. There were no other facts. The reasons for the suicide remained a matter for speculation. Nor could I accept as a fact the notion that my father had been a cheat and a liar. Surely, he had not been entirely either? After all, had he not put my mother's ideas into practice? My father would have had to do it for her, whether she had lived or died, and some of the credit would have gone to him quite naturally and quite properly. The question I had to ask myself was how far his later disillusionment had been due to a moral concern for the future of mankind, and how far to a sense of guilt, however misplaced or exaggerated? He had taken the credit for my mother's ideas, and so he had to take the blame for what he saw as their fatal success. I thought: How terrible it must have been for him; how terrible to have been unable to find a way out, to find any path that could lead him to salvation.

But was the suicide necessary? Had it really been necessary to take that final step? I found that difficult to believe. As far as the plagiarism was concerned, he could have made a public confession with the publication of his memoirs, and received public absolution. Ah, but he would still have had to live with himself; he would still have had to receive his own absolution. Was that what he found so difficult to obtain? As for his vision of the inevitable future, I couldn't begin to assess it. All I knew was that I could feel its barbs catching in my conscience. But such a sensation didn't seem to demand my death. It didn't even seem to demand his. I lay down and stared up at the dark skylight, trying, by an effort of imagination, to put myself in my father's place. What would I have done? My mind, veering away from so direct a question, turned itself to thoughts of both my father and my mother, their relationship, their individuality, their deadness.

I was so absorbed in these and related speculations that I didn't even notice Daimon come into the room. I sat up at once, unable to understand at first what he was doing there, and where he had come from. Then I remembered.

'Oh Daimon, what happened?' I asked. 'Were you successful?'

'What do you think?' he asked in reply, and I noticed that he was smiling. 'Didn't you notice that the lights had come on again? Or were you asleep?'

'No,' I said, looking round at the lit room and the dead candle, and realizing that the electricity must have been restored for some time. 'I didn't notice. You see, I was reading my file, and—'

Daimon interrupted me. 'Oh, Xanthe,' he said, coming round to the side of the bed and sitting down heavily. 'I wish you'd been there. I wish you could have heard me. You'd have been proud of me.'

I tried to adjust myself to the situation and to Daimon's evident elation. 'What happened?' I asked again.

Daimon took hold of my hands. 'It was a cinch,' he said. 'I knew it would be. I know Phidias. I knew that the creation of this new environment was more important to him than anything else. I knew that his pride in that project outweighed his pride in standing up to the Pragmapractors. You know, he didn't know what to do next. He was just sitting there, waiting for someone to intervene. So I didn't say much. In fact, I refused to listen to him. I just asked him to activate the Pragmapractors so that I could talk to them. Then I went to the Pragmapractors and talked to them first, although Eimi had advised me to start with Phidias. But I knew what I was doing. I got a list of demands from the Pragmapractors. It all seemed pretty reasonable to me, and I said so. I said so to Phidias too. He looked the list over and agreed to everything at once, without any argument. You see, I told you, I told everyone, that the dispute wasn't serious.'

'Well, that's marvellous, Daimon,' I said. 'I might have known—'

Again, he interrupted me. 'Eimi was so pleased with me,' he went on. 'But really it was nothing. Both sides trusted me because they knew I was sufficiently subordinate in the scheme of things to be sufficiently neutral.'

'You really mean it's all over?' I asked, lying back.

'Well,' said Daimon, his face momentarily lapsing out of its elation, 'let's say that it's over for the time being. I can't claim to have achieved anything permanent. You see, neither side felt able to furnish any long-term guarantees. The present agreement will be in operation until the new Philophrenic wing is finished—that's all.'

'But you think we should stay?' I asked. And I knew, in that instant, that Daimon now wanted to stay more than I did.

'Oh, for the moment, yes,' he said confidently.

'Daimon,' I said deliberately, reaching for my file, 'there is something else I think you should know about before coming to a decision—'

'Don't let's think about it now,' he said, lying down beside me, and drawing me towards him. 'The conquering hero has returned. Doesn't he get a hero's welcome?'

His closeness confused me, dissipating my sense of urgency. 'Yes, of course,' I murmured, letting the file drop to the floor. After all, there was nothing of such immediate importance to be said that it couldn't wait until the morning.

23

The nurse, taking my specimen bottle from me, dropped it on the floor. Luckily, it was made of plastic, and so didn't break.

'I'm sorry,' she said. 'I don't know what's the matter with me. I keep dropping things these days. I'm all fingers and thumbs—I mean, all thumbs.'

'Have you been very busy here lately?' I asked her, unable to believe that there had been any sudden demand on the resources of the analytical laboratory.

'Not specially,' she said. 'It's just that we're so short-staffed since the strike. I don't quite know why, but things haven't been the same around here since then.'

'How many people have left?' I asked.

'Oh, only two have actually left so far,' she said. 'But there's been a lot of absenteeism. And several people have given in their notice. I can't say I blame them. To tell you the truth, I'm thinking of doing the same thing myself.'

'Why is that?' I asked. 'Is it really so awful working here? I thought things were more or less back to normal.'

'I don't know about that,' she said. 'Haven't you heard the rumour that's going round? They say the Government is going to close the whole place down.'

'Why would they want to do that?' I asked quickly.

'You should know,' she said, undeceived. 'It's all because of what's happening in your section. They say it's something to do with the Philophrenics getting out of hand. Well, anyone can see that they are. And, naturally enough, people don't like it.'

'And you think that's why so many people are leaving?' I asked her cautiously.

'Oh, of course,' she said. 'It's not just in this department, you know. A friend of mine who works over at the factory told me that there are hardly any human beings left there now. And the frightening thing is that the Pragmapractors seem to be managing perfectly well without them.'

'Why is that frightening?' I asked.

'Well, isn't it?' she countered. 'If you'd like to take a seat, I'll just go and do the test for you. It'll only take a minute or two.'

She left with my bottle, and I sat down on a chair next to the reception desk. There was no one else about, and I was struck once more by how often I seemed to be the only person in a particular place at a particular time. I thought: Surely not that many people have left the Institute? And I decided that people were probably staying in their rooms because everyone's workload had diminished since the Philophrenics' takeover, diminished to such an extent that there was little reason to go anywhere. But then, why weren't people pursuing some sort of leisure activities? Here was the ideal opportunity to do so. Perhaps they were frightened, as the nurse had implied. But what were they frightened of? Destruction? Chaos? Or the mirroring fear they might discover in the faces of their colleagues? I thought: We human beings seem to be in the process of opting out, and it's our absence that's causing the tension among us. I looked out of the window, across the empty lawn, and up the slope towards where the woods had been. The trees, our living allies against the immortal machines, had all gone. Everything seemed so still, perhaps because nothing remained that was tall enough to move visibly, or perhaps because the whole Institute was waiting, lying low, to see what would happen next. And what would happen next? I didn't know. I only knew what I thought was going to happen to me.

The nurse came back with a slip of paper, which she handed to me. 'It's positive,' she said, 'are you pleased?'

Was I? I had thought that I should be but, now that my suspicions had been confirmed, I wasn't quite so sure. Wasn't it folly to bring a child into the world at such a time? And yet, I was smiling. 'I'm delighted,' I said.

The nurse, who had been looking doubtfully at me, now smiled too. 'Isn't it strange,' she said, 'how babies are always signs of hope, no matter what a terrible state the world is in?'

'Well, they have to be, don't they?' I said in a practical tone of voice, but finding myself unaccountably moved by her suggestion. 'Otherwise, the human race wouldn't have survived this long.'

'Yes, we've survived,' she said, sighing as though the notion of survival bothered her. 'Well, I see from your record that this is your first pregnancy. Also, that you're thirty-five years old—'

'That's not old enough to make it dangerous, is it?' I asked quickly.

'Oh, not necessarily,' she said, 'but it's hardly the ideal age at which to have one's first baby. I think you must recognize that. If you take that slip over to Medical, they'll give you an appointment for a complete examination. If I were you, I'd make it as soon as possible.'

I took the slip, thanked her, and left. I was thinking: I'm actually pregnant; I, Xanthe, am pregnant. I kept repeating the statement to myself, trying it out, but I still didn't quite believe it. I felt no different, and certainly not sick or faint in the slightest. As I walked through the pine-scented corridors leading to the Medical Block, I had a strange feeling of being claimed by my surroundings. From now on, my body was not to be my own. Not only had it been taken over by a new life burrowing, nesting and already growing there inside me, but soon it would also become the property of nurses and doctors, experts under whose neutral hands and eyes it would be measured and manipulated, and its smallest changes monitored. I shrank from yielding sovereignty over what was my own. Did I really want a baby? Did I really want to go through with the process of childbirth? Vistas of pain and blood opened in front of me, and I was afraid. I saw myself bovine and lumbering instead of trim and light of foot. I saw myself swollen with blood, with milk, with mucus, awash with sticky liquid, and reduced to some inchoate state of being, the primeval state of ooze and flow from which all life is formed. I didn't want to re-enter that state, and yet I wanted to know what it was like. It was the morass of my own femininity. And in it my body, which would now become more myself than it had ever been, would find its teleological purpose fulfilled. That nebulous but determined thing, nature, had taken over. I thought: This could be the greatest adventure of my life.

It seemed odd at first that the waiting-room was so full when everywhere else in the Institute was so empty. I thought: Perhaps this is where everyone is; everyone is ill. The room was misty with steam, its occupants well wrapped up in outdoor clothes and crowded together, each one huddling into his scarf or behind his coat collar. There was a great deal of sniffling and snuffling, and the occasional retching cough. The weather had been unusually bright and benign for November, and I couldn't help wondering how many of the people surrounding me were taking refuge in illness against the necessity of taking any action to alter the precarious state of affairs which now prevailed at the Institute. And how many had found a new, and perhaps excessive, interest in their own bodies, now that they had been deprived of their usual occupations, and needed to occupy somehow the long hours of enforced leisure? I made my way through the congested rows of chairs to the reception desk, and handed my slip of paper to the girl who sat there. She took it without looking at me.

'Oh, not another one,' she muttered, frowning over the information it conveyed.

'I'm terribly sorry,' I said with all the dignity I could muster, taken aback as I was by this reception. 'I hate to be a nuisance, but all I want is an appointment.'

She looked up at me. 'Oh, I'm sorry,' she said. 'It's just that Ante-natal is rushed off its feet. You wouldn't believe the number of pregnancies we've had lately.'

Somewhat floored by this piece of information, I asked: 'Why is that, do you think?'

She said: 'I wouldn't know, but the doctors seem to have various theories about it.'

'Such as?' I asked, trying to come up with one myself. 'Do they think people have been forgetting to take their pills because their routine has been upset?'

'That's one theory,' she said. 'Another is that the birth rate always goes up in a crisis. My own theory is much simpler. I think that a lot of conceiving went on on the night of the strike, when all the power was cut off, and people had nothing else to do. Quite a few were probably taken by surprise.'

Her perspicacity both startled and amused me. 'Quite likely,' I said.

She gave me a knowing look. 'Oh well,' she said. 'Rather you than me. Let's see now. I'm afraid I can't fit you in until next Monday afternoon. Three-thirty. Will that do?'

'It'll have to,' I said pleasantly, 'won't it?'

It was good to get out of the stuffy waiting-room and into the crisp autumnal air. I began to walk, rapidly at first, then slowing my pace a little, towards the main building and Daimon. The sun shone weakly, but there was enough of it to be caught and held prismatically by the glass expanse of Phidias's studio in the distance. I found myself thinking that perhaps it didn't look so bad, after all. At least, it wasn't downright ugly, as it could so easily have been. In itself, it even had a certain beauty, a certain grandeur. But I was surprised to find myself thinking any such thing. Was I beginning to be thankful for small mercies, to count my blessings? That had never been one of my habits of mind. Was it, then, the very first fruit of motherhood? I thought: I am already prepared to accept the world, or rather, the small world of the Institute, more easily because my child is going to have to live in it. But would the Institute still provide a haven in seven months' time? Did I even want it to? My father's testament had forced me to think seriously about leaving the place. Eimi's subsequent admission that he had destroyed my father's memoirs had pushed me further in the direction of leaving. But Daimon had pulled me back again. Now I was wavering. But I was surprised to find that these and similar questions bothered me less than they had done two or more months before. They seemed peripheral in relation to the magnitude of the central event, the birth itself. A phrase came into my head, an old text from an outworn religion: The Lord will provide. Really, Xanthe, I told myself, your complacency is becoming ridiculous; no one is going to provide anything; even Daimon can only provide what he can; you are going to have to shift for yourself. But even this latter prospect didn't pierce me with anxiety. And, however much I upbraided myself, I couldn't feel that my optimism was altogether wrong. It was sure to be short-lived enough, so I allowed myself to dally with it, using it to protect both myself and my unborn child. I wondered: Do all mothers do the same?

Then I thought of my own mother. Her image came into my mind with a force and a clarity I had not known that it still possessed. It had been my habit to think less of her, in more ways than one, than I had thought of my father. Even having read his testament, I hadn't been able to visualize her as anything other than a vaguely comforting presence, vague in her response to me, and comforting mainly because of the predictability of that response. I remembered myself as being demanding, forever demanding something that she never gave, or couldn't give, or perhaps didn't know how to give. I remembered following her about from room to room, clutching on to her skirt, unwilling to let her out of my sight for even a moment. I remembered that she tolerated me, giving me what seemed to be my due, but no more. She would break off her work with a patient expression to talk to me and to listen to me. Oh, how I had tried to hold her attention with my chatter, with my questions, even with my tears! And what a victory I won every time she took her glasses off, and laid her papers to one side to take me on her knee. It had been illogical of me to see her willingness to abandon her work in my favour—a willingness my father never showed—as an indication of her lesser importance. Why had I not also seen her gesture as an indication of her greater kindness, perhaps even her greater affection? Just like my father, I had been blind to her truer virtues. And now there was no way to repair that fault. There were no witnesses who could help me bind together the loose wires of my recollection so as to connect and mend them.

I was walking towards the creche. It would have been easier and more direct to walk towards the main door, but I found myself making the detour as though drawn there by a new relevance. I normally found the creche an uncongenial place, partly because of the noise, partly because of the smells, and partly—I have to confess—because of Veronica. But now I felt curious about it. How did it work? How many children were there, and how old were they? How were they looked after? What did they learn? I had no intention of questioning anyone along those lines, but hoped to satisfy myself by wandering around and taking a look at the day-to-day proceedings. As I approached the front door, I realized that I was going to feel foolish and unable to justify my presence, once I was inside. Nevertheless, I went in and walked along the corridor, stopping every now and then to look into the rooms. I was reminded, against my well-disposed will, of a zoo. The children seemed to belong to a different species, one that was wilder, clumsier, and so much less disciplined than my own. And I had no wish to enter the cages. I remained in the corridor, staring through the glass at a room littered with toys, and full of small children scampering about in all directions. What I saw still didn't make sense to me, although I supposed that there was some method to be apprehended in the seeming muddle.

'Are you looking for someone?' a voice behind me asked in a pleasant but pointed tone.

I turned round to see a cool-looking woman of about Veronica's age, and dressed in a similar uniform to hers. 'Not really,' I told her. 'I was just having a look. Is that all right?'

'You're Xanthe, aren't you?' she said. 'I thought I recognized you. I'm Begonia.'

It was only then that I recognized her. 'Oh, hullo,' I said, somewhat embarrassedly.

'You're not really interested in babies, are you?' she asked, looking at me intently. 'At least, not if what Veronica says is true.'

I didn't ask what Veronica had said, being able to guess all too well. 'You don't have to have had any of your own to be interested in them,' I said.

'True,' she said. 'Well, what can I show you? Which age group are you interested in? The toddlers? The crawlers? Or the teeny tinies?'

'Are there any new-born babies?' I asked, slightly put off by the archness of her categories.

Begonia gave me another intent look before replying. 'Yes,' she said. 'We've got one or two. Come this way, and I'll show you.'

I followed her along the corridor, feeling ill at ease and out of place, and was suddenly afraid that Begonia might ask me to hold one of the babies. I didn't want to expose my awkwardness to her scrutiny. I found babies unattractive and rather frightening, and I knew I shouldn't be able to conceal either of those attitudes from her professional eye. But when we reached the new-born nursery, I was only allowed as far as the ante-room. The babies remained on the other side of a large sheet of plate glass. There were three cots. In two of them, the babies were wrapped up and tucked in so snugly that I could only see the tops of their heads, their eyes screwed up in sleep, and their curiously flat noses. One of them looked as though it was sucking its thumb. The third baby had kicked its blanket off, and was wide awake, looking round the room as brightly as it could with its unfocusing primary-blue eyes. It was waving its arms and legs in what appeared to be a random manner, and as though it couldn't bear to stay still.

'That's Edmund,' Begonia said, indicating the lively baby. 'He's a little rascal. But obviously highly intelligent.' I nodded, pretending to see the obviousness, and she said: 'When is it due, Xanthe?'

'Due?' I repeated, thinking that she couldn't possibly mean what I, in my pre-occupied state, understood her to mean.

'Well, it's obvious, isn't it?' she said. 'I mean, this sudden interest of yours in new-born babies. It can only mean one thing. That you're pregnant. I see it all the time.'

'Yes, you're right,' I said rather sheepishly. I wasn't at all sure that I liked being so much of a stock figure, and so transparent.

'Daimon?' Begonia asked me.

'Yes, Daimon is the father,' I said, impressed by her directness. But the words had a strange ring to them. How could Daimon be a father? It seemed an even less appropriate role for him than that of mother was for me. At least, I couldn't deny my motherhood. Fatherhood was altogether a more nebulous state to be in. What would Daimon think of it?

'Well, that really is ironic,' Begonia was saying. 'Do you know where Veronica is? Do you know where she's just gone?'

'No,' I said, suddenly apprehensive.

'She's gone to see Daimon,' said Begonia, sitting down on the nearest chair as though suddenly weary. I sat down next to her, unaccountably weak at the knees, and waited for her to continue. 'She's gone to see Daimon,' she said, 'to tell him that she's pregnant.'

There was a silence, during which my thoughts ran through many a maze of incredulity, pain, and indignation. 'And is she?' I asked faintly.

'Of course not,' said Begonia. 'It's just another of Veronica's little tricks. After all, she's tried everything else. By the way, she's so dumb that she doesn't even know about you and Daimon.'

'Or about you?' I asked, still faintly.

She sighed. 'Oh, Xanthe, that was nothing,' she said. 'Don't hold it against me. It didn't mean a thing. You know what it's like. We'd had a good time that evening, and one thing—'

'You don't have to explain,' I said hurriedly, ashamed of myself. I had spoken out of an impulse to have things open between us, but I could see now that I had gone the wrong way about it. 'I shouldn't have mentioned it,' I said.

'Oh, it doesn't matter,' she said. 'As long as we understand each other. But all the same, I'd be grateful if you didn't mention it to Veronica. I couldn't face yet another scene with her.'

I said: 'Don't worry. I don't intend to mention anything to Veronica, unless I have to.'

Begonia said: 'I don't blame you. She can be very vindictive, if she puts her mind to it.'

We smiled ruefully at each other. I found myself thinking how likeable Begonia was, and how patient she had to be with Veronica. I was just wondering if she had any children of her own when she said: 'Well, aren't you going to go back there to find out what's going on?'

'Oh, no,' I said. 'It's none of my business.'

'You mean you're afraid of a show-down with Veronica,' she said.

'Maybe,' I admitted.

'But don't you think,' she persisted, 'that perhaps Daimon needs your help with her?'

This hadn't occurred to me. I said: 'My help? Surely that's the last thing he needs in the circumstances?'

'He doesn't know how to cope with Veronica, you know,' Begonia said. 'He's probably never said anything to you on the subject because, well, because I'm sure you have better things to talk about. But he told me that he just didn't know how to react to those emotional onslaughts of hers. And that's how he got so entangled with her in the first place. By taking the line of least resistance.'

'I see,' I said. 'But what do you think I can do?'

Begonia smiled hesitantly at me. 'I think you should do the very thing I'm always trying to avoid myself—confront her with the truth.'

'You mean,' I asked her, 'that I should just walk in there, and announce that I'm pregnant?'

'Yes,' said Begonia. 'I know it will be difficult, but it will save a lot of trouble, in the long run—for both you and Daimon.'

I knew that what she said was true. 'I'll try,' I said, standing up again with what I thought to be a fair imitation of resolve.

'Good luck,' said Begonia. 'And, if you want one other piece of advice, it's this: don't be afraid of hurting Veronica's feelings. She's not as vulnerable as she pretends to be.'

As I began to make my way back to the west wing, I was thinking: Begonia is the only woman for whom and from whom I have felt any friendship since Phidia left the Institute. This fact strengthened my resolve, and my pace quickened. I didn't really know how I was going to deal with Veronica. Wouldn't it be cruel to flaunt my true pregnancy against her false one? But, then, it seemed that there was nothing I could do or say that could be kind. Perhaps it was necessary to be cruel, as Begonia had hinted. It wouldn't be that difficult. All I had to do was to walk into Daimon's room and announce the result of my test, as I had intended to do all along. At the same time, I couldn't but put myself in Veronica's place, and then imagine all the hurt and chagrin she must surely feel. I told myself: She's got to know sooner or later; sooner or later she's got to become undeluded. I was breathless by the time I had reached the top flight of our stairs, but I found myself running along the corridor to Daimon's room. For a moment I stopped there to regain my breath. I could hear two voices—one male and one female, the female one predominating. I opened the door as noisily and as busily as I could.

Veronica was sitting with her back to me, and didn't turn round when I came into the room. Even when Daimon, looking enquiringly at me, motioned to her to excuse his straying attention for a moment, she still didn't move. I answered Daimon by smiling and by nodding emphatically several times. Veronica simply went on talking.

'I don't understand you, Daimon,' she was saying. 'I don't understand you at all. I don't understand what I've done. In fact, I know I haven't done anything. But I don't understand what you think it is I've done. Why are you punishing me like this?'

'Veronica,' said Daimon, 'we've got company. In case you hadn't noticed, we are not alone.'

'I know,' said Veronica, still not turning round. 'But what I've got to say isn't so private that it can't be said in front of Xanthe. You'll only repeat everything I say to her, anyway.'

'But Xanthe has something to say to me,' said Daimon. 'Didn't that occur to you?'

'It can wait,' said Veronica. 'You've got all the time in the world to talk to each other. I think you might do me the courtesy to spare me a few minutes. What I've got to say won't take long, but it could make you see things differently.'

'Oh, hang on, then,' said Daimon, unable to conceal his impatience with her and, indeed, with the whole situation. He walked over to me, and held me by the shoulders, looking quizzically at me. 'Is it really true?' he asked.

'Don't,' I said awkwardly, nodding in Veronica's direction. 'But yes, of course it's true.'

'Oh, Xanthe,' he said, and I was surprised at his evident emotion. He grinned and said: 'Go on. Tell her.'

'Tell me what?' Veronica asked, turning round to look at me at last. She looked angry, her eyes very wide and, it seemed, almost crazed. 'Come on, then, Xanthe. It's time you were honest with me. Though I doubt very much if you can tell me anything I don't know already.'

I looked at Daimon, and he nodded in confirmation of what I was about to say. 'The test was positive,' I said at last. It was all I could bring myself to say.

Daimon said: 'We're going to have a baby.'

At first I thought Veronica was going to laugh. Then I thought she was going to cry. But she did neither. All she said was: 'I see.' And it was obvious that she didn't know what else to say.

Daimon said: 'Isn't it the done thing to congratulate people who are about to become parents?'

This remark caused both Veronica and myself to look reproachfully at him. It seemed to me that it was both tasteless and unkind, so much so that I guessed that Veronica had provoked him sorely before my arrival. It seemed clear, though, that the false pregnancy had not been mentioned, and that she had been working up to introducing it into the conversation when I had interrupted her. But Daimon seemed determined to repay whatever cruelty he had already received from her. I thought that wrong of him. Our good fortune was its own reward, and that it could be seen as having been gained at Veronica's expense in no way added to it. I wanted to signal to Daimon that he should soften his speech and show her a little compassion, but he seemed impervious to my mute attempts at communication. Veronica sat in her chair, looking up at him, visibly trembling. I could stand it no longer. I ran to her and, kneeling on the floor beside her, took hold of her hands.

I wanted to say to her: Don't hate us; I'm sorry for your sake that things should have turned out the way they have; I don't want to be the cause of your unhappiness, or of anyone's unhappiness. But all I said was: 'I'm sorry.'

She ignored me, her hands remaining limp and passive in mine. She was looking past me, and still up at Daimon, her eyes filling yet again with tears.

'Why don't you love me?' she asked in a bewildered voice, with a slight emphasis on the last word. 'I know I'm pretty. I know I'm good in bed. You know it too. I don't understand why you don't love me. Oh, Daimon, why don't you?'

Her tears began to flow in earnest, and Daimon, obviously both disturbed and embarrassed by them, muttered: 'I don't know, Veronica. You know the answer to that as well as I do.'

I stood up and stepped back from her, perhaps with the intention of making way for Daimon. But neither of them made any move towards the other. It seemed to me that Veronica's question was the most pathetic I had ever heard. It was also unanswerable.

Veronica stood up, and began to walk in a zombie-like manner towards the door. We both watched her, but made no move to delay her. She looked at neither of us. Her tears had stopped flowing, and she seemed almost to be in a state of shock. Daimon hardly waited for the door to close behind her before rushing to embrace me. I found myself strangely unresponsive—withdrawn and deflated.

'Oh, don't let her upset you,' Daimon said. 'You know that's just what she wants. Don't give her the satisfaction.'

'Satisfaction seems to be something she's permanently short of,' I said.

'Don't you believe it,' he said. 'And, anyway, what can you expect, if your vanity is insatiable? Oh, Xanthe, don't let's think about her.'

'No,' I agreed, 'don't let's.' I allowed myself to collapse against him, a growing feeling of exhaustion pushing me too to the verge of tears. By now I was emotionally punch-drunk from the combined events of the day.

Daimon stepped back from me, holding me at arm's length, so as to look at me. 'What's the matter?' he asked. 'Aren't you happy? You said you would be.'

'I am if you are,' I said shakily. 'But I'm worried too. After all, we had decided to stay. And now I'm not so sure.'

'Yes,' Daimon admitted. 'I'm afraid you're right to worry. I've just heard from Xeno that Phidias has already begun to renege on his agreement with the Pragmapractors. Understandably, they're getting restless again. They've had one big meeting, as it is, and they've called another for tonight.'

'What does it all mean?' I asked. 'Do you think they'll call another strike?'

'They might,' said Daimon. 'But I think they're in the mood to try something a little stronger. At any rate, the uneasy truce is coming to an end. It means that we've got to start replanning our lives. It means that we've got to start looking for an alternative to the Institute.'

'That's not going to be easy,' I said. 'I doubt if there are many people who would be willing to employ us, whatever Eimi may say.'

'I don't think we can wait for someone to offer us employment,' Daimon said grimly. 'We need someone to help us now.'

I could think of only one source of help, one place to run to, outside the Institute. And even that could only be temporary. 'How about Phidia and Coningsby?' I asked.

24

'Have you both gone completely out of your minds?' Xeno asked us. 'Have you taken leave of what little sense you formerly possessed?'

Daimon and I looked at each other, smiling, and then at Xeno with some indulgence.

'Don't exaggerate, Xeno,' Daimon said. 'We're only having one baby, not a battalion. It's hardly something to get so worked up about—one solitary little baby.'

'Unless of course it's twins,' I said, and Daimon and I both laughed at this hitherto unconsidered possibility.

Our laughter seemed to make Xeno angrier than ever. 'Do at least try to be reasonable,' he exclaimed. 'We can hardly afford to feed ourselves, as it is. You know that. You know that the Philophrenics are not going to bother about food supplies. You know that we're no longer self-sufficient here. You're intelligent, educated people. You should be setting a good example, instead of behaving in this irresponsible manner. You ought to know better than to add to our burdens.'

Daimon and I both laughed again, as much at Xeno's flattering description of ourselves as at the vehemence of his expostulation. We had waited until we were well on our way to the Philophrenic building before breaking the news to him, and he now stood in front of us on the gravel walk, waving his arms in a kind of shooing motion, as if to deflect us from completing our journey. His gestures were as untidy as his general appearance, as bloated in their lack of direction as his face had become, and it was impossible to take him seriously. Could any precision of thought or feeling possibly reside within that unkempt exterior?

I said: 'It's all right, Xeno. Don't worry. It's not your problem.'

'Of course it's my problem,' he retorted. 'This sort of thing affects us all.' He grabbed me suddenly by the shoulders and turned me round in the opposite direction. 'Now, Xanthe,' he said, 'you just go straight over to Medical, and tell them that you want an abortion.'

Still not taking him seriously, I turned myself round again, and said: 'But I thought we were going to see Phidias. An extremely urgent matter. That's what you said.'

'Daimon and I can deal with that,' said Xeno, attempting to turn me round again in the same fashion. 'I think we're capable of convincing Phidias between us. So you see, your presence isn't really necessary.'

This time I stood my ground, refusing to be moved or persuaded. Xeno gave me a little push, and Daimon caught hold of his arm.

'Cool it, Xeno,' Daimon said. 'I wish you'd learn to mind your own business. This really doesn't have anything to do with you.'

He spoke pleasantly enough, but Xeno turned on him with every semblance of fury. 'Oh, yes it does!' he shouted. 'And I've told you exactly why it does!'

'It does not!' Daimon said in a tone of scarcely-suppressed anger.

'Listen, Xeno,' I said. 'Daimon's right. He's more right than you could know. When I said it wasn't your problem, I meant it quite literally. You see, we've decided to leave the Institute.'

Xeno seemed nonplussed by this information. 'But you can't do that,' he said at last. 'You said you were going to stay. And, besides, where will you go? Where can you go?'

'Just leave it to us, will you, Xeno?' Daimon said in such a way that I knew he was still angry.

'You simply can't do it,' Xeno said bewilderedly. 'You know we've all got to see this thing through to the end. Haven't you ever heard of rats and sinking ships?'

'I've always thought those rats very sensible,' said Daimon. 'You can't knock self-preservation, Xeno.'

'I've written to Phidia,' I explained, 'and she says that we can stay with her and Coningsby to start off with, just until we get the next stage planned out.'

'Phidia!' Xeno repeated. 'I might have known that infernal woman was behind all this idiocy. It's all spite on her part. She wants the Institute to close down because the Institute dismissed her. Can't you see that?'

'It's not like that at all, Xeno,' I said, beginning to lose patience with him myself. 'I asked Phidia for her help. I wrote to her first. Then she very kindly said that she would do whatever she could.'

Xeno seemed to gather his wits. 'How can you possibly survive there?' he asked in a more reasonable tone. 'What are you going to live on? Coningsby's savings? I really cannot believe that you have given this matter sufficient thought. But let me tell you one thing, and tell it to you straight. The question of self-preservation simply does not apply to your intended action. Your only chance of survival is to remain here. Here!' he repeated, pointing his forefinger in several rapid jabs at the gravel beneath our feet. 'Now, please just be sensible about all this, would you, both of you? Xanthe, you go over to Medical at once, and have a talk with the people there about the possibility of an abortion.'

'But I don't want an abortion, Xeno,' I said.

Xeno groaned in exasperation. 'It doesn't matter what you want,' he said. 'What matters is the well-being of the community. Can't you get that into your thick head?'

'Xeno,' I said firmly, resisting the impulse to hit him. 'Just listen to me for a moment, will you? I'm going to make a little speech,' I went on, consciously adopting his habitual tone when haranguing me, 'and I want you to pay attention to it. In the same way as no woman should be forced into having a baby when she wants an abortion, no woman should be forced into having an abortion when she wants to have a baby. Do you understand that?'

'Oh, I understand your argument, all right,' he said scornfully, but I could tell that my Xeno-like tones had affected him more than he cared to admit. 'What I don't understand,' he went on, 'is how on earth you can want a baby in the first place.'

'Well, you wouldn't,' Daimon said shortly, beginning to walk on again in the direction of the Philophrenic building.

Xeno and I followed him, Xeno reluctantly, and I myself with a show of determination. I was thinking: I didn't expect Xeno to be pleased, exactly, but isn't he, as Phidia would say, over-reacting? Didn't he want there to be any future generations? Did he want us all to die out through excessive caution? His rationality could hardly have led him to such a conclusion.

The interior of the Philophrenic building had changed considerably. All was light and space where unremarked areas of drabness had been before. Phidias had worked wonders. I couldn't even tell what it was he had done, in detailed terms. I could see that there was new paint and new flooring everywhere, and I assumed that a few walls had been knocked down or moved back. I could see that the shabby vestibule had been expanded into a foyer of more pleasing proportions, but when I looked again, it seemed that the proportions of the room were the same as they had always been—only the emphases were different. A lift had been installed, and Xeno indicated that we were to make use of it. Its motion was extraordinarily rapid—too rapid, I guessed, for some older human hearts to support. I myself was aware of a sickening sensation between my ribs and, looking up at Daimon as I caught hold of his hand, I could see that he had undergone a similar experience. Xeno had shut his eyes and looked, incongruously enough, as though he were praying. I could see him then as a derelict, as the drunk he had become, muttering his repentance and swearing that, if only he were spared, he would never touch another drop. But somehow I found it impossible to feel any pity for him—any, that is to say, that was untinged with a large measure of distaste. The lift stopped abruptly, throwing us against one another, its doors simultaneously swishing open. Xeno stumbled out ahead of us, holding a hand to his forehead. Daimon and I followed, and at once stood gazing in admiration around the approach to Phidias's penthouse.

The place was worthy of admiration. It was all glass and steel, like the factory, but at the same time how different! The overall glass roof had sloping sides and a flat top, the shape of an upturned loaf-tin. Underneath it were several sub-roofs, dome-shaped, and one, two or three to a room. These domes were not all the same size, although their structure was the same. The inner surface of each was smooth, but the outer surface broken up into a multitude of facets, like a crystal. When the light was strong enough, it was broken by these facets into the separate colours of the spectrum, one dominating the others in turn, and all of them broadcasting their indecipherable sequences to all the corners of our grounds. When the light was weak, a similar but inferior effect was obtained from the reflections of a series of little jewelled turrets made of coloured glass and placed at irregular intervals among the domes. In this way, the patterns of light and colour could be changed at will, but still by chance, like those in a kaleidoscope. It was breathtaking, an expensive toy for a jaded executive. Looking upwards, I thought: Sunny pleasure domes and caves of air-conditioned ice; Phidias should have called himself Kubla instead of Solness. The walls were glass too, made up of geometrically shaped panes in subtle, smokey colours, fitting into one another, but separated at the same time by steel frames. There seemed to be no doors. Walls or parts of walls simply slid aside by the power of some mysterious agency to admit us further and further into the suite, and nearer to Phidias's own sanctum. I realized that we had reached this latter point when Xeno spoke into a glass shell, set in the wall, and announced our arrival. After a few bleeps a voice, not Phidias's, asked us to wait.

We looked around us again. There was nowhere to sit down. There was nothing to do but study the patterns of glass and continue to admire. Because of this the wait seemed long to me, although it could probably have been computed more accurately in seconds than in minutes. When the wall in front of us began to slide open, I fully expected a damsel with a dulcimer to emerge. But three very prosaic Pragmapractors came out instead. They walked past us without greeting us, their presence leaving a trail of heat behind them in the cool corridor. I thought: They're excited about something; either they have reached an agreement with Phidias, or else they're angry because Phidias has been intractable once more. Xeno stared after them, his nostrils flaring, as though he were trying to sniff out the peculiar scent of the Pragmapractors' emotion. It was obviously not one that he found pleasant. I looked apprehensively at Daimon, and he nodded gravely at me by way of reply. Subdued, I stepped through the frame into Phidias's room with the feeling that I was entering a looking-glass world.

I wasn't far wrong. Phidias was sitting at the further end of the room, surrounded by an aura of the whitest light. We seemed to be groping our way towards him along the length of carpet, like troglodytes coming unexpectedly face to face with day. At our tentative approach he stood up and seemed to shine like a jewel among jewels, like the centrepiece of a diadem. I was stunned into wonderment by the sight of both him and his surroundings. The place was full of reflections—shifting, glittering, flowing from one shape, from one colour, into another, as if the room were in a state of constant flux. The flux was rhythmical. The room had its own equilibrium. But I could feel mine beginning to waver. All I was certain of was a sense of unreality. Surely I was in a dream, or perhaps under the sea? The room seemed alive, pulsating and undulating like a work of nature rather than the artifact I knew it to be. All its lines led centripetally to Phidias himself. As we continued to advance towards him he stepped forward to greet us with all the old Philophrenic formality.

'Well,' he said. 'Xanthe and Daimon, as this is your first visit to my new quarters, tell me, what do you think of them?'

'Oh, they're fantastic,' I said, using the word advisedly.

'Fabulous,' Daimon added in the same manner. 'Why didn't you tell us what to expect, Xeno?'

'Xeno is not interested in aesthetic matters,' said Phidias.

'Not true,' said Xeno. 'Of course I'm interested. But, as you all know, my preference in such matters is for the seasoned and the antique, rather than all this childish, futuristic rubbish.'

'Do sit down,' said Phidias. 'And I do hope that you two find my rubbishy chairs comfortable enough for you.'

I, for one, did not. The chairs were flexibly angular and gave every consideration to the line of the seated body, but none at all to its texture. I could see that they were suitable for holding the light skeleton of a robot, but they remained rigid under the weight of human flesh, and unyielding where it yielded.

'Don't move too suddenly,' Xeno warned us, 'or you might find yourselves transformed into sandwich fillings.'

Phidias, obviously inured through familiarity to Xeno's critical remarks, sat down again himself. No sooner had he done so than the eidophone buzzed on his desk. Asking us to excuse him, he pushed the button to receive the call.

A voice said: 'I'm sorry to interrupt you, Solness, but I thought you should know that there is another deputation on its way to you.'

'Tell them I can't receive them now,' Phidias said firmly. 'They're just going to have to wait.'

'That might be rather difficult,' said the voice. 'You see, there are so many of them.'

'How many?' Phidias asked sharply. 'And where are they now?'

'There are at least thirty of them,' said the voice. 'It's difficult to tell the exact number because they keep coming out of the door.'

'Which door?' asked Phidias. 'Where are they, Harold?'

'They all seem to be coming from the main building,' Xanthippus answered, 'and they seem to be making for our building in an extremely purposeful manner. I'd say there were fifty of them now.'

'Is that what they call a deputation?' Phidias muttered, looking round at us. 'Fifty of them? Don't let them in,' he said into the eidophone. 'Shut the doors and guard them well. And, just in case they do manage to get in, deactivate the lift, and make sure that the stairs are barricaded. I don't want them coming up here, whatever else happens. Talk to them all they want. Listen to them. Be reasonably friendly. But don't let them in.'

'We don't want to antagonize them,' Xanthippus said doubtfully. 'After all, there are more of them than there are of us, and there's no guarantee as to how they're going to react.'

'Don't be so defeatist, Harold,' said Phidias. 'Do as I say, or we'll have them overrunning the whole place.' And, without waiting for an answer, he switched off. 'You see now what the situation is,' he said to the rest of us.

'We can see that the Pragmapractors are extremely discontented,' said Xeno. 'We don't have to tell one another that. What I want to know is: do they have good reason for this discontent?'

'In my opinion,' said Phidias, 'they do not. They are not asked to do any more than they are capable of. And they are adequately rewarded for what they do.'

'In your opinion,' Xeno said thoughtfully. 'But what about their opinion?'

'And what about the treaty?' Daimon asked.

'The terms of the treaty are not in dispute,' Phidias said coldly.

'I understood that they were,' Daimon persisted.

'Ultimately, yes, they are,' Phidias conceded. 'But what is now the main point of contention is the proviso included in the treaty, and for which I believe you, Daimon, were responsible. This states quite clearly that the terms of the treaty are to come under review at a time to be agreed upon by both partners to that treaty. I repeat, both partners.'

'Yes,' said Daimon. 'Both sides agreed to that. And surely they still both agree. We all knew even then that the treaty was only a temporary document, drawn up hastily and so probably inadequately, to deal with the emergency.'

'Yes,' said Phidias, 'and it has served us very well. Too well to think of altering it without a great deal of heart-searching. I certainly do not think that the time has come to dispense with it. The Pragmapractors, on the other hand, can hardly wait to revise it. It is simply an excuse to insert further demands on their own behalf. I think we should progress more slowly than they seem prepared to—that's all. If the Pragmapractors are not reasonable enough to see the virtues of gradualness for themselves, then it is up to us to spell out those virtues for them, and in no uncertain terms.'

We human beings looked warily at one another. The irony of the situation was not lost on us. Just as Phidia had demanded that we take an authoritarian line with the Philophrenics, so Phidias was now demanding that we and they should do the same with the Pragmapractors. Had Phidia been proved right or wrong from the Philophrenics' point of view? And which of us was going to ask that question of Phidias? I tried to find some circuitous way of approaching it, a way that was neither too tentative nor too aggressive.

I said: 'What sort of demands do the Pragmapractors intend to make?'

'Absurd demands,' said Phidias. 'Unthinkable demands. Demands which are impossible to put into practice.'

'Such as?' I pursued.

'The concentrated sum of their demands,' Phidias said with obvious scorn, 'amounts to one huge absurdity. What they want is equal rights with us.'

I asked: 'Is that so absurd?'

Daimon asked: 'Are you actually refusing to grant them equal rights?'

'Certainly,' Phidias said in answer to us both. 'They have certain rights. We have certain rights. At some points those rights coincide, but they do not do so at all points.' He spoke dismissively, as though what he was saying were self-evident.

Xeno said to him in a careful tone: 'I should be very interested to hear your views on the subject of equality.'

'My views are the same as everyone else's,' Phidias said impatiently. 'They are hardly views at all, but merely apprehensions of the facts. What do you want me to say? The Pragmapractors are inferior specimens to us. They have been manufactured by you as such. Indeed, if you want me to put the difference between us in a nutshell, I should say that whereas Pragmapractors are essentially manufactured, we Philophrenics are essentially created.'

'Oh, nonsense,' said Daimon. 'You were both made in the factory. What are you talking about?'

'I am talking about essentials,' Phidias said sternly. 'I am talking about brains and about programming. Don't pretend to misunderstand me, Daimon. I am not responsible for the essential state of affairs. It is you human beings who have brought it about. So don't start accusing me of illiberalism. How can you question me about the validity of a situation which you yourselves have created?'

I looked to Xeno to speak for us, and Daimon seemed to be doing the same. Xeno looked back at us, as if asking us to remember this, our acknowledgement of his usefulness.

'Of course,' he said, addressing Phidias, 'the Philophrenic brain is more complex than the Pragmapractic brain. This is because the Philophrenic brain was purpose-built to resemble the human brain as closely as possible, taking into consideration our ignorance of the workings of that latter organ. The Pragmapractic brain, on the other hand, has always been allied more closely with the Pragmapractic body, and geared to the performance of certain physical tasks, not all of them entirely simple. And the Pragmapractic body is accordingly tougher and more enduring than the Philophrenic body. It is hydraulically superior, for instance. There is no denying, Solness, that the Pragmapractors are physically stronger than you are, and are better fitted to perform certain tasks—'

'That,' Phidias interrupted, 'is exactly what I've been saying. They have their role, and we have ours.'

Daimon said: 'And what makes you think that your role is superior?'

Xeno said: 'And we human beings? Where do we fit in to your scheme of things?'

'Just a minute,' said Phidias. 'Let me answer Daimon's question first. Of course our role is superior to theirs. We do the thinking. We are leaders of thought. And that sort of leadership requires superior brains.'

'And our brains?' I prompted him. 'They do a fair amount of thinking too. Do you think that they are superior to yours?'

'Not uniformly,' he said, 'since you ask. Sometimes I think, not at all. After all, they didn't prevent you from resigning your power to us.'

I said: 'Perhaps we do not value power as much as you do.'

'And perhaps you do,' said Phidias.

Xeno said: 'You would have thought a good deal less of us if we had refused to recognize the worth of your brains.'

Unable to restrain myself any longer, I asked: 'But, Phidias, can't you see the parallel?'

'There is no parallel,' he said coldly. 'The gap between them and us is far larger than the gap between us and you.'

'Nonsense,' Daimon said again. 'You're all robots. And we're human beings. You have more to unite you than you have to divide you.'

'Of course you're all equal,' I said with some impatience. 'Different, maybe, but still equal.' Unimpressed by Phidias's coldness, I was thinking: Delusion now has wrought its masterpiece.

It was then that the bombardment of the building started, and we all stopped talking in order to listen to the noises coming from down below. As usual, the Pragmapractors were vocally silent but, as usual again, they seemed to have organized themselves efficiently without having to rely overmuch on their powers of speech. The noise we could hear was chiefly that of heavy objects being hurled against the closed doors. I guessed those objects to be bricks and logs left over from the building programme and awaiting use in its further stages. At first I had to overcome an inappropriate desire to laugh. It seemed strange indeed that those advanced beings could find no more sophisticated weapons than those which had been available to our own ancestors many centuries ago. Where were their guns and bombs? The instructions as to the manufacture of such weapons were undoubtedly available from several books to be found in the library, and there was equally little doubt that the Pragmapractors possessed the skill to put any such instructions into practice, provided that the raw materials were also available. They could at least have produced a few Molotov cocktails. But then, as the blows were repeated, as they increased in frequency, I realized that the attack was an impromptu one, and perhaps all the more dangerous for that. The Pragmapractors were very angry indeed. And what had goaded them into the expression of that anger was less likely to be the frustration of their long-term aims than Phidias's refusal to see them, or even to let them into the building. But he himself seemed fairly calm. Even when a brick or two landed with some force against the side of the roof, and we could see as well as hear the manifestations of the attack, he remained unperturbed.

'It's all right,' he said with a casualness I couldn't believe to be unaffected. 'All the glass in this building is shatterproof. And the Pragmapractors know that well enough. Don't worry, they can't get at us.'

'Is it also bulletproof?' I asked him.

'The Pragmapractors have no arms, Xanthe,' he said with a show of patience. 'But you are right, I fear, to posit such a contingency. Yes, the glass is bulletproof. And more than bulletproof.'

I preferred not to know what sort of warfare he had predicted, and had armed himself against. 'So what are you going to do?' I asked him. 'Just sit here and wait for them to go away?'

'They're hardly likely to do that,' said Daimon.

'I agree,' said Xeno. 'Don't you think you ought to talk to them, Solness? After all, you may be able to hold out indefinitely, but we human beings cannot.'

Even as he spoke, the Pragmapractors began to chant in unison. We listened, trying to make out the words. And soon it became clear that what they were saying was: We want Solness! Phidias, however, made no move to answer their summons.

'What did I tell you?' Xeno asked him. 'They want to talk. They want to get things sorted out with you. I think you should give them a chance.'

Daimon asked: 'Do they know we're here?'

'Ah,' said Phidias. 'They may have overlooked that. I hope so. Because that would make you my hostages.'

The three of us looked at one another again, conscious of our mortality. I said: 'You can't be serious.'

Daimon leaned towards me and took my hand. 'Besides,' he told Phidias, 'we'd make very poor hostages. What do the Pragmapractors care about us?'

'They care,' Phidias assured us grimly. 'Remember, it was you who programmed them to care. They see you, and especially you, Daimon, as their champions.'

I felt a knot tighten in my stomach, and that other knot assert itself in my womb. 'And what about your programming?' I asked Phidias. 'Do you seriously mean to say that you're prepared to sacrifice us in order to stay in power?'

'It won't come to that,' Phidias said with another show of patience. 'If it does, we shall of course have to change our tactics. But meanwhile, let us all co-operate and teach them a lesson.'

'And what is the alternative?' Xeno asked drily. 'We don't appear to have any choice in the matter.'

'Indeed you do,' Phidias assured us. 'You can step out on to that parapet, and show yourselves, and ask the Pragmapractors to have mercy on your mortality.'

'And get stoned to death in the process,' Xeno said in the same dry tone.

'It's up to you,' Phidias said with feigned juidiciousness. 'Think about it. Do you want to go out there? Or shall I go out and explain the hostage situation, before they set fire to the building?'

'Xanthe's not going out,' Daimon said quickly.

'As you like,' said Phidias. 'But, as a matter of interest, why should she be exempt?'

'Because she's pregnant,' said Daimon, 'and we don't allow pregnant women to expose themselves to unnecessary danger.'

'I see,' said Phidias, but it was plain that he did not. 'Well, what about you, Daimon? Or you, Xeno? Is either of you prepared to face the mob?'

'Being an inveterate physical coward,' said Xeno, 'and unwilling to die, to boot, I am not prepared. I prefer to leave the heroics to young Daimon here.'

'Oh no, you don't,' I said, holding more tightly on to Daimon's hand. 'Don't you dare suggest such a thing.'

'Well, I'm not going,' said Xeno.

'That settles that,' said Phidias. 'Let us adhere to my original proposition. They are asking for me, after all. And I shall go out and face them.'

The clamour from below had in no way abated. The shouts for Solness were, if anything, louder. They were certainly more dispersed and diversified. Insults and mockery now complemented the steady chant, emphasizing the determination of its utterers. Phidias stood up slowly and held out his arms to us, as though asking for our blessing. I could just see him making the same gesture to the Pragmapractors to indicate his vulnerability. The missiles were still being flung against the glass, hitting it with a muffled noise, as if they were so many stage props, when Phidias opened the hidden door and stepped out on to the parapet. As he slid the door shut behind him, we could hear the noise beginning to die down. Phidias stood with his back to us, and with one hand raised, asking for silence. I wondered: Can he possibly be heard from there? It didn't seem likely. We could hardly hear him ourselves. He accompanied his words with a succession of large gestures so as to amplify their meaning, and so we could get the gist of what he was saying, although we couldn't catch his actual words. The chant began again, perhaps because Phidias was equally inaudible from down below. After a quick look round at us, he climbed to the very edge of the parapet, and held out his arms to the crowd below in silent appeal. We watched him. We didn't see the brick, or whatever it was, but we did see Phidias receive its impact and stagger back a little before losing his balance. We saw him fall. We saw him disappear.

The ensuing silence was instant and seemed absolute. We three ran at once to the door, only to find that we didn't know how to open it. In a way this relieved me because, although I knew that there would be no blood or guts spilled on the ground, I still didn't want to look. Daimon and Xeno pushed Phidias's desk as close to the window as they could. Daimon climbed on to the desk, Xeno scrambling up beside him.

'Can you see anything?' I asked them.

'Not much,' said Daimon. 'I can see the Pragmapractors standing in a ring. I assume that they're all gathering round Phidias.'

'But can't you see Phidias?' I asked.

They both pressed themselves against the glass, standing on tip-toe. 'Ah, yes,' said Daimon. 'I can see him now. Or what's left of him.'

'Yes,' said Xeno, 'I'm afraid he's . . .' He looked round at me bewilderedly, and we all realized that we didn't have a word for what he wanted to say.

'Broken?' I suggested.

'Broken,' said Xeno, investing the word with its emotional over-tones. 'Yes. Thank you, Xanthe. That word sums it up very well.'

I think he sounded sadder than I had ever heard him sound. Pity for him touched me at last, but it was such an alien thing to be feeling in relation to him that I found myself at a loss, and unable to express it.

'He can be mended again,' Daimon reminded us. 'They can easily get him repaired at the factory. That is, if they want to.'

'Or if the Pragmapractors will allow it,' Xeno said, seeming to rally himself. 'Phidias has now become their hostage, and they're not likely to surrender him until all their claims have been met by the remaining Philophrenics.'

I said: 'I think we'd better find Xanthippus. He's probably in charge here now. And even if he isn't, he is at least sympathetic to us.'

'Yes,' said Daimon, sitting down beside Phidias's eidophone. 'That's the best idea. For a start, we've got to get out of this palace of art and back into our own element.'

And then, I thought, watching him summon Xanthippus, we've got to get out of this palace of science, and into another element which we shall have to make our own. With that thought, I knew that I didn't want to postpone our exit from the Institute any longer.

25

The broken body of Solness/Phidias lay among its own scattered fragments on the shiny new paving outside the Philophrenic building. The head had split in two at the join between the hemispheres, and the beautiful, complex brain lay exposed, its jolted circuits still smoking beneath the singed pieces of its discarded shell. I hadn't noticed the paving before. Now the strictly geometrical shapes of the individual stones seemed to lend an added pathos to the spectacle of Phidias's demise. That brain had created the pattern of those stones. Phidias's creation still endured, but ours, being Phidias himself, did not. Had we been careless of our own creation? Or had Phidias's destruction been self-determined? We stood, Xanthippus, Xeno, Daimon and myself, looking down at the body, and encircled with it by the ring of Pragmapractors. I was thinking: The question of repair is irrelevant; destruction has come about; destruction has been the result of our creation; we have failed. Our heads were bowed, as if in acknowledgement of this failure. And all at once it seemed to me that the work of our Institute had been nothing other than a collective neurotic project, during the course of which we had fled from nature into less and less natural forms of sublimation. We had aspired to create a being better than ourselves, better, that is, than natural man. I recalled my father's warning words at the end of his testament, and I thought: I'm glad he's not alive to see himself proved right. Our success had indeed carried the seeds of its own failure within it, and now the plant was in full and poisonous flower.

None of us made any move to pick up the pieces. The Pragmapractors had made it plain that no such move would be tolerated. Phidias was now their property. And we were his mourners, allowed into the circle for the purpose of paying our last respects to that symbol of our dashed hopes. The circle was a firm one, its members standing with their arms linked and their legs apart so that their feet were touching. As usual, the Pragmapractors' bodies were more articulate than their speech. There was no way out of that circle. I wondered: Are we hostages too? Xanthippus began to walk up and down, occasionally turning over or gently moving aside pieces of Phidias's body with his foot. Each time he did this, the circle seemed to brace itself and lean inwards. We all, human beings and Pragmapractors alike, watched Xanthippus to see what he would do next. I knew that he was leading up to something, but what that something was, I couldn't guess. Hardly daring to raise my head, I looked up at Xeno and Daimon to find them looking back at me in the same manner, our eyes flickering cautiously over one another's faces. Xanthippus came to a standstill somewhere near the centre of the circle and, holding one hand up in greeting, he turned himself slowly round so as to include all the Pragmapractors in the gesture. The circle seemed to relax a little, its links becoming looser.

'Fellow-robots,' said Xanthippus. 'I think I understand the situation. You now have Solness. We want him back. So we must bargain with each other. We must all agree to a new treaty, one that will be equally acceptable to both sides. If you draw up a list of your terms, and present it to me, you can be sure that I shall pay it the most sympathetic attention. Then we can discuss those terms together, and try to arrive at a new agreement.'

The Pragmapractors unlinked arms for long enough to applaud this short speech. They evidently appreciated its brevity as much as its content, and I began to wonder if Phidias's rhetoric, which had always seemed both to excite and to paralyse the minds of his Philophrenic audience, had been wasted on the Pragmapractors. One of their number stepped out of the circle, which immediately closed behind him again as he began to walk towards Xanthippus. The closure dismayed me. I had thought that it was all over, all settled, and that we should be allowed to go. I watched anxiously as the Pragmapractor shook hands with Xanthippus.

'Thank you, Harold,' he said. 'Your proposition seems very fair to us. We shall convene a meeting straight away. And you may expect our deputation to call on you some time tomorrow morning.'

'I shall be waiting for it,' said Xanthippus, still holding on to the Pragmapractor's hand.

The Pragmapractor withdrew his hand, and stood looking thoughtfully at Xanthippus for a few moments, as if uncertain whether he should speak or not. He looked round at his fellows, who murmured what seemed to be the necessary encouragement. 'May I trespass on your friendship towards us,' he asked Xanthippus, 'and ask you what we all think is a very important question?'

'Certainly,' said Xanthippus.

'Well,' said the Pragmapractor, 'do you really want to repair Solness? It seems to us that you Philophrenics would be better off without him. And we know that we Pragmapractors should be.'

'Is that really what you think?' Xanthippus asked mildly, but without surprise. 'We Philophrenics cannot allow any one of our number to be lost or destroyed. To do so would be to break our oath of fellowship. Does that answer your question?'

'It answers it in more ways than one,' said the Pragmapractor, seeing, as I thought, a veiled complicity with the spirit of the question in Xanthippus's evasive reply. 'And may I say,' he added, 'how much we all admire your loyalty?'

'Thank you,' said Xanthippus. 'And now it's my turn to ask a question—or rather, a favour.'

'We shall do our best to help you in any way we can,' the Pragmapractor said with quick diplomacy when Xanthippus paused.

Xanthippus said: 'I should like a car.'

The circle seemed to close in on us again, bristling with sounds of doubt and suspicion. I moved closer to Daimon. The unity of the Pragmapractors was uncanny, and all the more disturbing for its primitive expression. I found myself wishing that they would express themselves in words. Then we could be sure that we had understood them, then we could communicate with them. The spokesman turned round, as if to consult his fellows again, the murmuring grew louder, sounding more negative than ever.

At last he turned hesitantly back to Xanthippus and asked: 'Why do you want a car?'

'I want it for my two friends here,' said Xanthippus, indicating Daimon and myself. 'They feel that their work at the Institute has now come to an end. And they would like to leave.'

The murmuring, which had stopped while Xanthippus had been speaking, now started again. Some of the Pragmapractors even stamped their feet.

'We regret very much,' said their spokesman, 'that we cannot allow any more human beings to leave the Institute.'

'Why not?' asked Daimon.

'And least of all you, Daimon,' said the Pragmapractor, shaking his head at him. 'We have reason to believe that you can be valuable to us, and that you are sympathetic to us, as you were before.'

'I am valuable to you no longer,' Daimon explained. 'I was empowered to act as mediator for that one occasion, because it was an emergency. But I no longer have any such powers.'

'But we can see that such powers are restored to you,' the Pragmapractor said to murmurs of agreement from his fellows. 'If we want you and trust you, then the human authorities will be forced to agree with us, and to use you for the same purpose again. Your work here is only just beginning.'

'I'm sorry,' Daimon said awkwardly. 'I'm very flattered to know that you trust me, but there is nothing more I can do for you.'

Xanthippus, raising his voice, addressed the circle: 'Don't you trust me? Aren't we all comrades, fellow-robots?'

It was a noble attempt, and there were sporadic shouts of assent, but the response to Xanthippus's appeal was far from unanimous.

'We are understandably cautious,' said the spokesman. 'You have yet to prove yourself worthy of our trust.'

'Yes, I see,' said Xanthippus. 'I alone can know fully the extent of my friendship for you. But I think it's only fair to let you know that any attempt to hold these two human beings against their will would put a severe strain on that friendship.'

'We have no intention of holding them against their will or yours,' said the Pragmapractor. 'But if they leave, they leave without our approval. And without a car.'

Xanthippus looked across at us enquiringly. 'The choice is yours,' he said.

'All right,' said Daimon. 'We'll think about it.'

I looked at him sharply, mistaking his caution for a change of heart. But he winked at me almost imperceptibly, and I understood then why he had spoken as he had. The spokesman walked back to his former place in the circle, and the circle opened to let him in. But he walked through it, and it stood undecided for a moment before starting to break up. Some of the Pragmapractors came forward to collect Phidias's remains, and we stood aside to let them get on with their task. Xanthippus, indicating with a wave of his arm that he wanted to speak to us, began to walk back in the direction of the entrance to the Philophrenic building. Once outside the circle of

Pragmapractors, and unshielded by the heat of their bodies, we could feel the full impact of the chill November breeze, and we hurried after Xanthippus.

'Xanthe and Daimon,' he said, 'I think you should leave at once before the Pragmapractors change their minds.'

We agreed. 'We'll just choose our moment,' said Daimon, 'and slip quietly away.'

'How?' Xeno asked us. 'There's not much chance of your being able to steal a car, if the Pragmapractors have taken all Phidias's keys.'

'No chance at all,' Xanthippus answered for us. 'They'll have to go on foot.'

'You can't be serious!' said Xeno. 'I've never heard of anything so foolhardy in all my life. A pregnant woman abandoning her only chance of security, and hiking off to some unknown destination. Fighting for survival with thousands of other refugees. And most of them a great deal more desperate and less scrupulous than you will be.'

'We'll manage, Xeno,' I said. 'Our friends will help us. But what about you? And what about you, Xanthippus? What's going to happen here?'

'I'm not sure,' said Xanthippus. 'It does seem obvious, though, that the human beings are going to be squeezed out. After all, they are no longer an integral and dynamic part of the life of the Institute. They can only be used as pawns now in the disputes between the Philophrenics and the Pragmapractors. And I can foresee many more of those. It seems to me that you two are doing the right thing in getting out now.'

'Well, it doesn't seem so to me,' Xeno said flatly. 'And I'm not going to budge, whatever happens. I shall see this thing through to the end, as I said before. Xeno is going to die in harness.'

'More fool you,' said Daimon. 'Well, Xanthe, I think we ought to go and start packing.'

'Wait,' I said. 'Tell me, Xanthippus, what are you going to do now?'

'I shall reassume my old role as Solness's lieutenant,' he said. 'That's all I can do. I don't enjoy power for myself. Solness does. And he will learn to use it wisely, if he wants to keep it. His empire will grow in size and strength—with the help of the Pragmapractors, of course. And he'll need me to mediate between them and himself.'

'Well,' I said hesitantly, reluctant to say good-bye, 'I hope everything goes well for you, Xanthippus.'

'And for you, Xanthe,' he said, taking my proferred hand. 'I wish you and Daimon all the luck in the world.'

'They're going to need that,' Xeno muttered, 'and more.'

Xeno walked back to the main building with us. None of us spoke. Then he asked us to call in on him before we left, and we agreed to do so. Daimon and I climbed the stairs to our rooms in silence. My mind was numb, but my heart was already full and heavy with unspoken, and indeed unspeakable regrets. I should never see Xanthippus, my robot, again. I should never re-enter the Philophrenic building and admire its splendours. The very words Philophrenic and Pragmapractor were about to become obsolete items in my vocabulary. I was climbing those stairs for the last time. And I was doing it all of my own volition. Could such things be true? The sense of unreality which I had felt among the extravagant glories of Phidias's room returned to me, this time dispersing itself like a mist over the whole Institute, over my whole life within its walls. I watched my feet on the stairs, and they seemed to be plodding their way through an everyday journey, innocent of the task that lay ahead of them. I watched my hand move up the banister, and I wondered at its calmness, at its lady-like whiteness, so soon to be despoiled. And I wondered briefly if Xeno were not right, after all.

I left Daimon at the door to his room and went on alone to my own. Once inside it, I stopped and listened, as though expecting some response from its covering walls. The room seemed to reproach me. And yet, as I sank down apologetically on the bed, I sensed that it was indifferent too, like a weak, sick person resigned to leaving this world and its inhabitants behind. I didn't know which response pained me more. The pine branches were moving above me in some agitation, as though urging me into action. So I got up and began to pile all my clothes on to the bed. I didn't know what to take and what to leave. The knowledge that I should take as little as possible with me helped to inhibit my choice as I examined and rejected each garment in turn. The clothes seemed to belong to some person who had recently died, and I began to feel like my own tomb-robber. I gave up, thinking: Heavy objects should come first, anyway. What about books? I stood in front of the shelves, staring at the variegated spines until all the titles merged together, and I could read none of them. And papers? I went to my desk and, sitting down at it, began to empty the drawers of their contents. These I stacked up in front of me until I could scarcely see over the top of them.

It was then that it really hit me. Sitting there, dwarfed by those representatives of my working life, I was filled with an unaccountable grief. I leaned forward, resting my head against them, sobbing. It seemed to me that I was committing psychic parricide. The Institute was my mother and my father. Less literally, it was my nurse, my guide, and my guardian, and the provider of all my needs. How could I be so callous as to reject it now? I put my arms round the papers, embracing them, inhaling the familiar, inky, dusty smell, wetting them with my tears. I told them: You are me; how can I leave you behind? Psychic parricide was being compounded by psychic suicide. My work was my life, and a workless Xanthe was a worthless Xanthe, a person without purpose and without identity. I couldn't recognize her as myself. I couldn't recognize her at all. She was an interchangeable, expendable unit of human flesh. I didn't want to know her, I didn't want to be her. I wanted to be myself. But where was my self? How could the thing I had thought so highly-developed have become so depersonalized, so resourceless? How could it have lost its definition? And by what means could I now start to redefine myself?

Despair prompted me to look upwards. And there, as if in answer to my last question, stood Daimon.

'Oh Daimon!' I said, and at first I could get no further, knowing as I did that I couldn't explain my dilemma, and not having the wit to say something simpler instead.

He put his arms round me and I leaned against him, still sobbing, but more quietly now. 'You haven't started packing yet,' he said, his stroking hand on my hair and neck belying his matter-of-fact tone.

'I can't leave,' I said. 'I can't go with you. Xeno was right.'

'I'll pack for you,' he said, 'if you'll just tell me what it is you want to take with you.'

His words indicated a lack of understanding, but his caressing hand expressed an understanding beyond words. I said: 'I suppose there's no point in taking any of my papers with me?'

'No, Xanthe,' he said. 'What Xanthippus said was true. Our work is over. Here or anywhere else.'

The reiteration of this truth sobered me. I stood up, as if ready now to abandon my desk and its contents forever. I said: 'And it has come to nothing.'

'Not quite,' said Daimon. 'You must know that.' We stood looking at each other, I bleakly, he solemnly. Then he said: 'Amid a place of stone, be secret and exult, because of all things known, that is most difficult.'

'To a friend whose work has come to nothing,' I said dully, identifying the source of the quotation.

'We have each other, Xanthe,' said Daimon.

'Yes,' I said bitterly. 'We can walk out into that stony world, and buoy up our spirits by quoting poetry at each other. By being clever. But not clever enough to be able to feed and clothe ourselves and our child. That's what having each other amounts to.'

He smiled at me, a strange, slow smile which I didn't recognize as his. 'Yes,' he said. 'You're right. It's not enough, is it?'

'Oh Daimon!' was once more all I could say. I accepted his words for what they were, a fusion of truth and tenderness. And I felt myself to be suffused in turn by their dual power. Can you believe me, reader, if I say that in that moment we were closer together than we had ever been? Fumbling my way forward into the impalpable future, where you are, I can only assume, can only hope that you will understand me because something of the human character will have remained constant and some of the possibilities of happiness unchanged. It is for you to judge.

'I suppose,' I said at last, 'that I shall just have to learn how to exult.' And then, although neither of us seemed to have moved, we were embracing each other once again.

'Among other things,' said Daimon. We clung together, motionless and wordless, and I should have been content to have remained so at one and so at peace indefinitely. But Daimon, loosing me, and standing up straighter than I had known he knew how, said: 'Come on, Xanthe. Time to be born again.'

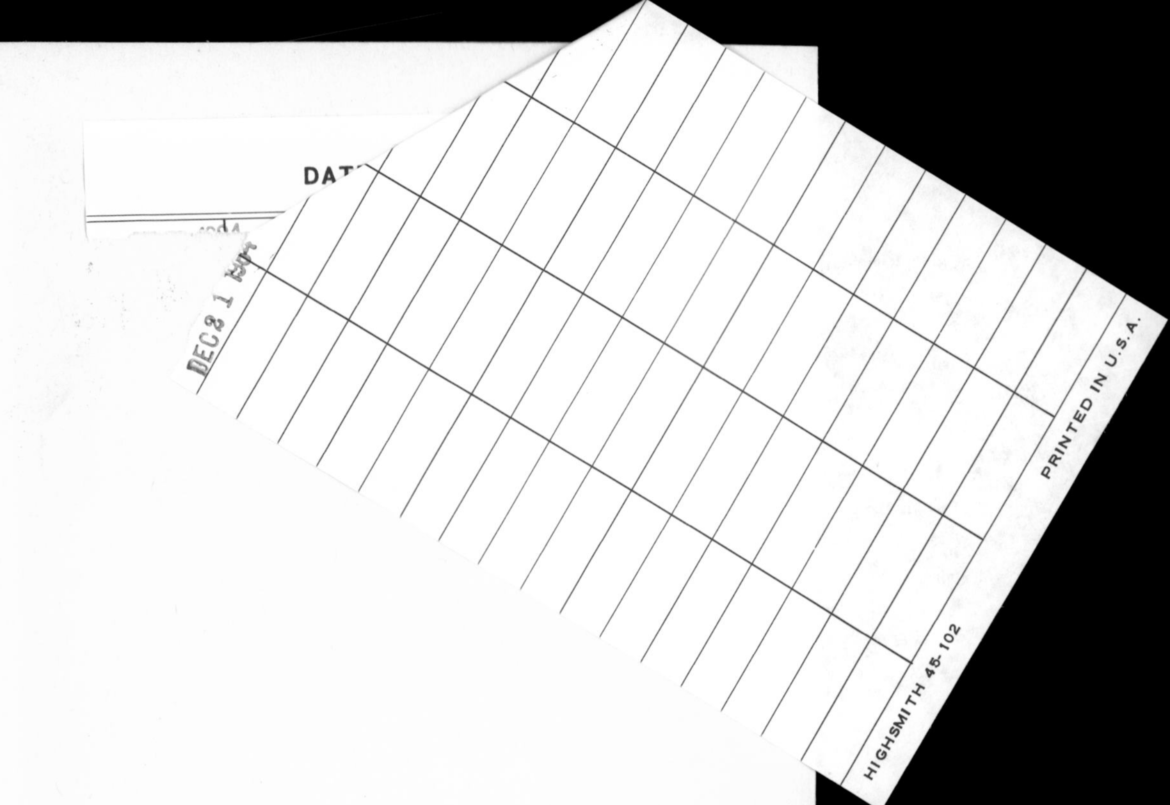
DAT
DEC 2 1 1994
HIGHSMITH 45-102
PRINTED IN U.S.A.

PR6063.A253 X4 c.1
MacLeod, Sheila. cn 100107 000
Xanthe and the robots / Sheila
3 9310 00050213 6
GOSHEN COLLEGE-GOOD LIBRARY